# PRAISE FOR *A STRE*

"Jess Wright's *A Stream to Follow* is a gripping reminder of the trauma of war and the healing power of family and love. A stunning and heartfelt debut."
— LINDA KASS, award-winning author of *Tasa's Song* and *A Ritchie Boy*

"This post-World War II novel touchingly and intelligently reminds us that no war ever ends. It survives in our minds and bodies, daring us to live and love alongside our memories of brutal history and unforgettable valor."
— SHELLY BLANTON-STROUD, author of *Copy Boy*

"In a thrilling account of the aftermath of wartime trauma, Jess Wright tells a story of heroism, love, and healing. Engaging and heartwarming. . . . A book you can't put down."
— ROBERT L. LEAHY, PhD, author of *Don't Believe Everything You Feel* and *The Worry Cure*

"An authentic portrait of working through traumatic experiences to develop resilience. At the same time, matters of the heart play an important role in the lives of the characters in this compelling family saga . . . an absolute joy to read."
— AMES SHELDON, award-winning author of *Eleanor's Wars*, *Don't Put the Boats Away*, and *Lemons in the Garden of Love*

"Jess Wright is a gifted storyteller who weaves the heartrending impact of PTSD into a novel that will resonate with all. It is a page-turner full of love, intrigue, and tested values."
— BARBARA O. ROTHBAUM, PhD, Professor and Director, Emory University Healthcare Veterans Program, and author of *PTSD: What Everyone Wants to Know*

# A STREAM
# TO FOLLOW

*A Novel*

# A STREAM TO FOLLOW

**JESS WRIGHT**

Published by SparkPress, a BookSparks imprint,
A division of SparkPoint Studio, LLC
Phoenix, Arizona, USA, 85007
www.gosparkpress.com

Published 2022
Printed in the United States of America
Print ISBN: 978-1-68463-121-6
E-ISBN: 978-1-68463-122-3
Library of Congress Control Number: 2021918339

Interior design by Tabitha Lahr

To Susanne Wright

And in memory of Captain Jesse Wright,
Jr., and First Lieutenant Donald Slep,
soldiers who had their own stories

# $\mathcal{C}$hapter 1

## HOMECOMING

———

*Pennsylvania*
*October 1945*

$\mathcal{F}$rom high on the main track of the Pennsylvania Railroad, his eyes locked on the mountain stream where it tumbled into the Juniata River. The train from New York had barreled through the gorge before it slowed at the curved stretch where the river went deep, snaking along the cliff and picking up the limestone spring–fed water from Spruce Creek. He had stood on the spot where the streams merged, casting to the fish that were strong enough to feed in the fast current and swirling pools.

When he was in France and Germany, Bruce had pictured this place to push his fear away. It was just a diversion—a way to lift himself away from the slaughter at the front line. But it nurtured a belief that he'd return here someday.

Bruce had been able to imagine with photographic accuracy since he was a boy. In medical school, he could scan pages in textbooks and seal them in his brain. In the war, he blocked out noise from exploding shells while he visualized each step of the surgery that was about to start. Until the battles in January had unnerved him, he could control the flow of his thoughts, take them where he wanted. Since then, imprints of the carnage tore at him.

Even now, when sight of the two streams signaled he was close to home, Bruce's thoughts ricocheted backward. It was the Zorn this time—the frozen river outside Rohrwiller. He could feel the ice crack as he reached out to his corpsman who had been hit in the face with the sniper's bullet. They fell under the surface before he grabbed a tangle of tree roots and pushed Carl through the ice onto the bank. His fingers were numb—they were losing their grip. But he heaved himself up beside Carl. Then the other corpsman ran forward, screamed, and dropped on top of them. The gun had fired again. The red crosses on their uniforms meant nothing to the Germans.

While he hugged the ground, Bruce rolled the dead soldier off them and found a hemostat in his frost-crusted pack. After he clamped the spurting vessel in the hole where Carl's jaw had been, he lay on his back, shuddering with cold, wondering if the sniper would find him. They hadn't needed to come out here to find the wounded men. It was a stupid mistake.

Bruce shook his head. *Enough*, he said to himself. *Shut it off.*

Sometimes he wished he had taken the amytal injection the psychiatrist had wanted to try on him. But the narco-synthesis theory—get semiconscious on a drug and spill it all out—was too Freudian for his taste. No, there weren't any good treatments. The memories gripped too hard for simple solutions.

Trying to wrestle his mind back to the present, Bruce focused on the river below him. It was early autumn, and the water level was low. He imagined wading into a shallow section by the bridge they were crossing. His fly rod began to move back and forth, spreading long loops that unfurled toward a riffle that could hold trout. The caddis fly bounced on the water, crossing from patches of sun to shade, riding along with the current in a natural drift. He lifted the rod and cast again. No strikes, but the rhythm of the casts settled him.

The train was picking up speed as it moved away from the river and toward Altoona, where Bruce would meet his mother and brother at the station. The war had tested all of them.

He could see his mother in his mind's eye now. She still had her angular beauty and erect posture from her years studying dance, but there were more lines in her face. Her laughter didn't come as easily. The car crash that killed his father in '43 had left its mark on her.

The photo Bruce pulled from his wallet showed his brother, Glen, standing in front of his P-51 Mustang. With such a good-looking, full-of-beans subject, the snapshot could have been scripted by Hollywood. His aviator's cap and flight jacket with a sheep's wool collar were worn with pride, as they should have been.

The confident stance showed a fresh-faced optimist. But the photo was taken at the beginning of Glen's war. Within three months, all seven of the other men in his tent died flying over France. And on Glen's last flight to Normandy, he took heavy shrapnel and barely made it back to England. The burns from the crash landing left scars that would last the rest of his life.

In the crowd of people meeting their families, the Duncans met at the center, standing taller than the others. Bruce held his mother first. She was lighter than he remembered. Not fragile yet. Older, but still elegant. Her voice was the same—rich and comforting, tinged with good humor.

"You'll squeeze me to pieces," Alice said. "Go ahead. I've been waiting for you to do it."

They laughed and pulled apart enough to take stock of each other.

"I just want to look at you, Bruce . . . take you in," she said.

As they started walking, they heard the sound of clapping. All around them, people had stopped what they were doing to watch their reunion. When Bruce turned to recognize them, the applause grew. Some of them shouted "Thank you!" and flashed the victory sign.

"That was an unexpected pleasure," Bruce said as he strolled arm in arm with his mother and brother toward the car. "I'm a lucky guy to be back here and have that kind of welcome."

*Not like some guys I knew*, Bruce thought.

"It's party time tonight," Glen said. "We invited everyone you wanted. And I found a few good-looking women in case you're ready to step out."

"Not yet," Bruce said. "Give me a chance to catch my breath."

"Everyone's bringing a bottle," Glen chimed. "So it should be a big blast. You're back home, the war's over . . . How could it get better?"

While they drove from the station in Altoona to their home in Hollidaysburg, Bruce tried to savor views of the places he had missed. But the satisfaction of returning home wasn't complete. There was a glaring absence.

He could imagine Amelia now in the back seat with his mother as his brother took them to the house on Walnut

Street. She was charming his mother, as she did everyone else she met. She was tossing that long ash-blond hair and talking with so much warmth that they were falling for her too. How could they resist? He had known from the first day that Amelia had a magnetic pull on him. There wouldn't be another one like her.

In the end, the barriers had been too high. Her father had treated him like an unwanted pest—someone to be swatted away. A doctor from a small town in Pennsylvania wasn't good enough for the daughter of a member of Parliament.

Amelia had stood up to her father for a long time, through the months before Bruce's unit left for France and beyond. Then Mark, her ex-boyfriend, returned from the campaign in Italy. With an impeccable background and connections, he was the easier choice. Her last letter arrived a month after the war ended. Full of guilt and regret, she said her father had won. Mark's offer of marriage had been accepted.

The slide into aching reverie wasn't helping Bruce. He had gone quiet for a while as they came into Hollidaysburg.

"Are you feeling okay, Bruce?" his mother asked. "Is this party a bad idea? We didn't ask if you wanted time to get used to being home."

"I'm fine, Mother," he said. Bruce snapped back to attention. "You don't need to worry about me anymore. It's blue skies ahead."


It seemed strange to walk into the house on Walnut Street without his father there to greet him. They hadn't been close, especially after Bruce turned down his offer to join the family hardware business. Still, he had respected his father and missed him. Robert Duncan's chair was in the same spot, but his pipes and tobacco were gone. He had vanished, as had so many.

In a way, the decision to practice medicine in Hollidays-burg after the war was a payback to his father—the long line of Duncans who worked in this town wouldn't be broken. His father's death had been an extra nudge to make the commitment to a place that called to him—a place where he would know his patients and mean something to them, a place where he would be near the mountains and streams where he belonged. The only option that could have lured him was to stay in England with Amelia. That door had closed.

His mother was at the piano, playing some of his favorite songs. Glen was in the kitchen mixing drinks. The windows were open, and a soft breeze was blowing at the curtains. The guests would arrive in less than an hour. It was time for a shower and a fresh uniform. This might be his last day in uniform, and he wanted to honor it.

*Chapter 2*

## THE TEST

—

### *Hampshire, England*
### *April 1944*

*I*t had been easier than Bruce expected. All that was required was a signature at the gate house to enter this fly-fishing mecca. The man at the gate even gave him a few flies, some Grannons, after apologizing that the river keeper was in the army and there were no guides to help Bruce learn the nuances of fishing the Test. Bruce had been astounded when he heard that the owner of Whitcombe Hall decided to open a few beats to soldiers waiting for the invasion across the channel and the push into Germany. Over fifty GIs had signed up for the lottery to be allowed to fish these hallowed waters, but Bruce's luck had come through. He had won the first chance to sample the Test.

When he was at Penn and wanted a break from studying medical texts, Bruce had read Halford's books about the Test. He could remember the description of the mill race, part of the Whitcombe estate and one of the most productive sections of the river. Unfortunately, Bruce's assigned part of the stream didn't include the mill race. He could see the weathered bricks of the mill while he walked toward his beat on the lower section of the river. Another fisherman was wading in the stream below the mill and had hooked a fish. From the bend of the rod and the heavy splashes, it looked like a nice-size trout. He would stay clear of the other fisherman as etiquette demanded.

The Test was almost too idyllic to seem real. Groomed through many generations, the banks were clear of the overhanging branches and the wildness of the streams he fished in Pennsylvania. With majestic trees rimming the stream and shading a brick mill with a waterwheel, the scene could have been captured in a painting like ones he had seen in the British Museum. Although the grass was rougher than it might have been before the war, the estate had escaped the turmoil that existed outside its gates. It was a haven from the furious buildup to the invasion.

The initial shock of being selected to be a battlefield surgeon, the most dangerous assignment for a doctor, had faded. A long haul of intensive training had converted him from a GP, just out of the University of Pennsylvania, into a specialist that the medical corps believed could handle the trauma of front-line warfare. Bruce wasn't sure how he would fare. So far, most of the surgeries he had done were for ordinary problems—hernias, appendicitis, and scrapes from training accidents. Soon he would need to handle injuries in a different league, first when men returned from the beaches in France to his hospital in England and then when his turn came to help carry the fight into Germany. Most of the men believed the invasion would start soon—in early June, when the tides and the weather would be at their best point for the attack.

If he couldn't find a little peace in this spot, he didn't know where it could be found. The soft bubbling of the stream and the rises he spotted on the surface were too inviting to be spoiled by premonitions of war.

The bamboo rod he borrowed at the gate house was a work of art. With nickel silver fittings and a walnut reel seat, it was much better equipment than he had ever used in the USA. Almost immediately, Bruce got the feel of the rod and could cast the line where he wanted in the river. It was good to sense the familiar tug when the rod loaded with a back cast and to watch the loop unfurl before the line hit the water. But Bruce assumed he would have to adapt his methods to have much success here. The Test was a slower-moving stream than Spruce Creek or the other waters that he usually fished. Those creeks tumbled out of the mountains and picked up speed as tributaries joined and springs fed the flow.

He had read about the challenges of getting a natural drift for dry flies in the chalk streams of England, and the Test was living up to its reputation. The trout were so wary in this ultra-clear water that there could be no drag or unnatural movement of the fly or the fish would refuse to strike. Bruce thought he was getting better at reading the stream and presenting the fly, but after two hours he still hadn't caught a fish. In the meantime, the fisherman in the mill race above him was connecting regularly.

It was tempting to move up the stream to ask the other fisherman for some advice—he obviously knew how to fish this stream. Bruce had given plenty of tips to other guys in the past. Yet he thought it would be bad form to approach the Englishman.

The major hatch appeared to be a species of mayfly that Bruce had never seen before. It was larger than any of the mayflies he had stashed in the box he brought from the States just in case he got the chance to try an English stream. And it had more pronounced yellow wings. None of the Grannons the gate keeper had given him were on the water, and all of the other flies in Bruce's collection seemed to be the wrong pattern for the Test. It was frustrating to be here in this spectacular setting and not be able to lure a fish to his fly. But Bruce had learned to avoid putting too much emphasis on the numbers or sizes of fish he caught.

Some days, the fish would take the fly readily. Other days he wouldn't have a single strike. Still, the essence of the stream, taking in the sights and sounds for a few hours, almost always refreshed him. It made him feel more alive.

When Bruce sat down on the bank to take a break, he let his mind drift along with the water. For at least a few moments, he wanted to feel that he was a part of this place. He had learned to burn pictures like these into his consciousness and to go back to them to evoke a sense of well-being. It was a simple strategy, a way to push troubling thoughts away for a while.

He was so intent on capturing the scene in front of him that Bruce didn't hear the soft steps of the fisherman who had walked down from the mill race.

A woman's voice woke him from his musing. "Good morning, Lieutenant Duncan. How do you like the Test?" she said. Her British upper-class accent was suffused with goodwill. "I can tell you know how to cast a fly rod, but I haven't seen you catch any fish yet."

Bruce turned and looked up to see a young woman dressed in full fishing gear.

Even wearing a baggy jacket and waders, she was stunning. Wisps of blond hair peaked out from under her wide-brimmed fishing hat and framed a face that made him stumble to find words.

Bruce flushed and said, "No, not much luck yet." Then he scrambled to his feet to introduce himself.

"I'm Bruce Duncan . . . but you already knew my name," he said. "How did you do that?"

She took off her hat, tossed her hair, and laughed in a friendly way. "I'm Amelia Whitcombe. I live here," she said. "I saw your name on the list your commander sent us . . . the men who won the lottery to get the beats. But I don't know anything else about you. Where do you fish when you are home in the States?"

Her easy manner began to relax Bruce, and her question about fishing helped relieve his awkwardness.

"Just the mountain creeks in western Pennsylvania . . . nothing like this gorgeous water," Bruce replied. "Your may-flies look different than the ones I brought with me. None of them have worked so far."

"Let me take a look," Amelia said.

"They're lovely . . . like little jewels. Tiny flies for your mountain streams," she said when Bruce showed her the box of flies. It was filled with sulfurs, caddis, and blue-winged olives. "Did you tie them?"

"A few," Bruce replied. "Tying flies is a family project . . . Most of them are my father's and brother's handiwork. I guess I have a piece of home with me in this fly box."


Amelia was normally reserved around the few strangers who fished on her family's estate, but there was something about this Yank that touched her. She had admired his smooth casting from a distance. And up close, she felt sponta-neous warmth toward him that she decided not to suppress. It didn't hurt that he was very good looking—not in the con-ventional manner of the men in her circles. He seemed fresh and natural.

*Show him how to catch a fish here*, she said to herself. *Daddy's in London. I won't get a lecture tonight.*

Her father would excoriate her for guiding this soldier on their stream—a definite breach of protocol for the heir to Whitcombe Hall. Since her brother was killed flying his Spitfire in the early days of the war, her father loaded more of his expectations on her. Because she was the only remaining Whitcombe descendant in her generation, he had ratcheted up the pressure to adhere to smothering dictates about their position in society. Her father didn't grasp that the war had turned everything upside down.

*What good are all the rules when you might die tomorrow?* she asked herself. *They didn't do my brother much good.*

"I'll tell you what, soldier. You're too good a fisherman to go away empty-handed. Let me be your guide for the afternoon. You're going to be fighting for us soon. You deserve to catch some English trout."

Bruce understood that Amelia was making an unusual offer—he doubted that she hung around the stream to guide other fishermen. At first he thought he should politely thank her so she could go back to her own beat. He knew his place as an interloper on this English estate. But he only made a lame attempt to decline when Amelia pointed toward the spot she wanted to start fishing with him.

"You're too generous," Bruce said. "If you could just loan me a couple mayflies and get me started, I think I'll be okay."

"No, I'm bored fishing by myself. After you catch some fish, you can teach me your American casting style. And maybe you can guide me sometime if I ever get to Pennsylvania."

"We have a deal. If you come to New York City after the war, it's a short train ride to Pennsylvania. It would be worth the trip."

Her prediction about catching fish didn't take long to come true. After she showed Bruce where the fish usually grouped into feeding lanes and suggested they use an emerger—a juvenile mayfly that rides in the surface film of the water until it sprouts its full wings—the Test began to boil with strikes. Before they stepped out of the stream to have lunch, Bruce caught eight fish—no trophies, but healthy brown trout with fight in them. And the action continued nonstop through the early part of the afternoon when many streams go to sleep.

"How do you like the Test now?" Amelia whispered as she gestured for them to move up the stream to a pool in the mill race. "I didn't fish the best pool this morning . . . wanted to give you plenty of room."

Bruce was transfixed by this woman. Of course he wanted to try out the pool and to keep fishing this legendary stream as long as he could. The cool, shimmering water was dimpled with rises now as the mayfly hatch was reaching an afternoon peak. The English spring was intoxicating with its deep greens and the scent of the irises along the bank. But these attractions paled against the experience of standing side by side with Amelia.

"I can't fish that pool. It's on your beat," Bruce said. "I'm doing fine here . . . best fishing day of my life. And no question, the best guide I've ever had." There was a bit of teasing in his voice as he tried to make some light-hearted conversation. His glance told a different story.

Bruce realized he was looking at her too much. He should be concentrating on reading the stream and making precise casts. Instead, he was stealing every opportunity to turn toward her.

Amelia wore her beauty in a comfortable, unassuming way. There was no posing or artificiality. Every word she uttered was on target—no wasted chatter. And she was making him feel wonderful.

It wasn't only her skill on the trout stream that surprised Bruce. When they took a break to have their lunches on the bank, he discovered she spent most of her time in an underground bunker in London. This day on the Test was as much a break for her as it was for him—a brief leave from her WAAF job analyzing aerial photographs of the German defenses.

"How did you get the job?" Bruce asked her.

"Cambridge," she replied. "I finished in 1941 at the end of the Blitz. And my mathematics professor advises the director of the Secret Service Bureau. The connection helped."

"I'm curious," Bruce said. "How do you analyze the photos?"

"It's not that glamorous. We use blowups and magnifiers but still squint at little dots on the page." She flashed a mischievous smile. "I've said enough . . . can't give away secrets."

"Understood," Bruce said.

Amelia had many layers, and Bruce liked them all—at least the ones he had seen so far. He wanted to know more.

"Tell me about Whitcombe Hall. Does your family live here?"

"For generations," she replied.

"It must be a treasure," Bruce said.

"This stream's a treasure," Amelia replied. "The rest can be suffocating . . . and sad." She paused and looked away.

Bruce could see that she was upset and decided not to press her to say more. "My family's had its problems," he said. "My father died last year, and my mother's trying to run our hardware store. It's a tough go."

"I'm sorry," she said. "Did you fish with your father? You said he tied some of your flies."

"Many times," Bruce replied. "How about your father?"

"Too busy . . . He's a member of Parliament. And he's too bitter. Since my brother got shot down, he won't come near the stream."

By the time they finished their lunch, Bruce learned that the rooms of Whitcombe Hall had gone quiet, her father sequestered in his study when he ventured out from his house in London. The staff had been cut to a subsistence level, and sheets covered the furniture. Losing Amelia's mother to cancer a decade ago had started her father's decline. And the killing of his son had broken him.

Bruce wanted to find words to offer some comfort but didn't know what to say. He settled for an awkward attempt at sympathy.

"You've lost too much," he said. "Your mother and brother gone. And your father so bitter."

"No worse than others," she said. "The girls in my office cheer me up. A day or two here, and I'm ready to go back to London."

Amelia shook her hair and smiled. "Enough tears," she said. "Come on, Yank. We're going to fish the mill race."

Soon they were casting over water that had been fallow for the hours they had plied the lower beat. And their styles were blending together—Amelia was casting more crisply, and Bruce had slowed his cadence. The rhythm of their casts seemed to feed on one another.

Both worked the far bank with delicate casts that dropped the fly inches from the grass in a chute where subtle rises were dimpling the surface. Amelia had told him that some of the largest fish stayed in this protected eddy, where they could sip the flies without much effort. She covered the head of the chute, while he fished the tail.

They missed a few hits, but then Amelia's rod bent almost in half and her reel began to scream. She had hooked the best fish of the day. It was Bruce's turn to help now. He backed away from the area where the fish was running and waded to the near bank to get the large net they hadn't needed to use before. The net had made him chuckle when Amelia showed it to him earlier. A two-handed giant that looked big enough for a salmon, it dwarfed anything he had ever used in Pennsylvania.

"Aren't you glad I brought that net?" Amelia said as she struggled with the fish. "I don't know how I could have used it myself . . . just brought it along because our guides always have one. If you can move downstream about fifty feet, I think I can steer this fish your way." Fifteen minutes later the glistening trout was in the net and Amelia's face was lit up with excitement.

"I want to let him go," Amelia said. "He'll be here another day for us to try to catch him."

Bruce heard the words that had slipped out of her mouth and was fairly certain she meant for the two of them to be together here again. But he was out of his element on the Test with an heiress. The war would take him away soon. *Cut the fantasies*, he said to himself.

"Yes, let's handle him gently," Bruce said. "Just hold his tail and let him swim in place for a moment to get his strength back. Then he'll be off." When the fish gave a quick flip of its body and flashed away, they looked at one another—not as fishermen who were triumphant after catching an epic trout, but as two people who had shared a special moment and wanted to share more.

Neither moved until Bruce said, "I think we've had enough fishing for today. Can we sit and talk a while?"

She put her rod over her shoulder, tipped her hat up, and gave Bruce a sparkling smile. "I think we can do better than sitting on the bank," she said. "I have the keys to the river keeper's cottage. No one's there."

Bruce didn't know what to say. He was getting aroused standing here in the water, and going with Amelia to the cottage was a delicious invitation. But his cautious side wondered if it was a good idea to sneak into a cabin with the daughter of the estate owner on the day he met her.

Amelia's next words hit their mark. "Who knows what will happen after the invasion? I might never see you again."

His caution began to crumble, and he reached to hold her hand.

"Let me hold you for a while," she said. "Don't worry, I'm not a loose woman. I've only had one real boyfriend, and he's out of my life. It's you that's making me act crazy."

The river keeper's cottage was a bit musty, but they didn't care. As soon as the door closed, they reached for one another. Even with their fishing garb still on, they melted together. With their hearts pounding, they helped each other slip off their clothes and looked with wonder. Amelia's long hair brushed the tops of her taut breasts, and her soft skin glowed in perfection. Bruce's lean body swelled.

He held her and whispered, "You're the most beautiful woman I'll ever see. I'm already in love."

"I'm with you," she said before she led him to the bed in the next room. "There's a lot I want to know about you, and I want to start now."

They spent the hours before Bruce had to return to his base exploring the contours, then the core of their bodies and minds. And when the evening began to cast shadows into the cottage, they clung together, trying not to let the richness pass. Now wordless, they stared into each other's eyes. Although they hadn't talked about the specter of what might come after the invasion, the immediacy of the war had driven them together. It hung over them now as they prepared to part. They would have two or three months before Bruce left England. Then no one could predict what might happen.

# Chapter 3

## REUNION

———

### Pennsylvania
### October 1945

The music that was playing when he walked down the stairs made Bruce smile. It was "Accentuate the Positive"—one of the cheeriest tunes written during the war. Glen must have chosen the record. He acted like he could take on anything—a good attitude for a fighter pilot. Bruce hoped civilian life would work out for Glen. He deserved a smooth trip.

The rubble and dust from Europe was still in Bruce's pores, but the sparkle that his mother had put on their home was giving him a lift. There was bunting on the front porch and decorations spread all through the downstairs. Vases were filled with roses and salvia from her garden, and incredible smells were coming from the kitchen. Alice and his aunt Pauline, both terrific cooks, had promised a feast for the ages. He suspected they weren't exaggerating.

Bruce was trying to settle into a mood that he hadn't felt for a long time—a sense of being grounded to something good, something solid. There were plenty of signs that his world could be that way again. Alice was more full of life than he had expected. His brother had some scarring from his burns but otherwise was brimming with vitality. And the town council had given him a strong endorsement to start a practice in Hollidaysburg. There was a place for him here.

"Hey, Bruce, get yourself a drink. You have some catching up to do," Glen yelled from the kitchen at the moment Pauline and Vic came through the front door.

Bruce was pleased to see that his aunt and uncle were the first guests. Pauline and Vic lived just two blocks away and were like an extra set of parents. Pauline, his mother's sister, was an irreverent pistol of a woman who was never afraid to speak her mind. Vic was a big man, six feet four inches and over three hundred pounds, who had gained weight since Bruce saw him last. "There he is . . . our hero," Pauline cracked when Bruce walked toward her. "Where did you get all the brass? Did they give out ribbons for bedding nurses?" Her warm embrace belied the playful words.

"Yeah," Bruce said as he picked up on Pauline's jesting without missing a beat. "This one is for setting the battalion record. No other guys came close."

Vic gripped Bruce's hand and gave it a bone-cracking shake. A manager at the Pennsylvania Railroad repair shops in Hollidaysburg, Vic was the kind of man who dived headfirst into everything he did. During his glory days as a tight end at Penn State, Vic was a heartthrob. Now in his late fifties, he was showing his age. Bruce noticed the popping veins in Vic's face.

There was no time for Bruce to relax with Pauline and Vic because Kate and Lucas Glover had arrived.

From his first glance at Kate, he knew that it was a mistake for Glen to invite her. They had stopped dating after

Bruce began medical school because Kate hadn't wanted to wait "forever" to get married—a good excuse for Bruce to make his exit. There had been plenty of heat between them in the last summer they were together, but Bruce had known he could never marry her. He needed something deeper—a woman who challenged him, someone who would fascinate him more as time went by.

As she hugged him tightly and whispered that she had missed him, he could see Lucas purse his lips—a hint that there might be trouble if Bruce didn't slip away from her soon.

"Hey, Lucas, good to see you," Bruce said after he moved away from Kate. "Are you playing any basketball? I'll bet you're still at the top of your game."

Bruce's attempt to break the tension seemed to be working as Lucas walked with him to the bar in the sun room. They had played together on the Hollidaysburg High School team when Lucas had excelled as a gritty guard and Bruce mostly rode the bench as a second-string forward. Until Lucas took Kate when she became available, they had been good friends. Lucas was finishing his ceramic engineering degree at Pitt and already was hired at Allegheny Refractories. So he had something to offer Kate that Bruce didn't—a marriage and a family right away.

Lucas was exempted from the draft because his company made silica linings for the high-temperature blast furnaces that were essential to the war effort. Now he was the superintendent of the Blairton plant for Allegheny Refractories—one of the largest companies in central Pennsylvania. Bruce didn't resent his spending the war in Hollidaysburg or moving ahead so fast in a career. Yet he could tell that Lucas was uncomfortable being at a party for a beribboned soldier. Two attempts to straighten a tie that didn't need straightening, a flushed face, and a trickle of sweat coming from a sideburn toward his chin gave him away. None of the other guests looked overheated

on this cool October evening. *Is he still jealous about Kate?*
Bruce wondered. *Guilt? A cushy life here when the rest of us served?*

They were awkward together now, when they had once had an easy relationship. Bruce hoped that the strain would be short-lived. He didn't want to mar his return to Hollidaysburg with a conflict with one of the town kingpins.

A rush of people arriving at the party gave Bruce a good excuse for breaking away from Lucas. Bess Runyon, his mother's best friend, was moving toward him now.

"So here you are," Bess said as she sized him up. "Good to see you, Bruce."

"And it's good to see you, Miss Runyon."

"Don't you think it's about time you drop the Miss Runyon?" Bess said. "You've seen God knows what in the war . . . and if I get my way, you're going to be my neighbor. The place next door just came on the market. It's a great house, just your size."

Bruce smiled. "I'm afraid my bank account is too thin now to buy anything."

"I saw that coming," Bess said. "McDonald, the owner, let the garden go wild. The weeds would scare off most people, but I told him I'd shape up the yard if he'd rent to you for a year. After you get your practice going, you can buy the home. It's yours if you want it."

Bess's garden was the finest in Hollidaysburg. Surrounding a Federal-style near-mansion on Elm Street, the landscape had been groomed by generations of Runyons since the house was built before the Civil War by one of her ancestors, a president of an iron-smelting company. Although Bess had worked as an English teacher and had never married, remnants of the family fortune allowed her to live in the antique-filled dwelling and maintain the expansive garden.

Bruce remembered the house that could be rented—a yellow clapboard-covered Victorian about half as large as the imposing structure next door. As Bess said, just his size. She had made a tantalizing offer. He would check it out soon.

"Bruce, you lead the way," Bruce's mother rang out as she pushed through the crowd. "We've been waiting for years to have this meal, and the table is loaded with everything you wanted."

True to her word, the dining room table was jammed with an abundance of food Bruce hadn't tasted since he left Hollidaysburg. Heaping casseroles of scalloped potatoes, simmered with cheese and cream, an Aunt Pauline specialty, sat next to roasted legs of lamb. And to Bruce's wonder, his mother had been able to find a late harvest of corn on the cob to make chicken corn pie—a soul-satisfying dish that had been created by his great-grandmother.

Before his uncle Vic started to carve and everyone could fill their plates, Bruce gathered Alice and Glen close to him as he prepared to deliver the words he had penned for the occasion.

"It's a glorious time for celebration, isn't it?" Bruce asked the crowd. "We've won the war, and life's getting back to normal. So here's to the USA! We all did our jobs . . . the people who served overseas and those at home. I raise my glass to all of you who kept the country running . . . You gave us soldiers the best support any army ever had.

"And here's to those soldiers," Bruce said as his voice began to tremble. "I can see some of their faces . . . great guys. They fought for what we have here tonight. The chance to be together with family and friends and to have a life after the war."

Bruce steadied himself and went on. "Well, the last thing I wanted to do tonight was to get maudlin or to tell war stories, so I guess I better get back on track. I think my mother wants us to join hands so she can say grace.

"It better be a short one. All these delights are waiting for us."

His mother was back at the piano now with the singers gathered around. Judge Clapper, a family friend, had just finished leading a raucous version, replete with innuendo, of Gene Autry's "Back in the Saddle Again" and had his hand on Alice's shoulder. Bruce had noticed a sparkle about Alice when the judge was near—a liveliness that reminded him of the years before the war.

The judge and his wife, Cecelia, had been fixtures at Duncan family events through the years, so there was a logical reason why he was at the party, even though Cecelia had died of cancer during the war. Yet Bruce's curiosity was piqued. Were the judge and his mother already seeing each other? He murmured under his breath, *Let her be happy. She deserves it.*

"Bruce, come on and join us," Alice called. "I have the Bing Crosby arrangement of *Don't Fence Me In.* You can take Bing's part, and the rest of us can try to be the Andrews Sisters."

The result was better than Bruce had anticipated. A member of the Penn glee club in his college days, he was a decent tenor and knew how to harmonize. Alice took the lead on the Andrews Sisters backing, while Bess and Pauline completed the trio.

"That was good, really good," Alice said. Tears welled in her eyes. "I can't tell you how many times I dreamed of having you back in this house, singing around this old piano."

Bruce sat down beside her. "Okay, Mom, we're ready for some more songs. How about 'Happy Days Are Here Again'? Everybody knows that one."

As the singing went on, the humorous and upbeat choices gave way to the softer ballads of love and yearning. Through most of them, Bruce's mood was more buoyant than it had been in months. Relief at being back in this welcoming place was trumping memories of the carnage in France and his longings for Amelia. But when they finally got to "I'll Be Seeing You," his resistance gave way. He turned his head as the words evoked memories that tore at him.

Alice knew about Amelia from Bruce's letters and could tell that the love songs were beginning to stoke the hurt. So she switched to some patriotic music she thought would ring out the party on a high note. It was after one o'clock in the morning when they sang the last strains of "God Bless America" and most of the remaining party goers drifted out into the night.

Glen and Vic were nursing beers on the front porch while Bruce helped Alice and Pauline put the kitchen back in order. He was glad there were chores to do. It had been an emotional evening.

The simple task of drying dishes calmed him. Work of any sort usually did that to Bruce. It was satisfying to channel his energies into something that he could measure, an activity where progress could be made. Medicine had been a good choice for him. There were always tasks to be done, problems to solve.

As he thought of the steps ahead of him—making the transition to civilian life, starting his practice, carving out a role in this community—Bruce wondered how the legacy of the war would play out.

In a way, 1942 through 1945 had been lost years—a piece of his life that he would never be able to make up. If the war hadn't happened, he would have already been in practice for three years. Maybe he would have been married by now. For certain, he wouldn't be carrying the painful memories that he hoped would fade.

Those channels of thinking never helped him. Going back over what could have been. Second-guessing himself about what he could have done to hold on to Amelia. Obsessing about mistakes he made as a rookie battlefield surgeon. Remembering the faces of soldiers who had closed their eyes for the last time. Trying to act like his old self tonight had worked. The dark thoughts had stayed away.

The rest of his life was ahead of him, and he was a more skilled doctor now than he would have been without the war. He needed to let the good cheer from tonight spill over him. He needed to tame the ghosts. More than anything, he needed to get to work.

*Chapter 4*

## GETTING STARTED

⌒

ollidaysburg was alive on this brilliant fall morning in 1945. The Diamond, in the center of the village at the highest point of Union Street, was busy with traffic. Fords, Chevys, and Plymouths were joined by pricier Studebakers and Packards coursing through the business section of town. Bruce was pleased to see so many cars in Hollidaysburg—the days of gas rationing were over.

Walking along the street toward First Trust Bank, he could hear steam engines from the tracks south of town and see plumes of smoke from the Pennsylvania Railroad repair shops. The shops had grown during the war years and now were massed between the town and Chimney Rocks Mountain. They surrounded the base of the mountain, as if they were about to start climbing it or fill in any open space around it. Prone to riffs of exaggeration, his uncle Vic claimed that the repair shops were the biggest and best in the USA. With the economy booming after the war and railroads needing to transport goods, Vic was speculating on land, hoping prices would rise for places to build.

Bruce's financial strategy was more measured. The pay as an army surgeon was Spartan compared to what he might have made in clinical practice, and he had sent most of it back home to help his mother with the hardware store. So his savings to start his practice totaled under a thousand dollars. He needed a loan to get going.

The façade of First Trust Bank was a pinnacle of the architecture on Union Street. Designed in an exuberant style of the late nineteenth century, the bank exterior was embroidered with mosaics of scenes from the history of the region—pioneers and Iroquois, early furnaces used to smelt iron ore, and at the top of the central arch, the canal and railway that had made the town a transportation hub. Bruce thought the designer had gone overboard to put a welcoming face on the building. All of the images were symbols of success. Even the Iroquois bartering with an early settler looked happy to be doing business. No scenes of bankruptcy, foreclosure, or poverty were depicted here.

Bruce tensed as he walked past the row of tellers toward the bank vice president's office. His father had struggled to pay back loans to keep the hardware store supplied. And when the store edged toward bankruptcy, his father must have taken this walk with a sense of doom. The store was at a low ebb in early 1943 when Robert Duncan died in a suspicious single-car accident. People were scrapping metal to help the war effort, not buying new hardware. His father's letters had skimmed over concerns about the store, but Bruce knew they were stretched to the limit.

Despite Bruce's trepidation, the banker, Jack Carter, gave him a warm greeting and had the loan papers ready to sign.

"Good to see a new doctor setting up shop," Jack said. "The bank is pleased to help you get started."

"I didn't want to do this," Bruce said. "I know the bank had problems with my father."

"Young man, you've got a smooth ride ahead. Magnuson is retiring, and you'll be the only doctor in town. You can be as busy as you want. What's there to be nervous about? You can pay back this loan in a year.

"It's a plus you aren't a partner in the hardware store. I wrote this up using just your financial history. No previous loans, no financial issues, just your stellar record in medical school and the army. You were a shoo-in for getting this loan. I'd give it to anyone with your promise."

"I like your confidence," Bruce said. "Where do I sign?"


As Bruce walked toward Duncan Hardware, four blocks down Union Street from the bank, his attention was focused on the storefronts with their corbelled tops and filigreed woodwork. He had missed this place, and he wanted to absorb as much of it as he could.

The buildings dated from the last century, when craftsmen had the skills to construct these solid, fanciful structures. One of his favorites was Suckling's Men's Store with its burnished copper fittings around the windows and brick patterns with crenellations that traced up to the eaves. The store windows were filled with fall suits, wool overcoats, and sharp-looking hats. He concluded that guys returning from the war must be buying lots of new outfits—Suckling's was thriving. After the practice got rolling, he might cross the doors to buy a new suit. His last one dated from med school graduation.

Encore Music, tucked into a small building beside the Manos Theater, was gleaming in the morning sun. Light popped off the facets of stained glass in the transom and across the display windows, glinting from the shiny surfaces of a trombone, a trio of brass cornets, and a French horn.

Then he spotted Pete Nicholaou, a family friend, who was looking out the front door of his restaurant, the

Ambrosia. After emigrating from Greece in the 1920s, Pete had become one of the major businessmen in town. Starting with a small candy store, he had added the Ambrosia and the two movie theaters in Hollidaysburg to his mini-empire. Bruce waved to Pete, who saluted back.

The Manos Theater, beside Pete's restaurant, didn't fit the mold of the historic district. With its fluted Ionic columns and bright posters, the movie palace had an over-the-top effect that mimicked a bit of Pete's Grecian homeland. Tonight's movie, *Anchors Aweigh* with Frank Sinatra and Gene Kelly, would pack in the customers.

Bruce's grandmother had told him of other theaters in Hollidaysburg that had closed after the movies took hold. The old opera house on the Diamond was long gone. Now converted to a department store, the opera house must have been a sight in its prime. It had attracted major acts of its era—Jenny Lind, the Swedish Nightingale, and Wild Bill Cody's Tom Thumb. Bruce's knowledge of this town was nurtured by his grandmother and mother—descendants of William Holliday, who had founded it in the 1700s.

Richardson's Pharmacy on the corner of Union and Wayne, only a half block from his new office, would be a convenient location for patients to fill their prescriptions. The Richardsons' collection of antique apothecary jars with exotic labels had fascinated Bruce as a boy. He had concocted mixtures of drugs like belladonna and digitalis in his imagination as a nine- or ten-year-old when he started to think of a career in medicine. By the time he left grade school, Bruce had learned that the white and blue canisters with their gold lettering were vestiges of the past and held worthless dust, if anything. The bottles were still there, however, and added a show of color and mystery to the pharmacy. He suspected these old bottles might have an unconscious influence on people picking up prescriptions. Despite the development of sulfa, penicillin, and other wonder drugs, the placebo response still was a significant part of medical practice.

Bruce wondered how his style of practicing medicine would be accepted. Honed by years in the service, his no-nonsense methods would be a change from the hand-holding that his predecessors used when they didn't know what to do. They were smooth and kind to a fault, not telling people the truth, and often hiding their ignorance behind an impeccable bedside manner. His family's own GP, Dr. Magnuson, had this laid-back attitude taught in homeopathic medical schools. The hack was probably the cause of a classmate's death when Bruce was fourteen. Magnuson was so slow to act that the boy's appendix burst, and he was dead of peritonitis within two days.

As he approached Duncan's Hardware, Bruce's thoughts switched from his medical practice to concerns about his brother and mother. He hadn't been in the store since returning from Germany three days ago. It looked just the same from the street—a formidable building, constructed by his grandfather, Matthew Duncan, in the 1890s as an emporium to dwarf other establishments on the block.

Glen had turned down a job offer to fly for Eastern Airlines, a fledgling carrier that was establishing a passenger network, and instead honored his promise to run the hardware store. From what Bruce had heard, an infusion of energy was needed. Without Glen's help, he feared their mother would have to close the business.

On this day, the store looked prosperous enough. The windows held an artful display of cornstalks and pumpkins woven around a selection of ladders. Pyramids of paint cans were festooned with photos of room renovations, and a lattice was strung with tools to tempt handymen. As he stepped across the threshold, Bruce felt a surge of emotion. The tiles on the floor at the entrance spelled out *Duncan*

*Hardware—1897*, the year his grandfather had returned from a mining adventure in Colorado to Hollidaysburg. As the story was told, the family was never as well off as when Matthew Duncan, who wasn't a very successful gold miner, got lucky in a poker game and put together the stake that allowed him to quit the mine fields.

He had built the store to last. The red brick edifice stretched over a double city lot, and the interior was fitted with oak cabinets and bins from front to back. With high ceilings and a loading dock in the rear, they could display heavy equipment other stores couldn't handle. The middle of the first floor had a cast-iron stove that was fired on cold days from fall to spring. A group of well-used rocking chairs were strewn around the stove to draw in customers. Glen and Alice were sitting there now, waiting for Bruce to arrive.

Glen spied Bruce coming through the door and jumped up to greet him. "What do you think of the store? Freshened it up, didn't we?"

"Looks great," Bruce said as he inspected the work. "I can tell you're putting your stamp on the place."

"He's been going almost nonstop since he got home," Alice said. "I get exhausted just watching him tackle his projects. There's so much more life around here. But we're having a little quibble about the stove. He wants to get rid of it and the farming equipment so he can use the space to start carrying washing machines and refrigerators."

"Yep. It's time we bring the store into the new world," Glen replied. "That stove goes back to the turn of the century . . . a vestige of the past. The factories will be pouring out appliances now that the war is over. We need to ride that wave."

"I suppose he's right," Alice said. "I just hate to end the tradition. Some of the regulars will think we've lost our way."

"Don't worry, Mom," Glen said. "A few of the men that sit around and drink our coffee might grouse. But they don't buy much of anything."

Knowing better than to inject his opinions into the discussion, Bruce moved the conversation along to plans for the rest of the day. "How about some lunch? I have an appointment with the architect for the office construction at one thirty, so we have to get moving. Pete's cooking a special meal for us . . . trout from his pond. He won't want us to rush through it."


The best part of dining at the Ambrosia was Pete himself—a small round man, always grinning, making people feel like honored guests. Pete had started as a cook at the Colonial, a restaurant that had occupied this space for many years. When he took over the Colonial, Pete kept the furniture and the old paintings of Hollidaysburg scenes on the walls. But he added a few touches of his native Greece—a section of the menu with traditional Greek dishes and some photos of the village where his parents had a taverna.

Moving through the lunch-hour crowd, Pete had a broader smile than usual.

"This is a big honor for me," he said as he tried to put his arm around Bruce's much higher shoulders. "Hosting a meal to celebrate the launch of your practice. I heard all of the paperwork got done today, and you're ready to go. Congratulations."

"It's not a big deal. We're just getting everything lined up to open the office."

"Bruce, it is a big deal," Alice said. "You've pointed toward this day all your life. You've worked so hard, you deserve everything that's happening."

"Come on back to the private room," Pete motioned. "I have some surprises for you."

Bruce entered a room with a table set for nine people and piled with brightly wrapped packages. "What's going on? I just asked for a table for the three of us."

"This is my treat," Pete said. "Your brother and I hatched the plan when we heard about all the things you're doing today."

With a chirping whistle, Pete summoned the others to enter through the back doors to the room. Aunt Pauline and Uncle Vic, Bess Runyon, Judge Clapper, and Helene, Pete's wife, spilled into the room, laughing as they surrounded Bruce.

"Just a little party to mark the occasion," Glen shouted through the babble.

"Helene and I are going to join you for this one—wouldn't miss it," Pete added.

Pauline waved her hands to get their attention and pointed to the pile of packages on the table. "Let's get these gifts opened before the food comes."

"We wanted to help with your new office, so we found a few trinkets that we thought you could use to decorate it," Alice explained. "You'll need some pictures on the walls and other things to make people comfortable . . . something better than those old anatomy prints that make Magnuson's office so grim."

"Vic and Pauline brought the biggest package. Start with that one," Glen said. "It's over in the corner, because it's too big for the table."

"I'm touched," Bruce said. "I had no idea that you were planning this. And I hadn't thought about what to put in the office to brighten it up. You're right, Magnuson's is deadly.

"So, Pauline, what's hiding behind the brown paper wrapping—something wild and exotic?"

"Nothing that wild. Something we've been saving for you."

Bruce tore off large swaths of paper to reveal three pieces of fine glazed stoneware. Whimsically drawn stags were on two of the pieces, a tall and well-formed jug and a large butter churn. The smallest of the pieces, a batter pail with a wooden handle and a tin lid, had four birds circling a beautifully scribed date of 1860.

"Where did you find these pieces? They're top notch. I love them."

"An auction in Harrisburg," Pauline answered. "When we saw them, we thought of you. A touch of country for your waiting room."

Each of the others had worked to find gifts that would delight Bruce. Glen produced a small brass scale that had belonged to their grandfather and had been used in the early days of the hardware store. Judge Clapper brought an oil painting of a fishing pool on Spruce Creek. Pete and Helene gave him a painted box with figures of ancient Greece and a rolled-up scroll of paper tied with a braided cord. The message on the scroll was their pledge to host an opening party at his new office.

Bess's package contained a simple, elegant glass vase from Steuben. Inside were two cards. The first said: "I'll keep this vase filled with flowers from my garden when they're in season. I wish you many years of a blossoming career." The second card read: "Would be lovely to have you as a neighbor."

The chance to rent the house next door to Bess solved one more of his problems. The small home had everything he would need. And it was one of the houses with character on the section of Elm Street where he had hoped to live. This day was shaping up to be one of the best for a long time.

The last gift was from his mother—a heavy flat box wrapped with hand-blocked paper she had printed herself. The blocking had a caduceus delicately woven into a pattern of suns, moons, and stars.

"I want to save this paper," Bruce said. "It's a work of art. I think I'll frame some of it for the office wall."

He opened the package and found a tasteful sign with chiseled lettering outlined in gold paint on a black background: *Bruce Duncan, M.D.*

"I had it made last winter when you were in that terrible battle in Alsace-Lorraine. I knew you'd get through the war and be able to hang it somewhere," Alice said.

"A gift of faith. Thanks, Mother," Bruce said before he kissed her on the cheek. "I'm lucky to have all of you behind me. I'd like to start tearing down some walls this afternoon and getting the office shaped up for business. I'm ready to go."

Walking from the restaurant to the house on Wayne Street that would hold his medical practice, Bruce's mind was churning. He was committed now. The part of him that wondered if he could ever find his way back to England and Amelia had to be tied up and bundled away. The searing traces of war had to fade into the background. He couldn't have better support for getting his practice established. It was time to throw himself into his work—to fulfill the promise of the sign his mother wanted him to hang in this town.

# Chapter 5

## GAME ON

———

The remnants of the fall leaves, their color fading in mid-November, tumbled around Bruce's feet as he walked toward his office. The wind was picking up, and the dense clouds were a steel gray that held a cold rain for later in the day. The signs of winter in the bare trees and the leaden sky stirred memories of a year ago in France when the battle of Hürtgen Forest was about to start.

Those memories were a trapdoor to a hell he wanted to forget. So he wrestled his mind back to the day ahead. Within the hour he would start seeing patients who weren't torn apart like the soldiers he had treated, who could sit calmly in his office talking about their symptoms.

The practice was getting busy faster than he expected, and Maggie Bailey, the nurse he had hired, would have patients lined up to see him. After being away from nursing while her children were young, Maggie had taken to her new job with gusto. Thick boned and compact, she ran the office like a field general. Yet there was a soft edge to her, a kindness that put people at ease. They had clicked from day one.

The first two patients were straightforward—easy to diagnose and treat. A man with edema needed an increased dose of hydrochlorothiazide and a check of his potassium level to see if a supplement should be prescribed. A woman with weight loss and overactive reflexes probably had hyperthyroidism. Bruce had drawn blood for definitive tests—ones he couldn't do in his lab but would send to the Altoona hospital for processing. He was just getting started with the third patient when Maggie snapped open the door and said, "I need you now in the next room—it's urgent."

A mother had brought her three-year-old son who had a high fever. He moaned a little but wasn't responding to questions. After a swift exam, Bruce told Maggie, "Call the ambulance. Tell them it's an emergency. Then get the spinal tap kit right away." The back of the boy's neck was tight, and he winced when his legs were lifted straight up from the examining table. Bruce had never seen a case of meningitis. This could be the first one.

Maggie rushed back with the kit, steadied the mother with a few words, and held the boy tight while Bruce slipped the needle between his third and fourth vertebrae to draw a sample of spinal fluid.

"Start an IV and give him an injection of penicillin G," Bruce said. "I'll be next door putting this under the scope. Call me if you need me."

He gave the mother a touch on the shoulder and comforted her as he left the room. "I think we have the answer . . . It's probably meningitis. Thank God for penicillin. He'll probably start doing better soon."

Within five minutes, the slide was in front of him—gram positive cocci of *streptococcus pneumonia*—a bacterium that penicillin would kill. He rushed back to the exam room just as the ambulance arrived. He would ride along to the hospital to make sure the boy got there in safe condition.

When Maggie left at the end of the day, she stepped in to give him a progress report. "Got to leave, Doc . . . Junior Varsity game starts at six, and I can't miss seeing my son make some tackles." After pausing for a moment, she continued. "That kid was lucky you came to town. I just called the hospital. He's waking up, temp is almost back to normal."

"Good news about the boy," Bruce said. "Couldn't have done it without you. If you hadn't made everything happen so quickly, we could have lost him."

Maggie smiled and said, "I'm glad it worked out. I wasn't quite as rusty as I thought I might be."

"I didn't see a flake of rust."

"Sorry to leave you with a couple more patients to see. I've got the charts started, and the patients are in the exam rooms. One of them is a young guy with a cut finger that needs sewed up. The other is a woman with a cough. Nothing complicated—you should be able to get out of here soon."

Suturing the finger took only a few minutes, and Bruce hoped he could wrap up his first week in the office with something simple like a cold. But when he picked up the last chart, he was startled to see the name Kate Glover. He hadn't seen Kate since the welcome home party when her husband, Lucas, got testy. Examining her would be awkward. Maybe he should have made a short list for Maggie of patients he couldn't treat. Now he was stuck alone with Kate in the office. And he had promised Glen he'd leave at five thirty to drive to Tyrone for tonight's varsity football game. He needed to get Kate out of the office fast and without a hitch.

When he knocked and opened the exam room door, he found Kate sitting on the table, draped in a hospital gown that barely covered her.

"Kate . . . I can't be your doctor," he said. "We were too close. You'll have to stick with Magnuson till he retires. Or you could see Steve Taylor in Altoona."

"I want you," she said as she flashed an inviting smile. "You're better than Magnuson or any of the doctors in Altoona. Couldn't we give it a try?"

"No. It's a bad idea. Lucas would be furious."

"I wouldn't mind if he got angry. Marrying him was a mistake."

The danger signs were blatant, and Bruce knew he needed to get Kate out of his office now.

"You need to go home to your family. We can forget this afternoon."

"I could see Sarah Avery, the woman doctor who's coming to town. But I'd still like to have you. Think about it. We can be friends. I won't bite."

Jolted by the news about another doctor, Bruce hesitated before leaving.

"I didn't know about the woman doctor. Who is she? When is she coming here?"

"I heard about her at the country club yesterday. She's graduating from Women's Medical College before Christmas. Supposed to open her practice in January or February. They said she's gorgeous . . . and smart."

"Good, you'll have a doctor you can see right here in Hollidaysburg. And it won't be me."

He turned and walked out the door.

It was half-time at the football game in Tyrone, and a cold rain was drilling down. The Hollidaysburg High School Band was slogging through the mud, giving a plucky performance of a John Philip Sousa march. But Bruce's attention was elsewhere. Kate's startling news had set off a torrent of thoughts. He'd been blindsided. Even the banker didn't know another new doctor was starting practice in Hollidaysburg. Would there be enough business for both of them? Could he pay back the loan? She was a woman—the first female doctor in the area. Would she pull the women away from his practice?

Kate's visit tore at him from another direction. Why would she come to his office unless she wanted something more than medical treatment? She knew Lucas would hate her being examined by an old boyfriend, and she knew a woman doctor was on her way. Was it a veiled invitation? He would never violate his medical oath, but the encounter had stirred him—not with desire for Kate. He didn't want her. He wanted Amelia.

Bruce could almost feel Amelia beside him now with her hand sneaking under his coat—she did that sometimes under the table at a restaurant or in the back of a taxi. Amelia came to him at odd moments. Sometimes he could hear her voice. Snippets of conversations they'd had. The last words she'd spoken to him—a hollow promise before he shipped out to France. The invitation from their first day together. "Let me hold you awhile." If Bruce hadn't been taught that grief could pull these sorts of tricks, he would think that he was going over the edge.

He knew he should start dating. It wasn't healthy to be obsessed with a ghost from the past and be without a woman for so long. But the prospects for finding someone who would make him forget Amelia were about as dreary as the sodden conditions on this wet November night. He had heard other vets say the greatest days of their lives were behind them—there would never be anything like the intensity of the war years. Would it be the same for him? Amelia was gone. Only the aching after-images remained.

Glen was taking out his flask regularly and was in high spirits. But Bruce was starting to shiver and was blowing into his hands to keep them warm. "Let's get out of here," Bruce said. "It looks like more rain is on the way, and the temperature is dropping. I've had enough."

"It's going to be a big mud fight in the second half," Glen said. "Don't you want to see these guys get really dirty? They'll be fumbling all over the place."

Bruce stood and took charge. "Time to go, brother. You can sleep off the Old Granddad in the back seat. You'll be in better shape by the time you get home."

"Come on, Bruce. Don't be such a prude . . . Loosen up. After what we went through, we deserve to have some fun. Here—have a slug of the whiskey. Drink to my tentmates. They're at the bottom of the English Channel. No more whiskey for them. And drink to your buddies. What are some of those guys' names? Teddy? And Blaise, the other doc you mumble about?"

Bruce grimaced. "Leave them out of this. I've had a hard enough day already."

"Sorry, Bruce. I need to celebrate. Honor those poor souls. Act like life is just a bowl of cherries."

"We each do it our way. You celebrate. I gnash my teeth."

Bruce thought of Amelia again. He'd been sitting in the cold, having pitiful fantasies about her being here. But she'd gutted him. *There's nothing to celebrate.*

Let's get moving," Bruce said. I have to make a quick stop at the hospital."


By the time they got through the streets of Tyrone and onto Route 220 to Altoona, the rain began to thicken and freeze. The Plymouth's defroster was roaring without much effect. It was hard to see the tail lights of the car ahead of them. "I'm going to skip the visit to the hospital," Bruce said. "It's getting slippery out there. I'll just take it easy and get us back to Hollidaysburg in one piece. I can call the hospital from home."

"I'd stay back from that car, give him plenty of room," Glen said. "I'll help you keep an eye on him."

"Rub the windshield when it gets fogged up. I've been trying to keep that guy in sight to stay on the road. Can't see much of the edge . . . Can you?"

"You're doing fine; just keep it steady," Glen said. "Glad you're driving and not me . . . had too many hits of the Old Grandad."

The driving got easier around the turnoff to Altoona, where there were businesses with lights blazing and streetlamps to cut through the murk. They passed the American Legion Post and the Rustic Isle restaurant and dance floor. A fair number of cars were still parked there despite the worsening conditions. People would get a surprise when they came outdoors to find their cars covered in ice. Next Bruce would need to veer left around the steep curve by Lakemont Park and would have only three more miles to Hollidaysburg.

"Almost home," Bruce said. "Tough drive at the end of a long day."

"Watch out," Glen screamed as they both saw a skidding car coming right at them from the opposite lane. Bruce jammed his foot on the brake and swerved to the right, just missing the other car. But there was a cacophony of sheering sounds and a thudding stop. The front of the car was buried to the edge of the windshield under the back of a truck parked on the side of the road. There had been nowhere safe to go. He hadn't seen the truck until seconds before they hit it. And there was a sharp drop-off into a gulley on the right side of the truck.

Glen had curled into a ball and crouched down in the seat when he saw the car approaching the back of the truck. His shins were bleeding from banging on the dashboard, and he was a little dazed. "I think I'm okay," he said.

"Get out of here quick!" Bruce shouted. "There's gas everywhere."

They scrambled out of the car after prying open the

driver's-side door—the only one that still worked. To Bruce's surprise, they weren't seriously hurt. Another foot or two under the truck and they both would have been dead.

Moving away from the Plymouth as it started to catch on fire, they realized that the other car hadn't fared as well. It was twisted against a utility pole that had broken off and was lying beside the road. Sparks were flaring from ruptured power lines dangling over the car. One of the men that had been in the car was sprawled beside the pole, groaning and bleeding heavily. There was no other sign of life.

"That car could be live with electricity; don't touch it," Glen shouted.

"Yeah, I know. It could blow too," Bruce shouted back. "But we need to check on the guy inside the car. Stay back. I'll take a look."

Bruce approached the car with quick strides. "He's dead—his head got crushed. Let's get the other fellow away from the car so I can work on him."

"Watch those wires," Glen said as they hurried toward the man who was now in a pool of blood.

Bruce spotted the source of the bleeding right away. "Give me your belt, Glen. I need to get a tourniquet on that left arm before we try to move him. That splintered bone was like a knife—cut open his brachial artery."

The man cried out when Bruce hitched the tourniquet against the mangled arm.

"Ahh . . . what are you doing?" he croaked. The pain had jerked him out of his stupor.

"Hang tight," Bruce said. "You were in a bad accident, but you'll be okay. I'm a doctor, so let me take care of you. We have to move you away from the car now."

Bruce and Glen used the fireman's carry to take him about a hundred feet across the road, where there was a house with a squat old woman standing on the porch.

"Call the police and an ambulance. This man needs to get to the hospital," Bruce said to her.

"Already did," she said. "I got some blankets on the floor in the living room . . . was ready for you. Bring him in."

"Get me more blankets or pillows," Bruce said. "He's going into shock. We need to get his legs into the air and push some blood back to his heart."

The bleeding was mostly stopped, and his legs were elevated, but he was sinking fast. Breathing was labored. He was starting to turn cyanotic. "Get me some scissors so I can strip this coat and shirt off him. Something's wrong with his chest."

He cut through the coat and discovered the problem. There were jagged broken ribs on the left side. And when he listened with his bare ear for breath sounds on that side of his chest, there were only faint murmurs—signs of a pneumothorax. The lung tissue must have been cut by one of the splintered ribs, and air was leaking out. His left chest cavity was full of air, compressing the lung and shoving the heart and aorta toward the right chest. If the pressure didn't release in the next few minutes, the heart would be squeezed out of commission. The only option was to stab through the space between the ribs with the scissors and to crank open a portal to release the air pressure.

"I'm going to cut into his chest with the scissors. He'll die unless we do it."

There was no time to worry about trying to sterilize the scissors. So Bruce found a spot between the fourth and fifth ribs and slid the scissors point over the top of the rib where it would miss the arteries and nerves. Then they heard a loud hiss, like air going out of a tire when it's cut, and gurgling sounds from around the scissor point. Soon the man's struggle to breathe eased and his color improved.

"Hold the scissors at an angle to keep an opening while I see if there's anything else wrong," Bruce directed his brother. "The hole I made needs to stay open until he gets to the hospital. Put your thumb on the scissors blade, right here, so it doesn't go in any farther and nick the lung. And tilt the blade down. It won't do any damage if you hold it tight."

Glen paused a moment, then slipped his hands over Bruce's and grabbed the blade. "Got it," he said as they heard the first strains of a siren.

Bruce's second ambulance ride of the day was more harrowing than the first. The man's blood pressure was barely detectable when they began the trip. But it went up to 80/50 after he started an IV and pumped the bag. The guy was still in shock—blood transfusions would be needed as soon as they got to the hospital.

He jury-rigged a chest tube with a large-bore needle and got the man's arm in a sling so it didn't flail around and loosen the tourniquet. Then the siren from the speeding ambulance seemed to shriek louder.

His mind was flashing onto another ambulance ride—Alsace in November 1944. He was driving this time because the driver had been killed. Bruce's clothes were soaked with blood, as they were now, and two soldiers were in the back, wounded and unconscious. The shell that had sent shrapnel into the driver had knocked Bruce out for a few moments. He was still dazed and wasn't sure if he was headed in the right direction.

His headlights were off in case he had veered into enemy territory. The only light came from artillery explosions that flared from the ridges and occasionally pierced the tightly woven trees. And the muddy ruts were frozen solid, bouncing him all over the road. He thought of his family getting news that he had driven an ambulance into a tree—an inglorious way to go.

Suddenly a rapid volley of shells incinerated part of the forest on his left. Through the fiery smoke he could make out the dull gray shapes of a formation of German 88s. From his right, he could hear the clanking treads of another group of approaching tanks—American Shermans that had set the forest on fire as they approached the 88s. He was caught between the lines of a looming tank battle. The bile rose in his throat and threatened to choke him.

He was stopped now, frozen in place. If he moved, the Germans were certain to see him. If he stayed here, it would be a miracle if they passed him by. He didn't have long to wait—a concussive blast threw the ambulance into the air and slammed it sideways in a deep trench. The 88s were firing through the woods and moving toward him. There was no way out of this one.

"Hey, Doc, I think this guy's going to make it," the medical technician said. "We'll be at the hospital in a couple minutes. Anything else we need to do?"

Bruce snapped back to the present. But he had been rocked by the memories that had swept over him. How long would these scenes continue to hammer at his mind? He had handled the emergencies today without letting flashbacks intrude. But could he end up like some of the GIs in his unit who had seen too much? He gritted his teeth and pushed the fears away. There was more to do tonight. A surgeon wouldn't be at the hospital this late. He would have to stand in until one arrived.

## Chapter 6

## NOEL 1944

*Alsace, France*

The fir tree was the only sign of Christmas in the aid station. Otherwise it was business as usual. Cots were filled with soldiers treated earlier in the day—a private with a gut wound that would lead to peritonitis if the penicillin didn't take hold, two with fresh amputations, another with a dressing on the remains of his shoulder. The operating tables were quiet now, cleaned up and ready for the next round. Maybe there would be a few more hours of calm on this December 24.

His friend Teddy had cut the tree down three days ago and decorated it with a few candles and some tin cans he punched out in swirls. They lit it for the first time yesterday. Then Teddy was cut down last night.

It was a ruse they had seen before—a German rifleman using a wounded GI as bait, trying to notch another kill. Teddy was wearing his medic's Red Cross sign and was dragging a litter to bring the soldier back. But the German used him for target practice. He waited until Teddy was starting an IV and then picked away at him so he could get the most pleasure from the murder. The first shot blew Teddy's left hand off where it was holding the IV bag. The second shot nailed his other hand when he grabbed the stump. The third ripped open his groin. The German took a break to watch him writhe and bellow in pain. After a few minutes, he let go with a fusillade that made Teddy's body dance and spatter into pieces.

The lull in action at the aid station gave Bruce time to think about Teddy. He had been the cheerleader in their group—a guy with a nonstop smile that made you think you could get through this war. If he was ever afraid, he didn't show it. If something tough needed to get done, he did it. He only had two years of pre-med before he enlisted. But he was already a wizard at managing trauma. Teddy was the one who rescued Bruce when he was dazed with a concussion after his ambulance strayed into a tank battle.

Now all that was left of Teddy was this small trace of his time on earth—a four-foot tree that was catching his after-glow. The tin spirals moved up and down as they rode the drafts in the small church they were using as a field hospital. Sometimes they reflected flashes of light from the chandelier in the rafters.

Bruce was carving a piece of wood with a scalpel, making an angel to put on the tree. It was the only memorial he could conjure now. If he made it back to the States, he'd visit Teddy's parents in Ohio.

What could he write to Teddy's parents that would ease their grief? All the words that came to his mind seemed canned—a hero, sacrificed himself for others, would have made a terrific surgeon after the war. Yet they were true. It would take some time to shape the letter. The way Teddy was killed was coloring everything now. Bruce would have to fashion a different end.

The shelling was getting closer again. Couldn't they take a break on Christmas Eve? Couldn't there be a gift of one "Stille Nacht"—a stop of the blasts that penetrated his brain? The concussion had doubled or tripled the intensity of the sounds. Explosions from miles away could feel like darts into his gray matter.

This Alsatian town with its half-timbered houses must have been pretty before the war. Tonight, fouled snow was crusted on a ruined village. Most of the houses were turned to rubble. No bells were being rung. The only semblance of a service in this old church was the chaplain visiting wounded GIs who were waiting to be evacuated from the front.

The days and nights with little patches of sleep were starting to loosen the corners of Bruce's mind. He thought he could hear singing now. It was the choir at the Presbyterian Church in Hollidaysburg, and his mother's clear soprano stood out. They were singing a familiar anthem, "O Holy Night." Alice always had the solo in that piece. She wouldn't have a drink until after the midnight service so her voice would stay true. Would he be there next year to hear her sing?

He needed to get some sleep. His thoughts were wandering all over the place, and another wave of injured soldiers would arrive before long.

A lieutenant from the command center rushed in before he could take a step toward his cot. "We need a surgeon right away," he barked. "Company C got powdered, and their docs are pinned down—can't help. Their captain, Weinstein, had some meat torn off his back. And they can't move him. He's stuck in a farmhouse right on the line. Cohen, the medic, called for help. He's got six other soldiers in trouble there and says he can't do the surgery the captain needs. Will you go?"

Bruce sharpened up. He knew Jake Cohen—a solid medic who had been with the division at Hürtgen Forest, one of the worst battles of the war. He wouldn't have sent out an SOS if he wasn't desperate.

"I'm your man," Bruce replied. He nodded to Blaisdell, the other doctor at the station, who gave him a thumbs-up sign.

Explosions on the ridges showered the sky with phosphorescent flares. So they were exposed—an easy catch if the Germans saw them and decided to take out an ambulance. But nothing happened until they neared the farmhouse. Suddenly, mortar blasts began to chew up the road behind them. Then he heard the American mortars firing back. Bruce muttered a little prayer: *Dear Lord, guide our mortars.* He needed help from anywhere he could get it.

Jake was hunched over the raw mess of the captain's back and was covered with blood. The other soldiers were slumped around the room, some moving slightly and groaning, some silent as stone.

"Three of them are dead," Jake shouted above the noise from the shelling. "The others will probably make it. But this guy's lost a lot of blood—stepped on a booby trap. I can't see what's going on. It's all shredded flesh and junk from the bomb."

"What have you done so far?" Bruce asked.

"Pumped him full of plasma and tried compression. Tied off some bad bleeders underneath what's left of his right scapula. Sorry to call for help, but it was too much for me."

"You're doing fine," Bruce said. "Let's pull off some of those compression bandages and see what we can fix."

When the sopping bandages were lifted, Bruce found a man who had large hunks of his back and his buttocks ripped away. Screws, ball bearings, and shards of barbed wire from the improvised bomb cluttered the wound. Blood pumped in arterial pulses from four points in the lower back and oozed from dozens more places. The captain wouldn't have much longer to live if they didn't stop the bleeding soon.

"Geno, get over here. You're going to assist," Bruce yelled to the ambulance driver. "Squeeze the plasma bag as hard as you can. When it's empty, grab that case of plasma we brought with us and hook up another bag. Keep them going."

"Jake, get every hemostat you can find. We need to get these bleeders first. We'll worry later about the hardware they shot through him."

Bruce piled up a stack of fresh bandage pads and pushed them into the captain's upper back, strapping them as tight as he could without clamping down on his breathing. Then he set to work on the worst part of the wound—the macerated lower back and buttocks. The blast hadn't penetrated the abdominal cavity. But the ridge of the spine was showing through in places, and nails and barbed wire were embedded in the bone.

Moving with speed, Bruce clamped the bleeders, cut off the flow with knots of suture material, and pulled out the worst of the debris so he could spot sources of oozing. Within fifteen minutes, they found the arterial tears and the captain had a fast, reedy pulse. They had bought a little time to plan the next stage of treatment.

"He's lost too much blood for plasma to do it all," Bruce told them. "He needs some whole blood soon. Geno, can you get us back fast to the aid station? Haven't heard the mortars for a while."

"No problem, Doc, if you don't mind a bumpy ride," Geno replied.

"You guys go ahead," Jake said. "I need to stay here until we can evacuate this whole crew."

Bruce's eyes met Jake's. They were both exhausted but flushed with adrenaline from their dash to stop the captain's bleeding. They knew that either one of them could be stacked in a pile for shipment home before this night was over.

"Yeah, you have to stay," Bruce said. He cuffed Jake on the shoulder. "We'll have a better Christmas next year."

The ride back to the aid station was jarring, as Geno had promised. He was hurtling over the frozen ruts as if he were in a race car, sliding and careening, but somehow staying on the road. Bruce had to tie the captain down to keep him from bouncing off the litter, and the rough ride was making it hard to keep the compression dressing in place. The captain had started Cheyne-Stokes breathing—an ominous cycle of deep and irregular breaths, then rattles and total pauses. Most people who got to this stage didn't make it. Bruce wanted to turn him over to help clear the airway, but he was afraid to jar loose the clots that had formed on his back.

A spray of shots banged at the rear of the ambulance when they took the turn by the bend in the river that pointed them away from the line and back to the town. Were they trying to stop the ambulance or just playing with them? The answer came soon enough when another shower of bullets hit them less than a minute later. This time, one of the shots hit the captain's knee and took part of it away. Another whistled by Bruce's head and split through the side of the ambulance back into the night air.

Geno floored the accelerator over a patch of better road, and the shots fizzled out as they moved closer to the town. Another close call. How many of these could a person have? Bruce didn't have time to ponder the caprices of fate, the inches that could separate life from death. He wrapped a compression dressing around the captain's knee and pushed more plasma into him. With luck, they would be at the aid station in a few minutes. He was crafting his strategy to pull the captain back from the brink.

Blaise was waiting when they pulled into the aid station. "Worried about you, Duncan—lots of shooting out there tonight," he said as they hoisted the captain out of the ambulance. "What the hell happened? The back of the ambulance is full of holes."

"Just some Christmas fireworks," Bruce said. "We're okay, but this guy's in rough shape. Probably lost more than half his blood, Cheyne-Stoking on the way here. I've got an IV going with plasma. Open a bigger port, a jugular vein. Then we'll transfuse him, two pints at a time."

The two surgeons explored the back wound under better light, searching for buried projectiles that could stab deeper and start the flow of bleeding again. And by dawn, their patient was ready for transfer to the field hospital. Infection would be a problem because the wound was so large and dirty. He would need extensive grafts. But at least the captain had a chance.

Bruce picked up the wooden angel and sat on the edge of his cot. The body and wings were shaped—the face was still a solid rectangle of pine. He began chipping away, visualizing Amelia. He was drained, weary to the bone. *No sleep before I finish this carving and write to her*, he said to himself. He wrestled with the part of his mind that wanted to circle back to Teddy's massacre, the captain's raw flesh, the Nazi murderers shooting at their ambulance. Following those channels would suck him under in a whirlpool.

*Keep your eyes on the angel . . . Close the door on what happened tonight*, he murmured under his breath.

"Hey, Duncan, that was a big-time save you made tonight," Blaise said as he moved past Bruce's cot to collapse on his own. "You better get some sleep while you can. They're going to attack the line again today . . . No holiday for us."

"Can't turn it off so fast, bud. Got to work on this carving a little while and then write a letter to my girl. I'll be right behind you."

"Okay. Call me if they serve the champagne brunch before you get to sleep."

Bruce cracked a small grin and said, "I'll buy you all the champagne you want when we finish this job. You've earned it."

"How about a champagne bath with my wife when I get home? Would you spring for that?"

"Sure, whatever you want," Bruce said. "Now let me finish this angel. I'll wreck it if I keep listening to your drivel."

The face didn't quite work out. He had a picture of Amelia in front of him. But his skills weren't good enough to capture any of her features. The angel had the look of a rustic carving from the backwoods of Pennsylvania. Still, it would do as a makeshift way to remember Teddy. He walked to the tree, bowed his head for a moment, and tied the angel on the top.

*December 25, 1944*
*Dear Amelia,*

*I'm sitting beside a Christmas tree in the aid station as I write this letter. A friend, Teddy Randall, found it and decorated it with bits and pieces of things he foraged from around the old church that's our home for a few days. In a way, it is the finest tree I ever saw.*

*You would laugh at my contribution to the tree. It's an angel I carved out of a block of old pine. Of course I had you in mind as a model for the angel. But my pitiful artistic skills were not up to the task. If I can, I'll hang on to the angel for after the war. I made it in Teddy's honor. He's had a rough time of it here in France.*

*When we put the angel on our Christmas trees, I'll think of Teddy and my other buddies. And I'll think of how your love kept me going in this hellhole.*

*We had a busy night last night, no sleep for us docs. But the Germans are taking a break this morning. All the guys we treated last night are in pretty good shape, so I'll try to catch some winks in a few minutes.*

*I didn't want to fall asleep without sending you my love on this Christmas Day. You are with me all the time, even in the thick of action when I'm on full alert. I can feel you beside me, willing me to succeed.*

*I worry about you in London with the V rockets still coming down. We don't get much news here close to the front, but we do hear that our troops will smash the launchers soon. Use those air raid shelters or get out to the country as much as you can until the rockets are silenced.*

*Where will we be this time next year? Whether it's England or the USA, the war is sure to be over. And we can sit by a roaring fire, holding one another with only good days ahead of us.*

*All my love,*
*Bruce*

## Chapter 7

## TONY

———

### Pennsylvania
### November 1945

The hospital was quiet early on Sunday morning. Night-duty nurses spoke softly to one another as they readied for the shift change. The operating rooms were dark. Lights were dimmed in the halls to give patients a better chance of getting some sleep. Bruce came before church to check on the two patients he had admitted on Friday. The boy with meningitis should be ready to go home tomorrow. Tony, the man from the car wreck, would have a dicey trip ahead.

He turned the corner and saw Steve Taylor, his obstetrician friend, coming out of the delivery room.

"Nice job on that guy from the car crash," he said.

"Didn't plan on doing any surgery after I came home . . . had enough of it in the war. But that fellow needed help right away, so I cobbled through it."

"Better than cobbling, I was told," Steve said. "Opened his chest and did a partial pneumonectomy. I would have been peeing in my pants. Last time I did any trauma was ten years ago when I was an intern. And I wasn't any good at it then."

"I hope it was the last time for me," Bruce said. "Keep bringing out those babies with first-class delivery . . . You're the master of that game."

"Have you met Sarah Avery, the woman doctor who's coming to Hollidaysburg?" Steve asked. "She's here for the weekend to scout out places for an office, and I'm meeting her at the Altoona Hotel for lunch. She wants me to do the OB from her practice."

"Am I the only one who didn't know I'm getting competition? I just heard about her on Friday."

"Don't worry about competition," Steve said. "Magnuson's done. There'll be more than enough patients for both of you. And you'll need someone to cover when you need a break. I was surprised too. Didn't know anything about it till last week when she called me. Join us at the hotel. She'll want to meet you."

"Can't do it. My brother, Glen, and I are going to Mastrioni's for lunch. He'll be here later this morning to see the guy from the car wreck. Glen helped me with the first aid."

"Bring him along. Sarah won't mind. She'll want to get to know all the players in Hollidaysburg."

"We wouldn't be in the way?"

"Nah."

"I suppose I should check out the competition. We'll be there." Bruce turned to walk to the surgery ward.


If Tony was awake, it would be time to start talking about his future. When he opened his chest, there was more than a torn lung to behold. The guy was only forty-two, but his lungs were brown and gnarled like walnuts. It had been risky business to resect the segment with the wounds and tie him up to stop the bleeding. The post-op X-rays showed fibrous constrictions on both sides of his chest. In some places emphysematous swellings pushed out like bubbles on an inner tube.

Tony must have been having trouble breathing even before the accident. With six broken ribs and a hunk of his left lung removed, constant oxygen had been needed since the surgery. Bruce had learned that both of the men in the accident worked at Allegheny Refractories. One was dead and never going back to work—the other looked doubtful.

Tony was propped up in the hospital bed, sipping some juice through a straw. He greeted Bruce with a pained smile and set the cup down with a slow arc of his right arm, guarding his movements to not rasp the edges of his broken ribs. His left arm was encased in plaster and was hanging from a pulley to keep it elevated. A chest tube drained some turbid fluid that gathered in a bottle on the floor.

"Still hurts like the devil," he whispered in a hoarse voice. "I can't get comfortable. Every time I stir in bed, it feels like a knife stabbing me in the ribs. How long will this last?"

"You're over the worst of the pain. It'll get better every day. Those broken ribs have already started to heal. Can't put a cast on them or your lungs wouldn't move. I want you to breathe deeply, even if it hurts. You have to expand your lungs . . . keep them from getting congested. We're pumping you full of sulfa and penicillin, but we don't want to give pneumonia a chance."

"Thanks, Doc, I'll try. When did I wake up? Was it last night? I remember seeing you and hearing the nurse tell me that you saved my butt. Am I going to make it?"

"Sure, you'll be out of here by next weekend if we can wean you off the oxygen. I need to listen to your lungs and make sure everything's okay. Then can I ask you some questions?"

"No problem as long as I don't nod off with that pain medicine they give me. I think I'm about due for some."

"In about an hour," Bruce explained as he began his examination.

The only problem that needed attention was the cast on his arm. It was too tight because his arm had swollen more in the past twenty-four hours. The radial pulse was still strong, and there was no sign of cyanosis from damping off the blood supply. But Tony would be more comfortable if he split the cast and taped it up until the edema went away. He called for the nurse to bring him the cast saw.

"Feeling a bit better now?" Bruce asked.

Tony nodded. "Yeah, my arm was aching bad."

"Just a few questions, and I'll come back later." Bruce turned a chair toward Tony and settled into it. He delivered his questions with a slow, gentle cadence. "When we took an X-ray, it showed you had some lung problems before the accident. Did you notice any trouble breathing before you ended up here?"

"Haven't run any races lately," he said. "Yeah, I cough a lot, bring up some junk every morning. I didn't do so well with deer hunting this year . . . had to drag myself up the ridge behind our house. Probably scared the deer away with all the huffing. Do I need to cut down on the cigarettes?"

"You need to stop . . . especially with a piece of your lung gone. Still, I don't think smoking explains everything. You work at Allegheny Refractories?"

"Yeah, since I was eighteen. Got hired on when I finished high school."

"And what do you do there?"

"Foreman on the first shift now. A great job. I can take it easy and tell the other guys what to do. Started as a dust devil . . . moving the sand and clay into the mixing bins."

"Do you wear a respirator or anything else to keep the dust out of your lungs?"

"Nah, we chew tobacco and spit on the floor. That keeps the dust down. You couldn't breathe at all with one of those respirators. They're for the white shirts. The managers wear them when they come out of their offices in their suits and ties. We'd get laughed off the floor if we showed up with that nose gear stuff."

"Get any instruction on how to manage the dust?" Bruce pressed a bit further.

"They call it the smell of money. It gets in your face and makes your clothes reek like a sand pit. But no dust, no bricks . . . no pay."

"Is there a doctor who checks to see if you have lung problems?"

"We got a company doc we can see for colds, the clap, or things like that. He's not bad. Never had a chest X-ray in his office."

"Did he ever mention checking you for silicosis?"

"We know that word. They say that silica is the reason most of the guys are done by the time they hit their midfifties. But what can you do? We got to work."

"I understand. There aren't enough jobs around here. It's pretty much the railroad or the brick plant unless you have a trade. Ever tried anything else? Can you do carpentry or wiring?"

"I don't like the way this talk is going, Doc. Are you telling me I shouldn't go back to the plant? I've got a family that needs to eat."

"It looks like you have silicosis, Tony. You'll need to stay off work for at least a month to recover from the accident. We'll talk then about what's best for you. I'm going to put you on medical leave until we can figure this out."

"No you're not," a voice said from the doorway. Lucas Glover stood there with his eyes trained on Bruce. "Our company doctor is the only one with authority to put someone on medical leave. When Tony's discharged, Dr. Fenelli will take over."

Lucas posed in a commanding stance, pushing himself to stand as tall as possible as he interrupted Bruce. He was puffed up today. Bruce had seen this sort of behavior from officers who were scared, who didn't know what they were doing. The good ones had an easy authority with the troops. The bad ones pressed too hard and made mistakes. They thought bravado would carry them through. It rarely did.

"Sorry to break in," he said in an acid tone. "I came to visit Tony and overheard you talking about Allegheny Refractories. We don't allow outside doctors to tell our employees or our supervisors what to do. So devote your energy to your practice. I'm sure there are hordes of women patients vying for your attention."

At first Bruce was puzzled by the swipe about women patients. Then it made sense. Kate must have said something about their encounter. Had someone told Lucas she had been the last one out of his office on Friday afternoon? Did he suspect there was more to the visit than a doctor's appointment? The questions about silicosis also seemed to light him up. Was the company trying to hide the problem? Bruce saw no clear path out of the tense situation other than to feign graciousness and make a quick exit. Tony Giordano didn't need a fight between his doctor and his boss right now.

"Have Fenelli see Tony anytime you want," Bruce said. "I'll bow out when he's stable from the surgery."

"Be careful about telling my men your half-baked ideas. You're no lung specialist—just a GP. And you don't have the morals to be any kind of doctor. Stay out of it."

Bruce felt the blood creep up his neck. He could shrug off one crack. But Lucas had gone too far. There was more at stake here than a return-to-work decision. He wouldn't be threatened—told how to practice medicine, have his reputation maligned.

"Let's go out in the hall, Lucas," he said.

After the door was closed, a twitching around his left eye sent a warning signal. *Be careful*, he told himself.

But his voice rose as he took on Lucas. "I'm Tony's doctor . . . for the time being. You can't barge in here to dictate what I do. And cut the snide remarks about women in my practice. I took an oath to do no harm. I've always kept it." Bruce's jaw was set, and his knuckles were clenched. The war had given him a raw edge. "What did she tell you?"

Lucas stiffened and pounded back. "Enough to know you're a slippery bastard. Stay away from her. You'll pay if you don't."

Two nurses walked by, looked at them, and whispered to one another.

Bruce realized this confrontation could explode and wreck his career before it got started. By the end of the war he had been as violent as any of the GIs. Killed Nazis attacking his aid station. "Lucas, we've got to calm down," he said. "We're in a hospital. I didn't touch Kate. Never would. "

Lucas glowered at him. "Not what I heard."

Bruce riveted his eyes on Lucas. "What did you hear?"

"I got home early that day, and she straggled in about five thirty . . . flushed, looking like she'd been laid. Didn't have her nylons on straight. Wouldn't tell me anything till I put the squeeze on her."

"There was nothing to tell."

"Said you know what to do with a woman."

Bruce took a step toward Lucas. "Bullshit. I'll bet you roughed her up until she said something to make you stop. If I hear you hit her, I won't keep quiet."

Lucas sneered at him. "Say a word and you're done."

"You little prick," Bruce spat out. He wanted to pin Lucas to the wall, see him squirm. Wipe the sneer off his face. But he checked himself.

"Now shut up and listen to me," Bruce said. "The guy in that room escaped by a thread, and he's still in bad shape. He can't go back to work in the dust when his lungs are shot. He's got severe silicosis . . . He'll be dead in a couple more years of sucking in that stuff. You're his boss—save him."

"Save yourself," Lucas said before he pivoted away and walked down the hall.

Bruce almost followed him to his car. It would have been easy for him to nail Lucas. He had been trained to do much worse in the war. But he turned a switch in his mind. *Enough. You're better than that. Treat your patient.*

He opened the door to Tony's room and entered, struggling to regain his doctor's persona. Bruce smiled before he pulled a chair over to sit by Tony's bedside. "Let's finish our conversation. I'm not discharging you until you're ready to go."

# Chapter 8

## CURRENTS

———

*B*ruce stared ahead in silence as he walked with his brother. They were on their way to the restaurant to meet Dr. Sarah Avery. But his mind was in another place. He was replaying Lucas's blistering attack at Tony's bedside, trying to understand what had happened.

"You're ignoring me," Glen said. "If you don't want me to hang along, I'll butt out so you can have the lady doctor to yourself."

"Don't get jumpy. I've got a problem . . . almost got into a fight with Lucas at the hospital this morning. He thinks I screwed his wife. Kate showed up at my office the day we went to the game in Tyrone, but I got her out the door quick. Nothing happened."

"I can see why he'd be jealous," Glen said. "The little piss-ant dodged the war. And he knows you and Kate had it going when you were in college."

"He was full of piss this time. Spit it out at me. Like I was a hack with no morals. Then he threatened me—tried to shut me up about silicosis. One more insult and I would have hit him."

"I never saw you hit anyone," Glen said. "Did the war make you edgier?"

"Maybe it did," Bruce said. The veneer on his nerves was thinner now. The anger hadn't been there before.

Steve Taylor was waiting for Bruce and Glen as they walked into the hotel lobby. "The lady doctor's a pool shark," Steve said. "When she saw the billiard room, I couldn't keep her away. Watch her sink a few balls before we have lunch. You'll be impressed."

They followed Steve to the billiard room, a spot usually frequented by men only, and stood in the corner to watch a woman with light red hair, dressed in slacks in Katharine Hepburn style. She was taking on one of the regulars at eight-ball with only two of the striped balls remaining. The doctor pocketed the ten ball from an angle that left the cue ball in an ideal position, hit a smooth bank shot around three of the solid-color balls to sink the thirteen ball, but was left with a long reach to the eight ball to win the game. She signaled to them and broke into a grin. "Any bets on this one?" she asked.

Steve replied. "Ten bucks says you can't make it."

"I need the money," she said.

She chalked her cue, took a sighting like a surveyor toward the path of the ball, and then stroked the cue ball with confidence.

"A pleasure to settle the bet," Steve said as he moved toward Sarah with Bruce and Glen trailing behind. "I hope you're as good at medicine as knocking a pool ball around."

"So do I," she said. "Are you Bruce and Glen?"

"Yep," Steve replied. "The Duncan brothers."

Sarah shook Bruce's hand with a firm grip. She had long fingers that looked delicate but felt powerful. Standing erect now, wearing low heels, she was only a couple inches shorter than Bruce. He figured she was about five nine without shoes—a thin woman with an athletic body and graceful moves. She wore no lipstick or other makeup. But her lightly freckled face didn't need decorating.

*Beautiful in her own way*, Bruce said to himself. Her easy confidence and rich voice would put patients at ease, make them feel understood, lift their moods. There was no artifice here.

"I've wanted to tell you how sorry I am to crowd in on you. The timing's awful. When I made the decision to come to Hollidaysburg, nobody was sure what you were going to do after the war. I had to find a place to practice, and with Magnuson winding down, this looked like a good opportunity. I hope there'll be plenty of work for both of us."

"I guarantee more than enough action to keep two of you busy," Steve said. "The railroad's going strong, and people are kicking into gear after the war. I'm counting on lots of babies over the next few years."

"No apologies needed," Bruce told Sarah. "I did waffle about where I was going. Even thought about staying overseas. But I'm glad I'm here."

"Have time for a game before lunch?" she asked.

"Another day," Bruce said. "I'm doing some fly-fishing this afternoon. First chance to take a break after a busy week. Let's get a bite to eat."


The hotel restaurant had filled with after-church diners, so they found a table on the edge of the crowd where they could talk. Bruce and Sarah had side-stepped details of how the two of them would practice in the same town and had been talking about the chances for a flu epidemic. When they exhausted that topic, Bruce decided to try to learn more about the unusual woman sitting across from him.

He didn't know much about women doctors. There had been none in his class at Penn, and the men had been skeptical about Women's Medical College, where Sarah went to school. He did know that women who chose medicine swore off the prospect of getting married. And they weren't known for their glamour. Yet Sarah had the most appeal of any woman he had seen in months.

"What got you into medicine?" Bruce asked. "Any doctors in your family?"

"No doctors. Only lawyers," Sarah replied. "My father and uncle run the firm my grandfather started in Williamsport . . . Avery, Avery, and Avery. A pretentious name, but the men are a good lot. I couldn't see myself as an attorney . . . enjoyed science too much. Camped out at the anatomy lab in college. How about you? I hear you're a great surgeon. Why are you working as a GP?"

"Didn't do a surgery residency. The army put me through a crash course to do front-line trauma work, so I learned some advanced first aid. We patched the guys up so they could be transported to the field hospitals."

"From what Steve told me, you did some amazing work on that brickworker that almost died."

"A fluke," he said. "Happened to be there when the accident happened. And the guy needed help before a chest surgeon could get there. He was bleeding out from a torn lung."

"You did thoracotomies in the war?"

"We'd open a chest when there wasn't any other option. But I've always wanted to be a GP in Hollidaysburg. My family's lived there since the town was founded . . . in the hardware business for the last few generations. Glen's got the hardware store now."

The doctors had passed on drinks, while Glen had downed three whiskey sours. When he heard Bruce mention his name, Glen straightened in his chair.

"Yeah, I got the store . . . not much of a gift," Glen said as he motioned to the waiter for another drink. "You docs will have it made in Hollidaysburg. Throw me some crumbs when you have the chance."

Glen's bitterness surprised Bruce. He hadn't tried to bring Glen into the conversation—a mistake, he could see now. Still, Glen's rude interruption was way off base. Bruce could see the lunch with Sarah unraveling if he didn't stop this problem now.

"Cap it," he said. "We'll all be okay—just go easy on the drinks."

"Quit sniping about me," Glen spat out. "All I hear about is drinking too much. Hell, all I've had is a few whiskey sours. We had pitchers of them in England."

He paused and glared at Bruce. "Doctor perfect . . . mind yourself. You almost lost it today. Don't knock me."

Bruce hadn't seen Glen act like this before. The flash of ill temper—like a faulty circuit went off in his brain—triggered a sudden memory of their father. His mercurial changes could come from nowhere.

"I wasn't sniping at you," Bruce said as he tried to find a way to defuse the situation. "Tony's accident riled both of us. Let's cool down and get back to talking with Sarah."

"Smooth, isn't he?" Glen asked Sarah. "Won't work today. I'm going home . . . I've had enough." He stood, drained the remains of his drink, and left the room.

Bruce turned to Sarah and Steve. "I'll apologize for him," he said. "Glen saw some rough action over the channel. Lost most of his buddies . . . got burned in a crash landing. We usually get along fine. I don't know what set him off today. Guess we were talking medicine, and he was left out . . . hit the whiskey sours too hard. We'll patch it up."

He noticed that Sarah had put on her wrap and gathered her purse to leave. "I hope this won't make you think we're too wild to trust," Bruce said.

"Plenty of men came back from the war with raw nerves," she said. "We have to understand, not criticize. Send him to me when my office opens . . . I'll do what I can. I studied some psychiatry at Eastern State Hospital."

"He'll never tell you what's bothering him—too proud. But he might let you check his burn scars. They're ugly. Scorched skin over most of his chest and legs. He's in pain most of the time."

"I suppose he drinks to cut the pain," she said.

"One of the reasons. But the drinking started before his plane crash. The chances of making it back to the States were so slim the fighter pilots got loaded most nights. And the next morning the docs pumped them up with Dexedrine to keep them sharp. I think he's hooked on the booze. He can't get Dexedrine now, as far as I know."

"Hard to blame him," Sarah said. "Who knows what I'd be doing if I were in his place? I thought of joining, being a nurse. I'm a little guilty I had such an easy ride."

"Same here," Steve said. "I was old enough to avoid the draft. Could have signed on."

"Drop the guilt," Bruce said. "We needed you here to keep the States humming." He looked at Sarah. "And Hollidaysburg will need both of us. I hope we can help each other."

She stood and shook his hand. "I think we can."

# Chapter 9

## WINTER STREAM

⸻

His feet were the first to follow this path to Spruce Creek since the storm two days ago. He broke through ice-crusted rime where the sun couldn't penetrate the evergreens and the thick stand of oaks. Deer tracks were the only sign of movement down his route to the stream.

The crunch of ice and the touch of his boot on the patches of leaves underneath absorbed him. He was thinking about where he placed his feet, in part to avoid slipping, but also to savor the experience. Bruce wanted to be here in the woods, approaching the stream, away from Lucas and Glen, away from his haunting memories of Amelia and the war.

The leaves were packed down—already turning to humus where they touched the dirt. A month ago, they were in full color, rustling and skittering as he pushed his feet through them. Today they had a different beauty—intricate patterns of leaves and twigs, decorations of ice crystals and desiccated berries, and earthy smells of the forest renewing itself.

Soft moss appeared underfoot as he hiked through a narrow section where rivulets of water threaded their way down the path. The spring on the hill above was one of the reasons Spruce Creek never ran dry. All along this valley, underground limestone streams cracked open here and there to feed the creek four seasons a year.

The moss cushioned his feet, leaving an indentation for a few moments until it bounced back into shape. With its vibrant green bracts and thousands of anthers bobbing above the mat, the moss seemed more alive than the brown and gray trees ringing the trail. Yet he could feel a pulse from the whole forest. He thought of the turkeys that weren't showing themselves now but could be scratching out calls any minute. He thought of the cicadas hibernating beneath the trees.

Last winter he only had fancies of being in places like this again. Now he might have fifty more years to soak up these mountains and valleys.

Bruce came to the bend in the trail where another path led to the ruins of a pre–Civil War iron-smelting furnace. For a few moments he pictured the furnace and the clearing beside it where he and Glen used to camp. Then he turned left and moved down the trail to the stream.

How many times had Glen been in trouble? When they were boys, Glen was expelled from the Boy Scouts for a prank that backfired and ended with a kid minus a thumb. Then he burned a hole through Vic's garage when he played with magnesium flares. Glen could be the nicest guy one moment and go off on a tangent the next. Being with him was like riding the Leap-the-Dips roller coaster at Lakemont Park.

By the time he saw him again, Glen would probably slough off the outburst today at the restaurant—nothing to ruffle their relationship. But the signs were frightening. Getting lit with whiskey at lunch. An angry tirade with no provocation. Lightning shifts in mood like their father had.

*What can you do?* Bruce asked himself. *Stop fighting back. He needs a brother.*

The murmur of water tumbling over stones told him he was close to the turnoff that would take him down over the bank to a spot where he could start fishing. He would have to hug the bank so the fish wouldn't see him coming. The water was low and clear this time of year.

The descent to the stream was tricky. In summer months, poison ivy jutted into the path at the top of the slope and needed to be skirted with care. The leaves were all dead now, and the stems were shriveled. But he knew not to grab any of the trees for balance if they had vines crawling on them.

Using his wading staff for balance, he scrambled around some large boulders and down the slope for about a hundred yards.

He stopped to watch and listen at the stream's edge, searching for signs of activity. The water gurgled around some smaller boulders. Then it tailed off into shallow riffles. When the spring rainstorms hit, the riffles could hold some trout. The fish would be in deeper water now, in runs where insect nymphs are swept by the current into their mouths, or the occasional winter hatch gives a reason to break the surface.

From his vantage point, he couldn't see rises dimpling the water—a disappointing observation, but not unexpected. Dry fly action was spotty in colder weather—a bonus when it occurred. With no rising fish, he decided to try a caddis nymph for a few casts while he waited to see if the afternoon sun brought some flies into the air.

The tug of the nymph at the end of the back cast and the power of the loop as it arced forward soothed him. This simple stroke had a meditative effect. And the unfolding of the line as it carried the nymph under a tree branch and dropped it into the head of a pocket of rushing water added pleasure to the mix. The sweet feeling of making a spot-on cast hadn't lost its hold.

The pocket of water, tucked behind swirling currents from a partially submerged rock, was only about a foot wide.

But it was a prime feeding lane for trout—one that had produced some vigorous fish in the past.

The nymph hit the water at an angle that drove it down—then a flash of silver and a strong hit. He had connected on his first cast. The fish wasn't a big one, ten inches or so. Still, it put on an acrobatic show of jumps as it tried to throw off the fly.

Bruce played it gently until it was tired and slipped easily into his net. He rinsed his hands in the cold water before handling the fish and then used a hemostat to remove the hook and set the trout free. *No damage done to that fish*, he said to himself. *I'll see him again another day.*

Fifteen minutes later, there had been no more strikes. So he began wading upstream toward a bigger pool. The stream was shallow in this section, and he could see straight to the bottom through the brilliant water. He stepped around the bunched gravel of the redds, the spawning beds where the big browns laid their eggs in the fall. The fry were gone from the redds, but there was an elemental sanctity of these spots he didn't want to disturb.

It was almost four o'clock by the time he reached the bottom end of the big pool. The air was cooling, and the narrow shafts of sun were moving up the banks away from the water. He knew this pool better than any of the others. It was the first place his father took him when he was six to start learning to read a stream and manage a fly rod.

A pang of longing struck him as he thought of a day like this when he and Glen were teenagers. It was another afternoon at Spruce Creek after Sunday dinner. His dad caught a trophy-size trout that day, and Bruce netted the fish after a long fight. The stream was the same, but it had no memory of Robert Duncan. The rocks, the water, the forest showed no stamp that he had been here. His father's life seemed as ephemeral as the insects that hatched for one day and then were gone forever.

His mind was spinning now with faces of others who had disappeared. Amelia, whom he had let slip away. A soldier who would have lived if Bruce had done a better job treating him. And Blaise, his best buddy. Nothing could be done about the dead but try to live for them—do some penance. But Amelia was still in England. Why hadn't he gone there after the war? Tried to win her back? Had the carnage in France and Germany warped his brain? Made him expect and tolerate the worst?

There was a loud splash from along the far bank. Then another rise by the roots of the old willow. The flurry of activity brought Bruce's thoughts back to the stream. *Forget it*, he said to himself. *There's no answer*.

It was difficult to see what they were taking. The fly was small and dark, maybe a blue-winged olive or a gray midge. With the water this clear, the fish would spook easily if he muffed the cast.

He started with the downstream fish, hoping not to scare off the others feeding closer to the tree. His tiniest blue-winged olive passed by the rising fish five times without drawing any interest. Both of his darkest colors of midges had the same result. The drift looked natural, so he was probably using the wrong fly.

There were a few small Adams patterns in his kit that he had used in England. The little gray fly was a master imitator. It wasn't an exact match for any fly on the chalk streams of Britain or the limestone creeks here. But fish would take it sometimes when they were hard to attract.

On the first cast, the Adams bounced into a seam lit by some flickering rays from the waning sun. A subtle bump, and the fly disappeared beneath the surface. He quickly raised the rod tip to set the hook—a solid brook trout was on the line. The fish had its fall colors, brilliant red splashed over silver and brown. He stepped back down the stream a bit and steered the trout away from the place where he saw more rises. There was enough light to try for another fish.

Within a half hour, three more trout fell for the Adams, and the fly was so wet he was having a hard time keeping it afloat. It was time to go home. He reeled in the line, clipped off the fly, and held it in his hand. It was one of the flies he took to England. Amelia spotted it in his box on the day they met on the river Test. He could almost hear her voice now in the dimming light. "Little jewels, tiny flies for your mountain streams," she said.

Amelia could have coursed through these woods, had their children, loved his family. She could have found ways to thrive in his world. She could have held him right now, in this spot.

Being with Sarah today had opened a vein that was spilling freely now. The tall, good-looking doctor was unobtainable. He knew they would remain professionals. No romance was possible. Yet she had substance—like Amelia.

His musings about Sarah stopped when he looked again at the Adams nestled in his palm. Amelia was the one who should be with him on the stream now. *No one can replace her*.

All that was left was the dark hole where Amelia had been. So he tried to wrest his mind back to the experience of luring those fish to his fly. The excitement of catching trout on a winter day was fresh. But it was no match for the melancholy creeping into him. Bruce sighed and kneeled down to the stream. He blew on the Adams to dry it out as much as he could, reached into the current, and set it adrift.

# Chapter 10

## GLEN

---

### Pennsylvania
### December 1945

Glen's rented house, a red brick two-story, was perched on a hill overlooking the park. On most days, the view across the open land down to the river wasn't dotted with much human activity. A few riders on their horses might duck in and out of the trees ringing the central meadow, or some families could be seen using the playground. This afternoon Bruce watched as a stream of people moved toward a skating pond that was opening for the first time.

"I didn't think it would work," Glen told Bruce as they finished their coffee. "That dirt curb is only eighteen inches high, and they had to fill the dikes with water from fire trucks."

"Did you sharpen your skates?" Bruce asked.

"Yeah, I'm all set. Ready to go."

Glen pushed his chair away from the table, then turned back toward Bruce. "There's something I want to talk about before we go to the pond—something I've kept to myself."

"Sure. There's no rush to get on the ice."

He hesitated before beginning. "I've been seeing a woman . . . Mimi Cochrane. She's a new teacher at Highland Hall. Just finished college. Mimi's from Hollidaysburg, but you never met her. When I was a senior, she was in the seventh grade. So I'm like an old man."

"Cut the old man stuff. You're only twenty-seven . . . still a kid. What's the problem?"

"Tough thing to admit, even to myself." Glen walked to the window and stared into the distance. "I've been as celibate as a monk. Wonder why?"

"Never crossed my mind. I figured you were waiting for the right woman."

"I wasn't waiting. Didn't want to saddle a woman with a cripple. That dustup at the lunch with Sarah was only a little crack into my soul."

"The dustup is forgiven," Bruce said. "There's nothing wrong with your soul. You just need more time to get over the war . . . and control the drinking."

"I hope you're right. I let my guard down with Mimi, thought a few dates wouldn't hurt. Met her at the store when she came in to buy some paint, saw her after church a couple days later. Walked her home, went out to dinner in Altoona, drove to State College to see a play . . . fell in love, if I know what that is."

He grinned. "She's like a Tinkerbell. Short, five foot one, a million smiles—just what I need. And really cute. She holds her head high, has a lot of spirit."

"Perfect for you," Bruce said.

"She doesn't know much about what happened over the channel. Just the good stuff . . . hasn't seen my burns. I've been playing the happy vet. Not drinking. But it can't last.

"So here's my question. Break it off now . . . save the hurt? Or jump in with everything I have? I'm torn in half, and it's driving me nuts."

Bruce motioned for them to move to the easy chairs by the fireplace. He couldn't tell Glen what to do. Still, he didn't want to dodge the question. Glen's fears were real. If he started drinking again, he could come apart fast. If he had inherited their father's instability, a world of trouble might await. Yet Glen had a chance. Could this woman lead him away from these dangers? A simple answer wouldn't be enough.

"I don't know, Glen. You might be asking the wrong person for advice. I'm still raw from that breakup with Amelia. Let me think about it for a while."

"You're my brother. If you can't guide me through this, nobody can."

Bruce took his pipe out of his pocket, ran a cleaner through the stem, and tamped down some of the mixture his tobacco shop in Philadelphia had sent. He didn't smoke the pipe much, but the ritual of filling the briar and lighting it with the Zippo that his father gave him before the war helped him focus his mind.

"I can tell you're in deep already," he said. "How about Mimi? What does she say?"

"Says she could love me," Glen said. "It's moving pretty fast."

"She hasn't seen anything like what happened at lunch with Sarah? The mood shifts like Dad had? Doesn't know about the nightmares, the pain from the burns?"

"Not yet."

"You just answered your question, Glen. Tell her about your problems. If she wants to keep this thing going, she'll say so. It could be worse for her to have you walk away than to help you fight the ghosts. If she wants out, at least you'll have company . . . me."

Glen tightened his lips and sat upright in the chair, hands on his knees. "That's the answer. Thanks."

"After you stormed out of the lunch with Sarah Avery, she stayed to talk," Bruce said. "She wasn't put off at all. Offered to be your doctor. Sarah studied psychiatry in Philadelphia. Go see her, Glen. She'll be open for business after New Year's. Find a way to shape up. Mimi or no Mimi."

"Okay, Doc."


By the time they arrived at the skating pond, it swarmed with people checking out the new ice. The high school dance band, Santa caps on their heads, chimed out Christmas carols from a shelter heated with a wood stove. Banners waved above the concession area, where the town's restaurants were out in force. At each stand, customers were sampling entries in a contest to choose the best soup in Hollidaysburg. A large bonfire, surrounded by benches, drew a crowd to watch the skaters.

"There she is," Glen pointed toward the center of the ice after they had moved through the crowd.

Bruce recognized her immediately—a pixie with muffler and fur hat twirling by herself, an excellent skater, smooth and in control.

"Let's go out to meet her," Glen said. "Never saw her skate before. She's way better than me."

Their hockey skates got the job done in sliding over the ice. And in a few minutes they were beside her. "Didn't know you were a Sonja Henie," Glen said. "Can you put up with some guys who can't do any twirls?"

"Delighted," she said with a smile. "Is this Bruce? I'm glad Glen finally got around to introducing us. I think he's trying to keep us a secret. I'm not sure why. But today's the day we go public."

"Good to meet you, Mimi," Bruce said. "Should we make an announcement?"

Mimi laughed. "Not yet. If you don't mind, I'm going to skate away with this fellow. Lose him in the crowd and spin him around until I have him in my spell. How about we see you at the bonfire in an hour?"

Bruce watched them skate off—hand in hand, with a tenderness he hadn't seen for a long time. The couplings the GIs had after Germany surrendered were fast and easy to find, at least from the way they bragged about them. Nothing like the scene in front of him now.

The tenderness had been there with Amelia almost to the end. He realized now that she had begun to change after VE Day, when he was stuck at the rehab hospital in Germany and Mark, her old boyfriend, was back from the war. Her letters had been full of worry for Bruce and dreams of their reunion. Then they changed to talk of the post-war changes and how she was adrift after leaving her job with the Secret Intelligence Service—work that had been essential until Germany was defeated. Mark wasn't mentioned, but Amelia's father became a regular subject in the letters. He was trying to groom her to take over managing the family holdings, including Whitcombe Hall—a development that should have worried Bruce more than it did at the time. Amelia had seemed more inclined to parlay her wartime service and her Cambridge connections to find an opportunity in London. Her degree had been in economics, and a boom was expected.

Bruce had been blinded by the intensity of the few months they had together before he left for France. But Amelia probably had already decided to end it. Too many hurdles—a marriage to an American doctor who wanted to go home would get in the way of any of these plans. Chalk it up as a great wartime fling, nothing more. Too bad he couldn't see it that way.

Bruce skated back toward the shore, his thoughts returning to Glen. *Don't let him get hurt*, he said under his breath.

His aunt Pauline's cackling brought him back to attention.

"Skating by yourself, are you? Can't you find a girl?"

Pauline skated arm in arm with his mother, Alice, and their friend Bess Runyon—three women pressing sixty but still in fine form from their days on the skating team as high school students at Highland Hall. They split, and each did a backward spiral before coming back together again.

"Nifty trick," Bruce said.

"We heard about the new doctor at the Women's Club yesterday," Pauline said. "They say that the girls will have to be the ones to support her because a man will never let the doctor put her hands on him."

She cackled again and said, "Can you imagine her doing a prostate exam? That would be something to see."

"Shush, Pauline," Alice said. "Put a lid on the dirty talk."

"Nothing wrong with a little dirt now and then," she replied.

"I think you've shocked the doctor," Bess said.

"Does it bother you the new doctor's a woman?" Pauline asked. "I thought doctors were an all-male club."

"Nope. The woman part isn't a problem. None of them have come here before, but there are plenty in Philadelphia. Women's Medical College graduates a class every year."

"Don't worry, Bruce," Bess said. "Magnuson won't last much longer, and a woman doctor could lighten things up around here. You could share night call or something—work together." She broke away from Alice and Pauline and motioned for Bruce to skate with her. Since Bruce had moved next door, they had been eating some dinners together and playing cribbage afterward. A friendship had been struck.

"Haven't skated with a man for years," Bess said. "Thanks for giving an old lady a quick turn around the ice."

"A pleasure, Bess. Much better than skating alone."

"Pauline was ribbing you about not having a girlfriend. But she's right. I hear the new doctor's prettier than you might expect—so sharp she doesn't need makeup. If you want an interesting woman, someone with character, she could be it."

Bruce smiled. "She won't be in the market for a boyfriend . . . too busy being a doctor. Now let me steer you back to Mother and Aunt Pauline. I'm going to warm up at the bonfire."


With his skates off, and a cup of soup in hand, Bruce mulled over Bess's foray into matchmaking. He hoped Sarah would be a good replacement for Magnuson—someone he could trust to cover his practice if he took a vacation, nothing more. An attractive woman, but out of bounds.

His seat on a bench by the fire looked out on the ice, where he could see Glen and Mimi skating slowly on the southern fringe of the pond, away from the crowds. Seeing them nudge together stirred images of Amelia. He could see her side by side with him on the Test on their first day, the rhythms of their casts pulling them closer. He could hear the sweetness in her voice when she invited him into the river keeper's cabin. But as Glen and Mimi skated toward him, he shrugged off the useless reverie. His brother needed him here now, not on a futile ride through the past.

*December 15, 1945*
*Dear Bruce,*

*I'm writing with trepidation, fearing you are so angry with me that you never want to hear from me again. I've regretted my decision every day since I wrote that pitiful letter to you in Germany. I knew that if I saw you again, I couldn't have broken it off. Your first leave after the war and a few days in Paris together; there would have been no turning back.*

*I hid the real reason I stepped away. It wasn't my feelings for Mark. He's a wisp compared to you. I'm ashamed to admit that I threw away our future to keep a family tree alive. It was worse than you knew. Daddy was drinking and couldn't get over losing my brother. He got more and more strident about his plans for me, and he laid out my options in black and white. End it with you or lose everything else.*

*Daddy said it would kill him if I went with you. The irony was that he died anyway, in October after another heart attack. So now I'm the owner of Whitcombe Hall, the house in London, and the trimmings that go with the estate.*

*Mark pressed his case after he came back from the Pacific. And again, I'm ashamed to confess that I accepted his proposal. Daddy wanted me to marry Mark so much, and Mark has all the credentials to run Whitcombe Hall. The wedding was to be at Christmas time, but it's on hold now.*

*I'm a confused, guilty, and lonely woman who would like nothing more than to wade into the water again with you. Could you forgive me?*

*Love,*
*Amelia*

## Chapter 11

## NOEL 1945

———

First Presbyterian Church was full on this Sunday before Christmas, and the Duncan brothers were together in their pew, wearing their uniforms as the pastor requested. The church was celebrating the first Christmas after the war with a tribute to the men and women who served and returned. In May there would be an unveiling of the plaque for the four soldiers who would never sit in these pews again.

Bruce was skeptical about prayer. The battlefields had made him doubt that God paid much attention to the fate of humans. Still, he muttered some words under his breath when there was time for silent prayer. *Guide me with Amelia.*

A pure and sonorous tenor voice started to ring out a message that caught Bruce's attention. The words from Handel's *Messiah*, "Every valley shall be exalted, the crooked made straight, and the rough places plain," stirred thoughts of what might be. The triumphant, joyful mood of the piece began to wash over him—a contrapuntal force against the doubts that had torn at him since the letter arrived yesterday.

Amelia's letter had rocked him—opened him up to hopes that had shriveled to nothing. He could take a couple months off to go to England, as soon as possible if he wanted to stop her marriage. Or he could ask her to come to New York City or Pennsylvania. They could be together for a few weeks to see if their rift could be healed. Images of a reunion were so vivid he could almost feel her with him. But questions flooded his mind. Could he ever trust her again? What did she want? A last tumble with him before settling into her life with Mark?

His practice was just getting started. He couldn't abandon it to go to England on a lark that Amelia meant what she said. His place was here in Hollidaysburg. If Amelia came here, the pull of her home at Whitcombe Hall would win out. She wouldn't stay in small-town Pennsylvania, and he would have the same crushing grief as the last time she left him. It would have been better to have never received that letter. He had started to carve out a life without her.

It was two days before Christmas, and he was thriving in his practice. He was surrounded by people who cared about him. The music was glorious. The church was decked with garlands of pine and full of the warmth of the season. Against this backdrop, Amelia was an interloper who could derail his career, shunt him away from his life plan. Yet the elemental draw to her was as strong as ever.

They came out of the church with the bells pealing the plaintive carol "I Wonder as I Wander." The minor key of the song and the dark skies with swirling snowflakes struck Bruce as good matches for his mood. He hugged his mother and set off to walk down Elm Street to his house.

"Bruce, slow down so I can walk with you," he heard Bess call out to him from across the street. "It's getting slippery out here, and I could use a strong arm."

He turned to see her scooting along without any difficulty. She was a fit woman from her gardening labors.

"You're looking pensive today. A tough case or something?" she said as she approached him.

"No, feeling fine. Just happy to be back in Hollidaysburg this Christmas and walking through the beautiful snow."

Bruce and Bess had been growing closer since she brokered the deal that helped him afford the rent on the small house beside her mansion. His house had "good bones," as Bess put it, but it had been rented for more than a decade and had deteriorated. The yard held a thicket of overgrown, wild-looking plants that would need to be attacked in the spring. In contrast, Bess's garden was a showpiece—a standard stop on the church garden tour each May. Today in the snow, the neatly clipped evergreens and the winding paths showed the thoughtful layout of the garden. A cherry tree at the end of the main path had a cloak of white, dressing it for Christmas.

Bess had an uncanny way of freeing Bruce up to talk. After a few hands of cribbage, the cards might be laid down as they segued into reminiscences about the war or philosophical discourses. Bess's intellect appealed to Bruce. And her pledge of privacy—"not a word to your mother or anyone else"—moved them toward being confidants.

"How about a pre-Christmas lunch?" she asked. "I've got some wonderful soup I made with the tomatoes I canned last summer, and I can do a quick soufflé while you read the paper."

Bruce didn't want to talk with her about Amelia—a topic he had avoided so far. But he didn't relish spending the afternoon alone with a dilemma that seemed to have no good answer.

"Okay, if you let me pay you back by shoveling your walk," he said. "I need some exercise now. The paper can wait."

The snow was coming down more heavily by the time he finished shoveling their walks. He would need to clear them off again before nightfall, but felt better having accomplished something he could see.

After he gave a hasty knock and entered the front door, he heard "White Christmas" being warbled by Bing Crosby from the record player. Bess's home was a feast for the senses. Relics of the canal days covered the walls and the floors—old paintings of the packet boats with the grizzled pioneers and boat operators, tables and chairs that had come on the boats from East Coast cities, cabinets with china and curios from the early 1800s, and worn oriental rugs. Crystal chandeliers hung from the twelve-foot ceilings.

For Christmas, Bess erected a tree that reached to the top of the ceiling and decorated it with glass ornaments that were family heirlooms. Evergreens were festooned on the circular banister that ran from the foyer to the third floor of the house. Electric candles were placed at each of the windows. And a bevy of music boxes was arrayed in the library. She made these Christmas preparations every year so she could host a party on the second Saturday of December.

Bess came out of the kitchen with a cheery welcome.

"Don't have to dream about having a white Christmas . . . It's here," she said. "Let's go back to the kitchen. The soufflé is in the oven, and we can start on the soup."

When lunch was finished, they played cribbage in the library, not talking much. Amelia's letter seeped back into Bruce's mind whenever he was quiet.

"Come on, Bruce, there's something going on here," she said. "You've been moping around and not saying anything. I have two ideas. Either I'm boring you, and you should go home; or you're chewing on a problem that you don't want to tell me about. Which is it?"

"You're never boring, Bess. But I probably should shovel the walks again and go home to work on some things."

"That's a dodge if I ever saw one. I think it's about the woman in England. I shouldn't snitch on him, but the postman told me you got a letter from England . . . He doesn't see many of those. I have my ways of finding out what goes on in this town."

Bruce smiled. "I guess you do."

"Your mother worries about you all the time. She says you can't get over Amelia. Told me Amelia's father claimed a doctor from the USA wasn't good enough for her. What a bunch of crap. You're good enough for any woman . . . Could be royalty, I don't care."

"Can't keep secrets in this town," Bruce said. "Please don't tell Mother or anyone else about the letter I got today. I should just shuck it off and find someone here."

"Not so easy to do when you're bitten by the big one," she told him before she paused to think. "Since we're talking about secrets, I'll share my deepest. Even your mother doesn't know about this part of my life. Don't let it slip, or I'll be an outcast."

"Don't tell me, Bess. I don't need to know."

"I need to tell somebody before I die—somebody who will understand and still accept me. You'll do that, Bruce, and I'll help you talk about Amelia. I'm the person for the job. You'll see.

"This doctor stuff makes you play a role. You can't be vulnerable, can't show feelings . . . can't let people know about your fears. You don't have to be the strong, silent type with me."

"You're right about needing to protect my reputation," he said. "But everybody needs to do that."

"How true." Bess stood, walked to her bookcase, and took a large leather-bound tome off the shelf. She leafed through the pages and pulled out a yellowed photo. "My hiding place. No one would think to look in *The History of the Juniata Canal* to learn about my past.

"Did you ever wonder why I never married? I was decent looking, had a nice figure, had more money than most, was popular at Bucknell. It would seem like I'd be a good catch for lots of guys. And I tried to date. It never worked. When a man touched me, I was numb. No feelings at all, or even repulsed. Then there was my college roommate—Mary Hobbs from Philadelphia's Main Line. Here's a photo of the two of us in our swimming suits. Beautiful, wasn't she? One night at the end of our junior year I crawled in bed with her, acting like I was sleepwalking. Things happened that night that scared both of us. And in a few days she went home and transferred to another school for her senior year. We never spoke again. I thought so many times about writing her, or getting in the car and driving to her home. Never did it . . . no guts. I never touched another woman. I came back here and taught school for all those years, lonely as hell. Poured myself into the garden—my salvation. Took care of my father when he faded, did volunteer work, made friends. You're probably wondering about my feelings for your mother. Sure, I desired her, but I never let on that I'm attracted to women. She's as attracted to men as I am to women. She loved your father even though he drank too much and had his spells. And she still has some life left in her for the judge.

"So there it is. I'm a fish out of water, a woman who only fumbled in the dark with someone she loved on one night in all her days on the planet. Do I disgust you? Can you still like me?"

Bruce touched her chin and tilted her head up to look in her eyes.

"Yes, I like you more than ever. You're the most honest person I know.

"I should take a lesson from you and stay away from Amelia," he continued. "The way it ended left me in bad shape. I got a note the day before I was going to Paris to see her for the first time after the Nazis surrendered . . . Told me there was another guy, her old boyfriend who came back from the Pacific. Her daddy and the guy are buddy-buddy, and I don't fit into their grand plan.

"A letter from her came on Friday, the first since the one before Paris. Now Amelia says she isn't sure about the other guy. Her father died, and she inherited everything. So she's put off the wedding. She wants to see me again . . . Looks like danger to me."

Bess hugged him. "Oh, you poor boy. Still in love, aren't you? Want to hold her so badly, but scared you'll get burned. Mary was only a few hours away on the train, and I never saw her again. My chance is long gone. Yours is still alive . . . tenuous, but very much alive."

"I can't decide what to do. Ignore the letter and never see her again, dance around a bit with the reply, or book the next boat to England."

"You could invite her here. She could stay with me, and I could check her out. All those years of teaching helped me spot the genuine articles in the crowd. It would look like I was a chaperone, so people wouldn't talk about you having a lover in town. You could sleep over here with her, whatever you want to do. If you don't take the chance, you'll never know what could have happened. Even if you decide to go different ways, at least you would have tried. You wouldn't end up with all of the regrets and maybes that I have."

"I don't know, Bess. I'd like her to show up here tomorrow, but it probably would make it worse for me in the end. I think it's time to tackle the snow again."

After he cleared the paths, Bruce stood erect with both hands cupped over the shovel handle, sighting into the thickness of the storm. Then he walked toward his dark house.

*Christmas Eve, 1945*
*Dear Amelia,*

*Your letter surprised and unsettled me. I've been trying to throw myself into this new life and forget you. Sometimes I can push the memories away, especially when I'm deep into work. Other times the sweetness of our time together is too powerful to ignore. I can be having a smooth day, focusing on something that seems important, when a little trigger, maybe a song or a smell or a way a tree blows in the wind, takes me back.*

*Yes, there is anger. Seeing pictures in my mind of us being together got me through that damned war. And the anticipation of meeting you in Paris was so strong that my heart was bursting for you. Then it did burst in a horrible way. Yes, I did figure the pressure from your father was the real reason you broke it off with me. I could salvage more self-respect with that explanation than thinking I came in second place to another man.*

*I guess there wasn't enough love to sway you from your legacy. Having your brother die and being the only heir must have been harder than I realized. I've tried to understand your dilemma and forgive you so I can hold on to the richness of our few months together without it torturing me. I was partway there, and then your letter arrived two days ago.*

*Of course I want to be with you again. But I don't want the suffering when the inevitable happens and we go back to our corners of the world. I was close to concluding that you made the right choice. I was trying to understand that the war bred intensity that couldn't survive afterward. I was starting to find my way here in Pennsylvania. Now I have no idea what to do.*

*Last Christmas Eve, I was in Alsace having one of my hardest days of the war. I wrote a letter to you that night. Do you still have it? I've kept your letters. I'll add the new one to the cache.*

*For now, all I can say is Merry Christmas from one whose soul still leaps at a word from you.*

*Love,*
*Bruce*

# *Chapter 12*

## PURSUED

⸺

he air was clear and crisp, but Bruce couldn't recognize the man tailing him. He wore a dull green coat and a brown hunting hat with ear flaps obscuring his face. There was nothing else to identify him. With only a block to go before he arrived at his house, Bruce took a quick left turn into an alley and ducked behind the first garage. The Christmas snow had melted yesterday, so he would be able to hear the crunch of footsteps on the cinders that had been spread in the alley.

Crouching low, he scanned the area for places where he could hide and still see the man when he turned the corner. All he could find was a stand of viburnums with bare branches. The tangles of stems would give some cover, but the stalker could punch right through the gaping holes between the shrubs. *Think fast*, Bruce told himself. He wanted to be the hunter, not the hunted. Then he saw the answer in front of him—an old wooden ladder lying on its side against the back of the garage. A rickety piece of equipment, probably left outside because it was ready for the junk heap, but it would do. In a few seconds he was in place—his head peeking over the crest of the roof so he could watch the man approach. The ladder was pulled up beside him. A loose rock was in his hand.

Five minutes went by without any movement in the alley. After another five minutes, Bruce began to wonder if his mind was playing tricks. The war had made him edgy. Had it made him paranoid? Probably the guy was just walking home—veered off at Walnut Street in another direction.

Another string of thoughts popped into his mind. *What if someone sees me on this roof? They'll think I've gone nuts . . . Maybe I have.*

When he edged down to reach for the ladder to get off the roof, a scuffle of footsteps stopped him cold. The man was coming through the alley toward him. Bruce's pulse started banging in his carotids as an image from the battle at Rohrwiller flashed in his brain. He was lying prone in the bombed-out aid station. Nazis at the door. Nowhere to go. In a reflex, he grabbed for his rifle. But all he found was the rough edge of the old ladder. *Steady yourself. This isn't the war. Be ready for him.*

The top of the brown cap came into view first. The man was looking away from Bruce, pausing for a few beats, then walking on. He glanced ahead, not toward the roof line where Bruce was lying flat to narrow his profile against the night sky.

Then he turned and stared back toward the alleyway entrance. He was a boy—Larry Bailey, his nurse's fifteen-year-old son, already close to six feet tall. The kid looked confused and scared. He glanced down the alley one more time before he started to walk away in the direction of Bruce's house.

Larry wasn't a threat. But why was the boy tracking him? Bruce relaxed his hand around the rock, slipped it into his pocket, and moved the ladder into position to climb down from the roof.

"Wait up," Bruce called to the kid when he found him. "Did you want to talk with me?"

Larry held his coat tightly around him, and his head hung down. Bruce saw him trembling as he got closer. "What's the problem?" Bruce asked.

Larry pursed his lips and looked away. "I was trying to get the courage to ask you something."

"Yeah, I saw you following me—didn't know who it was. So I tried to shake you. Why didn't you come to my office? I was there till six o'clock."

"I knew you were in there," Larry said. "I was waiting outside. Couldn't let my mother know what's wrong. She'd kill me.

"I . . . I'm in trouble. Messed around with a girl last week and caught something bad. The rash is all over me. Can you give me a shot and keep it quiet?"

"First let's find out what the problem is," he replied. "Then we can decide what to do. You can tell me what happened while we walk to my house. When did the rash start?"

"About a week ago, a day after a Christmas party at Sally Gwin's. I saw a big red blotch on my belly. I thought it was a hickey. Her cousin from Tyrone took me to a bedroom and did stuff I never saw before. The guys told me she had a reputation. We didn't go the whole way . . . I've never done that. But I touched her down there. She took my hand and made me rub her really hard till it hurt my hand. I went home right away and took a shower—really scrubbed myself. I guess it didn't work. The big blotch is still there, and the rash spread the whole way up my chest . . . started showing on my neck this afternoon. Is it syphilis? I heard about rashes from syphilis in my health class."

Bruce suspected the rash wasn't from a venereal disease. The rash from syphilis comes on much later. However, they had arrived at his house, and Bruce needed to examine Larry to be sure.

"I think you're going to be fine, Larry. I doubt it's syphilis. Let's take a look. Show me that blotch you talked about."

When Larry took his shirt off, the diagnosis was obvious—pityriasis rosea, an innocuous rash that starts with a scaly patch about two to three inches wide. Larry's patch was still prominent, and smaller red spots were studded in the fir-tree pattern that clinches the diagnosis.

Bruce explained the situation to Larry and comforted him. "There's no need to mention a word about the girl to your parents. It will be between us. But we should talk about sex and protecting yourself. Okay?"

"Anything you say, Doc. Thanks."

After Larry left, Bruce brewed coffee in the old tin pot that Bess gave him and sat at his kitchen table. He wasn't ready to cook dinner. He needed to take stock of the paranoia that had washed over him. *Dumb*, he said to himself. *No one could have been after me. The only enemy I have is Lucas. And he wouldn't try to tail me—too much to lose.*

He thought back to his last days in Rohrwiller when the town was almost taken by the Germans. If there were seeds of paranoia anywhere, they had come from that hellhole. A Nazi rifleman could be around any corner; a shell could crash through the roof of their aid station anytime. Even the miserable German prisoners they had treated and tied to their cots had to be watched. One of them worked his way loose, grabbed a gun, and tried to shoot his way out. Twenty-four hours a day through most of last January—never safe, never at ease. Always on guard.

A loud rapping at his front door startled him. At first he wondered if he was starting to hear things. Then the knock was repeated. It wasn't Bess's discreet tap. Glen would knock once and barge in. It was Friday night at seven thirty. He wasn't expecting anyone, and he'd already had enough surprises tonight. Part of him wanted to play possum—let the person knock and then go away thinking no one was home. But after the rapping got more insistent, he went to the door.

Tony stood there with two other men from the brick plant, holding a large box. They were still covered with dust from their shift at work and smelled of sweat and tobacco juice. "Sorry about coming to your house," Tony said. "We didn't want to show up at your office—thought our boss wouldn't like it. We had some dinner at the tavern and waited till it was quiet to come into Hollidaysburg."

"Good to see you, Tony. You back at work?"

"Yep. Fenelli only gave me three weeks for my ribs to heal. Cleared me, said I was fine. Didn't even check my X-ray. Lots of bullshit out there, Doc. But I know you can't treat me. I heard Glover threaten you."

"Wish I could, Tony."

"Anyway, me and my buddies—George Haskell's the big guy and Slim Pike's the scrawny fellow with the gap teeth—brought you something to thank you. You can have a wildlife feast, Doc. A wild turkey and roasts and whole loins from two deer. They're still fresh. Shot 'em on Christmas Eve and Christmas Day. Packed in ice. We'll drop off some venison burger and sausage after we get all the butchering done."

"A big gift. Thanks, fellows," Bruce said. "Come in so we can talk."

Tony and George took seats beside Bruce, while Slim stood nearby. "Don't tell anyone about the venison," George said. "Just missed the season, but Tony wasn't strong enough to go out until a few days ago. He had to do it for you, even if it put him under. He's a stubborn SOB . . . been talking about bringing you some good meat since he got home."

"We hauled him up on the ridge and got him in a blind he built last year," Slim explained. "Shot the two deer himself."

George continued. "We wanted to help after we heard what you did for him, Doc. He told us what you said about his lungs. Fenelli doesn't tell us anything."

"Yeah, Fenelli's a company man. He'll do anything they say," Slim added.

"What's the truth about the brick dust?" George asked. "Will we end up like Tony?"

Bruce knew he shouldn't get involved. Lucas had warned him away. The best decision would be to thank them again for the wild game, wish them luck, and send them on their way. Yet he couldn't ignore their plight.

"I'm not an expert on lung disease," Bruce said. "But I read up on silicosis after I diagnosed Tony. You don't get this illness unless you work around the kind of brick dust you guys breathe all the time. Not everybody has it as bad as Tony. Some men can work for twenty or thirty years and not have much change in their lungs. How about you two—George? Slim? Do you get short of breath?"

"Yeah, can't run the bases in softball any longer," George replied.

"Same for me," Slim added.

"Tony told me he doesn't wear a respirator. How about the rest of you?"

"Nobody wears them," Slim answered. "We have to buy them ourselves, and they slow you down."

"Do you have any exhaust fans to control the dust? Any other way to suck it out of the air?"

"That's a joke," Tony said. "We have a couple old fans that keep breaking down. Most of the time they aren't working. The worst time is when we sweep up the silica to put it back in the bins. No fan could handle that cloud of dust."

"Is your union looking out for you?" Bruce asked.

"We don't have a union," George replied. "They said they'd close the plant if a union got in, so the men voted it down."

"You have a tough situation," Bruce said. "The dust has millions of little silica particles with sharp edges, and they stick in the lung tissue where they can't get out. Before you notice much change in your breathing, the damage can sneak up on you. If you get advanced silicosis, there's not much that can be done except to get away from the dust and stop smoking. I told Tony he shouldn't go back to work in the plant."

He pulled his chair closer to Tony. "I can't imagine why Fenelli cleared you. They should put you on disability or get you a job in the main office away from the dust. Do you want me to write a letter to the plant manager? I used to play basketball with him. Glover told me to stop treating you, but he can't shut me up. And I don't mind calling Fenelli and telling him what I think."

"Time to confess," George said. "Bringing you the meat wasn't the only reason we came. We need someone on our side. Someone who can help us do something about it. Glover is vicious . . . He could hurt you. So we don't want him to know anything about us coming here. We want you to be a silent partner—find other doctors who could help us, give us the medical dope we need to convince them the problem needs to be fixed. Maybe you could help us write some letters so it looks like they came from us."

Bruce had underestimated them. They were ahead of him in thinking of ways to break the stranglehold of the company. "Are there other men at the plant who are thinking about these problems? Or is it just you three?"

"The car wreck with one of us dead and another in bad shape stirred guys up," George replied. "When Tony told us that Glover threatened you . . . cut you off from treating him, it snapped a cord. We've had enough of being bullied around. Hope you won't turn us away."

"I'm just a GP trying to treat the people who come to my office. Changing a company's policies is way over my head . . . but you're working in a death trap.

"The only answer I know is prevention," Bruce continued. "There must be other companies that are doing a better job protecting their employees. I'll write to one of the experts on lung disease I know in Philadelphia and ask him what he knows. And I'll get a librarian at the University of Pennsylvania to dig up some articles on preventing silicosis. Don't tell anybody I'm feeding you this stuff."

"Could you get X-rays or do some lung exams on some of the men so we can prove there's a problem?" George asked.

"You're pushing me too far with that one, guys. Let's start with researching on silicosis. And I might be able to get one of the doctors from Philadelphia to volunteer some time to help you out. Fenelli's never going to give you the results of his tests."

George nodded with appreciation. "Just what we need, Doc. Find us some experts to build our case."

"We better get out of here," Tony said. "Our wives might start looking for us. No one knows where we went tonight."

"Before you leave, let's split up that wild game," Bruce said. "One of those loins and the turkey are plenty for me. I'll give them to my mother to cook a family dinner. Spread the rest of the venison around to your families."

"Happy New Year, Doc," Tony said as they left. "1946 will be a better year."


After the men departed, Bruce walked down Elm Street toward the Ambrosia for a late dinner. He didn't want to be alone and cook for himself after what had happened this evening. Pete would be at the Ambrosia till closing time, and the mood would be light. Some banter with Pete would be a good diversion.

The encounter with Larry Bailey had shaken him. He had conjured a menacing stalker out of nothing but an innocent boy who needed to talk. Like a fool, he had climbed on a roof with a rock in his hand. Even if an adversary had been following him, he should have turned and walked toward the man. Fear had ruled.

Then, within an hour, he had jumped in with an offer to help the brickworkers. The offer should have scared him, but it didn't. George had said it—Lucas could hurt him. Was he thinking straight? Or had the war bent him in ways he couldn't understand?

Bruce's idyll of an easy-going medical practice—a tranquil life after the war—had faded. He hadn't been prepared for the roiling disruptions: the flashbacks and nightmares; Amelia's letter; Glen's instability; a near assault on Lucas; and tonight, a brush with paranoia and a risky decision to get involved with the men from the brick plant. Army training had prepared him to know what to do if a leg had gangrene or a finger got shot off. But he didn't have a manual for these other trials.

*Chapter 13*

## YEAR'S END

———

$R$eggie Shackleton's band was pumping out "Penn-sylvania 6-5000," the Glenn Miller tune, and the crowd was loving it. They echoed the *hey ohs* and the *na nas* in full-throated, boozy voices. Only ninety minutes and they would be in the New Year—1946, the first year without a war since '40. The country club was jumping.

The band had all of its boys back from the service. With five saxophones and four trombones, they made a big sound. The ballroom with its vaulted ceilings shook with energy from the band and the swarms of dancers. The days of rationing were over. They partied to make up for lost time.

Bruce was enjoying himself, despite having reservations about going to the dance. As promised, his date for the night, Mimi's roommate from college, was an attractive woman. Dressed in a jade-green sheath with a bare glimpse of breast peeking from the top, Becky had a forward, exciting look. Guys had already tapped him on the shoulder to cut in for dances. He didn't mind. There wasn't much of a connection with her, and her prattling about her friends in Manhattan struck him as a bit snobbish. It was good to be out dancing with a woman again, but this would be their last date. He was waiting for Amelia's next letter.

After the "Pennsylvania 6-5000" excitement, the band-leader took the mike and announced a ladies' choice. "Time to mix it up, friends. Pick someone else to spin around this star-flecked dance floor. Let the mirrored ball take you away to a distant land. Add some mystery to the night as we play 'Moonlight Serenade.'"

Becky was diplomatic. "Mind if I dance with your brother? Some of these other men are coming on a little strong."

"Sure," Bruce replied. "Mimi and I can sit this one out." Glen had been drinking champagne all evening. Better to have him on the dance floor than at the bar.

As Bruce walked with Mimi to their table, he felt a squeeze from behind him. Familiar hands, a familiar scent— it was Kate Glover. She whispered in his ear. "Lucas is in the men's bar smoking cigars. How about a dance?"

Bruce shook his head and walked on with Mimi. But Kate followed him and tapped on his shoulder. "Come on, Bruce. It won't hurt to give your old girlfriend a twirl."

Mimi turned to see Kate, a woman she didn't know. "Go ahead, Bruce. My feet are sore. I need a break."

"Sorry, Kate," Bruce said. He was getting irritated with Kate but tried not to show it to Mimi. "This lady needs some rest and someone to keep her company."

Kate called out to Glen as he swayed by them with Becky. "Look who I found for the lady's choice. Your big brother, and he's dragging his heels."

"Get with it, brother! Bad form to refuse a lady," Glen shouted over the swelling music.

"I'll be fine," Mimi said. "Enjoy the dance."

Bruce was fuming. But to avoid more attention, he took Kate's hand and steered her toward the middle of the dance floor. He hoped they would get lost in the crowd and Lucas would stay in the men's bar until the dance was over.

Kate smiled, held him lightly, and started dancing in a prim style that Bruce hadn't expected. "Don't worry. I'm reformed . . . no more surprises in your office. It was a mistake. Will you forgive me? Can we still be friends?"

Bruce kept a stiff posture and plenty of air between them. "Yes, I forgive you," he said. Her apology had started to soften his anger, but he wanted to get away from her as soon as he could. "Why did you ask me to dance when Lucas left the room?"

"He wheedled an explanation out of me after I left your office. I was flushed from running home . . . didn't put my nylons on straight. He asked me where I had been, and I panicked. I didn't know what to say. So I made a silly excuse about needing to see you for a bladder infection. His jealousy is out of control. I've never cheated on him, but he gets wild when he thinks I'm flirting with someone else."

"What did you tell him?"

"He asked how the pelvic exam felt, and I got so mad I lied . . . told him it felt great. It was a shouting match for the next couple hours. But I never told him what actually happened."

His anger flared again. "Come on, Kate. Why did you do that?"

"It was stupid."

"Yeah, it was."

"Should I be afraid of him?" Bruce asked.

"Not really. He's mostly bluster. Pushed me around a couple times but never hurt me. I don't think he'd go after you. But he's drinking hard tonight. I'd stay out of his way."

They danced silently for the rest of the song as Bruce thought about Kate and Lucas and how they had pulled him into their fight. His two old friends were locked into something volatile. If he tried to help, it would backfire. Staying out of the way was the best plan.

"An honor to dance with you, soldier," Kate said as the band started playing "Tuxedo Junction" and the crowd pulsed to the faster beat. "Time to scoot away. See you around town."

Steve Taylor waited for Bruce as he came back to their table. "If I can take you away from Becky for a little longer, there's someone in the billiard room you should see. Sarah's been holed up there all evening, cleaning up on bets. She's here to stay now. Arrived with the moving van yesterday. I'll smooth things out with Becky and the rest of the crew. You and Sarah should have a dance together—show the town that the two new GPs will be friends."

When Bruce entered the billiard room with Steve, he saw Sarah with her simple black dress hitched up so she could try a difficult shot with the pool cue behind her back. Her athletic legs looked terrific—like a dancer's. They waited until she finished the game, then approached her.

"I found your competition out on the dance floor," Steve said. "Thought you and Bruce should give it a try. If you are going to cover for one another, you might as well dance a number or two. Do you have a date we should ask?"

"No dates for me," she replied. "My real estate agent and his wife brought me. They wanted to introduce me to some of their friends."

Bruce was having second thoughts about dancing with Sarah. Seeing her in that tight black dress and catching a glimpse of her figure had triggered some desire. Not a good thing for two doctors working in the same town. But Steve was pressuring them. It would be awkward to back out now.

"Have time for one spin?" he asked. "Steve thinks it would be good to show people we're not enemies."

Sarah flushed a bit. "I'm afraid I'm not much of a dancer. I played a lot of basketball and tennis . . . tall girl sports. But eight years at a women's college and med school didn't give me much dancing practice. Could we meet for coffee instead . . . talk about a coverage plan? I'll need to go back home to Williamsport for a weekend now and then. How about the Ambrosia sometime on Saturday?"

Bruce was relieved. "I have office hours Saturday morning. Is seven a.m. okay? I'll show you the office before I get started at eight, and I'll introduce you to Maggie, my assistant. She's a genius. You'll need one like her."

The ballroom was packed now with revelers dancing away the last minutes of 1945. He couldn't spot Becky for a few minutes. Then he saw her dancing with a man he didn't know. As he walked toward them to cut in, Bruce heard Glen's voice over the band. His brother was on the bandstand with the mike waving in his hand.

Glen was acting like he was still in the service, partying with the abandon of a soldier who might be dead before the next evening. He was trying to sing along with the band with risqué lyrics that he must have learned when he was stationed in England. The effect wasn't humorous. Reggie Shackleton tried to ease the mike out of his hand, but Glen wouldn't be deterred. Some of the dancers stopped to watch the scene on the stage. Mimi stood at the edge of the crowd, grimacing.

Suspecting the embarrassment could get worse, Bruce jogged to the bandstand and motioned to Glen with a cross-handed chop to cut the singing. The gesture didn't work, so he stroked his finger across his throat with a flourish. Finally, he got his brother's attention. Reggie grabbed the mike. And Bruce jumped on the stage to put his arm around Glen and ease him away.

To provide cover, Bruce acted like they were having a light-hearted chat as he steered Glen to the veranda overlooking the golf course. The crowd quickly got back to celebrating, but Bruce saw Mimi tracing their exit from the room.

"Why did you pull that stunt?" Glen asked when they stepped outside. "You made me look like a fool. What's your problem? Have to control me? Do I have to fit into your perfect little world? Act like the good brother to the good doctor? I'm going back up there to tell them all you're full of shit. No wonder Amelia dumped you . . . A prig. That's what you are."

Bruce tried to tamp down his anger, but the muscles around his left eye were twitching. His thoughts were racing in the wrong direction. *He's a jackass. Cuff him like Dad used to do. Show him he's wrong.*

He rubbed the spasms around his eye while he struggled for control, for words that would defuse the conflict. His first attempt misfired. "Yeah, I get embarrassed when you go off. Who wouldn't? You're acting like a jerk. Now zip it up and lay off the booze."

"Afraid I'll end up like Dad? He never had any fun, and look what happened to him . . . You want to be the big shit? Lord it over us like he did? Well, go ahead. But I'm not a little boy. You can't push me around."

Glen shoved him aside and moved toward the door. "I'm going back in there."

Bruce stumbled for a moment, then regained his footing. "No you're not," he said as he tackled his brother and sent him crashing across an urn and onto the stone surface of the patio. Both of them were stunned.

Glen's forehead was bleeding, but he was alert.

"Are you all right?" Bruce asked him.

"Yeah," Glen said. "I shouldn't have shoved you. I asked for it."

Bruce reached for his brother's hand and pulled him up. They hadn't fought like this since they were boys. "Let me check your head," Bruce said. "I didn't mean to knock you so hard."

As he examined his brother, Bruce bit his lips and tried again. "I was trying to save your reputation. The band wasn't going along. They hated it. And Mimi hated it. The war's over, Glen. You can't act like you're back in England and getting soused with your buddies. You hit the booze too hard to know what you're doing."

Glen shrugged and motioned for Bruce to join him on a cold stone bench. "Yeah, I'm a little lit tonight. But what the hell? It's New Year's Eve. Try working in that hardware store all day. Sell a pound of nails and think you've had a great hour. You'd want a few drinks when you had the chance."

Bruce sat on the bench, both of them staring ahead into the night. "I don't blame you for wanting to have a good time. You saw enough in the air over France to make any guy want to let loose. And I know the hardware store's a struggle. It sank Dad. I don't want it to sink you."

Glen dropped his head. "Ah crap, just take me home and put me to bed. I'll be better tomorrow. A new year, a new man. I'll get past this stuff. It's not the store. I keep seeing the burning plane, trying to bail out, my jacket on fire. Whiskey settles me down for a while. Got to stop it."

Steve burst through the veranda doors and shouted to them. "Come on, guys, three minutes to midnight. Countdown's started."

"Let's go back in for a while," Bruce said. "We've got some scars, but we'll be okay. I want you to stand by me when I watch the fireworks. I'll tell you why before the show starts. Becky wouldn't understand."

They joined their party for the confetti throwing, horn blowing, and singing of "Auld Lang Syne." Bruce apologized to Becky for not being attentive. Glen held Mimi and asked her to stick by him. Then the crowd surged toward the bank of windows that spanned the south side of the ballroom. In daylight, the large windows opened to a sweeping view of the mountains surrounding Chimney Rocks—the natural formation that was a lookout for Iroquois before the town was settled. Tonight there was no moon, and only a faint outline of the rocks appeared. Dim reflections bounced off their white surfaces from the street lamps and house lights in Hollidaysburg.

Mimi primed Becky for the fireworks that would be launched from Chimney Rocks while Bruce took Glen aside and spoke softly.

"My war was easy compared to yours. But I've got a problem. Anything like a shell explosion, a rifle shot or a flash of light, can set me off. Makes me go back to the front. I don't know why those scenes haunt me."

"Not so easy to forget, is it?" Glen said. "So what are you doing here with the fireworks ready to go off?"

"I'm going to watch the fireworks with my eyes wide open—try to get over this crap. Will you stand with me?"

When the rockets started going off from Chimney Rocks, there was an unexpected addition to the show. Some partygoers from the country club set up their private display and fired off blasts from the eighteenth green, about 150 feet from where Bruce and Glen stood. The concussive blasts shook their ears, and the acrid clouds of smoke surrounded them.

Bruce's brain was pounding. When he was in a dental chair, he could fantasize scenes that would transport him away from the pain. He knew to not use this trick now. Still, fantasies darted through his mind—a perfect day with Amelia, touching her body, blond hair tumbling over his face. Her arriving in Hollidaysburg as Bess suggested might happen. But he wrestled his attention back to the explosions. Gritting his teeth and sweating in the cold night air, he pushed deeper to relive the night he was trapped in the aid station with shells cracking everywhere. German tanks were bearing down on them. The doctors grabbed their rifles. What good would rifles do against the fire spewing from a Panzer? The roof ripped off the building, and bricks tumbled over him. He stayed with that image and told himself, *Let it go . . . Let it go.*

When the fireworks sputtered to an end, Glen clapped Bruce on the shoulder. "Did that help? You stood in there—didn't flinch."

"I don't know. I'm rattled. It's been a strange night."

"I'm sorry I pushed you," Glen said. "No more heavy booze for me . . . a New Year's resolution."

"We need to stay together," Bruce said. "Make '46 a good year for both of us. Now I need to get back to Becky. Let me dance with her a couple times. Then we can go home."

# $\mathcal{C}$hapter 14

## SILICA

———————

### January 12, 1946

Dear Bruce,

I received your letter on the day after New Year's and got to work right away on your request. Miss Daniels, the librarian, told me you also wrote to her. We've been collaborating on a bit of background research on silicosis and precautions that can be taken.

You are correct in concluding that lung damage from silica is irreversible and the only option is prevention. Despite reams of evidence that workers exposed to silica dust have a high risk of lung fibrosis and emphysema, the companies that employ them typically dismiss the risks and avoid the steps that could give some protection.

The worst example was the Hawk's Nest debacle in the early '30s. Of about 2,500 men who dug a tunnel through silica-laden rock under Gauley Mountain in

*West Virginia, 764 died from acute silicosis. Another 1,500 developed chronic silicosis by 1936. There was an outcry, which led to hearings and some ineffective, largely ignored regulations. By the time the war started, it was business as usual at brick plants and quarries. It's hard to get data on the risks at a brick plant, but I estimate at least 50% of men that work there get silicosis.*

*As to prevention, the recommendations are to implement these steps. First, there should be ample ventilation of work spaces, including large-volume exhaust fans, vacuum devices, or other mechanical methods to remove as much dust as possible. Second, there should be liberal use of water to settle down silica particles in the air. Third, respirators should be required at all times, even if workers complain they're unwieldy or uncomfortable. Fourth, silica concentrations should be monitored routinely, and standards should be met for permissible levels in work environments. Fifth, workers should be examined at least yearly for signs of silicosis. One would think that an enlightened company would take these steps and move workers with early silicosis to a job with limited or no exposure to this hazard. However, I suspect such precautions are rarely taken.*

*In regard to your specific dilemma in helping the men at Allegheny Refractories, I think I could cajole some colleagues in pulmonary medicine to cosign a letter from me to the men, and possibly to the company, about ways to make the work environment safer. It would be best to have some firsthand information about the current conditions at the plant. You could ask them to take some photos, keep logs of working conditions, and so forth. The more data we have on actual conditions, the better. I might also be able to tip off a reporter from the Philadelphia Inquirer to write an article.*

*I gather you are in a delicate position after having been "fired" by their boss. So I won't do anything unless you tell me to proceed.*

*It was good to hear from you and learn that you're engaged in more than treating colds and sewing up lacerations in your new practice. I predicted you wouldn't shy away from the serious business of being a doctor in a small town. It looks like my prediction has come true.*

*Regards,*
*Phil*
*Phillip Silverman, M.D.*

*B*ruce sensed that Phil took some time deciding what to say to him. The challenge was unmistakable. In their meetings at Penn, Phil had often steered the conversation away from the mechanics of medicine. Segueing from case histories to discourses on the life of a doctor, he spoke of nuances that weren't covered in classroom teaching—the importance of spending extra time with someone who needed to talk, giving a tip or suggestion at the time a person was ready to accept it, and knowing how to deliver bad news. And he counseled Bruce on how to take care of himself, staying fit and involved in pursuits outside medicine so he wouldn't become a one-sided drudge or be unable to sustain a long career.

The stories Bruce remembered most were the personal ones Phil told about dilemmas he had faced—blame and self-doubt after the suicide of a young patient with depression, fear when he developed hepatitis as an intern and discovered firsthand the impact of having a disease with lethal potential, disappointment when his testimony at a hearing for coal workers with black lung didn't sway the judge. Phil didn't trumpet his coping skills when he told the stories, but Bruce could tell he took his lumps and grew from the experiences. If there was a unifying message, it was that unpredictable challenges will come your way and the way you respond to them defines you.

Tony Giordano, George Haskell, and Slim Pike were already in the private room at the Ambrosia when Bruce arrived for their meeting. Pete had provided them with beers, as Bruce requested. It was Friday afternoon at five thirty. As first-shift men, their week's work was done.

"Hey, Doc, thanks for the beers," George said. "Get one yourself."

"Those Yuenglings look good. But sorry, I can't have one. I have to go back to the office to run some lab tests."

"You work too hard, Doc," Slim said. "If you had a job like us, you could go fishing every day."

"We kept quiet about coming into town to see you," Tony said. "What's happened? Do you have some news?"

Bruce pulled Phil's letter from his jacket pocket and spread it out on the table. "The expert I told you about in Philadelphia wrote back. Read it and tell me what you think."

George and Tony sat down at the table and read the letter.

Slim stood back. "Need glasses or something, Doc. Can't read so well these days. They can tell me what it says."

"We don't have any of that stuff except those old fans— and they're garbage," George spat out. "The air testing's a good idea, but I doubt they'd ever do it. Wouldn't want to know what it showed. The only thing they test is the mud to make bricks and mortar. They make sure the mud's good, or they'll lose money when bricks fail in the blast furnaces.

"We're cooked worse than their lousy bricks. Read what it says right here. Fifty percent chance, and there's no treatment. Just hook us up to oxygen and let us suck air until we rot. Did you read that one about an enlightened company? I'm not sure what that word means, but I don't think it fits Allegheny Refractories."

"I'm one of the fifty percent for sure," Tony said. "Not much anyone can do for me except get me transferred to a job outside driving one of the trucks or something."

"Sounds like it's all bad news," Slim said. "Thanks for trying, Doc."

"Bad news for us, Slim. I know I've got a lot of silica in my lungs," George said. "But this Dr. Silverman offered to write a letter to the company and get some other doctors to sign it. And he might tip off a newspaper."

"We'd get fired if Glover or the other bosses found out we're behind this," Tony said. "But what the hell, somebody's got to stand up to them and take the chance. I'm pretty close to disability now. I can let Silverman use my name when he writes the letter."

"If he wrote the letter, nobody's name would need to be used," Bruce said. "Still, they could trace it back to me, and they'd know I treated Tony. People could talk and tell them that you met with me. It's hard to keep secrets in this town. I won't ask Phil Silverman to write that letter unless you all know the risk and want me to do it. I have no idea if the letter would do any good. So we could be asking for a lot of trouble with little chance of getting any relief for the men.

"I have another idea that has a chance of working and wouldn't be as dangerous as a letter. I'll ask to meet Lucas Glover at his office. We were friends in high school, so I don't think he'd refuse to see me. I'll be straight with him, tell him I can't stop worrying about Tony and the other guys who work at the plant. Explain that I checked the research on ways to prevent silicosis. I won't criticize him or push him into a corner. Just give him the chance to do the right thing."

George raised his eyebrows. "Glover's a tough man. He was better at first, when he got hired as an engineer. But after the war started and the pressure built to produce more bricks for the blast furnaces in Pittsburgh, he got promoted. Then he ordered everyone around like we were in the army. Squeezed every drop out of us. Some of the guys said he was guilty for taking a draft exemption. Now he's sitting on top of the world . . . plant manager with a company car, gorgeous wife, big house. He's not going to change."

"He needs to change," Bruce said. "It can't be good for a company to have its workers get sick. He's a smart guy. He'll be better off if his men are better off."

Tony looked up at Bruce and smiled. "I say give it a try. If you don't get anywhere, ask Silverman to write the letter. What do you say, George? Slim?"

George spoke first. "It could get hot for us. But yeah. Do it."

Slim took a long pull from his beer, moved to Bruce, and shook his hand. "I won't spoil the party. I'm in."

"Are you sure you understand the trouble this could bring?" Bruce questioned. "I don't see many problems for me. I don't work for the company."

"We know what could happen to us," George replied. "When we brought you the deer and turkeys, we knew what we were doing. We hoped you might be on our side. The three of us are worn out. The silica's got us. But maybe we could start something that would help the younger guys."

Tony closed the discussion. "The decision's made, Doc. How about another beer and a bite to eat? We don't come in town to the Ambrosia very often."


A week later, on another Friday, Bruce drove along the bank of Otter Creek on his way to the Allegheny Refractories plant in Blairton. There hadn't been time to hear back from Amelia, but he was thinking of her as he moved along the stream. Bess was giving him more encouragement to invite her to visit Pennsylvania. And if Amelia came, he would steer her clear of this terrain that had been eaten away by the two industries in the valley—the brickworks and a paper mill farther upstream. The first sign of entering this wasteland was the smell of the effluent from the paper mill that turned the stream oily black and left sulfur-tinged rime on the banks.

He remembered a camping trip with the Boy Scouts when they forded the river to follow a path toward the mountain lake at Blue Knob. It had been the middle of the summer, so they could take off their shoes and socks and wade across at a shallow point. The low waters from a dry spell must have concentrated the mill's discharge, because they had raw skin and scabby sores on their lower legs and feet for days. They stayed away from the polluted river afterward.

The brick plant's impact on the land came into view when he turned away from the river bottom toward Blairton. The road crested a small hill, and the sweep of the mountains ringing Blairton was all around him. He hadn't driven on this road since before the war. The holes on the ridges where the silica had been removed were larger. And there were more of them—like teeth that had gone to rot. Bruce knew that the plant had been at full capacity, three shifts a day, during the war. But he didn't expect as much devastation to the mountains.

The company houses, stacked closely together, lined both sides of the main street. They had a dispirited appearance as the light faded in the waning afternoon of a gray winter day. Paint flaked off the clapboard on most of the houses. Only a few appeared to have been freshened recently. The tiny yards were devoid of greenery. There were no traces of the boxwoods and yews that fronted the houses in Hollidaysburg. In a few spots some dried-up tomato vines flapped in the breeze. The ballfield was empty, much too cold for the baseball and football teams from Blairton High School or the softball players from the plant. He passed the center of the town with its company store, a Methodist Church, and Darrell's Cafe. The bar at the cafe was the busiest place in the town. He figured the crowd was mostly first-shift men who headed straight there before winding home with their pay for the week.

The brickworks dominated the south side of Blairton. Domed kilns, perhaps forty of them, each at least thirty feet tall and twice as wide, surrounded the main plant and company offices. Workers scuttled around several of the kilns, either loading them or disgorging the silica firebrick. Smoke poured out of the kilns that were being fired, and spurts of flames licked around the fireboxes.

From his readings, Bruce knew about the process of making firebrick. The silica bricks made here were different from the ones used for houses. Silica from quartz-embedded rock mined here could withstand temperatures up to three thousand degrees in blast furnaces for making steel. The Blairton plant, built in 1905, produced silica brick used to line the steel furnaces in Pittsburgh that had helped win two World Wars. All of the workers were deferred from the draft because the industry was critical to the war effort. It was a rough job. Cold in the winter, boiling hot around the kilns in the summer, silica dust in the air, and an ever-present risk of getting maimed by heavy equipment.

Approaching Lucas Glover to complain about working conditions was a dicey thing to do. Now that he had arrived at the plant, Bruce questioned the wisdom of making the appointment. Would this foray make it worse for the men? Would he be dismissed again as a naïve doctor who was in way over his head? Would Lucas's vitriol about Kate's office visit explode again?

The administrative complex stretched over at least a city block. Built of yellow brick in an Art Deco style and surrounded by clipped shrubs and tall maples, it seemed out of place among the kilns, corrugated iron–sided manufacturing facilities, warehouses, and rail lines where the working men spent their days. Bruce surmised that top brass of this company wanted a statement of power and influence. But he saw the design as a mark of excess in this industrial outpost far away from any major city.

Lucas greeted him with a firm handshake and a hint of a smile. His corner office with a big mahogany desk, red leather chairs, and sofa was stacked with folders, brick molds, and models for projects. A heavy odor of cigar smoke filled the room.

"I'm glad you came to see me, Bruce," he said. "I felt bad about the hard time I gave you at the hospital. You were just doing your job. Sorry for trying to push you around. I was worried about my guy."

Bruce shook his hand and smiled a bit in return. But Lucas's stinging rebukes in the hospital and Kate's revelations about the way he treated her swirled in the background.

"Thanks, Lucas. I thought we could get past that argument. We played a lot of ball together."

Lucas motioned him toward the two leather chairs that were pulled up to a low table. "Let's sit down. Cup of coffee? Or something stronger? I keep some bourbon handy for late afternoon meetings."

"Coffee for me," Bruce replied as he took one of the seats and tried to appear calm. "I want to continue the talk about silicosis we had in the hospital. I couldn't let it fester."

"Do you want me to lift your ban from treating our workers? Sorry, I can't do it. Emergencies or specialty care only. It's company policy—nothing against you. I'm sure you're a lot sharper than Fenelli. He's from that homeopathic school where they don't get very aggressive with treatment. He's got the contract, so I have to stick with him."

"No, I'm not trying to take over Fenelli's job. I've got plenty to do in my practice in Hollidaysburg. It's the worry that's been brewing about how bad your guy, Tony, is stuck with silicosis. His lungs are about eighty percent gone from silica. And I couldn't stop thinking about what might be happening to the other men at your plant. If there are a lot of them with silicosis, couldn't it come back to haunt the company?"

Lucas replied with a firm voice. "The working conditions are the same in firebrick plants everywhere. They've been this way for as long as anyone remembers. There's nothing I can do or anyone else can do to make it safer. It's a choice the men make when they sign on. They all know about silicosis. It's like working in coal mines. You can't take the dust completely out of the air. We do what we can to cut it down. If we stopped making the brick, the blast furnaces couldn't function, and the steel industry would die. So we keep going, doing our part."

Bruce paused and sipped his coffee. "I did some research on safety standards in plants that handle silica. Would you give your old teammate a chance to discuss what I learned?"

"Yeah, I'll listen. Tell me what you think we should do," he said as his back stiffened and the furrow between his eyes narrowed. Bruce recognized the tension and sensed that his opportunity might be slipping away. He moved ahead anyway.

"Phil Silverman, one of my professors at Penn, is a national expert on occupational lung diseases—black lung and silicosis. He recommends a five-point plan: big exhaust fans to clear dust away from the workers, watering to force silica down to the floor where it can be washed away, respirators even if workers complain about them, routine monitoring of air quality to reach target levels of silica concentration, and yearly lung exams for the workers. The goal is to reduce silica levels as much as possible and to move workers to less exposed jobs at the plant if they start showing signs of silicosis."

Lucas scowled. "Your ivory tower professor has probably never been in a brick plant, never worked a day of hard labor in his life." He reached for a cigar in the box beside him but didn't offer one to Bruce. "Sure, we can have fans and hoses. And we have respirators for anyone who wants one. You should work a day on the floor yourself . . . see what we have to do to get the product out the door."

He lit the cigar and continued, picking up steam. "Do you have any idea what it would cost us to do all that monitoring and reach some minuscule level of particles in the air that your researchers tell us is safe? Hell, we'd be out of business in a couple months. And none of these men would have a job. You have no idea what pressure I'm under to cut costs. Company headquarters is breathing down my neck every day. So if I blow up every now and then, you'll know why. If we fall behind, they'll cut me loose in a minute."

Bruce knew that Lucas was revealing more than he intended when the meeting started. If he kept pressing, he didn't know where the conversation would lead. Would Lucas show more concern? Would he toughen up and shut down their dialogue? As he did with patients, he tried to show some empathy.

"Lucas, I understand you have a hard business here. I appreciate everything you did during the war to keep the steel flowing. Those tanks that kept me alive in France never would have been built without your bricks. I know we need this industry. But isn't there a way to make it safer for the men? There has to be a solution that would satisfy all of you."

For a moment, Bruce thought his logic might be working. Lucas grabbed a thick pen and twirled it back and forth, looking like he was framing a serious response. But in a sudden move, he stabbed the pen toward Bruce. He was back on offense.

"You need to back off. If you weren't an old friend, I never would have met with you or listened to this crap. You don't want to be a 'do gooder' who tries to shut down one of the state's best employers. And by the way, I'd watch your reputation. I heard you danced with Kate at the New Year's Eve party at the club. Nuzzled up to her pretty close, they said. I don't think a doctor who messes with other men's wives will get very far in Hollidaysburg."

Bruce had almost lost control once before with Lucas, and he wasn't going to let it happen again. Recognizing that the conversation was over, at least for today, Bruce thought of ways to make his exit with as much grace as possible. Lucas's jealousy had clouded the opportunity for him to think of doing anything positive for the men. "I told you I have no interest in Kate . . . and I mean it. I'm in love with a woman I met in England, and I'll see her again soon. So drop the accusations about Kate. See the truth in what I said about protecting the men . . . You could save some lives."

"It's time for you to leave. Stay away from Allegheny Refractories and my wife. Go back to England to fiddle with your honey." He walked out of the office before Bruce could reply.

*January 10, 1946*
*Dear Bruce,*

*Your letter was the best Christmas present I have ever had. To hear that you still care, even though I acted so badly, means everything to me. I think about you so much of the day that it's a wonder I can get anything accomplished with the mound of responsibilities that have come my way.*

*I've been busy thinking of ways we could meet, and I have a proposal for you to consider. When Daddy died, I inherited his investments in the USA. He could see the war coming and shifted a good deal of his stock to a place where he thought it would be safe. A trip to New York to meet with his brokers on Wall Street wouldn't raise any eyebrows around here and would help me take better charge of the estate. The Queen Mary is being refitted from her troop carrier days and will sail to New York on May 5, arriving on May 10. Is the invitation still open to fish with you in Pennsylvania?*

*Whitcombe Hall is cold and drafty this time of year. I spend most of my time alone, sorting through the mess that Daddy left when he had the heart attack. I wish he had talked with me about his business affairs. The tax bills are daunting, but I think I'll be able to hold on to the old house and the section of the river Test where we had those idyllic days last spring.*

*I wasn't so honest with you before. I'll tell you every-thing now. My love for you is stronger than ever, but I'm still engaged to Mark. His family has the money to keep Whitcombe Hall running, and he has an import-ant position with Barclay's Bank. I keep putting off the wedding, and I don't see much of him because he's so busy with his work in London. My passion is all for you, not for him.*

*I didn't want to meet you in the USA without you knowing the truth about my situation here. My dreams are of finding a way for us to live our lives together. Could it be? Probably a small chance, but I want to try. Except for the miles between us, we are a perfect match.*

*Love,*
*Amelia*

# Chapter 15

## ROCKETS

———

### *London*
### *August 1944*

*T*he train moved through the outskirts of the city, through the heavy industrial zone pummeled during the Blitz and humming with activity now. Except for the random flying bombs—the V rockets that started falling after D-Day—Germany couldn't touch London now. Having given up the air war over this island, the Luftwaffe was trying to repel the Allies' advances toward Germany. Bruce would see them soon enough, probably by the end of the month, when his unit deployed to France.

From accounts he patched together from returning soldiers he treated, the Germans had a lot of fight left in them. It had been two months since D-Day, and the Allies had just broken out from St. Lo. Today's news described a heavy counterattack by columns of Panzers at Mortain. Bruce didn't know where his unit would be deployed or the exact date they would ship out. He did know they were trained to man a battlefield aid station. So they would be close to the action. His war was about to get interesting. Glen's was over. Bruce's visit yesterday to his brother might be the last until after the war. Glen was in an evacuation hospital north of London, waiting for air transport to the USA. Three weeks ago his P51 Mustang caught fire when he landed back in England. The controls were damaged so badly during a strafing attack in France that he had to limp back at low altitude, skimming the ocean and then tearing onto the runway with a skid that ignited the flames. Glen's experience and skill had paid off. But he had some severe burns on his legs and chest.

Bruce had arrived in time for the afternoon debridement and wound dressing. The burns still looked grisly with weeping, granulating tissue. Even though the raw skin must have been very painful, Glen had looked chipper. After the morphine for the dressing change wore off and Glen had dinner, they played cribbage and swapped stories until the nurse dimmed the lights and told Bruce visiting hours were over.

Another farewell, this one more difficult, awaited him. This two-day break in London could be his final chance to be with Amelia before shipping out. They had been fortunate to have so much time together since they met. He got away from the hospital almost every week. And she met him at the cottage at her estate if her father wasn't home. They had spent other weekends in London, where Amelia worked analyzing aerial photographs of the bombing war. She was bound to secrecy, but Bruce could tell that she was helping guide the planes to where they would have the most success. Today he would meet her in Bloomsbury at her flat on Bedford Square.

He reached into his pocket and felt his grandfather Duncan's watch. It was a refined piece with a solid gold case and filigreed engraving. Bruce had found a jeweler who added a B.D. & A.W., May 4, 1944, the day they had met, to the inside of the case. His father had given him the watch before Bruce left for basic training. Amelia would have the watch before the leave was over.

As the train slowed to pull into St. Pancras Station, he looked through the dusty window to see if there had been any flying bomb damage since his last visit. The newspaper articles claimed the defenses—barrage balloons with their cables rigged to snag the missiles, and the anti-aircraft guns that were popping now—were intercepting most of them. But the optimistic reports of success didn't stop his worry about Amelia. London was still a dangerous city.

From his vantage point on a middle track, the soaring glass canopy for the station didn't appear to have new holes. The rail hub was hit hard during the Blitz, and the repair work had focused on keeping the tracks open, not on cosmetics of the Victorian lid to the station. Another arriving train and two departing trains moved past him. The new scourge of rockets attacking the city wasn't interfering with the regular train schedule—one of the prides of Britain.

It was only a twenty-minute walk from the station to Amelia's flat, where she would cook breakfast for them after her night shift in the bunkers at Westminster. As she did in the past, Amelia volunteered for a solid twenty-four hours of duty on Friday so she could be free for the weekend. After they ate and had some time together, she would take a short nap and then be ready to go.

The early morning sun sent shafts of light through the ruins of the buildings along Gower Street. Bruce liked to take this route because it took him through the center of the University of London. It reminded him a bit of Penn—an intellectual haven in the middle of a bustling city. Even pockmarked with the aftermath of the Blitz, the campus gave him a sense of calm, of being anchored into a tradition of learning that would outlive this insane war.

The angled crossmembers of the old structures had settled since the Blitz ended. The gaping holes still had a jarring effect. But the structures were stable and were lying fallow until the shooting stopped and rebuilding could begin. He hoped the classic features of these buildings would be restored and not blasted to make way for some of the nondescript façades that had started to appear in London.

Bedford Square had taken a few strikes early in the war, but most of its brick houses were still in pristine form. A large crater in the middle of the small park showed how much impact German bombs could have. In early August, trees shaded the crater, and grasses and brush, pushing back after four growing seasons, softened the ragged contours of the hole. A few children were finishing an early morning game of kickball on a flat area, close to the crater. The city had been cleared of most of its children at the beginning of the air war. Now they were starting to return from the countryside, where they had been taken for safety.

As Bruce neared the house where Amelia lived, two of the children, a boy of about seven and an older girl, probably his sister, ran up to him. They had flushed cheeks from the game and stopped for a moment to catch their breath before talking.

"Hey, Captain," the girl said. "We like American soldiers. You're the reason our dad will be home soon. He's in France. Are you going there?"

"Yes, in a couple weeks. What's your dad's name? If I see him, I'll tell him I met you."

The boy answered, "He's a captain too. A tank commander. I'm Tommy Wheaton, and my sister's Hope Wheaton. My dad's name is Thomas. I'm a junior."

"Well, Thomas Wheaton Junior and Hope Wheaton, I'm sure your dad is proud of you. We'll wipe up the Germans so fast he'll be on his way home before you know it."

"What's in that box with the ribbon?" Hope asked. "It's really pretty. Got a girlfriend?"

"You guessed it," he replied. "I'm sure she wouldn't mind if you sampled the candy. Let's open it up."

Tommy's eyes widened, and he flashed a big smile. "We don't get treats like this very often. I'm sure glad we spoke to you, sir."

Bruce held out the box and opened the ribbon with a flourish. "I count two dozen chocolates. You can take six each. We can save twelve for Amelia. Don't eat them all at once. Maybe your mother would like one."

Tommy and Hope were well mannered. They wiped their hands on Tommy's handkerchief and then carefully selected four chocolates each. "Four is plenty for us," Hope said. "Two for each hand, so they won't get smashed together. Thanks, Captain. Have a nice visit with your girlfriend."

Amelia was watching Bruce talk with Tommy and Hope from her second-story window and could hear the warmth of his voice as he talked with them. She gathered the curtain around her like a blanket. *I want to have his children.*

He was coming toward her flat now, and she bounded down the stairs to greet him. The frayed feeling from working through the night had left her. She had planned this day to take them deeper, to carry them through the absence that loomed just ahead.

"You make me want to cry," she said as she reached to hold him. "That was the sweetest thing to do for those children. You have a gentle touch, soldier."

"How could I not share that box of chocolates?" He laughed. "They're cute kids, and they're missing their father. Do you know them?"

"Yes, their mother, Miranda, is a WAAF . . . looks after

barrage balloons. The children have had to grow up fast. Hope looks after Tommy when their mother's at work. She's probably there now."

"Let's find them another treat when we're out today," he said. "What do you think they'd like?"

"More candy. But fruit would be better. None of the kids are getting enough fresh food. I'll bet they eat out of tins most of the time."

She squeezed his arm as they went inside. "I have a treat for you. Ever had truffles? I lifted the last jar from the pantry at Whitcombe Hall just for us. We won't see any more of them till the Germans are out of France. We're going to have a meal to remember, and then see what happens."

"I followed your instructions, no breakfast. So I'm starved. The truffles sound wonderful, never had them before. But I'm starved the most for you." He grinned. "The more I taste, the more I want."

The small table in Amelia's kitchen was set with a bright yellow tablecloth, plates with painted folk scenes from Brittany, a vase with blue salvia and white daisies, and wine glasses. "I know you don't like to drink during the day, but this is a special occasion," she said. "I'm going to cook a Brouillade . . . a classic with eggs and truffles. And we need to have just a sip of a Montrachet from '38 that I found hidden away in a shop down the street. We're going to have some flavors of France before you head off to help win it back."

He took a seat at the table and continued the easy chatting as she started to work. "I'm a grateful customer, chef. I'll take all the delicacies you offer."

Amelia took an earthenware bowl from the counter and showed Bruce the contents. "Before I went to work yesterday, I shaved half of the truffles into the bowl and cracked the eggs on top of them. Can you smell the truffles? They infuse the eggs with smells the French go wild over."

She lit the gas burner and placed a double-boiler on the stove. After it heated up, Amelia placed the eggs and truffles, some butter, and cream in the top part of the pan. Then she whisked the mixture gently until it congealed into soft curds. "This is a simple recipe. It's the ingredients that sing. Anyone could make it."

She finished by shaving the extra truffles on top of the eggs and served it with toast and some rashers of English bacon. "Our neighbor at Whitcombe Hall cured the bacon," she said. "I was lucky to get some."

Bruce tasted the eggs and truffles first. "Best thing I've ever eaten . . . heaven on earth." They ate the meal slowly, hanging on to the moment. An undercurrent of anxiety about what was to come in the next few months amplified their senses, making the tastes more intense.

After Amelia led Bruce to her bedroom, they began to dance slowly and tenderly. Soon they were skin to skin, feeling the delicious rise of their bodies. He kissed Amelia's breasts, and then pulled her close while she rubbed her softness against him. As they fell to the bed and melted together, words of endearment gave way to cries of desire. Volleys of pleasure and caring surged through them until Amelia drifted into sleep with her head nestled on Bruce's shoulder.


Bruce closed his eyes briefly, but then opened them wide. He didn't want to miss any of his time with her. He carefully slipped her head onto the pillow and gazed over her body, trying to store an image of each curve, each fold, each finger, each toe. He brushed blond wisps of hair away from her face with a delicate touch and absorbed her with every ounce of concentration he could tap. His lips touched her forehead lightly. Tears began to trickle down his cheeks.

Two hours later, Amelia was up, showered, and ready to go. "You had a French meal, and now we're going to a shop that's pure England. I want to give you something you won't forget when you're on the battlefield." She tossed her hair and laughed. "It will be too big to fit in your duffel. So after the war, you'll have to come to Whitcombe Hall to claim it. I'm not going to let you escape home without seeing me first. Any guesses on what it is?"

He picked up on her teasing. "No. But even if it's a piece of Big Ben, I won't need an excuse to bring me back. You're the draw."

They set off at a brisk pace, walking past the fortifications in the open areas around the British Museum. At St. Clement Dane's Church, a bombed-out hulk of a majestic structure, they saw a line of children waiting to be given one pear each. "We need to find some fruit somewhere to take to Tommy and Hope," Bruce said. "Do you know anyplace we can stop on the way back to your flat?"

"Don't worry. There's a little market in Bloomsbury that should have peaches and pears. The owner has a brother with a farm in Kent. Our eggs came from there, and she usually has fresh things that are hard to find anywhere else. She beats Fortnum and Mason in my book."

"You know your way around London, young lady. The guide service is impeccable."

Twenty minutes later they were on Pall Mall Street at the door of Hardy's fly-fishing shop. "The temple of fishing equipment," she said. "We're going to find the perfect rod for you . . . no more borrowed stuff. We'll have the beauty signed with your name and hang it on the top rung of the rack in the stream keeper's cottage. The rod will be there, a few paces from the Test, when you return."

"Only if you let me give you something before we go in there." He took a small velvet pouch from his pocket. "My grandfather came back from the Colorado Gold Rush in 1884 with this pouch. The watch was in his vest pocket every day I saw him. Open it up and take a look."

Amelia held the pouch carefully and then loosened the drawstrings. The outside of the gold watch had an engraving of a fisherman bringing a trout to the net. "My grandfather had the engraving added after he got back to Pennsylvania. It's a Waltham watch . . . made in America."

She smiled. "Could have guessed there would be a fishing scene. You Duncans love your streams."

"Check inside," Bruce said.

Amelia saw their initials in engraved letters filling the center of the case. "There's too much love to let a war or an ocean stop us," Bruce said. "Will you keep the watch for us?"

She took the watch to her lips and kissed it. "Yes, I'll hold the watch. Our initials are carved to stay . . . Come back safe. I lost my brother. I can't lose you."


In the evening, after dinner at the Hotel Russell, they strolled through Bloomsbury as the sun was setting. At least for now, the city had a comforting presence. They hadn't heard any air raid sirens since Bruce arrived. And the leafed-out trees sheltered some hardy birds—survivors that were flitting about. The salmon sky was streaked with gray-bordered, fast-moving clouds.

They continued down Montague Street, taking the long way back to Bedford Square. Someone had planted dahlias in planters in front of one of the houses—an incongruous sight in the middle of London. Bruce thought of his mother's friend, Bess Runyon. Her garden in Hollidaysburg would be brimming with dahlias now, getting ready for a late summer and early fall display.

"Come back and see these flowers for me when I'm in France," Bruce said. "We can plant some next year."

Before Amelia could respond, they heard the buzzing, ominous sound of a V rocket coming from the south toward them. It was low-pitched with a raspy overtone, like gears were being chewed up inside the engine. There was no place to take cover, no underground stations nearby. And the rocket sounds were growing louder.

When they looked up to try to decide which way to run, they saw the rocket pass not more than a hundred yards above their heads. The vestiges of light from the last rays of sun hit its dull surface, silhouetting the swept back wings against the darkening sky.

"It's headed straight for Bedford Square," Amelia shouted. A few seconds later they heard a thundering blast and saw a fireball erupt about where Amelia's flat was located.

They looked at one another, shocked out of the cocoon of their peaceful day. Bruce held Amelia until her trembling calmed. "Hang on to that watch," he said. "It may be our charm. That rocket could have wiped us out."

Sirens began to wail. The British ambulance corpsmen would be on the scene soon. "We need to get there fast," Bruce told her as he grabbed her hand and started to run. "We might be able to help."

A few minutes later they saw how close the rocket came to hitting Amelia's flat. Flame-tinged clouds of black smoke streamed into the air from the center of the explosion, just two or three blocks to the northeast of Bedford Square. Dense, choking dust was enveloping the square, making it hard to breathe. Shattered glass crunched under their feet as they moved past her building. Other than broken windows, the row of houses on the east side where she lived looked intact. But the corner of the square nearest to the point of the rocket fall hadn't fared as well. A crowd of people stood outside the houses there, milling around.

Tommy and Hope's house was damaged the worst. The top floor, where they lived, had most of the roof blown away. In the failing light, Bruce and Amelia could see that rafters hung at precarious angles. A bathtub was turned on end against the remnants of a brick chimney. Bruce put his arm around Amelia and stared at the damage. A sickening dread washed over him. "The bomb sucked the roof off like a tornado. I don't see how anyone could survive."

Then Bruce felt a little hand in his. It was Tommy. "My mom's over there screaming to get somebody to find Hope. Can you call for the firemen or the police? None of them are here yet."

"Tommy, I'm sure glad you're okay," Bruce said as he knelt down and hugged him. "What happened?"

"I was out playing, and my mom came to call me in for bed. That's when the bomb went off. Hope's still in there. Our neighbors are safe, but no one knows what to do. Captain, I'm scared."

Amelia looked at the people who had come out of their flats. They were mostly older men and women, dazed by the attack. "We can't wait till the firemen come here," she said. "They tackle the biggest problems first. It could be hours before we see them. Let's take Tommy to his mother and check out the building. These people won't go in there."

"No, you stay with Tommy, and I'll look for Hope. The army trained me to search through wreckage. I'll be careful. If it's too dangerous, I'll back off until the firemen get here."

He kissed her and sprinted toward the house. After scanning the entry hall for stability, he took the stairs two at a time past the second-story flat until he reached a fractured door with a number three dangling loosely from its front. A shaft of moonlight gave the brass a dull glimmer. There was nothing left of the roof behind him, but he could see a dark cavern of twisted beams and fallen slate behind the door.

Pausing to decide on taking the risk to enter, he heard a soft groan just inside the door. "Hope, is that you?" he shouted.

"Yes, I can't move my leg. It hurts too much to pull it out. And I'm bleeding a lot."

"Do you feel woozy like you might faint?" he asked.

"I don't know how I feel . . . Yes, I guess I could faint."

"Don't try to move. Stay still, and I'll open the door very slowly."

"You can't do that," she told him. "My head and shoulders are against the door. You'll just push me and twist my leg off. I was trying to get down to the basement when the bomb went off. I heard the buzzing. Everything fell on top of me."

Bruce tried to soothe her with a steady manner. "We'll do it another way," he said. "The door is torn apart at the top. I can chip it away and climb in there to free you up."

A beam of light came up the stairs, and he could hear Amelia calling to him.

"I'm up here," he yelled. "It's safe if you stay in the stairwell. We have a girl that's trapped."

The sounds of multiple feet rang on the tread. Soon she arrived with two men in their sixties with flashlights and crowbars. "Found a couple neighbors who wanted to join us," she said. "Harry and Luther, meet Bruce."

With reinforcements and tools at hand, Bruce organized a plan to extricate Hope from the debris of her ruined flat. "We need to move quickly," he said. "She may be losing blood."

They shored up the doorframe to protect against collapse when it was breached, then used the crowbars to rip the door apart. Her head and shoulders spilled over the threshold when they pulled the last parts of the wood away.

Using rapid movements, Bruce examined her for sources of major bleeding.

"You have some cuts from the broken windows," he told her. "But they're clotting on their own. We can sew you up so you'll look like new . . . pretty as ever. Now let's free up your leg so we can get you out of here."

With great care, they lifted a rafter that had fallen on her left leg and slid her out the door onto the landing. Amelia pulled from under Hope's arms while cradling her head against her chest. Bruce steadied the leg, which he was sure was broken. There could be extensive bleeding into a crush injury like this one, but being young would give Hope the reserve to heal.

The rest of their night and next day were consumed by the aftermath of the attack. Bruce helped the ambulance crews stabilize victims that were found in the rubble. Amelia took in neighbors who couldn't return to their flats. And she helped the Red Cross distribute food in the shelter at the British Museum, three blocks to the west of Bedford Square.

When it was time for Bruce to return to his camp, they stood on her front stoop looking toward the devastation. Twenty-seven people had died. At least that many were still missing and were probably incinerated or buried so deeply they had no chance of living. Hope was in a hospital with a femur smashed into many pieces.

"I want you to live in that bunker at work until we take out those rocket launchers," Bruce said. "You should sleep there and eat there . . . Don't take any chances. I want to see you in one lovely piece when I return."

"Same advice to you, soldier. If you can stay away from the front, do it. If there's a bunker, dig in. And get back here as soon as you can."

She took his grandfather's watch from her pocket and placed it in his hand. "Take the watch with you, Bruce. You'll need it more than I will. I've seen the newsreels of the Germans shelling hospitals and strafing ambulances. A part of me is in the watch now. It will bring us back together again."

He looked at her and knew it wouldn't help to argue back and forth about who should carry the watch. So he took out his pocket knife and pushed a small button to let the pin slide out of the hinge on the case. "The cover for me, and the works for you."

Amelia laughed. "You're a genius, soldier. How could any woman resist you?"

"Plenty have, but there's only one who counts now. She better resist the other guys while this fellow does his duty."

Dropping the jocular tone, she held him tightly. "Only you, Bruce."

"Only you, Amelia."

He walked to the corner of the block, turned to see her sitting on the stoop, and then disappeared.

*January 26, 1946*
*Dear Amelia,*

*My answer is yes. The invitation to visit me in Pennsylvania still stands. Since your last letter, it has been hard to think of much else except seeing you again.*

*I'm struggling to understand your situation and picture what the future might hold for us. A wild-eyed fantasy has you liking my little town (and me) so much that you break it off with Mark, mothball Whitcombe Hall, and give the USA a try. But being realistic, I know that you are an engaged woman who is anchored to another place.*

*Although we probably won't have more than a little bit of stolen time from our separate lives, I can't step away from the opportunity to be with you. I'll take what you can give me and treasure it.*

*In May, the mountain streams should be alive with rises from trout. I won't have any truffles in the cupboard, but we can harvest a few of the smaller fish to give you a good taste of this corner of the world. You can stay with my next-door neighbor, Bess Runyon. The Hollidaysburg gossip mill would be humming if you bunked with me. Bess is on our side. She knows about us and will make it easy to be in a spot where others won't pry.*

*I may be assuming too much by planning ways for us to be together. The engagement puts us in a different realm than before. Still, I can't help wanting to be as close to you as I possibly can. Please give me your instructions on how to proceed. A chaste reunion would be tough, but I could manage.*

*After you fell asleep the last time we made love, my senses were in overdrive, searing you into my mind to take with me to France. That evening the V rocket hit, and we worked nonstop until I had to return to camp.*

*Now I know those images won't be the final ones I'll have of you. Whatever happens in May, or afterward, you'll always be the one for me.*

*Love,*
*Bruce*

# $\mathcal{C}$hapter 16

## SMEAR

---

**Letter to the Editor**

*January 29, 1946*

*Have you wondered why our new doctor doesn't have a wife or a girlfriend? I discovered the reason the hard way.*

*Watch out, husbands. If your wife is his patient, she may get more than a medical exam. Keep your family away from Duncan. Go back to Magnuson or wait till the lady doctor opens shop.*

*A Wronged Husband*

The pleasantries were over. Bess's carrot cake had been eaten, and they were seated around her kitchen table, ready to begin. The room went quiet before she took the lead.

"You know why I invited you here today. We can't ignore those letters in the *Hollidaysburg Register*. It's some crackpot. Must have a grudge or something. Before I write a letter myself, I wanted to get our little circle together. Plan how to fight back."

Bess fixed her gaze on each person in turn. Bruce at the far end of the table. Glen, Pauline, and Vic from the family. And Judge Clapper, nominated by Bruce's mother, who was too upset to attend. Bess nodded to Bruce. "Tell us what you know. Anyone you suspect?"

He paused before speaking. "I'm glad you're here. Thanks for coming." The awkwardness of being accused showed in his tense, measured tone. He could feel his underarms moisten. "I haven't said much to you about the letters. Just that they aren't true." After taking a deep breath, he continued. "I hoped the problem would blow over, but the fallout's getting worse. When I walk around town, people cross the street so they don't have to talk to me. We've had half the number of patients in the office that we had the week before."

"We'll get this thing fixed; don't worry," Vic said.

"I'm not so sure anything can be done," Bruce replied. "When your reputation is sullied, it can take a long time to repair it."

Glen tapped his empty coffee mug on the table. "I say we keep it simple—find out who wrote the letters, expose the slander, and correct the record."

"Well put," the judge said. "Of course we have to be sure that Bruce is telling us everything. Any lawyer knows not to build a defense before discovering the facts."

He stood and walked behind Bruce, placing a hand on his shoulder. "If there's any piece of the letters that has substance, you need to explain it."

Bruce stiffened. "There was one incident. A married woman sort of made a pass at me after Maggie had left for the day. I can't give you her name. She could get hurt if the word got out. I didn't touch her, and I got her out of the office as soon as I could. Told her she could never come back. Absolutely nothing happened between us. Since then, we make sure Maggie's in the room anytime a woman's there."

The judge continued his queries. "Could her husband be the one writing the letters?"

"I don't know who's doing it," Bruce replied.

"Let's try a different tack," Judge Clapper said. "Bess mentioned a grudge. Anyone who might want to hurt you?"

"I know the answer to that one," Glen said. "Lucas Glover. He's been jealous ever since he grabbed Kate on the rebound after Bruce broke up with her. I had to push Bruce to dance with Kate on New Year's Eve, and he handled her like a hot potato."

"Makes sense to me," Vic said, turning toward Bruce. "Rumors are going around the shop that you've been helping some men with silicosis at Allegheny Refractories. Our foreman saw you coming out of the Ambrosia with the guy you saved in the car wreck and a couple other men from the brick plant. I'll bet Lucas would be furious if he knew you were working with them."

"Okay, fess up," Pauline said. "Kate was the woman that came on to you, wasn't she? I saw her nestle up to you at your homecoming party. I'd say that woman still has a lot of heat in her for you. And her husband's a mean SOB. I wouldn't blame her for wanting out."

"I'm not saying," Bruce replied. "I promised the woman I wouldn't identify her. As for Kate . . . I have no interest in her. And there's nothing between us. Can you keep your suspicions to yourselves? It would make things a lot worse if people started talking about Kate and me."

Bess tried to break the tension. "Sure, Bruce. We can keep mum about Kate." She moved her eyes around the table, gaining assent from each of them. "We shouldn't push you any further. You're in a delicate position. Let's find some positive things to do. How about my idea of writing a letter to the editor? Or maybe lots of letters."

"In court, testimonials from family and friends don't

help much," Judge Clapper noted. "But I don't know about the court of public opinion. Probably wouldn't hurt unless it draws more attention to the problem."

Pauline raised her hand. "I know some women who would vouch for Bruce. They aren't family, and they sing his praises. Bruce, if you approve, I'll ask a few of them to write letters."

"I'm going to write one myself," Bess added. "We can't stand by while Bruce is being dragged through the mud."

"Go ahead," Bruce replied. "But don't mention anything about the woman who flirted with me."

"I think you could do some damage control by meeting with other doctors," the judge suggested. "Magnuson still has a following. He could use this opportunity to undercut you. Or he could defend you if he thinks you've been wronged. He's not much of a doctor, but he's honest. And how about the new doctor, Sarah Avery? It would be good to have her on your side. Weren't you going to work out a way to cover for each other when you're out of town? Sealing that deal would show she trusts you and endorses your practice."

"I'd also call your friend Steve Taylor," Vic said. "Try to bring him on board. Don't go at this alone, Bruce. You'll need all the help you can find."

"All that stuff is fine," Glen said. "But the silicosis mess could wreck everything. It's not only you that's losing here, Bruce. The hardware store wasn't doing great before the letters. Last week, we only sold a few tools and some paint. That was it. One of the days, we had three customers. What are you doing with those guys from the brick plant?" The edge in Glen's voice was palpable.

"It started with treating Tony, the guy in the car accident when we were coming back from the football game. His lungs are full of silicosis. I didn't know he was that sick. Lucas chewed me out in the hospital. Told me to stay away from his men and let their company doctor make all the decisions.

Then Tony brought his friends to see me. I couldn't turn them down. They're dying in their fifties, choked by the dust. And the company doesn't do anything about it."

"What did you do? Ride to their rescue?" Glen asked. "You should know not to take on Allegheny Refractories. They'll crush you like a fly. Already started from what I can see."

"I did some research, talked with an expert I know at Penn. The company could make it safer for the men, but they won't do it. Says it costs too much. I went to see Lucas. I thought we were making headway. He understands what's at stake. But he's under the gun. Has to keep profits up or he's out. He got huffy at the end of our talk, ushered me out the door. In a few days, the first letter appeared. I figure he's trying to silence me."

Glen put his head in his hands and groaned. "You've got to back off, Bruce. Tell him you're done with the crusader business. Tell him you won't tinker with their precious company if he writes a letter of apology to the paper. Write it for him. Say that he found his wife lied and had never even been a patient of yours. There's too much risk for us if you don't stand down."

"Glen has a point," Vic said. "The bosses at the brickyard didn't get their jobs by being friendly. The PRR is a playground compared to Allegheny Refractories. I know some fellows who could play tough with Lucas. Put sand in his gas tank or cut some tires. But it would probably make him more vicious. I'd pick fights with somebody else."

"Knock it off," Pauline said. "You're trying to bully Bruce. Make him feel guilty for doing the right thing. We can survive these petty letters. Anyone who knows Bruce understands he's a straight shooter. Bruce, get a girlfriend quick, and we'll organize a campaign to support you. Don't listen to these doomsayers."

"Thanks, Pauline, and thanks to the rest of you," Bruce said. "I like all of your ideas but two of them. I can't let Lucas scare me away from trying to help the brickworkers. I won't back off." A slight smile spread over his face. "And a girlfriend is out of the question. Amelia Whitcombe, the woman I fell for during the war, is back in my life. She'll be here for a visit in May. I hope I'll still be in one piece to see her."

The revelation broke the tension. Vic grinned widely, while tears gathered in Bess's eyes. Pauline bolted upright and chortled. "When they see that beauty, they'll know Bruce wouldn't diddle with our housewives."

"Good for you, brother," Glen said. "She's amazing, folks. I've met her. Bruce, you better lie low with your brick plant mission so you don't screw up her visit."

"Bruce told me about her," Bess said. "I don't think she'd want him to lie low for anything."

Bruce put on his coat, walked toward the door, and turned back to them. "There's a lot to do before May. We'll get this letter problem resolved before then."

# Chapter 17

## SARAH

⌇

*T*he letters in the *Hollidaysburg Register* worried Sarah. Three from the same angry man were published, followed by a bevy of letters from the doctor's supporters, who claimed someone was trying to slander him. The missive, signed by a dozen females who dubbed themselves the "grateful young women patients," described their trust in a war vet with inviolable character. One of the letters, from a mother of a boy he had rescued from meningitis, was especially touching. Whatever had happened, or not happened, with the wife of the "wronged husband," Bruce Duncan had made at least one rabid enemy and a large number of friends in the short time he'd been practicing here.

She asked herself why she was meeting him. Would it have been better to avoid being seen with the beleaguered doctor? She had only been practicing for a month, and here was some noise that could distract her, sour her attempts to get a foothold in this town. Yet she was curious. What would Bruce say, if anything, about the uproar? She had liked Bruce immediately when she met him. He saw heavy action during the war, Steve Taylor told her. Got decked with medals but never talked about it. Maybe the "wronged husband" was wrong. Sarah hoped so.

Walking on the main street, as she was doing now on her way to the Ambrosia, would be a daily pleasure. The downtown streets had more charm than those in Williamsport, her hometown, and the care of the shop owners was obvious. No cracked paint or dusty windows here. Her apartment, in the big house on Union Street, was only four blocks from the Diamond at the center of town and another two blocks to her office. With train service in Altoona, she almost could have done without a car.

She passed Richardson's and waved to the pharmacist who had stepped outside for the mail. They met a week ago to set up some of Sarah's special prescriptions—compounds that weren't standard fare. So far, everyone had been welcoming, even Magnuson, an old-fashioned doc who hinted he would be on his way to Florida soon. Said he was happy to exit the scene and leave the town to people with more energy and patience than him.

Pete Nicholaou, the fellow who owned the Manos Theater and the Ambrosia, was a colorful character. When she told Pete that she would be eating at his restaurant often because she didn't like to cook, he offered to deliver dinner if she were too busy to get away. And his wife, Helene, volunteered to give her free cooking lessons. Both short, chubby people with gray hair, their Greek origins were stamped all over their little empire. Pete's movie theater was a jumble of Hollywood-inspired excess with a pseudo-Athenian façade, while the Ambrosia held an odd combination of paintings of Hollidaysburg's history, Windsor-style chairs, and a huge antique wall clock, mixed with a hodgepodge of photos of famous ruins from their homeland, and diplomas with gold seals and faded ribbons.

With Valentine's Day approaching, Pete and Helene had used their candy molds to make hundreds of cupids and hearts in chocolate or brilliant red, crystalline concoctions that probably had enough sugar in them to send a person into diabetes on the spot. She couldn't imagine anyone other than a child being able to eat more than a small bite of the glistening red cupids and hearts. Still, the candies, grouped on pyramidal stands in the front window and dotted all over the tables and counters, gave the place a festive air.

She could see Bruce waiting for her at a back table as Pete greeted her. The doctor sat upright, with his hands gripping a mug of coffee. Didn't look as relaxed as the last time they had met here, in early January.

"Can we order some lunch?" she said. "I'm famished. Worked all morning finishing my lab setup."

"Sounds good to me," he replied. "I'm done for the day. Had an easy Saturday. Just a few colds and some routine stuff. Wrapped up by eleven thirty."

Pete delivered the menus and trumpeted his special— roasted pork loin. "Too much for me," Sarah told him. "The tuna salad will be fine, and I'll save room for one small scoop of your cherry vanilla ice cream."

"I'll take the pork loin," Bruce said. "Going fishing this afternoon, and I'll need to fill up to keep me warm."

"You fish this time of year? Aren't the trout hibernating for the winter?"

"It's quiet on the stream in February," he replied. "I don't stay very long. You have to put so many layers under the waders that it's hard to move, and the ice cakes on the rod if you don't keep knocking it off. But it's beautiful there with snow on the banks and no other footprints to see. I usually get a few bites, even catch a fish now and then. Does me good to get away for a while."

"Never tried fishing," she said. "My dad takes his boat out for bass in the summer. My mother and I went to a movie or did something else when he went on those trips. I know what you mean about getting away. Tennis is my escape. I play it when I can."

Bruce paused and looked into his coffee, interrupting the flow that had begun so easily. "Sarah, I'll get to the point. I asked you to meet me because of the letters. I'm sure you've seen them. If we're going to work together in any way, you have to know what's going on. Can I tell you what I know about the letters?"

"Of course," she said. "I can imagine it's been a nightmare. But if you're breaking your doctor's oath, you'll need to leave Hollidaysburg. Straighten yourself out. Try again in some other town or give up medicine."

"I can't prove it now, wish I could. Give me a little time. I'll show you and everyone else that I'm the one who's the victim. The letter writer is trying to scare me off from something I have to do. I didn't take advantage of his wife. I never did that with any of my patients—never would. I'm trying to figure how to expose him now. Get him to recant the letters."

"What did you do to him? Was he blackmailing you?"

"No, he doesn't have anything to blackmail me about. I suppose he could have threatened to send those letters if I didn't back down. He didn't make any threats, just the onslaught of letters. It caught me by surprise."

Bruce explained his dilemma, telling her about the rampant silicosis at the brick factory; how he discovered the disease after treating Tony's injuries; the visits from his buddies, George and Slim; and the contacts with Phil Silverman.

"Someone at Allegheny Refractories is sending the letters. And they're telling me to shut up, mind my own business."

Sarah was becoming convinced that Bruce was giving her a straight story. She had pressed him to tell the truth, showed him she wouldn't be a pushover. And he came through, hadn't been ruffled when she mentioned blackmail. But wasn't he naïve about the risks of taking on an industrial juggernaut?

Maybe a bit grandiose believing he could save those men from silicosis? She admired him for taking a stand but wondered if he was being foolish. Or maybe she was just trying to talk herself out of how much she was starting to like him. He was exactly the kind of man she would have sought out if she hadn't chosen a career for a single woman.

"So will you capitulate? I wouldn't blame you. Or will you keep fighting them? If you get reporters to publish exposés in the *Philadelphia Inquirer* and the *Pittsburgh Press*, who knows what the backlash might be?"

Pete arrived then with their food. "I wanted to serve you myself, my honored guests. You're getting the best from our kitchen." He waved his hand like a magician, sweeping a napkin across another serving tray his wife, Helene, passed to him. "And here's an extra treat from our own pond—smoked trout with whipped cream and horseradish sauce." He leaned over to whisper into Sarah's ear. "Our boy needs friends. Whatever he says, believe him."

After they sampled the trout and gave their host a volley of compliments, Pete bowed and returned to the front register to greet other diners. His theatrics had diverted them from the question about capitulating or moving ahead.

"So we were in Philadelphia at the same time, but never met," Sarah said in a matter-of-fact way. "I don't think any of the women at my school ever set foot on the Penn medical campus."

She wondered if he realized that she was checking him out. Did he have the usual biases against women doctors? Prejudices that forced them to have their own medical school and struggle for acceptance?

"Yeah, it's a shame that Penn won't admit women medical students," Bruce said. "In a way, it's like segregation." Sarah cocked her head slightly and looked at him, anticipating more. "I'm probably as blind as any other guy about how hard it is for women doctors. But I can learn. If I don't, let me know."

Sarah had heard enough for now. She would wait to see if he would follow through. "If we're going to cover for one another, I can't have you undercutting me. So I'll hold you to your promise."

"Fair enough," he replied. "How about updating me on polio. You'll be the expert here. You mentioned a surge of cases in Philadelphia during the war. I haven't seen polio since medical school. And that was a minor brush with paralysis. The girl was back on her feet in a few days."

"When the weather warms up, we'll see some polio here. Not as much as in the big cities. Still can be deadly, though. I've met with the president of the medical staff at the Altoona hospital about ordering some iron lungs. We need to be prepared."

She went on to describe the tragic outcome of an eight-year-old boy who didn't have the muscle control to move air, even with an iron lung. Infection roared through him, despite penicillin, while his parents and doctors watched him die. "After a few cases like that, you start to feel helpless. If polio catches on here, it'll take all of us working together."

They went into doctor-to-doctor mode, talking about ideas for prevention, debating the value of braces after the infection subsided, and agreeing that the Sister Kenny method—gentle exercise instead of the conventional immobilization that could freeze muscles and joints—should be taught to the rehab staff at the hospital. Their back-and-forth about polio broke the tension, put them on common ground.

As the lunch wore on into the early afternoon, they nibbled on dessert and circled back around to key questions. "Before Pete brought our food, you asked me if I was going to cave in to the smear letters or if I was going to give the green light to Phil Silverman to contact the reporters. You should know which way I'm heading before you agree to cover my practice when I'm away."

"You couldn't live with yourself if you let those men down. You'll do it."

She didn't give him time to respond. "And the coverage thing is just common sense. In a few months when Magnuson heads south, we'll be the only two doctors in Hollidaysburg. Your aunt told me your girlfriend's coming from England for a visit in May. I'm sure you'll want some time off when she's here. So let's just tell people how it is, post some notices. The *Register* is doing an article to introduce me. I can have them spell out details of what happens when I'm out of town."

Bruce smiled. "Thanks. I've lucked into having you as a colleague."

When Sarah left the restaurant, she began to question herself. Had she made a mistake? Given too much, too fast? Although she doubted Bruce had taken advantage of a woman patient, other men had lied to her. She had cultivated a toughness to get as far as she was today. But he had seemed so genuine that she let her guard down, decided to work with him when his reputation was troubled.

At the beginning of Bruce's account of the dangers of silica and the callousness of Allegheny Refractories, his struggle for the workers seemed Quixotic. Then it began to make more sense. After Pete had brought them lunch and they relaxed into talking medicine, she realized she would probably make the same choice that Bruce had made. Fighting polio, fighting silicosis—they had trained to take on these challenges. Not dodge their responsibilities.

An undercurrent of anxiety tugged at Sarah as she neared her apartment. She wondered if she had strayed—let a swell of feelings for Bruce cloud her judgment. He had been so easy to like that she couldn't let him dangle. Couldn't tell him to get his problems sorted out before she'd announce their coverage plan—an endorsement he needed now. Part of her hadn't wanted to leave Bruce at the Ambrosia. Their conversation had been the most stimulating she'd had since coming to this village where she had known no one.

Then she clicked through all the reasons she had opted for a medical career instead of marriage and a family. Her parents' incessant screaming at each other. Her dreams of being a woman doctor. The jerk who mistreated her in college—a linebacker who pushed her out a car door when he didn't get what he wanted. A deep-in-the-gut need to be independent.

Sarah entered the darkened room, turned on the light beside her wing chair, and opened the novel she was reading. *Stay true*, she told herself as she tried to pick up the thread of the story. *There's no room for a man in your life.*

# Chapter 18

## BROTHERS

⸻

They stopped talking at the top of the rise as they looked down the snowy road leading to the cabin. These deep woods had a reverential hold on Bruce and Glen, and they hadn't walked this path since before the war. They had parked their car at the first gate, by the White Deer Camp, when the conditions became too slippery to keep driving over the hilly and rock-strewn road their grandfather had helped clear out of the forest. During this year's hunting season, they stayed away from this place, their taste for shooting gone. Today they planned to be on the mountain by themselves.

The hemlock grove where they had spent summer nights around campfires with sparks flickering against the green fronds was cloaked in thick robes of white, the branches dipping in graceful arcs. With a brilliant blue sky and no wind, last night's snow was pristine, untouched except for the tracks of animals. They took a detour down a familiar chute into the heart of the stand of evergreens. Deer had spent the night in the clearing, protected from the storm. Their hoof prints and droppings, still fresh, showed they had moved on in the early morning, after the snow stopped.

Glen kicked some of the snow away from the ring of large stones. He spoke in close to a whisper, not wanting to spook any of the wildlife they might see as they walked on to the cabin. "I wanted to see if anybody moved our rocks. Last time we camped here, Dad was with us." He looked at Bruce and gave a shrug. They didn't talk about their father. But loss was written on their faces as they stared at the formation they had helped Robert Duncan build when they were boys. "Let's follow those deer for a while," Glen said. "See where they're going."

Their grandfather and two of his friends bought this land around 1890, over three hundred acres that had been logged in the early 1800s, when charcoal was needed for the iron furnaces at Etna on the Juniata River. The second-growth oaks, maples, and walnuts were mature now. Only the tree-studded shelves of leveled ground where the charcoal was burned gave any sign of the industry that had thrived here.

The log cabin their grandfather constructed before the turn of the century was a classic—a two-story structure of poles cut from the woods, a huge fireplace that could hold pieces of wood four feet wide, and trophy-size deer racks on the walls. They had used old-fashioned methods to build the cabin, only compromising the pioneer style to add a tin roof, a wood-burning cook stove, and a kitchen sink connected with pipes to a spring on the mountain. Bruce and Glen could see the cabin now as they came up from a gulley where the deer had passed on one of the game trails that dotted the land.

Pausing to listen for movement of the deer, Bruce caught sight of something ahead. He signaled for Glen to look toward the lower part of the tree canopy. Almost hidden from view among the snow-crusted limbs were some bulging shapes—wild turkeys with their bodies tucked against the cold. "Let them be," Glen mouthed silently. The snow cover had muffled their approach. So they had almost walked into a flock of roosting birds, a skittish quarry that usually frustrated hunters trying to get close enough for a clean shot.

When Bruce turned to detour around the birds, his foot pivoted in the snow and snapped a branch. Suddenly a cacophony of yelps and squawks pierced the afternoon stillness. Mini-explosions of snow threw up storms of crystals, and the beat of the big birds' wings pulsed through the air. They had flushed at least twenty turkeys, which were scrambling in their awkward but powerful way, flying low under the branches, at first in all directions, some over their heads. Then a semblance of order took over as most of the flock regrouped and made its way toward the ridge to the south. The birds that scattered in ones and twos would be calling later that day to find their way back to the group.

"Good job, eagle eye," Glen said. "I didn't see them. Never got so close to wild turkeys. I thought they were going to fly right into us. You could have reached up and snagged one with your hand."

Bruce motioned toward the cabin. "It's time to get warm," he said. "This dose of snow's been enough after last winter."

Without warning, a chill went through him. Just a few words about last winter and the exhilaration was gone, replaced with a scene he wanted to forget. His numb fingers were struggling to stitch the tepid flesh of a frost-bitten soldier. The generators were screaming at capacity, but the heaters were outmanned against the cold. Hypothermia was creeping over the wounded patients. All they could do was pile on more blankets and cluster the men closer to the fleeting streams of warmed air. Trying to avoid hypothermia themselves, they kept moving, huddling for a while by the single stove in the middle of the operating area, then back to work, every sweater and coat in their kits under their gowns.

Bruce took a deep breath and tried to erase the stubborn traces from his mind. As the months had gone by, he was getting better at shutting off the flow, usually by willing himself to stop the thoughts, other times by evoking images of calming scenes. He used this tactic now. *Think of a smooth cast with your fly rod. The line unfolds in a long, gentle loop till it settles at the base of the willow tree. Cast again till you're in the clear.*

Getting closer to the cabin, they could see that the deer herd had come within fifty yards of the log structure on their way to a higher spot on the mountain. "Granddaddy would be pleased," Glen said. "The cabin's so much a part of the land now, the deer walk right past it."

"I doubt anyone's been here since early December, no tire tracks, no sign of life," Bruce added. "Plenty of firewood, though. Let's get a fire started and heat the place up."


A half hour later, they were sitting close to the fire, in rockers that had been there as long as they could remember. "I wonder if there's still a stash of booze under the stairs," Glen said. "I wouldn't mind a sip to take the chill off."

"Maybe just a small sip . . . I'll check it out," Bruce replied as he padded across the worn plank floor to the base of the stairs. He reached behind the primitive newel post with its knobby surface stripped of bark and worn smooth. Feeling for a small lever, he got a handful of cobwebs before locating the latch his grandfather installed when the cabin was built. After a light tug, he could hear the spring release at the bottom of the post. Glen was on his feet now with a flashlight in his hand.

"I'll bet Dad left a bottle in there," Glen said. Their grandmother had been a teetotaler, and the only time Grandfather Duncan touched whiskey was when he was at the camp. Their father had carried on the same tradition of hiding a stash.

Glen got down on his knees and pivoted the bottom stairs away from the landing. He turned on the light and splashed it over a dusty cache—Old Overholt, Early Times bourbon, and a bottle of Gordon's gin. "There's Dad's rye," he said. "He'd want us to have it." He grabbed one of the bottles and gestured for Bruce to join him back in front of the fire.

They drank the whiskey neat, not saying much for a while, each of them having private thoughts about their dad. Bruce took a few sips while Glen drained his glass quickly. "Let me top you off," Glen said. "The rye's got enough age to be really good."

"This is plenty for me. I'll go light so I can drive us home. " Bruce swirled the whiskey in his glass and set it down on the floor. Not wanting to talk about his father, he steered the conversation toward their mother's budding relationship with the judge. "Mom's looking younger these days, isn't she? Seeing the judge every day, I hear. What do you think will come of it?"

"Yeah, it's moving along. She thinks she's fooled everybody. But I know she went up to Eaglesmere with him last week. Spent the night there in his brother's cottage on the lake. She took her skates and said she was staying with a friend in Altoona so they could be close to the pond at the college. They're sneaky things . . . like a couple of kids."

They both grinned as they thought about the future of their mother's romance with Judge Clapper. "Good for them," Bruce said. "He was lonely by himself on the big farm. And Mom's got a lot of zip left in her. I don't see any reason why they shouldn't get together." He paused to touch the whiskey glass lightly to his lips. "It wouldn't hurt her finances either. Supporting Mom and yourself with the hardware store must be tough."

Glen sat upright. Mention of the family store had stirred him. He rose to throw another log on the fire, then turned back to Bruce. "It's hard now. But if the crap with the smear letters stops, and we get through the winter, we'll be fine. Once the weather breaks, they'll be swarming the store. Inventory's stocked up, ready for the crowds." His face flushed from the whiskey and the fire, Glen began to wave his hands in expansive, sweeping movements, pointing at imaginary stacks of marvelous goods. With a loud and rapid staccato, he pitched his wares like a circus barker. "Welcome to Duncan's Hardware, my friends. Best selection in central Pennsylvania. Come right along with me, and I'll show you the mysteries of a modern washing machine. Press a button and your work's done. Need an installment plan? Layaway? No problem. Want a lilac bush, a peach that will bear fruit in a year? We have it all."

An angry edge to Glen's pressured delivery was unmistakable. His brother's moods shifted so quickly now. It didn't take much to set him off. Regretting that he'd mentioned the hardware store, Bruce tried to defuse the situation. "You're doing a great job, Glen. The store's never looked better."

"Not that you've helped much. Those letters in the newspaper torpedoed our business." He filled his glass, gulped the whiskey, and began pacing in front of the fireplace, his body outlined by the flickering light. "I hope you're finished with that stuff with the brick plant. It was driving Lucas nuts. Did you tell him you'd lay off?"

"You heard what I said when we met at Bess's house. I've got to help those guys."

"So you didn't lay off?"

"No, we've upped our game. Had to do it. Phil Silverman from Penn has been helping me."

"What've you done?" Glen asked as he twirled to face Bruce.

"There'll be an exposé in tomorrow's *Inquirer*. It'll ask for a hearing in Harrisburg . . . but the hearing is already set. One of Phil's friends is a state senator."

Glen drained his glass in one swallow and threw it inches over Bruce's head, smashing it against the wall. "Call it off, you dumb shit! They'll gut us."

Glen was unhinged—dangerous. He needed to be calmed now. With slow, careful moves, Bruce rose and opened his palms in a gesture of reconciliation. Then he went to Glen and held his shoulders, trying to settle him. "We'll be fine. Stay with me through this."

With a sudden jab, Glen punched Bruce's jaw, toppling him against a rocker that spun in a circle and crashed into the middle of his spine. Dazed for a moment, Bruce stayed prone on the floor while his brother stood over him.

"You deserved it," Glen said.

Bruce's head began to clear, and he started to reach toward Glen's ankles to sweep him to the floor and pin him. Then he checked himself. "I'm getting out of here . . . You hurt me." He pulled on his coat. "I'll take a hike to the brook. Let you cool down."


Agitated by the encounter, Bruce set off at a brisk pace to put some distance between himself and the cabin. He had wanted to fight back but knew it could ignite more violence. His brother had scared him.

Bruce was struggling to understand what had happened. Yes, Glen had guzzled the booze hard and fast. His war wounds were still festering. He was afraid the store would go under—furious because the silica battle was hurting business. But was his wildness a sign of something more malignant? Manic depression?

Their father could talk so fast it was hard to follow him.

He could stay up all night hatching half-baked schemes to make money. Then some kind of switch would go off, and he'd grind to a standstill. Other times he had such a hair trigger that it took nothing to cross him. He would say vicious things—cut his boys down in a merciless way. Within a few hours he could be bragging about his sons to the neighbors. It was hard to predict which Robert Duncan they would find each day.

As a kid, Bruce had assumed he was the reason his father got mad. Some of those cruel words came back to him now. *You're a little snotnose . . . All you do is make us worry . . . Can't you ever do anything right?*

Bruce stared into the icy waters of the brook—a stream where he and Glen had played as boys. Answers weren't coming. He was choking with anger that had no place. Stepping onto a sliver of land that jutted into the brook, Bruce picked up a large rough-edged rock from under the snow. With both hands, he held it above his head and threw it with concussive force into the stream. Three more rocks hit the water. Then other sounds pierced the frigid air.

Someone was firing an M-1 Garand, the rifle he had learned to use in the war. Eight shots rang out in rapid succession—an entire clip. Eight shots later, he located the source. It was close, at the east border of their property. The gunman was either target shooting or massacring a deer herd out of season. With another volley of bullets, Bruce's thoughts careened from pictures of deer being slaughtered, their chests exploding with the impact of the big 30-06 shells, to a gun battle in Alsace.

Infuriated at the gunman, Bruce charged across the brook toward the sounds of gunfire. Before he made much progress, one more burst of shots stopped him. His mind flooded with memories of snow-covered bodies, lying still where they fell, congealed blood marking wounds that would

never heal. He sank to his knees. *I'm the one who's going insane
. . . Will it never end?*

Bruce found his brother sitting on the floor, his back against
the overturned rocking chair. He was curled up with arms
around his knees, his face turned away from Bruce. His shape
was taking up the least possible space in the room.

"Are you okay?" Bruce asked.

Glen shook his head and remained silent.

"Look, I know you couldn't help it. You weren't thinking
straight."

Glen shuddered and pulled more tightly into himself.

"Is it the war? The burns? The damn hardware store?
Speak to me."

"All of them," he said in a soft voice, depleted after his
burst of aggression. "I can't do it. Can't get over the war.
Can't make the store work. I'm worse than Dad. I could have
killed you when I threw that glass.

"I'm a shithole . . . Everybody knows it. The only time
I feel good is when I'm plastered."

"You're not a shithole. But when you hit the booze, you
act like one. It blows your brain . . . makes you a terror. You
have to quit."

Glen whimpered. "I know."

"As long as you're quitting—ditch the store. It took Dad
down. One of us dead is enough. Get a job flying. Maybe at
the airport they're building in Altoona. Or move to Pittsburgh and work at the airport there. No whining . . . Break
out of it, bud."

Glen didn't budge from his shrunken position, so Bruce
continued. "You have to stop hammering yourself. Talk with
me. Talk with Sarah Avery. She knows psychiatry. God knows
you need that kind of help."

Glen started to unwind from his tight ball while Bruce waited for his response. They heard the M-1 shots start again.

"I've heard enough of that guy's target practice," Bruce said. "Let's go home."

"I can't close the store," Glen said. "Won't give up . . . but I've had my last whiskey."

Bruce motioned for his brother to follow him. "We'll see."

$\mathscr{C}hapter\ 19$

## TESTED

———

*Pennsylvania*
*February 1946*

t was a little after five o'clock on Sunday morning. Bruce had been awake since a nightmare rattled him two hours ago. A gory scene of a woman with her back ripped apart, bleeders spouting in so many places that he would have needed a dozen hands to control them, had jolted him awake. In the dream, the blood was choking Bruce. It was in his mouth and his nose, so he couldn't catch his breath. It was in his eyes, so he couldn't see to work through the red haze. Then the flesh bubbled up and acted like a whirlpool, sucking him into the middle of the wound.

The dream was a brutal twist on his attempt to save the captain at an Alsatian farmhouse last year on Christmas Eve. But the woman in the nightmare was Amelia.

The threatening messages that triggered the dream had arrived in yesterday's mail. A postcard was on top—a scene along Main Street showing Duncan's Hardware with licking flames pasted all over it. The second piece was much worse. It was one of his favorite photos of Amelia. The bastard had cut wedges into her face and painted *Whore* in a lurid shade across her breasts. Gobs of dried blood were smeared over her body. This violation was sick—and frightening. The only way anyone could have gotten hold of this photo was to break into his house. It had been stored in the kitchen desk drawer along with her letters and some other snapshots they had taken before he left for France. Lucas, or whoever was responsible for this assault, had gone too far.

It was no coincidence that the threatening letter arrived yesterday. Phil Silverman's ideas had worked—a legislative hearing was scheduled in Harrisburg a week from Tuesday. And Bruce was listed as a main witness. His job was to explain the risks the men faced from silicosis—tell real-life stories of the devastation. Bruce had the materials he needed. X-rays from Tony and other victims. Plenty of damaging proof. Someone was trying to scare him. Stop him from testifying.

After the nightmare, Bruce had given up trying to go back to sleep. He needed a mechanical task—work that would get his hands and his mind busy enough to push his apprehensions aside for a while. So he had taken a brisk walk through the darkened streets to his office. There were some lab tests to be done before he began to see patients on Monday morning.

As he settled into the routine of pipetting the reagents into test tubes, his thoughts turned toward Amelia's visit. With letters coming now at least once a week, and the details of her trip arranged, her presence was almost palpable. They decided she would travel by train from New York, arriving here on May 15.

His mother, Bess Runyon, and his aunt Pauline had appointed themselves as a welcoming committee. Bess was in charge of housing Amelia, as she had promised on a snowy evening in December. Never having had children, she was relishing the role she assumed for herself—an auxiliary mother with an agenda to make Bruce's relationship with Amelia work. Her main focus was setting up a room for Amelia. It would be a bower that would make her like Hollidaysburg so much she would never want to leave.

Bess was scouring magazines looking for designs and stopped by almost every evening to show him her finds. His attempts to have her back off on the renovation had failed. He didn't want her to dig deep to spend on a decorating job that wasn't needed. Her big house had character, faded from the years of living there as a single woman with dwindling finances, but comfortable and authentic. He was certain Amelia, who had little pretense despite living at Whitcombe Hall, would like Bess and her historic house.

His mother and aunt were organizing a picnic with American and British music played by the town's brass band. Pete Nicholaou was already engaged to cater the affair. Bruce appreciated their kindness, but he didn't want Amelia's visit to be consumed with social events. And he didn't want to overwhelm her with a heavy dose of local characters until they had a chance to get to know one another again. On the first day he would meet her at the train station and get her to Bess's house to rest from the trip. He could see her stepping off the train now.

From her letters, he could tell she was wrestling with a decision that would bring them together for more than the time in May. But he had been stung too hard the last time to drop his guard and hope for too much. As he had done many times in the last few months, he cautioned himself, *Slim chance we'll stay together. No more than ten percent. Just be grateful for a couple weeks with her.*

An escalation of banging from the pipes in the radiators caught his attention. The sound was like ball-peen hammers hitting the cast iron in waves. The banging started in the waiting room, circled around the two radiators at the far end of the main office, and peaked as it reached the single, larger radiator in the lab area. The weather had turned cold again, even though it was the first week of March. And the old furnace that had been converted from coal to oil was straining to do its job. He could hear hisses and sighs coming up from the basement stairwell.

With the lab work finished, Bruce needed something else to fill his mind before he went home for breakfast. So he pulled out a textbook, *Practical Clinical Psychiatry*, he thought might help him understand his brother. The cases in the book described problems worse than Glen's. A woman who thought she was Eve from the book of Genesis had gone on a month-long spell of stripping her clothes off and walking through her village. A man who had previously been a reliable plumber became convinced that he had the secret to produce the purest water imaginable. His delusions seemed innocuous until he began to break into houses to tear out old pipes and piled the broken remains in the mayor's yard to make his point.

Although the cases were more dramatic, the list of symptoms in the book seemed to fit Glen. He had a manic rush at the hunting camp when he rattled off the virtues of the hardware store with the pressured, agitated style described in the book. Then he exploded with anger—another classic symptom of mania. The depression after the wildness was short-lived.

Most of Glen's symptoms were on the manic side of the illness. If there were any long or deep slides into melancholia, Bruce hadn't seen them. He thought back over the past few months since he arrived home. There had been the embarrassing outburst at the lunch with Sarah Avery and the manic surge at the bandstand on New Year's Eve. Two weeks ago

Glen had been pumped up for a 10:00 p.m. to 2:00 a.m. sale at the hardware store—free hot dogs for anyone who made a purchase. He ran out of hot dogs around midnight and had to roust out the store manager at the A&P to get more supplies. Glen was on a roll that night. He hung around the store till dawn drinking beer, reveling in the experience, until Vic came to check on him and drove him home.

Closing the book, Bruce mouthed a few of his thoughts. *Don't let him be one of those. He's suffered enough already . . . the burns, all his buddies who died.*

As he steadied himself to leave the office, Bruce heard a new sound—a piercing whistle from the basement. The clanging in the radiators had stopped suddenly. *The whistle must be coming from the furnace*, he concluded. Checking the radiators, he saw they were so hot he could hardly touch them. The temperature of the room had jumped while he was absorbed in the book. *I have to get down there and turn it off.*

When he opened the door to the basement, a whoosh of hot steam hit him in the face. The whistle was louder. So loud he thought it might burst his eardrums if he didn't get the furnace shut off soon. As he bounded down the steps, his ears were throbbing with pain. It was hard to breathe with the steam all around him. Then a gigantic blast—everything went black.


Bruce didn't know where he was. Only that he was in another battle zone. He tried to move and felt jagged pieces of metal and hunks of plaster fall to his side. Acrid smoke was choking him. And blood was pouring down his legs. He had to escape or he would suffocate.

When he stood in the pitch dark, his feet slipped on debris-strewn stairs and a lancinating pain shot through his right leg, up into his groin. His mind was fogged, but the pain made him reach down to check for a wound. A spike of torn steel was embedded in his thigh.

*I can't run. Can't walk, or it will cut an artery. I'll crawl on my back. Drag the leg behind me. No, I'll pull it out. I have to get out of here now.*

He was shaking, so he grabbed the spike with both hands. Touching it sent an electric jolt deep to the bone, making him scream. But he forced the metal upward till it was free.

*Why are there steps in the aid station? Where's Blaise? Why can't I hear any corpsmen? Should I go up the stairs or down?*

Bruce clamped a hand on his torn thigh and took a step.

# *Chapter 20*

## ROHRWILLER

⌇

### *Alsace, France*
### *January 1945*

The stars and stripes on the jeeps snapped in the crisp wind as they made their way into Rohrwiller. At last, a sunny day after slogging through the ice and muck to this picturesque, untouched village. With the French out to greet them, cheering from the fronts of their half-timbered houses, there was a heady sense that the war was almost won. They were here to knock the Germans out of Herrlisheim and back across the Rhine.

Blaise was whooping it up, circling his arm like a cowboy with a lasso and shouting over the roar of the engines. He looked over to Bruce with a wide grin. "Got 'em cornered, buddy. We'll be back home by Easter. Rolling eggs on the lawn. Eating ham and apple pie."

An ex-cheerleader from Penn State, Blaise plied his spirit-building skills whenever he had the chance. Bruce liked the guy. He appreciated his upbeat attitude and respected his work. They had been in med school in Philadelphia at the same time, Bruce at Penn and Blaise at Jefferson across the Schuylkill. But they hadn't met until last summer, when they became surgeons for their battalion.

"Hope it will be that easy," Bruce said. "The colonel says the Germans are jammed into Herrlisheim, loaded with 88s and ready to fight. This could be the big one for us."

"Look at these guys," Blaise said. "Best in the USA. Ready to go. The Krauts don't have a chance."

The soldiers did have more bounce to their step, more wisecracks, more talk about getting home. The hero-like welcome provided an elixir the men needed. And the well-kept town with blue and pink stucco houses gave an aura of normalcy. There were no rubble-filled streets or collapsed walls to remind them of the hellish scenes they had left behind.

After the grinding battle at Christmas, they had been exhausted. Thirty percent casualties, and no reinforcements. How the men could take so much battering and still pick themselves up to fight again astounded Bruce. He wondered why more of the soldiers hadn't snapped, their brains sucked dry of the will to go on. Yet here they were, looking fresh, ready to push ahead and finish the war.

They approached the town hall, the thick-walled structure that would be the command post for their attack on Herrlisheim. The annex, a typical Alsatian house that butted up against the main building, had been commandeered for their battle aid station. A corpsman was painting a red cross on the roof—probably a wasted effort. The Germans had ignored their hospital and ambulance markers too many times to take comfort in the signs.

The mini-parade into town was over, and the mood of the men sobered. They began to unload the trucks and ambulances to set up another temporary hospital. Bruce thought to himself, *Herrlisheim is only two miles away. Wouldn't take much for them to be on top of us.* He touched the last letter from Amelia in his pocket and mouthed a little prayer. *Give us the strength, Lord. Give us the strength.*

His colonel wanted him to attend command meetings when Bruce could get free from the aid station. Usually he enjoyed being included, being asked for his opinions. But this meeting wasn't like any of the others. It was embarrassing, brutal, and dangerous. A bully was pushing their battalion into a battle they were sure to lose.

Reeking of cognac, the commander had arrived at almost midnight to give orders for an advance to Herrlisheim. While he strutted around the room in his dress uniform and twirled his baton, he was insulting the colonel. "No guts," he said. "Bullshit, you need reinforcements. If you can't get your pecker up to do the job, I'll find someone who will."

Bruce thought his colonel was right. The intelligence showed three to four thousand Germans with a heavy concentration of Panzers around Herrlisheim and many more south of the town in the Stainwald forest. With only 750 troops and a smattering of Shermans, he said it would be suicidal to attack now, before they had more tanks and men. The commander blew off the concerns. Claimed there were only a few ragtag soldiers left there. "Time to claim the victory," he blustered. Bruce wanted to back up the colonel but kept his mouth shut. The other officers in the room did the same.

The colonel tried again. "Soften them up with air strikes and wait a few days till we have enough Shermans to crack through the line. Then we can do it. These men have come through too much to get slaughtered for no good reason. Stay here at the front, get to know the men—you'll see for yourself."

The dig at the commander for not being at the front set him off. He grabbed the colonel by his lapels and jutted his chin inches from his face. Spitting out his words, the commander said, "Do what you were taught to do. Get this fleabag unit shaped up and ready to fight. You have one day before we attack." He raised his baton, struck the colonel on his chest, and stomped out of the room.

Ice crystals on the domed helmets shed an eerie glow over the predawn gathering. Company B was lined up with their Shermans, ready to move toward Herrlisheim. The men were quiet, each deep into his own thoughts about what was to come. Their breath escaped in small white clouds against the frigid night air. For many, the breaths were winnowing down to the last few they would take. The advance would start as they emerged through the woods around Rohrwiller and hit the open fields, over a mile long, before reaching the edge of Herrlisheim. No cover there, nothing but stalking behind the tanks. If the tanks blew, they would be totally exposed. The soldiers knew what they faced. It would be a shooting gallery for the Germans.

The shelling started as they moved through the thinning trees. The stark emptiness of the fields, mowed down to winter stubble and dusted with drifting snow, was lit by the starbursts of the shells from the American side, and now the return from German batteries. Dim shapes of Panzers stuck up from the rim of the sightline across the fields. The enemy wasn't surprised by this attack.

Bruce stayed at the edge of the trees with his binoculars fixed on the unmoving German line. They must be dug in deeply, he concluded. Even with the high-powered glasses, all he could make out through the swirls of remaining fog was the dull gray of the tanks and the outline of houses on the outskirts of Herrlisheim. He counted at least twenty of the Panzers. More would be lurking out of sight.

He estimated ten minutes before the GIs would be in range of enemy rifles. They were crawling from rut to rut in the fields, staying as low as possible, only getting up to run in short surges. The German shells were falling behind him, tearing up the old forest. It wouldn't be long before they started to find the range.

He knew he shouldn't be here. The colonel would rip him if he found out. Bruce's gesture of going with Company B to the start of the attack was reckless. He should be back in the aid station, waiting to play his role. But he had an ominous sense about today's battle. He couldn't stay away.

It wasn't the first time he took chances. There had been dozens of ambulance runs under fire. He could have avoided most of them. There were the trips in reconnaissance planes over enemy territory, the rides in tanks when the enemy was close. Blaise thought he had a death wish. Asked him if he was suicidal. The question had made him pause. It was hard to explain. "No," he had replied. "Don't want to miss the action. Want to be able to tell my grandkids I saw this war."

The truth was more complicated. Part of him thought he should be out there with the men. It was a stroke of good fortune that he was a little older and was almost through med school when this war began. If the war had started a few years earlier, he would be one of the guys crawling toward the Germans.

He had a good chance to make it through to the end of the war and have a nice life. The men on the frozen ground weren't so lucky. They were the ones who did most of the dying. He had listened to their cries for their mothers, their screams before the morphine took hold. He had gotten too close to them, seen too many of them drop. They were his brothers. And they were about to be sacrificed on the whim of a shit-faced commander.

Shafts of early morning light began to show through small breaks in the clouds. Like spotlights they appeared here and there, turning on and off, catching the metal of a tank or muffled glints from rifles being pushed ahead of the men.

The Germans didn't hesitate for long when the light changed. Their artillery exploded with staccato belches of fire, the pace quickening with accurate hits 150 to 200 yards in front of Bruce. Two of the Shermans were in flames. He could see soldiers trying to climb out of the nearest tank. The infantrymen who had been behind the tank were scattered. Some lying motionless on the ground, others peeling off to find a tank that was still moving forward. Panzers were closing from the town and out of the Stainwald Forest.

His lips set tight, Bruce turned from the scene and scrambled down the hill toward his jeep. When he rounded the corner of the rocky path, he saw splintered trees with the remains of the jeep smoldering at their base.

A wave of shock gave way to derision. Now his choice to see the start of the battle seemed frivolous, even selfish. *What did you think you were doing?* He began to run toward Rohrwiller, hoping that he would get there before the first ambulances arrived.

Beaten back three times, the men were trying again. The first P-47s they had seen in weeks had strafed the Germans before the fog descended. Tank reinforcements were finally on their way. And a group of Nazis had been captured north of the canal around Herrlisheim.

One of the enemy soldiers, a lieutenant who was in the aid station getting his wounds treated, was speaking in

English. Coming out of a morphine haze, his words were slurred at first. Then they sharpened so Bruce could understand him. "Get me out of here," he said. "Take me to prison camp. This town is gone. Zerstört . . . dead."

Blaise heard the soldier sputter and came over as Bruce worked on the German's right thigh. The shot had torn most of the quadriceps away but had spared the bone. There wasn't enough skin left to close the wound. The only option was to clean it up and let the tissue granulate and partially fill the hole.

"What are you saying?" Blaise asked. "Do you know something?"

"Blitzkrieg heute," he blurted in German. Then he switched to English. "More Panzers. More soldiers. Waited till we can crush you. Orders no prisoners. No Rohrwiller."

"Lies," Blaise said. "We've got you licked. We'll be in Herrlisheim by tomorrow."

"Believe me," the German said as he winced at a deeper plunge of Bruce's cauterizing tool. "You didn't let me die. We wouldn't do the same. Move the hospital. I warn you."

Bruce shook his head. "I'm giving you more morphine so I can finish this job."


Two hours later, frost-encrusted GI casualties streamed into the aid station. Shells rocked the town. The electrical supply flickered, and the generators began to fire. A full-scale attack was under way.

The German timing was impeccable. The snow and fog were giving them cover to move toward Rohrwiller. The P-47s were grounded. Supplies were tenuous. The German counterpunch might do what the lieutenant warned. Bruce steeled himself. *Keep working. Do your job. We're too close to fail now.*

A sandy-haired soldier yelled and tried to get up from his stretcher. But he collapsed, his left arm and leg useless at his side. The reason was obvious—a cavernous gap in his skull. A bullet had torn through the parietal lobe of his brain, destroying nerve centers for muscles on the left side of his body. Jellylike pieces of tissue matted his head. Bruce locked eyes with the corpsman. They knew this soldier couldn't be saved. He nodded to the corpsman to inject enough morphine to ease him into permanent sleep. The soldier would be left to die while they tried to help the men who had a chance.

These moments were the hardest. Too many wounded men to handle well. Decisions to make that would haunt him later. Just Blaise and him and a few corpsman and nurses for a whole battlefield of injuries coming at them. Bleeding, moaning GIs were all around him. *Where to start? Start anywhere. Keep moving. Don't think. Yes, do think. Stay alert. Do your best.*

"Doc, am I going to make it?" asked a soldier who didn't look older than sixteen. His groin wound was a bloody stump—his penis and testicles gone with shrapnel from a mine. The lower part of his abdominal muscles was shredded, and the shimmer of intestine could be glimpsed through the slits. "Is my cock okay? I can't look." Bruce couldn't tell him now. It would be a challenge to save his life. "You'll be fine, soldier. Stay still while I stop the bleeding and get you ready for surgery. We'll put you back together again." The sickening reality of the wound grabbed Bruce for a few minutes. Then he moved to the next soldier.

The German artillery strikes were getting closer. Surgical instruments shook with the explosions. Plaster flaked down from the ceiling. Any pretense of a sterile surgical field had been abandoned. There was no time to change their crimson-soaked gowns. It was a furious dash to stabilize as many as possible.

A shell hit in the street in front of the aid station, blowing open the timbered door. Acrid smoke and a thick cloud of dust spilled through the gap. "Get some stretchers, anything," Blaise shouted. "Block it off. Keep this place as clean as we can." Two of the corpsmen rushed to plug the tear in their flimsy defenses. Bruce stole a quick glance before the blown door was covered. The house across the street had disappeared. Flames licked around the rubble. He shivered and returned to suturing an arm that had been amputated by a tank shell. He suspected there was no time now for a retreat—to pack the injured men and leave Rohrwiller.

His prediction was confirmed soon when their colonel entered the aid station and gathered the officers. After a two-week battle with no relief, he was still trying to inspire his men and give them a plan. "The Panzers have broken through. They're close to the edge of Rohrwiller now. It'll be door-to-door fighting, but the tanks will have trouble in the streets. Our guys will ambush them with grenades and bazookas. Give us some time till our Shermans get here from the north. Fog and ice have slowed them. All we need is to hold out for a day.

"The Germans will come after the command post as soon as they can. But we're not moving, and neither are you. We don't have the troops to haul you out of here. So I'm sending you some machine guns and bazookas. Any of the wounded who can handle a gun should get ready to use it. If the Krauts run down our street, start shooting. I'll be out there with you. We're going to win this war."

When the colonel left, Bruce put his arm around Blaise's shoulders. It was the closest thing to a hug he could muster. "Good luck, buddy," he said. Blaise replied with a half-hearted laugh. "Next stop the Ritz. Drinks are on me." They turned and went back to work.

The shelling continued through the night, but no Panzers had appeared. No German soldiers had stormed their corner of Rohrwiller. The flow of injured men had slowed to a trickle. Corpsmen couldn't get through the streets, so the wounded were out there somewhere by themselves. The fog had gotten thicker. Where were the Panzers that were threatening to run over them?

Grenade and mortar explosions from the American side punctuated the night air, signaling where battle spots flared. Then the telltale sound of a Panzer cannon caught their attention. The German tanks were getting closer.

The soldier who had his genitals shot off was resting now. His abdominal slashes were tied together with sutures. His stump was packed with gauze and sulfa. The GI who had his brain ripped apart was barely breathing. Chokes and rattles told the story that he wouldn't see another day. The wounded Germans were in the corner of the room, hand-cuffed to cots if they were conscious. One of them had beady eyes, which he hadn't closed all night. Bruce worried about him. Could he spring on them? Try to grab their guns, wipe them out, and fight his way back to his troops?

His thoughts were interrupted by a sudden blast, a deafening roar and flash of blinding light. He grabbed a gun and dived to the floor. All the lights were out now. The generator hum had stopped. Then he looked up. A corner of the room was open to the sky. He could see only an outline of the shorn rafters through the cloud of smoke that was escaping. *Where did the shell hit?* he thought. *Did it take out any of the men?* The Germans looked safe. The cots in their corner were untouched.

He began to crawl toward the oil stove. There was no sign of light from the stove. Was it incinerated in the blast? They would freeze soon without its heat. He could already feel some snow blowing through the hole in the roof. "Blaise," he called out. "Where are you? Is everybody safe?"

The two nurses cried out, "Safe here."

Some of the soldiers who could speak replied, "Safe here." One of them began sobbing.

Bruce kept crawling till he touched a searing piece of iron. He pulled his hand back. It was from the stove. He turned to the left, nudged forward, and felt a body in his path. He found the radial artery—no pulse. There was blood all over the head and neck. A shard of stove metal had sliced the jugular and torn most of the face off the soldier. With a sense of doom, he slipped his hand into the man's back pocket. His fingertips traced a caduceus stamped on the wallet. It was a twin of the one in his pocket. Just a month ago, a soldier who had been a shoemaker made them the wallets for Christmas.

He put his head on Blaise's chest. No heart sounds, no breath. A good life was over.

# Chapter 21

## AFTERMATH

*Pennsylvania*
*February 1946*

They found Bruce staggering out of his office, ten or so minutes after the explosion, his skin fiery red, hair singed from the heat, pants shredded, and blood covering his legs. Sarah and Glen had arrived at the same time, both knowing that the blast was too close to Bruce's office to ignore. The town's fire alarm was ringing, but the men hadn't appeared yet.

"Let's get him down on the ground fast," she said. "Spread your coat out. Lots of bleeding from that right leg."

"I'm okay," Bruce squeaked in a dry, raspy voice. "Put some pressure on those cuts. I'm a little wobbly, that's all."

"You're more than wobbly," she said. "Do what I say. I'm the doctor now. We'll take care of you."

"What happened? Did the SOBs bomb you?" Glen asked as Sarah eased Bruce on top of the coat and began to examine him for more injuries.

"Before you start asking questions, take my coat and rip out the lining," she said. "Tear it into pieces and hold a couple big ones on that wound on his right leg. It's the only one that's bleeding badly."

"The furnace must have blown," Bruce said. "It was screaming like a banshee. I was going down the stairs to check on it, and pow! Blew me against the stairs. Knocked me out for a while."

"Take it easy, Bruce," she said in a calming voice. "No need to talk. You took a pretty big hit. Your leg looks like some shrapnel tore into it. We'll need to get you over to my office to check the wounds and sew you up. And you have some second-degree burns. Just rest till we have some help to move you. We'll put you back together."

She turned to Glen and raised her eyebrows. "Lucky he wasn't a few steps closer to the furnace. No damage above his legs. Could have been a lot worse."

"Are you all right, brother?" Glen asked.

"Making it. Be back in the office tomorrow if they can fix the furnace."

"You're going nowhere near your office tomorrow," Sarah said. "You'll need to take some time off, let yourself heal. Now keep quiet and let us do our work. The firemen will be here soon. They can put you on a litter and walk you down the street to my office."

"Then you're coming home with me for a while," Glen said.

The sirens of the fire engines told them the trucks were near. Bruce closed his eyes. His bravado was fading.

"So what do you think of my little operating room?" Sarah asked Bruce to divert his attention from her digging the metal fragments out of his legs. She had already sutured the largest puncture wound after irrigating it with sterile saline. "I set it up for doing minor surgery. Give me a critique."

He lifted his head and twisted his upper body to look at her. "Can't beat the service. Highly recommended." He could see her red hair swept back under a hospital cap. Strands of it poked through the edges. Her eyes flashed away from his legs for a moment and caught his glance. The furrowing of her eyebrows softened.

"Stay still, Bruce. I need all the help from you I can get. No squirming around while I finish this job."

He lowered his head and closed his eyes. Joking with Sarah had helped for a while. But the flood of images from the past returned again. They came at him with violence. His body tightened, and his skin turned clammy.

"The explosion took me back," he said.

"Back where?" she asked.

"To France. A stove blew. It was hit with a shell. Killed my friend Blaise—another doc. It was a miracle I made it."

The pain showed on his face. It was a deeper pain than the hurt from today's blast. He began to relive the scene, tensing and grimacing, then shaking his head back and forth. Tears began to streak his cheeks.

"I'm sorry, soldier," she said as she tried to comfort him. "You can tell me what happened. I'm a good listener."

Bruce didn't respond at first. The memories had been held tight for months. Until he slipped and told Sarah about Blaise, there was only one person who knew anything about what had happened. But his letters to Amelia had shielded her from the worst of the losses. No one had entered the darkest corners of his mind.

Sarah's deft caring was tempering his resolve to keep the memories to himself. Yet he had to shut the door. "You've listened enough," he replied with a forced smile. "Thanks for the offer." He closed his eyes again and kept quiet while she completed her work.

The wounds Sarah could treat were dusted with sulfa and sutured. But she felt helpless to heal the ones that were haunting Bruce. She slipped off her surgical gloves and leaned over the man who had suffered more than she had realized. She hesitated, then caressed his cheek with a light touch of the back of her fingers. Under normal conditions he would be too proud, too stubborn to show his vulnerability. And she would never let her guard down to touch him in this way. The accident in his office had opened a stream from his past and brought them to this intimate moment. *Dangerous*, she thought to herself. *Stop it. Be his doctor, nothing more.*

"Okay, Humpty Dumpty. Your pieces are back together again. Let's get some salve on those burns, and you'll be ready to go. Your family's waiting. They'll be happy to see you walk out of here."

"I'll need a pair of pants," he said. "See if Glen can bring me some clothes."

She could tell he was back to the present, at least for now. "You should keep those wounds open to the air for a couple days. Let's rig up a hospital gown like a skirt. It's too bad I don't have a gown with a tartan print. You could act like it was a kilt. Aren't the Duncans Scottish?"

A smile creased his face. "Good job, Doctor. Make me a skirt."

News about the explosion had traveled quickly. When Bruce opened the door to Sarah's waiting room, he saw a group of his family and friends. His mother moved to him first. She threw her arms around him and began to cry.

"Oh, my boy," she whispered.

Glen came to their side and held both of them. "He's safe, Mother. You don't have to worry. We'll fix everything."

They stood there for a few beats, not moving. Then Bess Runyon and his aunt Pauline joined the tight circle, their hands stretched around the three at the core. In progression, Judge Clapper, Maggie Bailey, and Mimi came forward. The close call had shaken all of them.

"Give Bruce some air," Sarah said with a lift to her voice. "Let him sit down for a while. Then he needs to go home to get some rest." As they started to break away, she continued. "He wants to go back to work tomorrow. Don't you dare let him do it. We'll check him back here in three days. Glen, can you take charge? If you don't hold him down, he'll be seeing patients in the morning."

"You're never going back near that office again," Alice said. "I should have known not to trust that old rat trap you rented. That furnace must have been there before I was born. You needed a better place with a new furnace. I should have helped you with the money."

"Mother, you've done everything for me. It was just bad luck. I heard the furnace whistling. I could've called a repairman instead of looking at it myself."

"Classic second-guessing," Judge Clapper said. "It won't do any good to blame yourselves. Solve the problem. It's all you can do now. Alice, come over and sit beside me. Let these younger folks plan what to do."

"I'll corral the landlord," Glen said. "Make him tear out that old furnace and put in a new one. If he balks, we'll threaten to sue."

"Bruce can share my office until the repairs are done," Sarah added. "It will be tight, but we can manage."

"I've got a better idea," Maggie said. "I'll bet we could borrow a couple rooms at the church. If we use the church's folding chairs and tables, we won't have to move the whole office. And if Sarah lets him use her lab, the only big thing we'll need to take is his examining table. I think it could work."

"I'm on the property committee," the judge said. "I'll get it approved." He turned to Alice. "Your family has been going to the church since it was founded. You deserve some help now, and the church will step up. I know they will."

"There's a pair of rooms in the basement that should work," Pauline said. "Our scout troop uses them to store camping gear. We can haul the equipment over to our attic. Then Bruce can set up the rooms like one of his field stations. If he could do surgery on the battlefront, he can hold out in our church for a little while."

Glen nodded. "I can borrow a truck and ask some of my friends to help with the move. Bruce, all you'll have to do is tell us what stays and what goes. Maggie can supervise, while you stay at my house to recuperate. You'll be back in business by the end of the week."

"I'll get a crew to clean the rooms," Bess said. "We might want to put a quick coat of paint on the walls. The scouts have been in there for years. It could look shabby when the camping gear gets cleared out."

Their rush to help was moving too fast for Bruce. He was still mulling over the furnace explosion. If he had walked down the steps ten seconds earlier, the damage would have been much worse. He could be dead. Another part of his mind was trying to push away the images of the endgame at Rohrwiller. He was lucky there too. Why did the shell take out Blaise and not him?

The mask he had to wear—a mask of calm over the noise—wasn't covering so well. The epinephrine surge from the accident had faded, and the burns and punctures had started to hurt. Though he was surrounded by people, a strange sense of aloneness was tugging at him. Amelia's visit was a long way off. Death was too close. He had to regain his equanimity. Thank them, tell them he would be at work soon. Show them they had nothing to fear.

He rose and then faltered as he took a step. A wave of nausea and lightheadedness came over him. For a moment he thought he might drop to the floor. *Vasovagal response*, his doctor persona told him. *You lost some blood, had a big shock. Steady yourself on the arm of the chair. It will pass.*

He felt disconnected. His body wasn't listening to his brain. As he looked around the room, the others were turned toward him, waiting for him to speak. Their shapes were blurred, out of focus. He froze for a few seconds, then sat down again in the chair. Sarah walked to him to check his pulse.

"He's been through too much to work out a plan now," she said. "His heart's racing. Could have lost more blood than I realized. He needs an IV and some fluids."

"Is it worse than we thought?" Alice asked. "He looks like he can't talk. Is he having a stroke?"

"No, nothing serious. A bit of fluid and a few days of rest and he'll be fine."

Bruce steeled himself. "Sorry, folks, I got woozy for a minute. Couldn't concentrate on the plans."

He sat up in the chair while Sarah started the IV and brought a pole to hang the bottle. When he felt the cool stream in his veins, a pulse of vitality went through him, and his command experience in battlefield aid stations gave him the presence to spell out the action steps. "Glen, go ahead with pushing Smythe. Tell him we want a new furnace within two weeks, no later. Judge, can you visit Reverend Capers before you talk with the property committee? Be sure he's on board."

As Bruce finished his instructions, Vic appeared at the door. He held a dirty canvas bag at his side. "Where have you been?" Pauline asked.

"Talking with the firemen. Checking things at the office," he replied. "I secured the place. Got it locked down."

"So what's the verdict?" Bruce asked. "Can we get it cleaned up soon?"

"You're looking better," Vic said. "I figured Doc Avery wouldn't need me while she patched you up. So I got my hard hat and poked around the scene." He tucked the canvas bag behind a chair and walked toward Bruce. "Can I give my nephew a hug?" he asked Sarah.

"Sure, but be careful. He's got some burns, and he's pretty sore now."

Vic folded his meaty arms around Bruce, only touching his back. He whispered into his ear, "When we have a minute, I need to talk with you alone."

He sat down in the chair next to Bruce and gave his report. "The furnace is blown apart. There's no way it can be repaired. So there won't be any heat unless we rig some kerosene stoves. I already called to the shop for the foreman to bring one for each floor and get them fired up. And I hired some of my men to watch the place. The basement looks like a battle zone, but there's no damage upstairs except for some broken glass in the lab. Smythe came by to see what happened. He told me he'll start the cleanup tomorrow. I'll ride him to see he gets the job done right."

"Thanks, Vic," Bruce said. "Glen was going to put some pressure on Smythe. Do you think it's needed?"

"Maybe later," Vic replied. "Let's see how it goes over the next couple days."

Sarah folded her arms and spoke. "I'm going to have to break up this party. Our patient needs to finish his IV and go to Glen's house and stay in bed all day."

"I'll stay a little longer and give Bruce a ride," Vic said. "He can lie down on the back seat of the big Chrysler. Pauline, you can go with Alice, Bess, and the judge to church. There's still time to make the eleven o'clock service. Should be lots of prayers of thanksgiving today. I'll catch up with you later."

After all of them left, and Sarah went into her office, Vic retrieved the canvas bag. "There's something else you need to know," he said. "Are you feeling strong enough now to take another hit?"

"Yeah. What's going on? What do you have in the bag?"

Vic opened the drawstrings and pulled out a gnarled piece of metal. "You probably don't know what I've got here. I see these kinds of valves at the shop. It's the steam release valve for your furnace boiler. I discovered it after the firemen went home. I was sifting through the litter, trying to figure out why the boiler exploded. The answer is right here in this twisted hunk of iron."

"What is it?" Bruce asked.

"Can you see this brass screw near the outlet? It shouldn't be there. Someone drove it into the valve. It's sabotage, Bruce. The explosion was no accident."

Bruce took a deep breath. Flushed with anger, his face began to twitch. "Allegheny Refractories . . . they want to silence me. And they almost did. I'm supposed to testify in Harrisburg in ten days."

"I've been putting together a timeline," Vic said. "From what I know about boilers, I think they broke into your office a little after midnight, jammed the valve, and then turned up the regulator so the boiler would overheat. It should have taken four or five hours for the pressure to build to the point that it would blow. I don't think they wanted to kill you. They must have planned to rip your office apart when nobody was there. They didn't know you would come to work so early on a Sunday morning. Another scare job, but this one could have been lethal.

"I didn't want the others to know about this," Vic continued as he rolled the metal in his hands. "All we have is this valve. There's no other evidence to prove who did it. If we keep quiet for a while, they might believe we think it was an accident. It would give us some time to investigate."

"Yeah, keep it quiet. Trace it back to Lucas," Bruce said.

A picture of Lucas sitting in his office came at Bruce in a sudden jolt, and a volley of spasms grabbed at his face. He stood and rubbed his face hard. The spasms wouldn't stop. "You bastard," he said before he kicked a chair, which bounced off the wall and landed at Vic's feet.

"Whoa," Vic said. "What are you doing?"

"I was fighting him."

"You've had enough," Vic said. "Let me take you to Glen's house so you can get some sleep."

"Not quite yet," Bruce said. The spasms had stopped after his explosion. "Let me cool down. Think about what we can do."

He took a few deep breaths and continued. "Let's say we can track the sabotage back to Allegheny Refractories. Or even if we can't find more evidence, we can claim we have it. We could get Lucas's attention real fast. Hold it over his head. Make him stop harassing me and do the right thing for his men."

"Might work," Vic said. "But you need to watch out. They could come after you again. I wouldn't want to lose my favorite nephew."

"None of us would like to lose you," Sarah said.

The men had been so absorbed in their conversation that they hadn't seen her come from behind them. "Sorry to eavesdrop," she said. "I needed to get that IV out and see if you're ready to go home."

"What did you hear?" Bruce asked.

"Something about sabotage and your crazy idea to use it against Lucas Glover."

"Will you seal your lips?" Bruce asked. "We need to keep this between ourselves."

"Bruce, this isn't a game," she said. "You're an amateur at this kind of business. Go to the police. Let them handle it."

"Can't do it . . . not now. We need this chance to squeeze Lucas."

"I don't know if you're so full of pride you can't back down, or if you're just foolhardy. But I'm your doctor now. I'll keep the secret."

"Good," he said. "I'm going to tell Glen and Tony about the valve. There'll be five of us that know. Enough to track down any evidence we can find. And five whom I can trust. Vic, you and Glen can look for clues. Tony can be our ears at the brick plant. There are bound to be rumors, and someone might talk about what they did. Sarah, you can make sure I'm well enough to visit Lucas soon. We're going to make the most of this mistake."

*February 25, 1946*
*Dear Amelia,*

*Something happened yesterday that makes me worry that you might get hurt if you come to the USA. Although I've told you a bit about my work with the men at the brick plant, I haven't let you know how dangerous it's become.*

*The furnace in my office exploded yesterday, just when I was going down the basement stairs to check on it. The pipes had been banging, and I heard a whistling noise that I hadn't heard before. Fortunately, I only got some cuts in my legs and some minor burns. Sarah Avery, the other new doctor in town, came right away and took good care of me. I'm resting today and plan to be treating patients again tomorrow in a temporary office at the Presbyterian Church.*

*It looks like the explosion was an attempt to frighten me away from my little campaign to help the men. We've had exposés published in the Philadelphia and Pittsburgh newspapers, and I'm scheduled to testify soon at a hearing at the state capital. We've put enough heat on the company that they're fighting back.*

*Because the furnace was rigged to blow up around five on Sunday morning, I don't think they meant to have it happen when anyone was there. I hadn't been able to sleep and went to the office to do some lab work. While there's some comfort in knowing they weren't trying to put me under the ground, the situation is full of risk. I don't know what they'll try next, and one of their clumsy attempts to intimidate me was a crude letter that had defaced photos of you (which they stole during a break-in at my house) with some threats toward both of us.*

*I have a plan to get the company to stop their attacks on us and do the right thing for the men. But it could take some time for the situation to settle down. In the meantime, it would be best to delay your trip. Even if you stay in New York and don't come to Hollidaysburg, they could try to pull some tricks.*

*It hurts way more than the wounds from yesterday to ask you to put off your visit. Visions of what could be are stronger than ever. They wash over me, giving me strength to get out of this mess I've created and build a future for us.*

*Love,*
*Bruce*

# Chapter 22

## DETERMINED

———

The men gathered in Vic's kitchen to report on what they had found since the explosion. They would have an hour or two to themselves before Pauline returned from a library committee meeting.

"Vic, what did you find?" Bruce asked. "Any more evidence?"

"We had the place to ourselves all day Sunday and Monday," he replied. "The workmen came today to start demolition, so I don't think we'll be able to do much more. They'll be there a while. It's a big job."

"Do you have enough to charge Lucas?" Tony asked. "I'd like to see the little weasel get caught."

"Glen and I pumped the water out and got the place as dry as we could," Vic said. "Then we sorted through every piece of the rubble. I'm not making excuses, but I'm telling you that clues would have to be obvious for us to find them. Half of the basement has a dirt floor, and the water from the broken pipes made it a mud bath. I was looking for a device that might have defeated the thermostat. Didn't see anything like that. And there was no chance of finding footprints. The whole floor was covered in muck by the time we got the water out of there. I got lucky when I found that pressure release valve right after the blast. It got thrown on the stairwell just below the place Bruce was standing. It's all we've got except for the jimmied window that Glen spotted."

"I checked all of the doors and windows," Glen said. "Couldn't understand how they got in for a while. I thought they might have had a key. Then I saw it. The iron grate over one of the basement windows didn't have cobwebs around it like the others. And there was chipped paint and splintered wood where they slipped a blade in there to loosen the latch. There could be fingerprints, but I'll bet they wore gloves."

"How about footprints outside?" Vic asked.

"The window they used is at the back of the house where the walk goes to the garage," Glen replied. "They must have stayed on the walk until they crouched down to crawl through the window. There were some faint marks in the ground, probably from their knees. I took pictures of the ground and the window where they scratched the frame. It's not much, but we have some proof that someone broke into the house."

"I think I know who did it," Tony said. "Some of the boys from Garnersville tore up a bar last night. Payday isn't till Friday. They never go out on Monday, and they wouldn't have the money to get lit this close to payday. They got extra cash somewhere, and it probably was from the boss."

"Did anyone hear them talk about the explosion?" Bruce asked.

"No one's talking," he answered. "The only thing I know for sure is that Shorty Mock called in sick today. He's the crudest of the bunch. Got kicked out of the army for hitting an officer. Every word that comes out of his mouth is filth. I don't know if the rumor's true, but they say his parents are first cousins. He's short, just like his nickname. And he's got weird-looking ears. They're folded tight and set really low on his head. You'd know him if you saw him.

"The other guy to watch is Jerry Ringler. He's the only one of the men from Garnersville that got out of high school. He's the assistant foreman in the maintenance shop—a company man. Never bitches about the dust. Has got himself a nice, clean job. Sends the other guys out to repair the machines on the floor and sits in his office most of the day. I heard he left the bar after one beer and told the other two guys, Shorty and a fellow named Hap Felker, to zip it up. Hap doesn't work at the plant. He gets by with trapping coons and mink. Spent time in jail for breaking and entering."

"We need some proof they did it," Bruce said. "Do you know anybody who could get them to talk? How about somebody who could buy them some beers and loosen them up?"

"The men I can trust would stick out if they showed up at the Garnersville Bar," Tony said. "It's a rough place. Fits right in with their shacks and the piles of junk in their yards. But I've asked George and Slim to listen without tipping anybody off about what we know. If we're patient, Shorty might say something at work. He's got such a lousy job, cleaning the toilets and sweeping the floors, I can see him bragging about some special work for the boss."

"We could wait a long time," Vic said. "And the hearing in Harrisburg is next week. Lucas could go nuts and pull another trick to keep Bruce from testifying. Even if he lays off for a while, Bruce's girlfriend is coming from England soon. He sent those threatening letters about her. We need to stop him now.

"Let's give him some of his own medicine. I know a couple fellows at the PRR shop who wouldn't mind putting some pressure on Shorty. I think Shorty's the weakest link here. Or if we want to go to the source, we could play our own tricks on Lucas. I've been hatching some ideas. Just fantasies at this point, but he's asked for it. We could set him up for a mistake at the plant. Get him fired. He's already under the gun because of the publicity about silicosis. It probably wouldn't take much for us to break him. What do you think, Tony? How could we get revenge?"

"I don't know about trying to get him canned," Tony replied. "It would take something big, like a string of ruined brick shipments. And they could probably trace it back to one of our guys. If we got caught, we'd lose our jobs. Hell, the plant could close if it was bad enough."

"We're not going to do anything to risk the men we're trying to help," Bruce said. "And we aren't going to commit any crimes. But let's keep churning out ideas. We can show the explosion was rigged and someone broke into the basement. All we need is a tighter link to Lucas. The Garnersville men getting drunk and tearing up a bar won't do it."

"We have enough to go to the police now," Glen said. "Let them look for fingerprints. Tell them about Shorty and that Ringler fellow. They can question them, find out where they were the night the furnace valve got plugged. If the police were hounding Lucas and his crew, he would have to back off. He wouldn't dare try to come after Bruce again."

Tony stood and began to pace. "If the police start snooping around, the bosses in Pittsburgh won't like it. They probably would get rid of Lucas. It could be good for us. Or it could be a lot worse. There's a hard liner, Elliott Price, they could send from headquarters. He's been here before. You wouldn't like him. Screamed at one of the guys who asked him about getting safety equipment for one of the brick presses. Told him to shut up and do his work or they would find someone who wanted the job.

"Lucas could be better for us than a new plant manager. We think he knows we're right about the dust, but he's getting crunched from Price and the other white shirts in Pittsburgh.

They can't admit there's any chance that silica's dangerous. If they did, they'd have to spend money on making the plants safer, and they might have to pay us damages. Could put them, and us, out of business. It's a fine line. Push too hard, and all of the men might be out of work. All we want are some reasonable precautions and a chance to get transferred to areas where there isn't any dust if your lungs start to go."

Bruce nodded in agreement. "Lucas couldn't have meant for anyone to be in my office when that furnace blew. He's done some bad things, but he's not a murderer. I still think he gives us the best chance to make some changes at the plant. If he could show the balls to stand up to the brass in Pittsburgh and take some steps to improve conditions, we'll have made a start. He knows that silica is harming his men. And he's not immune to the dust himself.

"If we could get inside his brain now, I think we'd find he's trying to rescue himself, undo what he's done, and find a way to get out of the trap. I want to give him the way out. But first we need to show him that he's caught."

"What about the testimony in Harrisburg next week?" Glen asked. "I agree with Vic that Lucas might try to stop you. Could you bow out? Tell them you're injured and you can't make the trip? Your friend from Philadelphia, Silverman, is scheduled to be there. He can make all the same points you would make. And he's the big expert."

"Yeah, take it easy," Tony said. "Don't take any more chances. You've done too much already."

"I'm going," Bruce said. "Can't miss it. Fenelli, the company doctor, will be there. When he does a cover-up, we can make him look like a fool. Phil Silverman can explain the science, give them the statistics. I'll personalize it so they'll see how the men suffer. I've got X-rays on Tony and some of the other men. Their names are blacked out to protect them, but I'll testify the films came from men at the plant. It won't take a medical degree to see the damage. It will stare them in the face."

Glen shook his head. "Stubborn. You've always been stubborn. Don't know when to stop."

"Yeah, he's stubborn," Vic said. "Gets him places. But I'm not sure Lucas can be turned around. I wouldn't push him at all until we're sure he's in our pocket. I still want to work on Shorty. Nothing that would alert the cops, just a little rough and tumble. What do you say, Bruce?"

"No. Keep your men at the PRR shops. If they cause trouble, it would be easy to trace it back to you and me. Our plan is set, and I don't want anybody going off on their own. Tony, you can be on the lookout for any more information that would help us. See if George and Slim can get Shorty to drink with them on payday. And maybe someone could get to know Hap Felker, the fellow that Tony thinks was with them. Glen and Vic, you can drive with me to Harrisburg if you can take the day off. And keep saying the explosion was an accident. When people ask about me, tell them I'm recovered and working on getting the office back in shape. Vic, I know you're trying to save my skin. But no trouble, please. Let me do it my way.

"We'll give it two weeks, close the loop around Lucas by testifying in Harrisburg. Then I'll go to see him, take the fouled release valve and the photos of the basement window and anything else we can find. If Shorty talks, we'll have everything we need. We've got Lucas in a pincer, like we squeezed the Germans."

Vic turned toward him with a grimace. "Be careful when you squeeze something," Vic said. "Try that with a snake and you can get bit."

# Chapter 23

## CONFESSION

---

*Pennsylvania*
*March 1946*

Kate walked into Sarah's office dressed in a sumptuous coat with a mink collar, her hair swept up in a pompadour, and her face heavy with makeup. The red on her lips was almost iridescent. Sarah wondered why Kate had gone to so much trouble to put on a show. She looked like she was ready for a night on the town in Manhattan. It was after five o'clock on a Wednesday. Why wasn't she at home cooking dinner?

It had been only two weeks since Kate's first visit—a straightforward consultation for a urinary tract infection. Sarah suspected that today would be different. The fancy plumage couldn't hide signs of a woman in trouble. When Kate came closer, Sarah could see the streaked mascara where tears had left their tracks.

Kate seemed to be trying to calm herself as she slipped out of her coat and perched on the chair. She offered a few pleasantries about the cold weather, but the tension was obvious. Her bottom lip was curling as she bit on it. The tenor of her voice wasn't convincing.

"Thanks for seeing me at the end of the day," Kate said. "I don't know how you have the energy to treat the hordes that come here. I hear your business is booming."

Sarah sat down at her desk, knowing the woman needed to talk. "We've got plenty of time. The waiting room is empty now, and my nurse put the closed sign on the door. What's bothering you? I can tell you're upset."

Kate looked away for a few moments and then plunged ahead. "It's a problem I can't admit to my gynecologist. You probably know him, Steve Taylor. He delivered my son. A good guy, but I don't think he'd understand. He'd probably think I'm a frigid ice queen or something. I thought a woman doctor would be more sympathetic."

"What's wrong?"

"It's hard to talk about," Kate said as she lowered her head. "I had to get dressed up to get the courage to come here. Didn't want to look like a worn-out housewife. You know the type. Can't make her husband happy, rotting away in nothing land until she looks like an old dishrag. I'm not there yet, but I'm on my way."

"You look fabulous, nothing like a dishrag. Tell me about the problem. I'll try to help."

Kate took a deep breath and brought her eyes up to meet Sarah's. "When Lucas makes love to me, it hurts so bad I can't stand it. I fake it when I can, but most of the time I have to push him away."

Sarah paused to gauge her words. "We'll do an exam later to check for physical problems, and there are some exercises I can show you. But let's start with a few questions. Is it okay if we're frank? I don't think we should tiptoe around the facts."

"Sure, let them fly. I'm not squeamish."

"Was it always this way with Lucas?"

"No, it was fine in the beginning. We were close until after the baby was born and he got the promotion to plant manager. I wasn't as interested in rolling around in bed with him after the baby, but it didn't hurt when we did it."

"When did the problems start?"

"About two years ago. He'd come home from work frustrated and would yell at me if I wasn't ready for him when he wanted me. It got a lot worse the last few months. He's afraid he'll get fired if he doesn't shut up the guys who are agitating about the silica dust. Lucas wasn't mean when I married him. He is now."

"I can imagine it's hard to feel romantic if he's mean to you. What happens when you try to have sex?"

"I'm dry as the desert, and my vagina is clamped shut. I usually can't get it loosened, so he does his own thing and calls me a bitch."

"Can you do your own thing? What happens if you stimulate yourself?"

"Works okay then."

Kate hung her head again. "I'm making him hate me, and I'm starting to hate him. And I think about how my son and I could make it on our own. Do you have some creams, or maybe a shot that would relax me? I can't drive him away. Who knows what he'll do?"

"Has he hit you?"

"Pushed me around a little. Treated me rough when we were trying to have sex. Never actually hit me. It's his words that cut the deepest."

"Are you afraid he'll harm you?"

Kate considered the question with care. "Not really. He's got a lot of bluster, but I don't think he's dangerous. At least not to me."

"What keeps you from leaving him?"

"Lucas Junior . . . being afraid to admit I made a big mistake." She hesitated. "And I guess I still love him in a way. He always comes back to me after he's bad, writes me apologies, tells me he'd be lost without me. He's got a huge job, makes a lot of money, could move up to the next rung and manage a new group of plants in South America. But he's losing his mind over this silica thing. If he could solve that problem, I think he'd settle down."

Sarah was learning more than she needed to know. Kate could have information that could help Bruce pin the furnace explosion on Lucas. It was tempting to ask more questions. But her job was to treat Kate, her patient. Not to be a detective for Bruce.

"I'm thinking about how I can help," Sarah said. "I can tell you're torn between wanting to leave and staying loyal. I can't tell you what to do, but I can listen when you want to talk. Just don't tell me anything that could get someone in trouble."

"Is everything I say confidential?" Kate asked.

"Of course," Sarah replied.

"Then I want to tell you why it got so bad this week. It was that accident at Bruce's office. I think Lucas was behind it. I overheard him talking on the phone after the blast. He was almost whispering, but I could hear him saying something about keeping a man named Shorty quiet. They could all go to jail if Shorty spouted off about what they had done. After the call, Lucas came after me, wanted to have sex. The last thing I wanted was for him to touch me anywhere. You can guess how it turned out. He did rough me up more than a little that time. This heavy makeup isn't my usual style."

Sarah had tried to avoid leading Kate down the path toward implicating her husband. Yet here they were. She knew enough to put Lucas away and ruin what was left of their marriage. If she didn't reveal the truth, would Kate get hurt worse? What would happen to Bruce? Could someone get killed?

Her mind swirled with indecision. Should she warn Kate that the abuse would escalate if she didn't get out now? Should she push her to go to the police? Or should she break her vow of confidentiality and file a police report herself? Sarah was thinking quickly now. She needed to respond to Kate's confession. There hadn't been any lectures in med school on this kind of conflict.

*Stick with being a doctor*, she told herself. *Be careful you don't take advantage.*

"Kate, I said our talk was confidential. And I meant it. I won't tell anyone. But why did you tell me about Lucas and the explosion? What did you want me to do?"

"I don't know. It just spilled out. I didn't come here to tell you about the explosion."

"Do you want me to help you leave him? Do you want to tell the police?"

"No, I can't divorce him. I told you why. I could never turn him in to the police. We'd lose everything."

Sarah nodded her head in understanding, but then pressed forward. "He's hitting you. So my priority has to be your life. Should I just be your sounding board? Or do you want me to give you advice?"

"What would you do?" Kate asked.

"Some creams or ointments aren't going to stop this problem. I'd leave him for a while. Tell him why you're going. Say you think you may still love him, but he has to stop attacking you. He can never hit you again or you'll be gone for good. I don't know about letting him know you overheard what he's been doing to Bruce. But he has to end that business or he'll get caught. Then everything would fall apart. Can you stay with your parents for a few weeks? Give him time to think about what he's doing?

"I said I couldn't tell you what to do. And I went ahead and told you exactly how I'd handle it. Sorry, Kate, I'm getting out of bounds . . . Do what makes the most sense to you."

"You're not out of bounds at all," Kate replied. "If I had the will, I'd do what you say. I should stand up to him. But I'll need to think about what I can do. I'm not ready to take him on quite yet."

"Okay, let me know when you want to talk more," Sarah said. "I'll be here when you need me. Now, do you want to go ahead with the exam?"

"Sure, in a minute." Kate hesitated, took a deep breath, and continued. "I've got another confession that needs to come out first. Do you have a little more time?"

"I'm not going anywhere."

"Do you remember the letters in the newspaper that accused Bruce of taking advantage of women patients? Well, it was all my fault. I was the woman who told her husband that Bruce made advances. And it was all a lie. I went to his office at the end of the day. Just like I did today with you. I had it all plotted out. Bruce and I were a couple when we were in college, but I couldn't see myself waiting for all of those years in medical school. And I didn't think he'd want to marry me after he got to Philadelphia. So I started dating Lucas. One of the dumbest things I've ever done.

"Bruce never touched me in his office or any other time since he came back from the war. Oh, I wanted him. And I was ready to throw myself at him. But he was absolutely correct. Never wavered. When I went home, I couldn't resist pestering Lucas. I tried to make him jealous so he'd treat me better. I told him Bruce grabbed me but I resisted. So Lucas isn't the only guilty one. There you have it. Should I slink out of here? Never bother you again? I've been such a despicable person. A real mess."

Sarah had suspected that Lucas wrote the smear letters. Who else would have had the motive to try to bring Bruce down? Now she knew why he'd chosen the smear tactic. Kate had inflamed her husband and probably set him off on the course that almost killed Bruce. Lucas must still think that Bruce tried to seduce his wife. It was more than the silica battle. The guy was fighting for his wife and his self-respect.

"Does Lucas know that you lied about Bruce?"

"No, I've wanted to tell him. But I've been afraid. What should I do? If he knew the truth, he might let Bruce alone."

Sarah caught herself again. *It's not your job to correct the lies. Back away. Let her decide.*

"I already said too much when I told you what I'd do about leaving Lucas. You have to make the choice, Kate. I'm just your doctor."

"You're already more than a doctor," Kate said. "I don't have anyone else I can talk with about these things. I can't even tell my mother what happened. Don't give up on me."

"I won't."

Kate put on her coat and fumbled to pull gloves over her shaking hands. "I am going to do something. I promise. I can't let this go on."

"You forgot about the exam," Sarah said.

"I don't need it," Kate replied. "We both know what's wrong. And keep the creams for now. I don't think I'll need them for a while."

"There is one thing you might do for me," Kate said as she moved toward the door.

"What could I do?"

A hint of a smile creased Kate's face when she turned to face Sarah. "You could start dating Bruce. It would make Lucas stop thinking Bruce is trying to take me away from him. And Bruce needs a girlfriend.

"You've probably heard about the woman coming from England," Kate continued as they stood in the waiting room. "She's an heiress, I'm told. A spoiled snob who took him for a ride during the war. The word is that she realizes she missed a gem and is coming here to lure him back to England. We don't want to lose Bruce. I'm not thinking of myself. I have no future with him. It's for our town and his family. Glen needs a steady hand. He's struggling. Bruce's mother has the judge, but she'd be crushed if Bruce left Hollidaysburg."

Kate reached to touch Sarah's hand. "The main reason I want you to date him is that you're a perfect match. You're beautiful and smart. And you're doing an important job. I always knew that Bruce would find a wife who had more to offer than me. I hope you're the one."

Sarah stood silently after Kate left. They had warned her in med school not to get personally involved with patients. And they cautioned that a woman doctor shouldn't try to mix marriage and a medical career. "You can't have both," they had said. "You'll be like a priest. Get used to it." Yet she had let her worries about Bruce influence her treatment decisions. She had led Kate to the brink of implicating Lucas. Even worse, she was fantasizing that Kate's parting words were on target.

She shivered a bit from the cold air that had moved through the room after Kate left. It was time to go back to her apartment to have a bit of dinner and then read some medical journals. The apartment hadn't seemed lonely before. Tonight she wished she had somewhere else to go.

# Chapter 24

## AMELIA

---

### Hampshire, England
### March 1946

*G*rant to all who mourn this pilot who flew to save our nation, a sure confidence in thy care, that casting all their grief in thee, they may know the consolation of thy love. Amen.

The Anglican priest left the pulpit after the benediction and walked down the center aisle of the chapel at Whitcombe Hall. The dedication service for the stained-glass window was over, and people began to say their goodbyes and drift away. The living had other things to do on this first Wednesday of March.

Amelia had greeted them all at the luncheon before the service—aunts, uncles, and cousins; neighbors and friends; and her brother David's classmates and fellow pilots who had survived the war. David had played on the tennis team and was a popular student at Oxford, but it had been four years since he was shot down. Many of his friends had met the same fate. His mother and father, Anna and Charles Whitcombe, were dead. Amelia wondered how many people who saw the window her father had commissioned would remember David.

*It's a shame it took so long to make*, Amelia thought to herself as she looked at the window. *I hope Daddy is somewhere he can see it.*

She turned back to Mark. "Sorry, I'm so distracted," she said. "It's the last service for David. In twenty years, people will come into the chapel, glance at the window, and have no idea what we lost."

"You're doing fine," Mark said. "You only shed a tear or two. If you get busy with the renovations, you won't mope around so much. The checkbook is open . . . Use it."

"Maybe in a few weeks," she replied. "I don't have the taste for it now."

"Are you dragging your feet?" he asked. "You postponed the wedding. You won't come to London with me. And I can't get a kiss out of you."

Amelia tried to hide a shudder as she thought of kissing him. She had been pushing him away for months and hadn't told him the reason. They were still engaged. He deserved at least a kiss. But she couldn't do it.

"I'm just trying to find my way."

He slapped his gloves in his open hand. "You've lost your way, Amelia. I've about had it with giving you time. You'd think I was a cousin instead of your fiancé."

"I'm sorry, Mark."

"I have to leave for London now. I can't miss the meeting at my club. It's the most important one of the year. Come with me. I'll get us a room at Claridge's. Pull you out of your gloom."

"No, you go on. I'll stay here. It's a day I want to remember."

After Mark sped down the driveway in his Jaguar, Amelia was alone—a state that suited her now. There was more to think about than Mark knew. She turned and walked back toward the chapel.

Bruce's most recent letter had arrived this morning. He was under attack—almost killed by a rigged explosion in his office. And he wanted to postpone her visit. With the press of hosting the day's events, and grief pulling with renewed strength, she hadn't been able to grapple with the news or decide how to respond. She wanted to solve that dilemma soon. But first she needed to be with her brother.

She entered the silent chapel that had buzzed with humanity thirty minutes ago. It was just the two of them now—David, a year older than she, a wonderful brother, immortalized in pieces of glass. A kaleidoscope of pictures of him flooded her mind—the two of them rolling like logs down the hill past the cherry orchard toward the river, learning to cast a fly rod on the Test, getting tipsy for the first time with a bottle of wine purloined from one of their parents' parties. There had been none of the rivalry her friends had with their brothers. He was her number-one fan. Pointed her toward Cambridge and a serious degree in economics, not the usual girl's fare. He would have been proud of her work with the aerial surveillance team but didn't live to see it.

The tears she had suppressed broke loose as she traced her hand over the bits of light-infused crystal the artist used to capture his image. *Gone*, she said out loud. *Gone*. Then she sat in the pew and bowed her head.

Prayers wouldn't come to her. Instead she thought of how David's death had changed all of them. Her father had the worst of it. A shadow of himself after his son's plane went down, he drowned himself with whiskey and port. She understood now that it was malignant grief that killed her father and made him force her to give up Bruce, marry Mark, and try to fill in for David. Her father had pummeled her with guilt. "If you go with Duncan, it will kill me," he had said. "It will be the end of Whitcombe Hall—everything we've stood for." He had put the weight of David's unfulfilled life on her, and Amelia had caved. Her own grief had been stoked, her sense of responsibility too strong to overcome. In the end, a marriage to Mark was the only way to save what was left of her family and Whitcombe Hall. When she had been offered jobs in London putting her degree to work, her father had vetoed those too. Nothing could stand in the way of her being the heir to Whitcombe Hall and its trappings—a fate that she had accepted, even when she realized it would swallow her.

*Daddy was sick*, she told herself. *And I was too weak to resist.*

She whispered words of forgiveness for her father and herself and then looked again at the image of her brother in the window. The thoughts she had been seeking came to her without hesitation. *David would want me to be my own woman. I will be.*


Drifts of crocus and snowdrops on the slope leading down to the Test began to cheer her as she walked through them, and on an impulse she gathered her coat around her and rolled the rest of the way to the river bank, just as David and she had done when they were children. When she landed on the swath of soft grass by the stream, she spread her arms and breathed deeply, savoring the fragrances of early spring.

After brushing the blades of grass off her coat, she started toward the river keeper's cottage, still unoccupied almost a year after the war. Jeremy Richards, an amputee from the Normandy invasion, was living with his parents, learning how to walk with a prosthesis. Amelia hadn't filled the river keeper's position yet, hoping that Jeremy might be able to return to his job.

The cottage door had stayed shut since the last time she was here with Bruce. It had been July 21, 1944—two weeks before their time in London when the V rockets fell. They had thought there would be more days in their hideaway on the Test, but his unit shipped out sooner than expected, less than a week after they parted on the stoop of the flat in Bloomsbury.

She brushed some cobwebs from the weathered oak door, pulled the iron key from her pocket, and inserted it in the lock. It turned without a hitch, and she entered the dark room. *Why didn't I come here? It was weakness. Bruce is here.*

Before Amelia could plot her course, she needed air and light. So she opened the windows and shutters, swept the floor, and cut some crocus blossoms to fill a small vase. *This place has to come alive again. Too many sweet moments to let it molder.*

She took the vase into the bedroom and placed it on the small table that held a leather-bound book of poems they had read together. The bedspread hadn't been touched since they left it. The sheets were the ones they had pulled around them on their last night here. She wanted to open the covers and slip into the bed. But she needed to remain clear-headed. A reverie of their touches in this spot wouldn't help her be decisive.

The hob on the gas-fired stove lit right away, and she put the kettle on to boil. The tea, stored in an airtight tin, was probably stale, but it would suffice. While Amelia waited for the tea, she checked the fly rods in the rack beside the fireplace. The bamboo rod with nickel silver fittings she had bought Bruce at Hardy's in London hung on the top rung of the rack. Two of David's rods were in the middle. And her eight-foot, lightweight rod nestled on the bottom rung. There was no sign of Mark there—only the two men she loved.

Amelia hadn't fished since the day she wrote that horrid letter to Bruce. *It was cruel*, she thought. *No warning. Full of lame excuses. I couldn't face him.*

With the whistling kettle drawing her back to the small kitchen, she tried to push the regrets away and plan how to go forward. The duplicity of being engaged to one man and traveling to see another had been tearing at her. *You've been hedging your bets. Afraid to jump in with both feet. Afraid to leave this place. Afraid of the unknown.*

Amelia took the mug of hot tea to the porch, where she sat on the stone steps and looked toward the mill race. While she had been waiting to travel with a cover story—a meeting in New York with her father's brokers—Bruce had almost died. Now he was telling her it was too dangerous for her to visit him.

The defaced photos worried her; the thugs at the brick plant knew who she was and could use her to get at Bruce. But she was ready to stop being put off by fear. She was at a crossroads. *Be honest with Mark. With Bruce. With yourself.*

The decision was made. Take the train to London tomorrow to see Mark and break the engagement, then book the next possible boat to the USA. She wanted to start fresh with Bruce, take time to know him in his home, with his family, far away from the war. Help him if she could. Be able to leave Whitcombe Hall if the path led away from here. Be able to go another way if she couldn't make a life with Bruce.

Amelia pulled on her wading boots and walked to the mill race. The cool air of late afternoon had slowed the hatch that was peaking when she arrived. But there were a few dimples on the water where the trout came up in gentle swells to sip blue-winged olives—miniature flies that were almost invisible until she was in the stream. She had chosen a reel with the fine line needed to deliver the olives with a natural drift.

The first cast slipped the olive down a chute where the fish were feeding. Because there were no takers, she decided to let that spot rest. With no wind and clear water, any unnatural perturbation of the mirror-smooth surface, even two swings of the fly in rapid succession, would spook the trout.

An upstream cast in another direction tempted a fish that flashed bright silver under the fly but didn't follow through with a take. The refusal was enough for her to try an olive that was one size smaller—an exact match would be needed.

She paused to scan the stream and saw a rise form about forty feet below her, still in the heart of the long pool but tucked close to the bank, under an overhanging wild rose bush that would have been trimmed back if the river keeper had been on his watch. Casting again to the first chute would be an easier way to see if she had chosen a right-sized olive, but the challenge of floating the fly under the thorn-encrusted branches of the rose grabbed her attention.

Amelia stripped line off the reel with each arc of her rod until she had gauged the length needed to reach the trout. After dropping the fly upstream from the fish, she guided the olive with a minute nudge to aim it straight down the channel where the trout had risen. With the afternoon sun angled to send torch beams through the water, she could see the fish emerge from its haven under the stream bank and swim toward the fly. It paused for a split second, then flicked its tail and surged upward toward the fly.

She set the hook and let the fish take its first run—a dash into a deep stretch of water, about eight or ten feet below the rose bush. Then she applied as much pressure as she dared to move it out into the stream. If the trout decided to race back in her direction, an acrobatic jump near the rose branches could snare the line and end the fight. At first, the trout followed her lead. She thought it was a twelve- to fourteen-inch fish—one that probably would not have the power to break the line if she continued to steer it into open water. But the fish turned in a sudden move and dived with a heavy thrust back toward the bank. She could see the slab side of the trout now and realized it was a larger fish—not a giant, but a trout that could snap the line if she didn't play it well.

The fish pivoted, raced farther downstream, and erupted out of the water, pulling the line tight against the rose branches. Keeping the rod tip down, Amelia let more line off the reel, giving the fish room to run until she could move again to lead it away from the hazards. *Patience*, she told herself. *Pull too hard and he'll be gone. Too little pressure, and he'll throw off the fly.*

After two more jumps, the trout had spent its energy and gave only light resistance as she brought it toward her. As she held the fish in the net, Amelia saw that the blue-winged olive was held by a slim fiber on the edge of the trout's lip. When she relaxed the line, the fly popped loose, and she eased the trout out of the net into the stream. It swam in place for a few seconds, then darted back to its home.

*Enough for today. The next time I catch a trout, I'll be in Pennsylvania. And I won't be alone.*

# Chapter 25

## BY THE FIRE

*Pennsylvania*
*March 1946*

Snow was coming down in thick flakes that stuck to Bruce's shoulders and nested in the coarse fibers of his Woolrich coat. The temperature was hovering just below freezing, so the snow was wet and clinging—good for making a snowman but tough to shovel. With fourteen inches on the ground and more to come, he was trying to keep ahead of the storm. His walk was passable for now. Bess's needed to be cleared.

The snowstorm was giving Bruce a bit of respite from his worries. With his testimony at the silica hearings scheduled for next Tuesday, he'd been wondering if Lucas would launch another scare attack. There were double locks on his windows and doors now. He was checking under his car before keying the ignition. *Good to be paranoid*, he told himself.

He shrugged off the intrusive thoughts about Lucas and moved up Bess's walk. The wide limbs of her saucer magnolia, loaded with swelling buds that would show pink within the month, were sagging with the weight of the snow. Her

prize rhododendrons were faring better. The broad leaves
sloped downward like slippery pitched roofs that shunted
the snow to the ground. He waded over to the magnolia and
pulled himself up beyond the crotch of the tree so he could
get leverage on the branches. A few stomps of his foot and
the white candles on the buds swished into the air. He would
come back again, after dark, to unburden the tree and save
it from splitting apart.

The snow that coursed over the tops of his boots and
was working its way down his socks didn't bother him. He
knocked at it a bit with his gloved hand and went on with
his work. There had been times this winter when the cold
had taken his thoughts back to France. But today there was
satisfaction in moving the snow off his neighbor's walk. When
the men came later for dinner, there would be some difficult things to discuss—plans for the silica testimony couldn't
be put off. But for now, Bruce put his concerns aside and
immersed himself in a steady rhythm of pushing the shovel,
releasing the load over his shoulder, and starting again.

By the time he reached Bess's front porch, she was out
to greet him. "You scampered up that tree like a boy," she
laughed. "I'm blessed. The town doctor is shoveling my walk
and saving my trees. Can I pay you back? Come for supper
and some cards?"

"Thanks, Bess. Can't do it tonight. Vic and Glen are
coming to prep me for the hearing in Harrisburg. I'm making
stew for them. My mother's recipe."

"Can I come over and whip it up for you?"

"No, I want to do it," he replied. "I rolled in the supplies
before the storm." He pushed the last of the snow off the
steps and moved up to clear the porch.

"They're coming on Monday to strip the old wallpaper
off the walls in the back bedroom," she said. "We'll have that
room looking like a palace for Amelia."

"No need to rush," Bruce said. "I told her to delay the trip until we get the business with the brick plant settled."

"Ah. I'm disappointed. You need to see her."

"I want to be sure it's safe for her to be here," he said.

Bess pulled her coat more tightly around her. "What happened, Bruce? Are you keeping something from me? Did someone rig your furnace to blow up?"

"I've said too much already." He worked in silence to move snow off the porch before turning to face her. "Can you keep your theories to yourself? We're trying to solve this problem, and we don't want rumors flying around town."

"Sure, I'll do what you say," she replied. "But I wonder what Amelia thinks about you putting her off. If I were a young woman that offered her beau a second chance, I wouldn't like being told to stay away."

He stood with the shovel at his side and spoke in a reassuring tone. "I've got to go now to get dinner in the oven. We can play cribbage tomorrow night, and you can tell me all about the bedroom. I want Amelia to be here as soon as we get this mess cleared up."


The kitchen in his house was old-fashioned. If he could buy the house someday, a new kitchen would be at the top of his list. The stove was an early gas model from the teens or early '20s. Refrigeration was from a zinc-lined icebox, custom built into the pantry. When he could afford a Frigidaire, the first thing to go would be that icebox.

The best place to work was on the scrubbed pine table. There were remnants of blue paint left on the legs from long ago. But the top was smooth from wear. Lots of pie crusts had been rolled out on that table.

Bruce put a record on the Victrola, a Benny Goodman swing tune, and began to cut the beef into pieces and dust them with flour. Until he came back from the war and rented this house, he hadn't done much cooking. Now it could be the most relaxing part of the day. He ate Sunday dinner with his family and caught a bite at the Ambrosia about once a week. But other nights that Bess didn't invite him for supper, he cooked for himself. Tonight was his first stab at cooking for others.

With the walks shoveled and the stew in the oven, Bruce slipped into his study to read a novel. He needed a bit more time to relax before he resumed his churning on how to trap Lucas and make his points at the hearing.

His study was a comfortable place. The room was paneled with dark walnut from trees that were cut almost a hundred years ago, and the view looked out on Bess's garden through two mullioned windows with a fireplace between them. It was a good place to build a fire and sit in the cracked leather wing chair beside it.

The novel was a best-seller—*Cass Timberlane* by Sinclair Lewis. Yet the words didn't hold him this afternoon. The book slid down on his chest as he stared at the fire.

A godsend of a coal stove in Rohrwiller began to shimmer in his mind. After Blaise was killed, they had to fight to defend their decimated aid station. But they had been fortunate. Under cover of icy fog, a counteroffensive of American tanks had penetrated the town. When the Germans found the odds were against them, they pulled back to Herrlisheim. By dawn the aid station had been moved to the village's Baroque church, where they were warmed by a towering ceramic stove that had stood there for centuries. Their rush to tend to the wounded would be their last for a few weeks. They were evacuated within a day when the replacement medical unit arrived.

On most days, memories of where he was exactly one year before flashed into his consciousness. On March 9, 1945, his unit was near St. Avold, readying for their push across the Rhine. Usually his reveries of the war were unbidden, but they were starting to lose their hold. He could let some of them float through his mind without stirring much commotion.

Was it just time passing? Anniversaries ticking off? Or did the blast in his office wake him up? Teach him that he was wasting his effort rehashing the past? He needed to use his energy on today's problems instead of letting it drain away in laments about the war.

The fire had dwindled while Bruce tried again to read the novel. So he got up to stoke it with more wood. As he turned back toward his chair, his eyes fixed on the picture of Amelia in her fishing gear by the mill race at Whitcombe Hall. The photo caught the afternoon sun, lighting her hair in gold against the ivy on the river keeper's cottage. They had just landed a trout they had been stalking since lunchtime, and she was radiant, pulsing with delight. In a few minutes they would be inside the cottage—their private place.

Sitting by the fire again, Bruce could feel Amelia's presence. She was teasing him now, brushing his face with a feather she had plucked from a streamer—one of her large trout flies. They were on the rug in front of the fireplace in the cottage. It was May, but there was a chill in the air after nightfall. A small fire was keeping them warm. She moved the feather down his body till it made him erect again. Then she touched her lips along the trace of the feather. When she turned and gave him the smile that always knocked him out, he was gone, lost in this wondrous woman.

The pictures in his mind coursed through that night they spent together. The scenes were vivid, almost real. After the last burst of lovemaking, they fell into a twilight of drowsy murmurs and touches. Her breasts relaxed into his skin like they were part of his body, each breath fusing her deeper into him. When she nuzzled her head against his shoulder, he reached to stroke her hair. She gave a sigh and began to drift asleep.

The sounds of a door shutting and stamping of feet startled him. Then he heard his brother's voice. "You're early. What's up?" Bruce asked.

"I was sitting looking at the snow and thinking too much. So I got in the car and slid my way over here. Need any help with dinner?"

"All done. The stew's in the oven. Come over here by the fire and warm up."

Glen settled in a Windsor chair and put a small notebook on the candle stand between them. "The letter to the editor was a surprise," Glen said. "Kate must have written it. Any other paper wouldn't publish anonymous letters. But the *Hollidaysburg Register* couldn't resist. A woman who admits she lied when she told her husband her doctor tried to seduce her. A story like that could be on one of those radio soap operas."

"If it was Kate, she helped my case. Vouched for me and said she was trying to make her husband jealous. I'll bet he went berserk when he saw the article."

"Mimi heard that she left Lucas. Moved back with her parents."

"A good idea," Bruce said. "I wouldn't want her to get hurt."

"You think he'd go after her?" Glen asked.

"I don't know. Remember when all of us were buddies? I never thought any of us could be a criminal. Funny how life takes its twists."

Glen put his hand on the notebook and looked at the fire. "Yeah, it does take twists. Lucas got the breaks. A scholarship to Penn State, big job right out of school, didn't have to serve in the war, a gorgeous wife, nice kid . . . He screwed it up."

"What's in the notebook?" Bruce asked. "Ideas for the hearing next week?"

"Nah, I've got some lists in there. The reasons I should break it off with Mimi and the few reasons I shouldn't."

"Break it off? I thought you two were solid. "

"You said I should tell her everything . . . let her decide. It was good advice, but I only went halfway. She's seen my burns. Heard about my nightmares. Knows I can get wild. She forgave me after that fiasco on the bandstand on New Year's Eve. She hasn't flinched yet."

"Sounds good so far. What are you holding back?"

Glen lowered his head while he gathered his thoughts. "I think I'll end up like Dad. You know how he was. Okay for a while. Then he'd explode—jump all over us. We couldn't figure it out. Thought it was our fault. But it wasn't. I've treated you the same way. Tore into you the first time we met Sarah. Went nuts when we were at the hunting camp. Almost hurt you bad. I don't see it coming . . . can't control it. Will I explode with Mimi? Hasn't happened yet, but it could.

"Remember when Dad was in those dark moods? Some days I don't want to get out of bed. I think I can't make the store work. Think I'm not good enough. But I cover it up and keep going. Dad ended up a failure. Dead in a car wreck . . . probably a suicide. Mimi doesn't deserve that kind of ending.

"I haven't had a drink since we were at the camp. I've been helping you with the brick plant mess. Acting sane around Mimi. But it won't last. You know me better than anybody. Should I cut away now before I do something crazy?"

Bruce rose from his chair and walked toward the photo of Amelia. His longing to be with her colored his thoughts about Glen. The risks his brother described were real. Yet Glen's doubts might destroy his best chance for love. He had lost enough in the war. He shouldn't have to lose this woman over fears he'd end up like their father.

"This is tough for me," Bruce said. "I want to say it's your decision and I can't help you make it. But I don't want to dodge your question."

"No dodging. I can take whatever you say."

Bruce turned to face his brother. "Tell her about Dad. You're not the same as him. You know what to watch for. You'll do your best to stay straight. Marry her if she'll have you."

"Thanks. I needed to hear those words."

"And meet with Sarah Avery, like I suggested. She knows enough psychiatry to help you stay straight."

"Yes, sir."

"Come on. We can stir the stew and pull the kitchen table in here for dinner. We'll want to eat by the fire."

# Chapter 26

## THE CAPITAL

hen they entered the capitol rotunda, the men stopped to view the sea of marble and gilt. Assuming the role of tour guide, Vic reeled off superlatives for Bruce and Glen, who hadn't visited the building before. "Teddy Roosevelt called it the handsomest building in America, and it has our history painted on those walls. Look at the pioneers building cabins in that mural. Could have been from the early days of Hollidaysburg."

"We need to keep moving," Bruce said. "I don't want to miss seeing Phil Silverman before the hearing."

"Is that him?" Glen asked. "There's an old fellow in a tweed coat on the balcony waving at us."

"Yep, that's the man," Bruce said. "He wants us to join him up there."

They set off at a quick clip to climb the white marble staircase. Phil and another man stood at the top, waiting for them.

"I thought we would spot you from this eagle's nest," Phil said as he greeted Bruce with a warm handshake. The professor had aged since Bruce saw him last in 1941. His hair was white, but he was still fit—a wiry man who had been a regular at the Philadelphia Athletic Club for decades. "Let me introduce you to Alex Barton from Cornell. He's a fount of wisdom on silicosis. Wrote the classic articles after the Hawk's Nest Tunnel disaster in 1930 and knows the pathophysiology better than anyone."

The men shook hands while Bruce introduced Vic and Glen. "They're my cheerleaders," Bruce said. "Wouldn't let me come here by myself."

"Let's find a corner where we can talk," Phil said. "I want you to hear what Alex will say when he testifies. It will be strong stuff."

They walked down the corridor and found an open door to an ornate room decorated with more paintings of colonial Pennsylvania. The familiar scene of William Penn meeting with Indians on the banks of the Delaware River stared down at them.

"It's a copy," Phil said. "I've been here before to testify about black lung. Didn't make much progress that time. Maybe today will be better. It won't hurt if we scoot in here for a few minutes."

"Don't hesitate," Vic said. "We pay enough taxes to borrow this room for a little while."

After they settled in chairs at one end of a mahogany conference table, Phil began. "If this hearing is like the others, they'll have stacked most of the senators against us. And they'll be brutal. The first time I testified, they came at me so strong I ended up with spit drooling down my mouth. They'll try to get under your skin. Make you overreact. Do anything to make you look like a fool. Their modus operandi is to discredit the witness. So you need to stay calm, stick to the points you want to make. Act like a doctor who can't be ruffled.

"The other thing they'll do is call some stooges the company's bought off. I don't know who they've found, but there'll be a pulmonologist who will say there's no research that proves silica causes fibrotic lung disease. There'll be a bogus scientist who will claim that silica doesn't destroy alveoli. So let the traitors impugn themselves. Let them pave their way to Hades."

"Well put," Alex said. "When I testified in West Virginia about the Hawk's Nest Tunnel, there were only two senators from Wheeling who were interested in finding the truth. The others gave the company a pass. Ignored testimony that they dry drilled the tunnel and only did wet drilling when the inspectors arrived. We did get some action in Congress. They had to pay attention to 764 dead. But the Labor Department standards are ignored. Only fifteen years, and Hawk's Nest is forgotten."

Their notes of caution didn't surprise Bruce. He had assumed that many of the legislators would be pro-industry. As part-time senators, most were businessmen themselves. And Allegheny Refractories had probably contributed to their campaign funds, if not more. He had read accounts of hearings when Union Carbide bosses said they hadn't seen dust clouds at the Hawk's Nest Tunnel, and congressmen didn't press to expose the lies. Yet the reports he had studied weren't all pessimistic. Some progress was being made. Granite workers were using water to hold down the powder from their drills. Exhaust systems were being used on bagging machines for pulverized silica. The brick industry was at the tail end of the improvement curve. It was time for them to change.

"I brought the X-rays," Bruce said. "Couldn't bring the man we X-rayed after his car accident here to testify. But I found something else that may get their attention."

He motioned to a satchel he had placed on the table. "Have any idea what might be in there?"

Vic laughed. "What kind of trick are you going to pull? Do you have a bag of silica you're going to blow in the faces of the senators?"

"You'll find out soon. It'll be a surprise."

Phil gave a thumbs-up sign in approval. "Irv Henderson, my state senator, got the hearing on the books. And he'll lead off the questioning. I'll tip him off that we have some drama in store so he should call you last. Irv can say that you're the GP who has seen the destruction, and you'll tell the committee what it's like to have silicosis. They'll have to listen."

Lucas was at the fringe of a group of company executives and lawyers who were gathering at the front of the chamber. Bruce could tell that he was on edge. Although he was trying to talk with Fenelli, the company doctor, Lucas's hands were in motion, straightening his tie, scratching at the back of his neck.

Glen grabbed his arm as he started to walk toward Lucas. "Don't go over there. It'll light him up. He hates you, Bruce."

He slipped from his brother's grip, moved across the room, and pulled Lucas aside. "There's still time for you to do the right thing," he said. "Fix the problems at the plant and stop coming after me. I know you had my furnace rigged, but I won't say anything if you make the right choices. Yeah, try to please your bosses. But you can save some lives. Do the simple stuff to cut the dust."

Lucas set his jaw as if he were about to go on the attack. He stood erect, stretching himself to his maximum height. Even puffed up, he stood six inches below Bruce. He was about to spit out a retort when he checked himself. After hesitating for a few beats, he bit his lip and responded. "For God's sake, Duncan. We're in the Senate chambers. Keep it quiet."

A hint of pleading in Lucas's voice and a sag in the ramrod stance told Bruce that he had got to him. "Let's sit down for a minute. They're not ready to start the hearing, and they won't hear us if we keep our voices down."

"I can't talk with you now. My boss is in the room. You guys are the enemy."

"No, we're not. If you want to stay in business, you need to take care of your men. We're doing you a favor."

Lucas looked toward the crowded table where the Allegheny Refractories men were gathered. They were huddled over their papers and hadn't seemed to notice his absence. "You didn't do me any favors with my wife. I'm going to get her back. Stay away from her."

"You saw the letter in the newspaper," Bruce replied with a steady tone. "She must have told you the truth . . . I'm innocent."

Lucas sighed. "Yeah, she tried to manipulate me. It backfired."

"I have no interest in Kate," Bruce said. "She's your wife; I'm trying to find my own. Believe me—I want your family to be together. And I want you to keep your job. You know what needs to be done. You're the one that has the answers."


The hearing was proceeding as expected. Irv Henderson had called Phil, who explained the pathophysiology of silicosis and showed photos of microscopic images of silica embedded in lung tissue. There had been some raised eyebrows when he demonstrated that silica crystals went straight through a sieve with pores so fine that they held water. "The lungs are close to defenseless," he explained. "The particles are so tiny they can go anywhere. Millions of the little darts get stuck in the lung and won't let go. Cough all you want, and they won't shake loose."

Alex explained how tunneling through the granite at Hawk's Nest with no ventilation and no water suppression had produced a dense fog of dust that ruined lungs at a rapid clip. Many of the men were sick in less than six months, could no longer do the job, and drifted off to die in some other place. The decline of a brickworker from chronic silicosis—a more insidious killer—could take ten or more years. But the result was the same. Lungs that could no longer pull oxygen from the air.

The senators from the rural areas—homes of the mines and brick plants—teed off on Phil and Alex; they questioned the link between Hawk's Nest and industries in their counties, impugned the witnesses as ivory tower professors, and claimed that stiff regulations would shutter the businesses that kept America strong.

The experts were unflappable. They had been through other attempts to demean them and were armed with the Department of Labor recommendations they had helped write after Hawk's Nest. "The solutions are simple," Alex testified. "Invest money in vacuum devices to pull the dust away from the man and his machine, use water wherever you can to keep the silica out of the air, require respirators when the other methods don't give full control, test the air to see if your precautions are working. Have your men checked by a doctor regularly, get chest X-rays, and pull men off duty, give them another job, if they show early signs of silicosis."

Bruce's turn came toward the end of the hearing. He thought that Phil and Alex had made a strong case for anti-silicosis regulations, but most of the senators seemed unmoved. They had become fitful or distracted as the afternoon progressed. He supposed they were thinking of what they would have for dinner or how their first sip of whiskey would taste. About a third of the congressmen had already drifted away when the tall clock in the room struck four.

"Dr. Duncan," Irv Henderson announced. "You've personally treated men with silicosis from the Blairton plant. Tell the committee what the illness does to a worker."

Bruce's impatience to get the story out and frustration with the ignorance of the senators had made him tense, ramped up his nervousness about speaking. The muscles around his left eye began to twitch, a warning sign that his anger was surging. *Cool down . . . don't let them get to you*, he told himself.

Bruce motioned to his brother, who wheeled a bank of screens to the front and plugged the device into the wall. Then he paused to look around the room at the senators and the executives from Allegheny Refractories. His unease began to fade as he coached himself on how to act. *Look them in the eye. You have the facts. Use them.*

"To give you a picture of silicosis, I asked the Harrisburg hospital to lend us an X-ray viewing box. If you watch closely, you'll learn to recognize the signs of silicosis so you could spot them yourself. The first group of films I brought with me are from people in this room.

"No, I'm not saying anyone here has the disease," he said as he moved toward the screen. "We need to start with recognizing a healthy lung. This film is from a fifty-two-year-old man with no known chest disease. It's an X-ray of Senator Henderson's lungs. He kindly consented to bring the film along so we can compare a man who has spent over five decades breathing Philadelphia air, which I found not too clean when I was a med student there, with X-rays of men who have had a different line of work—making bricks. The other two X-rays in the normal set are from my brother, Glen, who just hooked up the X-ray viewer, and from Dr. Silverman, another Philadelphia air breather. Glen got burned pretty badly in the war when his plane crashed coming back to England. His lungs got scorched, and he had trouble breathing for a while. But they healed with time. Something that never happens with silicosis. Dr. Silverman just turned seventy. I asked for his X-ray to show what older lungs may look like if they haven't had to breathe silica dust."

Bruce took out a pointer and demonstrated clear lung fields of people with no pulmonary disease, outlines of a healthy-sized heart, and uncongested hila where the major bronchi sprouted from their tracheas. "There are a few tiny nodules in Dr. Silverman's lungs. Probably scars from a bad chest cold from years ago. But nothing to worry about. He has lungs that are almost as vibrant as our senator's. All of them could probably hike the Grand Canyon if they wanted to do it."

The gambit of showing the senator's X-ray had caught their attention. The undercurrent of side conversations had stopped. None of the remaining senators and observers were readying to leave.

"The next X-ray is from a worker at the Blairton plant. He was in a car accident that happened right in front of my eyes. We were able to stop his bleeding, but I was shocked when I saw his chest X-ray. He's forty-three, a few years younger than Senator Henderson. But look at the differences. The roots of both sides of his lungs are loaded with nodules. Some of them are as big as baseballs. And out here in the main part of the lungs, there are streaky white fibers everywhere. The fibers are the big cords of scarred tissue you can see on the X-ray, but there are thousands of smaller cords that don't show up on a film. They act like nooses on the lung tissue. Strangle the life out of the tissue until it's screaming for oxygen. This man used to play basketball and walked up and down the mountains hunting deer and turkeys. Now he can't walk twenty feet without stopping to gasp for breath. He can't walk up the stairs in his house, so his bed is in the living room. His dream is to live long enough to see his son graduate from high school, but I doubt he'll make it."

He pivoted and looked straight at the men from Allegheny Refractories. "Don't blame this man for what I'm saying here. He wants to keep working at the Blairton plant—at the desk job he got since his accident. He has a lot of courage to let me show his X-rays."

A senator from Scranton stood up. "How do we know it's silicosis and he got it at the brick plant? Maybe he has cancer or TB. An X-ray from one man doesn't prove anything."

"You're correct, Senator. One X-ray doesn't make the case," Bruce replied as he put five other X-rays on the screen in rapid succession. "These are films from other men from the Blairton works. All of them were certified well by the company doctor but came to the Altoona hospital when they got sick. We don't know exactly how many men who work at Blairton have silicosis. But we tested two dozen of them, and sixteen had poor lung function."

He stepped back and waved his hand down the display of X-rays. "So which is the worst? If you were picking a film of a man who died of silicosis, which one would it be?"

The senators sat in silence, their eyes scanning the collection of pictures of fibrous lungs.

"Five men with silicosis whose traces are on this screen are all younger than fifty and still work at the Blairton plant." He tapped the pointer on the last film on the right. "This man had to stop work at forty-eight because he was so short of breath he couldn't do the job. Lasted three more years till he finally smothered to death. His family gave me permission to show you something very personal—his legacy, if you will."

Bruce moved back to the table and opened the satchel. "Here are his lungs. They're preserved very close to how they looked when the pathologist pulled them out of his chest. Gnarled like old dried-up prunes, shrunk to a shadow of this other set I brought to show you."

Bruce reached back into the bag to reveal another large bottle. "This man was sixty-four when he died of a heart attack. His lungs were in fairly good shape compared to the fellow who ended up in the first jar."

He moved among the senators so they could examine them closely. But most averted their eyes. When he approached the table with the Allegheny Refractories representatives, Lucas looked at the jars and gave a small nod of his head. Was he ceding the point? Was he acknowledging that something had to be done?

"We've heard enough from this witness," the senator from Scranton said. "Our time is up. Mr. Chairman, I request we adjourn and deliberate on this testimony at a later date."

"Hear, hear," another senator cried out. "I second the motion for adjournment."

# Chapter 27

## PARALYSIS

——————

After finishing his Saturday morning office hours in his temporary place at the Presbyterian Church, Bruce was in Sarah's lab, wrapping up his work and looking forward to his afternoon off duty. Repairs to his office had been more of a job than expected. So he was leaning on Sarah's kindness to muddle through till his suite was ready.

Her lab was more inviting than his Spartan setup. The bright yellow walls were accented with paintings of forest scenes in all four seasons. Her stools had comfortable, padded seats, covered in a blue-checked gingham. A radio sat on the counter to entertain her while she ran tests. He had never seen a lab like this, but he liked her touch. *Why not? I could learn a lesson here.*

While he prepared a slide for a blood count, he thought again about his performance at the hearing. He had gone over the testimony many times but couldn't let it go. Vic was full of compliments. Glen was more circumspect. "Too many of them yawning in there for my taste; you did your best to wake them up." The three doctors—Bruce, Phil, and Alex—conferred after their testimony and agreed they had made their points. Yet Bruce was troubled. Had it been presumptuous to bring the X-rays and the specimens? Had he gone overboard when he moved around the room like a professor teaching class? He had startled some of them when he pulled out the lungs. Then they had shut down the hearing without any deliberation. "Heard enough from this witness," the senator had said. It would be weeks or months before they learned the results, if any were to be had.

"Deep in thought, I see," Sarah said as she entered the room. "Too deep to take a break for a bite of lunch at the Ambrosia? I'm ready for my last patient, and she's only here for a blood pressure checkup. I'll be out of here in fifteen minutes."

Bruce turned to see a tall woman with a smile leaning against the frame of the open door. In her white coat and hair wrapped in a tight bun, she looked professional. Still, there was no hiding her beauty.

"You can't work all the time, and I want to hear what happened in Harrisburg. I think I deserve a firsthand account. Aren't I part of the team?"

He returned the friendly parry. "First team and a top player. The fifteen-minute warning is accepted. Let me do this blood count, and I'll treat you to Pete's best."

She laughed. "Offer accepted."

As he checked the slide to see if it was dried and ready for the microscope, Bruce thought of Sarah working next door. She had shown a deft touch in treating his lacerations and burns. Her technical skills were first rate; the suturing looked like the work of a plastic surgeon. The largest puncture on his leg had been a ragged mess, a stellate wound that needed careful debriding. She had kept him distracted with breezy conversation while she snipped the macerated skin from the margins and created a flap to cover the hunk of tissue that was torn away.

They were becoming friendlier as he visited her office each day to do his lab work. *We'll have to watch it,* he thought. There were iron-clad reasons why romance shouldn't enter their relationship. Sarah had told him about her commitment to a single life, oddly enough when she was removing his sutures. "Do you think I'm weird because I don't have a boyfriend?" she had asked. Without giving him a chance to respond, she answered her own question. "Don't spread any rumors, buster. I'm not a lesbian. But medicine and a family don't mix for a woman doctor." Was she putting him on notice? Laying down a law while she brushed over his skin with her gloved hands?

Even if Amelia wasn't coming to visit, Sarah would need to stay out of bounds. The small-town backlash against two doctors who were involved with one another could be nasty. Their lunch would need to be a businesslike gathering. Nothing more. With his office repairs nearing completion, they soon would be back in their separate spaces. A good thing.

Putting his musings about Sarah aside, Bruce focused on viewing the blood smear from his patient. If he was correct in his suspicions, the white-haired woman who had been one of his teachers in high school had pernicious anemia. The hemoglobin value was low, and her symptoms pointed toward this diagnosis. Miss Ayers had been one of Magnuson's patients and had come to Bruce for the first time yesterday. After she told him she was exhausted all the time and felt pins and needles in her legs, Bruce asked her to open her mouth. The telltale sign was in front of him, a beefy red tongue.

He put the slide on Sarah's Leitz microscope, a prewar model from Germany that was much better than his American-made Spencer, and focused on the cells he had stained earlier. As he sharpened the image, his sleuthing instincts surged. One of the pleasures of his work was the satisfaction of putting the pieces together to make a diagnosis, especially when there was a solution to the problem.

As Bruce expected, the red blood cells were misshapen. Many were ovals instead of round discs. And some were macrocytes, a juvenile form two or more times the size of a mature cell. A few hyperpigmented white cells added to the picture of classic vitamin $B_{12}$ deficiency and pernicious anemia. Miss Ayers was his first case. Some injections of $B_{12}$ and she should be able to enjoy her retirement.

"Help me right now; where are you?" he heard a man scream. "My son's dying. He can't breathe." Bruce ran through the door and found Sarah charging from the other direction. It was Lucas with his limp son in his arms. "I thought he just had a cold and let him sleep. Couldn't wake him up."

Bruce grabbed the boy and rushed him into Sarah's exam room with Lucas tailing behind. The man was frantic. "It's my fault. I should have checked on him."

"Sit down and let us work," Bruce said as he tore the boy's shirt off. The four-year-old was still moving air but not much. An ominous, cyanotic blue color was creeping over his face. The breaths were rapid and shallow. His pulse was racing.

"Was he weak yesterday?" Sarah asked. "Did he have trouble moving?"

"Yeah," Lucas replied. "I have him for the weekend. Didn't want to eat last night. So I put him to bed early. Didn't hear a squeak from him all night. Looked in this morning, and he was still sleeping. At least I thought he was sleeping."

Sarah did a rapid exam of his chest, listening and tapping to see if he had pneumonia, while Bruce scrambled to find a surgical kit.

"His chest is clear, probably not pneumonia," she said.

"Looks like polio to me," Bruce said as he pulled on rubber gloves. "The paralysis is going fast. We need to do a tracheostomy."

"Agreed," she said. "You do it. I'll hold the boy in case he feels any pain. No time for anesthesia."

"I can't watch you cut my boy's neck," Lucas said. "Go ahead. I'll close my eyes. Can I hold his hand?"

"Yes, come up here and stand beside me," Sarah told him. "We need to work fast."

"I did plenty of these in the war, Lucas. We'll get air in him real soon."

Bruce gave the boy's neck a quick scrub with iodine solution and plunged the scalpel into his trachea. Lucas Jr. didn't move. The hypoxia was shutting down his brain.

"Hand me that tray of trach tubes," Bruce told Sarah. "I'll need the smallest one."

He took the tube from her and slipped it into the hole in the boy's neck. Then, taking a syringe, he filled the cuff of the tube with air and turned the valve to seal the device.

"Now let's get him pinked up," Bruce said as he began to squeeze the ventilating bag. "Stay close to him, Lucas. When he gets some oxygen back in his system, he might start to move. We don't know where the paralysis has struck except on his breathing. You might need to hold him for a while. We don't want to jostle the trach till I can get it secured and stop the bleeding."

"I'll do the ventilation while you finish the surgery," Sarah said.

With the tracheostomy in place, the boy's color started to improve. It started in his face, which had been a ghostly blue, and then spread to his arms and legs. But he wasn't moving any of his limbs. Sarah held up his hand to look at his nail beds. "Still dusky but looking better. We're going to get him through this scare, Lucas."

"What will happen to him? Will he be able to breathe on his own? Will he be able to walk?"

"Hard to say right now," she replied. "We had some cases like this when I was in med school. That's why I stocked the office with trach tubes. Sometimes the paralysis goes away in a few days or weeks. For now we need to keep someone on that bag all the time till he can breathe on his own or we can get him into an iron lung. We'll teach you how to use the bag."

"The trach's secure," Bruce said. "I'm going to call an ambulance to take him to the Altoona hospital. They can send him to Children's in Pittsburgh if he doesn't shake off the paralysis soon. Sarah and I will go in the ambulance. Lucas, pick up Kate and meet us there."

"How can I tell her what happened? I almost killed our boy."

"It's not your fault," Sarah said. "I'll call her before we leave for the hospital. Your kid's in deep trouble. He'll need both of you."

"Oh shit—I deserve this punishment. And the guy I've screwed over saves my boy's life. What can I say?"

"Just thank him. And go get your wife. We'll see you at the hospital."


Salmon pink flames streaked the darkening sky as they walked down the hill from the hospital. Bruce and Sarah were on their way to Mastrioni's restaurant to make up for their missed lunch at the Ambrosia.

The boy was stable, his lungs inflated artificially by shifts of nurses and volunteers, an hour at a time until they passed the job to the next one. Hal Logsdon, the pediatrician, was in charge. Their job was over. Nothing more could be done now except keeping air moving in and out, praying, and waiting. The bulbar paralysis had come on like a storm with little warning. It could pass in a few days or get worse.

"Look at the glow around the cathedral dome," Sarah said. "The sun's behind it. Just in the right place. I'm not much for signs, but I hope that halo means something. The kid needs God on his side."

Bruce signaled to show he agreed, and they walked on. The grimy railroad city usually gave him twinges of sadness. Rows of dispiriting wooden houses with paint stained gray from coal dust were crammed together with only narrow concrete passageways between. Yet the excitement from the afternoon was still with him, and the shimmering light was transforming the city. The last rays of sun glinted off the windows of the YMCA where he had played basketball as a boy. The upper floors of Gable's Department Store, a nondescript tower of bricks during the day, jutted above the skyline with crisp shadows against a luminous red façade. The scene reminded him of a Hopper painting.

"Do emergencies get you pumped up?" he asked. "Push me to the limit and I feel more alive. Everything's extra sharp for me now." He pointed toward the department store. "I wouldn't notice the light playing on those bricks on an ordinary day. Leftover adrenaline, I guess."

"Yes, it's the same for me."

"You might think I'm crazy, but sometimes I miss the war. Never thought I'd say that. Lots of adrenaline."

"Is it boring to be back in Hollidaysburg?"

Her question made him pause. Most of his days he saw patients with ordinary illnesses—nothing like the excitement at the front. And he had jumped into a new battle at the brick plant. Was he looking for danger? Did he want to keep fighting?

"No," he said. "I've gotten myself into enough trouble to make it interesting."

Bruce thought of offering her his arm as they walked together—a natural thing to do. He was talking about things he usually kept to himself, and it was tempting to cultivate this intimacy of words and get closer. But he held back.

"You were in top form today," Sarah said. "Doing a trach on a little kid isn't easy. I'm glad you were there. I'm not sure I could have done it."

"You were the one who was prepared. Had a pediatric trach. That was brilliant. I would have had to improvise if he showed up at my office."

They talked more about their afternoon as they walked downhill until Bruce stopped and motioned to a low stone wall skirting a school playground. A lone boy was shooting baskets in semidarkness at the outdoor court. Otherwise the playground was quiet. The sun had just set. "Let's sit here for a while," he said. "We'll be at Mastrioni's soon, and I can't say these things there or in the cab going back to Hollidaysburg."

She stopped but appeared hesitant. "We shouldn't be talking about anything that couldn't be said in public."

"Agreed. But I have to tell you something. I can't hide it."

"Okay. Just a few minutes. It's almost dark. We need to get to dinner."

He reached to cover her hand as they sat on the wall. She didn't take it away.

"I like working with you," Bruce started. "And I like more than the work. It's easy to be with you."

He hesitated to decide how to parse his words. "Even if you weren't off limits, I have an English girlfriend. I would have married her if she hadn't given me the boot. Done anything to make it work. She's back in the mix. Coming here before too long, and I want to give it a chance."

"You don't need to explain. I know about her."

She stood and turned toward him. "You're right I'm off limits. If I was going to throw my career away, you would be first in line. But it's not going to happen. You're going to convince that English girl to stay in Hollidaysburg, and we'll go on being the two docs in our little town. We'll know what could have been. No one else will know. Just colleagues and friends. A deal?"

"A deal." He shook her hand and smiled. "Though part of me wanted you to say something different."

Sarah laughed. "You get one kiss from this dedicated spinster, and that's it. It'll have to last a lifetime."

"Make it a good one," he said.

She did.

# Chapter 28

## TURBULENCE

—

*B*ess was waiting. When he stepped out of the cab, she pulled a shawl around her shoulders and hurried past her dormant rose garden, taking the stone path to his house. Her flashlight darted on the creek rock and the creeping thyme swirling between the cracks.

She caught up to Bruce as he was opening his mailbox. "I heard about Kate and Lucas's boy. It's all over town. They say you saved his life."

Bruce shrugged. "It's polio. We'll see more of it."

"There's some dinner in the oven for you. A pork roast. Want to eat at my house, or can I deliver?"

"Thanks, but I had dinner at Mastrioni's after we got the boy settled at the hospital. It was a little celebration for getting the kid through the day."

"Do you have enough energy left for a game of cribbage? I want to hear how you got the boy breathing again. The word is that Lucas brought his son to Sarah's office and you happened to be there working in the lab. True?"

He laughed. "How do people in this town know so much about what I do?"

"It's not so mysterious," Bess said. "Your friend Dr. Taylor was at the hospital delivering a baby and called Glen to let him know what happened. He told your mother, and it didn't take long for all of us to know. We're your fan club, Bruce."

Bruce opened the mailbox and found a letter from Amelia. If he had calculated the number of days correctly, it would hold the response to his letter about postponing her visit.

"I'll take a pass on the cribbage tonight. I'm bushed, and there's a letter from England in my hand. Amelia gets top priority."

"As it should be," Bess said. "I'm invited to Judge Clapper's tomorrow for Sunday lunch with your family. You can tell us about your exploits then."

"I think I'll be upstaged. The judge hasn't entertained like this since his wife died. I'll bet he has an agenda."

"Could be. Your mother is smiling a lot these days. They eat dinner together every evening. He leaves by nine o'clock. Very discreet."

"The dinners aren't a secret. Glen and I stay away from Mother's house in the evenings unless we're invited."

"Same for me."

He held Amelia's letter to his chest. "I need to tend to my own business. We can talk more tomorrow."


The remnants of his day needed sorting out before he could open the letter. And the hard-seated Windsor chair by a cold fireplace seemed the best place to take stock of what had happened. His feelings whipsawed between guilt and excitement. Guilt for crossing the line Sarah drew. Excitement from the aftershocks of a kiss that would never be repeated. The once-in-a-lifetime qualification gave it extra meaning. He wouldn't forget it.

There was more remorse when his eyes moved to the unopened letter from Amelia on the table beside him. After an unexpected chance to be with her again, he was flirting with another woman. *Beyond flirting*, he corrected himself.

He went back and forth—a volley of thoughts castigating himself for attempting to weasel into Sarah's life; another blast for sullying his rekindled relationship with Amelia.

Then a new stream of ideas opened up. Had he put off Amelia's trip because of the danger? Or were the reasons more complicated? Sarah had stitched his wounds the day he wrote the letter putting a hold on Amelia's visit.

An undercurrent of anger began to surface. Amelia was still engaged and would come to the USA on a pretense that she needed to meet with brokers in New York. Was he fooling himself that she would want to live in this small town? She had crushed him once and was lying to her fiancé. Could he ever trust her?

The only certainty was that just two women had transfixed him, and both were impossible prizes. Was he on a quest to prove something to himself? Did he need to have the most precious jewel?

*Time to grow up*, he told himself. *Forget them. Something will come along. Just don't make it like Lucas and Kate.*

An hour later, he had built a fire and settled down in the old leather chair. His thoughts had turned for a while to the boy with polio and his chances of making it through the night. A call to the hospital had been reassuring. The ventilation bag was keeping him alive, and the trach he had placed was holding up well.

Amelia's letter was still on the table. He was ready to read it now.

*March 7, 1946*
*Dear Bruce,*

*Your last letter arrived two days ago, on the day we dedicated the window to my brother. Since then my mind has been filled with pictures of those men from the brick plant coming after you. If they tried to blow up your office, what else will they do? While I've been puttering around waiting for the Queen Mary to get refitted, you were almost killed.*

*Please, please watch out. I can't ask you to stop pressing them. I know your fiber. But you have so much more to give if they don't take you down.*

*Your warning to postpone my visit won't deter me. I want to be there now. We dodged the V rockets, so a standoff with a brick company shouldn't stop us from being together.*

*The earliest passage I can find is on the Drottingholm leaving Gothenburg on March 29 and arriving in New York on April 3. Because there are no other options, the roundabout route through Sweden will have to do. I'll spend just one day in New York before boarding the train to Altoona. You can expect to see me on Friday, April 5, with a beaming smile, ready for bodyguard duties.*

*A lot has happened in the last two days. Hearing that you are in trouble stirred me to action, and I've become an unencumbered woman. The ruse of my engagement to Mark couldn't go on a day longer. I told him about you and broke it off. Whitcombe Hall can sink into the ground, and my father will disown me from heaven. But I'll be free.*

*Who is the young lady doctor who is treating your wounds? Should I be jealous? Please remember, I'm coming to you, as fast as I can. We'll find a way, I'm certain.*

*By the time this letter gets to you, it will only be about two weeks till I arrive in Pennsylvania. Don't worry about having arrangements in place. I can stay in a hotel and find a car to drive. You can do your doctoring every day, and I'll keep myself busy until your last patient treks out of your office. We'll have a month to see what happens.*

*In my heart, I'm with you today.*

*Love,*
*Amelia*

*She did it again,* he said to himself. Like their first day on the river Test, Amelia surprised him with a gift so large that he could feel her warmth spreading through him. Could she have known that the letter would reach him when he needed it the most?

She had shown her courage. Broke off her engagement when it could mean she'd lose Whitcombe Hall. Her failsafe option had been jettisoned. Amelia was very serious now. It would be more than a brief reprise and another goodbye.

Could he match her resolve? He'd found that another woman could sway him. The ambivalence had been palpable. But Amelia's magic worked again. He would be ready for her.

When Bruce opened the front door to the judge's farmhouse, the aroma of roast beef wafted over him. He could see the sideboard loaded with pies and could hear the bustle from the kitchen. During the war, a meal like this was a far-off dream. Bruce remembered a scrawny chicken that a French farmer had given him after he had set his daughter's broken ankle. He and Blaise had stewed that bird to get every ounce of flavor out of it. A few carrots were all they could find to add to the pot. In December 1944, it had been a fine meal—the best they would have together.

An image of Blaise lying by the ruptured stove in Rohr-willer flashed into his mind. A thickness grabbed him in the chest, but he took a deep breath and moved on toward the kitchen. He was doing better at short-circuiting these unbidden memories. *Enjoy the dinner. Don't let yourself sink into that hole.*

The judge's voice bellowed over the clamor. "Bruce, you're late. Get out here right away. We've got some big news."

They were gathered around Mimi, who was showing off a diamond engagement ring. Glen stood aside with his face curled in a grin.

"A wedding next month," the judge said. "Your brother is going to beat you to the altar."

Bruce paused to absorb the scene. Mimi was glowing. Glen was coming toward him.

"I took your advice," Glen said as he hugged Bruce. "She knows the risk but didn't hesitate. Said yes right away."

"I knew she would," Bruce replied.

"We're not going to waste any time. We'll be on our honeymoon six weeks from today."

Bruce's smile widened. "When is the wedding? I might have a guest if it's after April 5."

"Presbyterian church. The full deal on Saturday, April 27. Who's the guest? Any chance she's English?"

"You guessed it. Amelia moved her trip ahead. Found a boat out of Sweden. I doubt Lucas will cause trouble now. How could he after we saved his son? But we'll still have to be careful."

"Hey, what are you two talking about?" the judge said. "Come on over here. I'm breaking out the champagne for a toast."

He produced bottles of Pol Roger while Bruce's mother passed out the glasses. "I just happened to have some of the good stuff waiting for a special occasion. Who wants to say some words over this fine couple?"

Bruce took a glass and stepped forward. "To Mimi and Glen. The brightest future for you."

After the glasses clinked and the bubbles slid down their throats, Alice was the first to speak. Her face was flushed, and her eyes were sparkling. "Brian Clapper, come here and hold my hand."

The judge joined her as the group fell silent. "This kind man wouldn't want to take anything away from the lovely moments we've just had. We're so happy for Mimi and Glen . . . but he stocked the champagne for another announcement.

I can't hold it back. He's asked me to marry him, and it's going to happen. July 4, right here at the farm. A good old-fashioned party. And the fireworks won't be just in the sky."

The room erupted with cheers as the judge leaned over to give Alice a soft kiss. "Young love and old love," he said. "It's all good."

A double engagement was more than Bruce had expected when he turned down the judge's lane less than an hour ago. And his revelation about Amelia's visit had added more cheer to the festivities. He had work to do to ensure the cheer lasted.

# Chapter 29

## RECKONING

———

*A*s Lucas promised, the lock on the timber gate to the Spruce Creek Trout Club was open. Bruce loosened the chain and swung the gate inward. Only the two of them would be here on a Wednesday evening in mid-March. In a few weeks when spring was in full force, the club would be busy with anglers who had the connections to join or were fortunate to be invited to fish here.

He closed the gate behind him so drivers on the mountain road wouldn't be tempted to trespass on the grounds of the storied club. J. Edgar Hoover was a member. Jimmy Stewart had fished there. And Allegheny Refractories had fishing badges to bestow on customers or politicians they were trying to influence. Bruce had passed the entrance many times but hadn't been inside the enclave until today.

The gravel road curved a hundred feet from the gate and then opened up to a hemlock-lined track that led straight toward the lodge. Unlike the forest roads Bruce usually traveled, there were no bumps to rattle his car or water-filled potholes to skirt around. The *Private, No Trespassing* signs were carved from wood with letters painted in gold like a doctor's shingle—not paper signs nailed to trees. The place reeked of privilege.

Bruce was edgy. The closer he got to the lodge, the more he thought it was a bad idea to meet Lucas here. The club was the kind of place that would grate on him any day. And it was Lucas's home turf. Seeing the beautiful stretch of trout stream in front of the lodge didn't help. Lucas was the only one who lived in the area who belonged. Locals were shut out of this prime section of one of the best trout streams in the East.

"What do you think of the place?" Lucas asked as he greeted his guest on the front porch. "Come inside where it's warmer. I have some drinks set up for us."

Bruce stayed on the grass. "Let's walk along the stream. No drinks for me tonight."

Lucas attempted a smile, but he dropped it quickly when he saw the tight set of Bruce's jaw. After Bruce watched Lucas squirm for a moment, he led the way toward the water.

They passed by wooden benches on the manicured lawn and crossed a footbridge over the creek. Bruce wanted some distance from the imposing lodge, so he pushed on through a stand of mature oaks until they came to a clearing where the stream swirled in a deep pool at the base of a sycamore tree. This part of the stream had been left in its natural state. The bank was covered with moss, and a half-rotten log gave them a place to sit. The mottled white and gray-brown of the peeling sycamore bark brightened the shadows as the sun angled over the ridge to the west.

"We have about a half hour before it gets dark," Bruce said. "You invited me here. What's your agenda?"

"I wanted us to be alone. No chance anyone could overhear."

"The fish won't be talking."

Lucas swallowed, got up from the log, and stared across the stream at the roots of the sycamore. "I did it," he blurted. "I wrote the letters to the newspaper, broke into your house, stole the pictures of your English girlfriend, hired the Garnersville men to scare you. I didn't think anyone would get hurt. It got out of control."

"I could send you to jail."

"I know. Why don't you?"

Bruce was calm now as he sat on the log and thought about how to leverage the opportunity. "I will if you don't listen . . . if you don't change."

After pausing to let the threat roil Lucas, he continued. "What good would rotting in jail be when you could be a father to a boy with polio? When you could save lives at the brick plant? I know you didn't mean to kill me. But it would look that way to a jury."

"The rigged boiler valve was Shorty Mock's idea—pure Garnersville stupidity. I didn't know anything about it until after the explosion. They were supposed to just rough you up a bit, cut some tires or trash your office. My bosses in Pittsburgh were pressing me. I had to make you back off."

"You made a big mistake. And you lost your wife along the way. You're at the bottom now . . . What are you going to do?"

Lucas turned back to Bruce. "The hearing got to me. When you pulled the lungs out of the bag, I got sick. My bullshit reasons for denying the risk fell apart. I can't get the pictures out of my mind."

"Good," Bruce said.

"But until you rescued my boy, I was going to try to muddle through. Pay the Garnersville men to keep quiet. On Saturday, when you and Sarah worked that miracle, I knew I'd have to tell you what happened. Try to clean up this mess."

"Start with calling off your thugs," Bruce said. "And never touch my family or me again. My girlfriend will be here in two weeks. Make sure she's safe. If anything happens to her, I'll know where to look."

The left side of Bruce's face was twitching. An image of the photo of Amelia that Lucas desecrated had flashed through his mind, and his anger was surging. *Stay in control . . . Pin him down.*

Lucas hadn't responded. He had sat down on the log and was holding his head in his hands.

"What's your answer? Speak up."

"She'll be safe," Lucas said.

"And how about the men at the plant? What will you do for them?"

Lucas looked up. "I sent a memo to Pittsburgh three days ago. Couched it as something we had to do to take the heat off the company. I couldn't ask for too much at first. So I asked for a watering system at the mixing hub. The dust is the worst there."

"Not enough," Bruce said.

"If I push too hard, they'll can me. Replace me with someone who won't make a stir. Let me take it a step at a time."

"There better be more steps . . . soon."

Lucas was trembling. "There will be."

Bruce stood and broke a rough piece off the decaying log. "You're full of rot . . . like this wood. Clear it all out of your life—everything."

He pitched the wood into the creek and paused to watch it float away in the darkening water, his anger beginning to ease as the branch moved downstream. "One more thing," Bruce said. "Fire Fenelli. You need a doctor who will tell you what you should know, not what you want to hear. Ask Sarah to help for a while until you can bring a new doctor here."

"Not easy to do," Lucas said as he regained a touch of feistiness. "He's a company man. Pittsburgh wouldn't be pleased."

"Get rid of him," Bruce said.

Walking back along the bank, they could see faint reflections from the porch lights on the stream in front of the lodge. In May this stretch of water would be alive with trout gorging on spinners—the egg-laying fly that darts on the surface of the water at twilight. Tonight there were no sounds of rising fish. The temperature had dipped further as dark approached, and the wind had picked up speed. If the fish were feeding, they were deep below the surface.

Bruce gave the stream only a passing thought. Instead he mulled over Lucas's responses. Should he push him harder? Or could he overreach and shut him down? Lucas got testy about Fenelli, but he hadn't said no. The chances of getting new regulations on silica from the legislature were dim. Too many senators were in the industry camp. So his influence with Lucas gave the best shot at getting something done. *Keep the pressure on, but don't break him.*

"I can help you with Fenelli," Bruce said. "A few complaints from workers to the medical board would give you the ammunition. I know some men who would write letters if you'll protect them."

"Pittsburgh doesn't like bad publicity."

"There's no way they could trace it to you," Bruce replied. "Who would think you'd expose your own company doctor?"

By the time they crossed the bridge, the plan was set: anonymous letters sent to the board within the week, Fenelli gone within the month. There was just one more question for tonight.

"You didn't pledge you'll call off the Garnersville creeps. Why not?"

Lucas paused and cleared his throat. They were on the front lawn of the lodge. There was enough light for Bruce to see he was struggling.

"You have my pledge. I don't want anyone harmed. I could fry in hell for what I've done."

He took a few more steps, then stopped. "But we need to watch out for the Garnersville men," Lucas said, his voice cracking. "They have a feud going with Tony and his friends. Shorty and his gang think the guys from Blairton lord it over them, make jokes about them."

After motioning to Bruce to sit with him on a bench, he continued. "Some of it's true. They pick on the men from Garnersville. Ride them for living on piles of rusted-out junk and having sex with their cousins."

"What scares you?" Bruce asked.

"I met Shorty and his buddy, Jerry Ringler, at the Garnersville Tavern on Saturday and told them to stay away from you and your family. Gave them a hundred bucks each to end the deal and shut them up. But I'm not sure they listened. Shorty pounded down two boilermakers and went on a rant. He thinks you're trying to get a big settlement for Tony and some other of your favorites and shut the plant down. Said the brickyard's the only place that would hire him, and he's not going to lose his job because of some do-gooder. After the hearing in Harrisburg, you were either a hero or a scumbag at the plant. You can guess which side the Garnersville gang took."

"Let's go inside," Bruce said. "I'll take the drink you offered me."


The lodge could have passed for an elite men's club in Pittsburgh or Philadelphia. It reminded Bruce of the Union League in Philadelphia, where the dean at Penn had hosted a dinner the night before their med school graduation. The ornate flourishes of the Union League were missing at this forest retreat, but the leather chairs, oriental rugs, and oil paintings were from the same genre.

Lucas showed him the wall of signed photos of celebrities who had stayed there and the bedroom where Hoover, the FBI director, slept. Then they stopped at the bar to pour neat bourbons.

"I won't clink glasses with you yet," Bruce said. "You have to deliver. Throttle Shorty and Jerry and do everything else you promised. You know what will happen if they come after me. Or, God forbid, they do something to Amelia."

After Lucas took a long draw of the Four Roses, he offered an answer.

"Maybe there can be winners. I'll find better jobs for them at the plant. Jerry won't be a problem. He's got some skills. Shorty's another story, but he might be able to handle loading the kilns. There's a good pay bump to do that work. If they don't follow along, they won't be working anywhere for Allegheny Refractories."

Bruce didn't respond. He could tell Lucas had more to say.

"The other winner will be you. Your silicosis crusade will succeed—at least in part. And there will be a nice gift for you if we can pull it off. Do you know how long people are on the waiting list to be a member of this club? It can be twenty years or forever. But there are ways around the wait. I have the clout and the money to get you in now. You'd love it."

The attempted bribe stunned Bruce. He hadn't expected Lucas to be this blatant in trying to ensure his silence. For a moment, the prospect of fishing these waters had enticed him. But the price to be paid was too high.

"I'm not for sale. You can try to buy Shorty and Jerry. Not me."

He slammed the drink down on the bar and walked to the door. It would be the last time he set foot in the Spruce Creek Trout Club.

# Chapter 30

## FIRST DAY

---

### Pennsylvania
### April 1946

Bruce paced on the train platform, glancing at posters that dotted the outside walls. It was his fourth or fifth trip past the Shriner's Circus notices that papered the Altoona station. He had arrived at 9:30 to await the 11:07 a.m. Streamliner from New York City.

With only a quarter of an hour to go, he was trying to call up a clear picture of Amelia. He replayed the last image he had of her—on the stoop of her flat in Bloomsbury as he turned to leave. They were exhausted that morning. After the V-rocket attack there hadn't been enough time to ready themselves for a separation that might be final. He remembered her words when he set off to the St. Pancras station. "Only you, Bruce." Those words braced him through the war. Then the crushing letter came three weeks after VE Day. A blow he didn't see coming.

For a few seconds, the letter slipped in front of him again. Then he imagined crumpling it into a ball, opening his hand, and watching it tumbling away in a gust of wind. *We were caught in a war. It brought us together. Tore us apart. Killed her brother and turned her father against her.*

A train whistle snapped him to attention. But it was a freight train loaded with coal, headed toward the Horseshoe Curve and Pittsburgh. After he watched the train move on, he surveyed the station from his vantage point at the end of the platform. It was an ordinary PRR building decorated with faded Victorian bric-a-brac. Coal-dust-stained paint gave the station a worn look.

*Shabby*, Bruce thought. *She'll want to get out of this backwater as fast as she can.* There was nothing here with the grandeur of Whitcombe Hall. Nothing like the stone mill on the river Test. Nothing like Hardy's fly-fishing shop in London.

Their letters, two a week, had been laced with anticipation. But they had avoided the most difficult question. What would happen after her stay? Could she love him enough to make this place her home?

He heard Amelia's voice before he saw her. A young girl, nine or ten years old, stood in the doorway of the train, wide-eyed and frozen in place. "Just pop down those stairs. I'll be right behind you, and we'll find your aunt in a minute or two," Amelia said with a warmth that tore into him, opening a flood of emotion. He bit his lips while he waited for her to appear.

Amelia reached for the girl's shoulder to reassure her and then stepped into the doorway. Her smile lit up the dark passageway as she spotted Bruce and waved to him.

"Rosalie, there's my friend. He'll take your bag and help you find your family. Stay with me while I give him a kiss."

With her little friend in tow, Amelia came to him, her long blond hair swirling in the early spring wind. She stopped to look at Bruce before she touched him. "Handsome, isn't he?" she said to the girl.

Bruce couldn't speak. His visions of Amelia hadn't come close to the real thing.

"I'd swim across the ocean to be with you," Amelia said.

For a moment the whistles of the train and the people staring at them didn't exist. Then the conductor tugged Bruce's arm. "Mister, you better take a break and grab her suitcases or they'll be on their way to Pittsburgh."

Amelia laughed and nudged Bruce toward the train. "And get Rosalie's big canvas bag. It's sitting next to the three I brought. Mine have yellow tags, and Rosalie's has a rabbit's ear on the handle."

Bruce ran up the steps to grab two of Amelia's leather suitcases while the conductor shuttled her other bag and Rosalie's army-issue duffel to the edge of the steps. By the time he transferred them to the platform, the train was starting to lurch forward.

Before he could hail a porter, he glimpsed Pete Nicholaou pushing his way toward them with his wife, Helene, a few steps behind. Heavy from their own cooking, they were struggling to speed along the train platform. Panting and red-faced, Pete was at his limit. Helene was trying to keep pace while giving her husband an earful.

"There she is," Pete shouted back to Helene. "Thank God we found her."

Bruce wondered why Pete and Helene would be here to welcome Amelia until he saw Rosalie jump up and down. In a few seconds the girl was enveloped by Pete and Helene. His two friends held her so closely that Rosalie was invisible till they broke apart and came toward them.

Holding hands with her two elders, Rosalie walked right up to Amelia. "Let me introduce my aunt Helene and uncle Pete. I'm going to live with them till my mother gets well."

"I'm very pleased to meet your aunt and uncle. And I want you to know my special friend, Dr. Bruce Duncan."

Bruce reached down to shake Rosalie's hand. "I happen to know your aunt and uncle quite well. They're the best cooks I know. They can't keep me away from the Ambrosia. "

Rosalie turned toward her aunt and uncle. "Miss Whitcombe rode with me the whole way from New York. She saw me sitting alone and offered me a seat in her compartment. She's the nicest lady. Told me stories and played games for the whole ride. Can we ask her to the Ambrosia?"

"With pleasure," Pete replied. "Her special friend is a special friend of ours. We'll treat them to a dinner after Miss Whitcombe rests from her journey. We heard she was coming from England to visit Dr. Duncan."

He bowed to Amelia. "Our deepest thanks for helping Rosalie. We were worried about her traveling alone."

"And my thanks to you for your open-hearted welcome," Amelia replied. "I'll be delighted to dine at your restaurant. Can we include Rosalie?"

"Of course," Pete answered before making their exit. "You must be tired after traveling so far. We'll move along with Rosalie so Bruce can get you settled at Miss Runyon's."

"Yes, it's been a long trip. Six days to cross the ocean before the train ride from New York. Next stop, Miss Runyon's. Then I want to see your beautiful village."

Pete pivoted to Bruce to give his endorsement. "She'll charm the town, Doc."

"I know," he replied as he put her hand on his arm.

Having asked Bess and his family to give them a few hours to themselves, Bruce eased down the alley in the car, parked in his garage, and led Amelia over the brick walk to his back door. The grass was vibrant with the lush green of spring, and the heady fragrance of Bess's saucer magnolia was strong enough to reach across to them. Daffodils he had clipped earlier in the day spilled over antique buckets on the porch.

He opened the door and ushered her into his kitchen. So far their touches had been discreet. The kiss at the station. Squeezing her hand in the car as he explained that her visit was big news in this small town. Brushing against one another as they walked toward his house. Now that they were alone, he reached to her face, his fingers tracing along her cheek, then under her chin. "I never thought I'd see you again," he said as moisture glistened in his eyes.

"Couldn't keep me away."

Like their first encounter at the river Test, the attraction was magnetic. As the rush of pleasure hit him full force, he showered her face with kisses—her eyes, her cheeks, her nose, her lips—his senses dancing to the edge. His hands slipped under her blouse, caressing her silky skin as he fell deeper into her.

But after they slid down on the soft rag rug under their feet, Amelia seemed to catch herself. She took a deep breath and nudged away. "Can I just lie with my head on your shoulder for a moment and tell you what I'm thinking?" she asked.

"Is something wrong?"

"No . . . but I need some time to get to know you again. To face what I did to you. To feel like I deserve you."

"I've forgiven you," he said. "Your brother was dead; your father pressured you . . . threatened you. I was headed back to the USA. Better to break it off before we met again."

"It's not easy to forgive what I did," she said. "You need to trust me again. And we need to see if we can make a life together. The day we met, we were reckless, lost ourselves without thinking. Then it all exploded. I don't want that to happen again. I want to be sure. Is it okay? Can you wait?"

"I'm starved for you . . . but yes, I can wait."

"It's not that I don't want to devour you. But we need a proper courtship."

"And we'll have one," he said.

"The last time I was in London you cooked eggs and truffles for me," Bruce said as he began to rise. "Are you hungry? We don't have truffles here. But I can fire up my old stove and make you something special."

"I'm famished. Put on your apron and get to work."

She moved to sit at his painted pine table, where she propped her head in her hands and watched him pull out pans and grab ingredients from his icebox. "I love watching you," she said. "I could sit here all day and do it. Could I tag along when you're in your office?"

Bruce nodded and began to sing a tune—"Begin the Beguine"—a Cole Porter number they had played on her phonograph when they danced at her flat. The lyrics told their story. Lovers who thought their chance was wasted. But the fire remained.

"One dance before lunch?" he asked. "I promise no monkey business. Only some courtship."

She laughed and held out her hand. "We're making headway already."

"Rosalie is only ten and had to travel by herself," Amelia said as they walked to Bruce's mother's house for dinner.

"A dangerous thing for a little girl," Bess said.

"They had no choice. Her father was killed at Iwo Jima—a stray bullet after they thought the island was secure. Her mother has breast cancer that's in her lungs, so she can't take care of Rosalie. She put her on the train with her father's duffel filled with clothes and a few toys. Rosalie thinks she'll be going back soon when her mother is stronger. It doesn't sound too likely to me."

Keeping a slow pace for Bess, they ambled along the tree-canopied street, passing by some of the grandest houses in Hollidaysburg. Not wanting to interrupt the flow of Amelia's tales of her journey, he resisted giving an account of the houses and the people who lived in them. There would be time later to take her around the town.

"I want to do something for Rosalie and her mother," Amelia continued. "Tomorrow, I'll stop by the Ambrosia to get her mother's address. The first thing is to write her a note telling her how her daughter is so brave and wonderful."

"I can help Rosalie with her lessons," Bess said. "I suppose she'll start school here. An old teacher should be good for something."

"I can check with her mother's doctors if we get their names," Bruce said. "But it will have to wait till later. Our guest of honor needs to get to the party."

Alice Duncan's home hadn't looked this festive since the day Bruce returned from Germany. It was her idea to have Amelia meet all of the family at once, and she wanted to make it a success. Bowls of sweet-smelling viburnum graced the tables. A tall vase with pink magnolia blossoms stood on the grand piano. The chipped gesso frame around her grandfather's portrait had been restored, and the brass door knocker was gleaming with fresh polish.

A daughter of a former member of Parliament, owner of an English manor, and graduate of Cambridge University was about to arrive. Even though her son had described Amelia's home, Whitcombe Hall, as a bit weary from neglect during the war, Alice wanted to show this blue-blooded woman that the Duncans were a presence in their own right.

Her sister, Pauline, and the judge had arrived after lunch to help with preparations. Vic left work after the first shift ended at three o'clock to start the fire in the backyard pit. And Glen and Mimi joined them as soon as the hardware store closed for the day.

Alice vetoed the judge's offer to have this party at his farm, but he had prevailed with his plan to roast a whole lamb on a spit in her backyard. Vic, Glen, and the judge had dug a pit in her vegetable garden and rigged a motorized iron contraption, built in Vic's shop at the railroad, to rotate the meat over the hickory coals. The fragrance of the wood fire with the meat juices dripping and sputtering on it came through the cracked open kitchen windows and mixed with the rich aroma of scalloped potatoes, simmering in cream with a touch of onion. Unless Amelia was a finicky eater, she should love this dinner.

As Alice lifted a bowl of viburnum to give it one more inspection, she heard voices on the porch, and the young couple stepped into the room—first Amelia, then Bruce beside her. A jolt of certainty hit Alice, and the bowl fell from her hands, shattering its crystal facets into hundreds of pieces. She had known in an instant why her son had suffered so much for this woman. Amelia was an uncommon beauty. With her shoulder-length blond hair swinging on top of an exquisite cashmere sweater, and her tartan skirt not showing a crease after a long trip, she exuded British class.

Ignoring the glass at his mother's feet, Bruce grinned and introduced them. "Mother, meet Amelia. Looks like she's already made an impression. Hope it's a good one."

"Yes, it is," Alice replied as she held out her hands to greet Amelia. She wanted to like this woman, but her admiration was mixed with reserve.

The crash of the bowl had summoned the others, who gathered at the periphery of the room, absorbed by the scene. "Are you going to keep her to yourself all night long?" Pauline asked.

"Of course not," Alice said. "Everyone, come here and meet Amelia."

"I want to visit you soon, Mrs. Duncan," Amelia said as she turned to Bruce, put her arm in his, and flashed a wide smile. "Especially to get the inside scoop on this guy."

Bruce had written to Amelia about each of the people that she saw around her—nuggets that she used to conjure a picture of how they would look and what she might say to them. So she recognized Pauline, the younger, less patrician of the sisters but with the sharper wit; Vic, the big man who had been a football star in his youth; the judge, dressed in an impeccable three-piece suit, as if he were attending a dinner party in Mayfair; and Glen, the brother she had met in London, standing at the end of the line with his fiancée, Mimi. With Bruce at her side, she greeted them all till she reached Glen.


He stood straight and swept his hand through his tousled hair when she approached him. The whiskey Glen had been nipping had done its business. Worried that he might slur his words, he slowed down and tried to speak as clearly as he could. "Good to see you again, Amelia," he said. "Those visits you made to the hospital after Bruce left for France were bright spots until I could ship back home."

It was an awkward moment. She hesitated, then held out her arms. "I've been bad, I know. Can you forgive me?"

A piece of him—a piece he was struggling to control—despised this woman for the way she had treated his brother. He had worried about seeing her tonight, thought he might let loose on her. Yet she was as gorgeous as ever. She filled a room like no one else. Bright and sexy as they come.

"I'm trying," he said.

With the spit rotating in smooth circles, Pauline knew Vic was in his element—pleased with the tricks he could pull in using the PRR shop to construct a one-off device for the family. The others around the fire, Bess, and the judge, were taking stock of Amelia as she helped Vic with the lamb.

Pauline talked with Amelia, probing her more than her sister, Alice, would have wanted. "How does our favorite doctor look to you after not seeing him for so long? Any warts or wrinkles? Has our small town rubbed off on him too much?"

"He's just fine, Mrs. Andrews. The small town is part of his charm."

"He and Glen are like sons. I hope you'll understand if I look out for him."

"Understood."

Pauline pursed her lips, then plunged ahead. "Seems like a long way to travel to see a beau," she said. "You couldn't do that very often."

"Amelia just got here," Vic said. "Give her a chance to get settled before you tee off on her."

"There's no need to hold back, Mrs. Andrews," Amelia replied. "Yes, it is an ocean away. But I'm happy to be here."

"England isn't the end of the earth," the judge said. "We're getting safe air service soon. And I'm going to fly there myself someday."

"Don't mind Pauline," Bess said. "She's crusty on the outside but soft inside."

Pauline chortled. "No one's ever called me soft before—not even my husband."

After Vic gave his wife a withering stare, he flipped off the switch to the spit motor and cut into the meat. "Perfect," he said. "Time to celebrate."

Bruce could see the danger signals. It was time to break up the party before Glen unraveled and caused damage. He had opened another bottle of whiskey while the others switched to coffee after dinner. Because Mimi had gone home early, nursing a cough, the constraint he tried to show around her was falling away. There was a telltale flush on his face, and he had gotten louder as he backed the judge into a corner of the room. Bruce could overhear snippets of Glen's fast-paced delivery—something about needing a loan for an idea that was a sure thing.

"We've been monopolizing Amelia," Bess said as she stood and gathered her purse to signal her readiness to leave. "With us jabbering in her ear, Bruce hasn't had a moment to talk with her all evening. We should let them go." Bruce hadn't been the only one to notice Glen's behavior.

Bruce understood Bess's ploy and was grateful for it. But he didn't want to end the evening quite yet. Amelia had won over all of them except Glen. Even Aunt Pauline had come around after the little dustup that Bess told him about. Pauline had been her usual self. She was testing the new person in the crowd, showing she wouldn't be a pushover. Glen was more of a problem.

He'd heard the skepticism in his brother's voice when he greeted Amelia, and he'd seen him act strange during dinner— last to come to the table, a sullen face as he talked with Vic and Pauline. There hadn't been a hint of negative feelings toward Amelia until tonight. Had he been hiding a grudge?

After Bess announced her imminent departure, Glen didn't budge from his position that blocked the judge from joining the group. He was in the judge's face, regaling him about the appliance business, rambling about getting a loan to invest in a new store, drawing graphs in the air with broad sweeps of his arms. He'd switched from low gear to over-drive while Bruce had been transfixed with Amelia's telling of fishing on the Test. Was this barrage an intentional slight of Amelia, or was it whiskey-fueled mania? Whatever the cause, he couldn't start this visit with a fracture between Glen and Amelia.

"Hey, brother," he said as he stepped between the two men. "Can you spare a few minutes with Amelia before we leave? You two haven't been able to talk."

The judge jumped on the opportunity to escape. "Yes, go ahead," he said as he motioned him toward Amelia. "Stop by the farm sometime, and we can talk about a loan in the light of day."

"Don't humor me," Glen replied with a touch of vitriol. "You were buttoned down here at the party where you had to listen. No chance you'd give me a loan if I showed up at the farm. Forget it."

The angry snap brought the others to attention, and the conversations went quiet. Bruce realized that Glen was too agitated to make any peace with Amelia now. "I think we've all had a long day," he said. "Let's cool down and say our goodbyes. Glen, I'll bring Amelia by the store in the morning. You two can catch up then. Everyone needs some sleep now."

"Sleep is the last thing I need," Glen shouted at his brother. "You can go to bed with the Queen of England. I don't care. Just butt out of my business. Don't tell me what to do."

He tipped an imaginary hat to Amelia, sneered, and walked toward the door. "Watch out for her. Burned you once, will burn you again."

Bruce lunged for him and grabbed an arm as he was trying to make an exit. "Stop right where you are," he said as he spun Glen around. "You're in no shape to know how much you're hurting us. How much you're hurting yourself." He shook him with both hands. "You're drunk, Glen . . . and you're mean. Picking fights. Insulting Amelia. Yeah, you got chewed up in the war. No excuse, buddy."

Then he backed away and pleaded with Glen, trying to find a way that his brother could repair some of the damage. "What are you going to say to these people? To make it better."

The effort to wring an apology from him seemed to work for a few moments. Glen looked around the room without speaking. His eyes darting from person to person. Then the manic fury took hold again, and he spewed invective in machine-gun style, hitting scattershot around the room until he came back to Bruce.

"Does Amelia know about Doctor Sarah?" He spat out the words. "Play with the Englishwoman and send her back where she belongs. Sarah's the one. My spies saw you two in Altoona after you saved that boy with polio. Longest kiss they ever saw. Confess it, brother." A peel of sardonic laughter burst from Glen's mouth. "Don't try to rein me in. I tell the truth. I'm the only one who knows the truth . . . the way."

With a flourish like he was pulling a cape around his shoulders, Glen signaled he was leaving and no one could stop him. "Into the night, my friends."

Alice rushed to the door and screamed out to him, "Don't drive, Glen. Walk it off and get to bed." Then she turned back to the room. Alice was struggling to hold back tears. She looked at Amelia, who had been silent, not defending herself against Glen's attack. Amelia's jaw was held higher, and her lips were tight. Glen's words must have stung. "He's a wounded man," Alice said to Amelia. "But a good man. He got shell-shocked in the war. We need to give him time to heal."

"I know," Amelia said. "I saw him with his burns in the hospital. They were gruesome."

"It's more than the war," Bruce said. "He has our father's melancholia. And he can flip into mania like he did tonight. Same as in the textbooks. Talks out of his head. Can say anything. Do anything. Probably went to the American Legion bar to souse himself to the hilt. It's his favorite spot when he's on a tear. I have to get to him before he causes more trouble."

"Go ahead, Bruce," Amelia said. "I'll stay here with your mother while you track him down. We'll be fine. Been through a lot worse."

"Thank you," he whispered before he left. Amelia had been gracious when Glen attacked—stood there and took the insults without flinching. But his brother had been cruel. He hoped not enough to turn her away.

# Chapter 31

## SPRING STREAM

—〜—

*B*ruce and Amelia were in a private anteroom at the Altoona hospital, waiting to visit Glen and talk with his doctor, Sarah Avery. After being told to stay away until Sarah could calm him with sedatives, the call had come that the mania had broken. Glen had slept straight for two days until early this morning.

"I have some explaining to do before you meet Sarah," Bruce said. "Bess told you to ignore Glen's spouting off about Sarah and me. She claimed Glen was paranoid. Making up stories. The paranoia part was true. By the time he got picked up by the police, he was a messenger from God. Put here to stamp out sin."

He paused to decide how to proceed, to find the best way to tell her. A faint flush appeared on his face as Amelia nodded for him to continue. "But I'm guilty . . . the kiss happened. I was wavering, not sure you and I could bridge the Atlantic. When you see Sarah, you'll know why I was tempted. She's gorgeous . . . and sharp. When I got torn up with shrapnel from the boiler, she put me back together. Very professional. Very skilled. And a very soft touch. Though she wouldn't admit it."

He gathered his resolve and pushed on. "It was an odd kiss. We had just saved a little boy's life. Hadn't intended to spend the day together. But we lingered, had dinner, walked through the streets of Altoona.

"Do you want to hear more?" he asked Amelia.

"Yes," she said with a faint smile. "I'm not a guilt-free woman. I have some things to tell you after you finish."

"It's not very racy. No heavy romance to confess. Sarah's committed to her career. Says she'll never marry. Can't get entangled with a man. I'm not sure what would have happened if she hadn't drawn that line. But the kiss was the only one, at least with me. One kiss before ending our little flirtation. She said it would be a good one, and she was right.

"Sarah's no threat to us. She's a colleague. Someone I need to have on my side, cover for me when I take a break. And she's a friend. She helped me over those rough days after my office got blown apart. Shared her office, teamed up with Vic and Glen to fight back. I hope she can be your friend."

He opened his palms and looked to Amelia for her reaction. "So there you have it. Am I in trouble?"

Amelia had listened carefully as he wrestled with telling her about Sarah. After he was done, she reached to him and put her hand on his.

"You're not in trouble," she said. "You could have sloughed off Glen's rants. There was enough noise there that I didn't make much of his talk about Sarah. I thought he was taunting me. And even if there was something between you and Sarah, I understand. I wasn't expecting you to be celibate while you waited for a girl from England who might never show up."

"I wasn't a monk," Bruce said. "There was a nurse in Germany after you sent me that letter. I was floundering—lonely and bitter. It didn't mean anything."

"Listen, soldier. I'm the one that should be confessing. I was engaged for ten months. You know what that means. While you were hurting from my bad decision, I was playing the merry fiancée of a rich man. The marriage would have been hollow—just a convenience. But I'd signed up for it."

Her lips curled in a slight smile. "We English can make the dumbest choices when we see our ancestors' paintings on the wall. Can't stand the idea our portrait won't be next."

"Let's bury the past," Bruce said. "It's time to make better choices."

When Amelia leaned to kiss him, the door to the anteroom opened and Sarah entered with quick steps.

"Sorry I'm late," she said. "It's been a busy morning. I didn't expect to have so many of my patients in the hospital."

Enveloped in her white coat, and with her hair pinned up to keep it out of the way when she examined patients, Sarah had the presence of a hard-working physician. Yet there was no mistaking her femininity.

"You must be Amelia," she said as she smiled and came forward. "I've heard how much you mean to this guy."

Amelia knew right away that she could like Sarah—a woman with the kind of presence she admired. But Amelia's thoughts were tinged with fear. *She's a knockout. Watch her.* Then she tried to calm her mind. *She's drawn the line. A career woman. Trust them.*

Bruce seemed wary of the risks in the first meeting of the two women, so Amelia wasn't surprised when he moved the conversation to the business that brought them to the hospital.

"I want Sarah to have dinner with us soon. Let you two get to know one another. But let's talk about Glen now. How's he doing?"

"Pretty well, considering what happened. If you hadn't come along, he might have fought with the police. He's lucky they only charged him with drunk driving."

"He took a couple swings at me before they handcuffed him," Bruce said. "Is he calmed down enough for us to visit?"

"Yes," Sarah said. "As soon as I tell you what to expect. Keep the visit short. He's still drowsy from the Seconal. Five minutes will be plenty. Then you need to get out of here and enjoy the day you planned at Spruce Creek. I'm covering your practice, and I want you to forget about work, forget about Glen for a while. I've got some ideas to help him."

"Don't spare us," Bruce said. "Does he need to go to the state hospital?"

"When I saw Glen on Saturday night, I thought we might have to commit him," Sarah replied. "I almost ordered a straitjacket, but we had two big orderlies who held him while we injected the sedative. It put him down right away. He was picking fights, baiting the staff, telling them he was invincible. Today he's contrite . . . wants to leave and go back to work at the hardware store. I was surprised the mania ended so fast. When I did my psych rotation at Eastern State, we saw psychotic breaks that lasted for weeks. We were lucky this time."

"Did he ever come to talk with you?" Bruce asked. "I asked him to do it, but I didn't want to pry."

She shook her head. "No."

"Can you work with him? Help him?" Bruce asked.

"I'll do what I can, but he needs a psychiatrist."

"I've thought the same thing," Bruce said. "But I don't trust any of the psychiatrists at the state hospital. It's a warehouse. No treatment—unless you consider shock therapy legit. I saw it when I was at Penn. It's brutal stuff."

"A doctor I know from Philadelphia is finishing his psychiatry training in July and is coming to Altoona. I dated him when I was at Swarthmore and he was a med student at Jefferson . . . before I decided to be a doctor. Jim went to Germany with Patton's army, saw a lot of cases of shell shock. He's going to work at the state hospital half-time and start a private practice. The first in Altoona. Jim's good—very good."

"Wonderful," Amelia said. "Glen deserves the best."

"Can you talk with Glen now, while he's raw from the other night?" Bruce said. "Convince him to see your friend?"

"We had that talk first thing this morning," Sarah replied. "Glen's ashamed, knows he went way overboard. He's ready."

Amelia nodded her head in gratitude and looked toward Bruce for approval. "We're having dinner tonight at the Ambrosia with a little girl, Rosalie, Pete's niece, who rode with me on the train from New York. Join us so we can talk about happier things."

"If I can finish my work, I'll be there. Step one is our visit with Glen. Then you and Bruce need to head for the stream so I can get to the office."


The drive to Spruce Creek had given them time to digest the morning's events. Almost punch drunk from the Seconal and the forced sleep, Glen had bounced back and forth between teary pledges to reform and mini-bursts of agitation. Sarah had sent them on their way with assurance that Glen would stay there for a few more days.

They were quiet now as they started down a trail from the small parking area about two miles past the Spruce Creek Tavern. Other than the few cars in the tavern's lot, the road had been deserted past the Little Juniata River, under the bridge and the mainline of the Pennsylvania Railroad, and on through the valley toward the stream. Bruce had chosen a trail with no human prints—one that would take them to a secluded stretch of water. The stream would be theirs alone today.

The path was soft from yesterday's shower. So their footfall was silent. The only sounds were from the rushing water as it bounced off the rocks in the side channel to their left. They were moving toward the confluence of three small branches that came together into a series of pools that should hold fish. The forest floor had turned from brown to fresh green since the last time Bruce was here.

Swirling heads of skunk cabbage jutted above swaths of trillium with their three-lobed flowers that signal the ascent of spring. The willows close to the water were cloaked with a glow of shimmering lime that would fade as summer approached, while the unfurling leaves of the maples held red samaras that sparkled in the sun. Two chipmunks scooted across the moss-covered path in front of them and disappeared in the burgeoning understory. The forest was pulsing with life, shot full of the color of new growth.

Bruce carried a picnic basket that Bess had packed for them, two bamboo fly rods, and a wicker creel loaded with a supply of caddis imitations that he hoped would match today's hatch. With only a few clouds in the morning sky, a sun-warmed stream, and little wind, conditions were ripe for trout rising to snare caddis flies emerging from the water.

"When we come to the waterfall where the creek comes together, we'll detour downstream for about a half mile," Bruce said. "Circle around through the woods so we won't spook the trout. Then we can work our way up through the prime riffles and pools. The stream's smaller than the Test. So we'll have to be stealthy, keep a low profile, talk in whispers."

Walking behind him, she tugged at the back of his fishing jacket and gave him a quick kiss on the back of the neck. "Lead on, guide. Stealthy I'll be."

"If you do that one more time, we'll never get to the stream," he said as he turned to laugh with her. "This is serious business, Amelia," he said with faux sternness. "I've waited a long time to go fishing with you again, show you a few trout on this side of the Atlantic. And we're going to do it."

"Yes, sir, we're going to do it."

As they came to the first pool, they paused before the break in the woods to gaze through the trees at the water. The first rise was at the lower edge, only a few inches from a small cascade where the steady flow of the pool ended with a sudden gush around a clutch of boulders, then careened down through a dense thicket of brush. Could they put a fly in that narrow space without it swinging out of control? Near to impossible, he concluded.

Scanning upstream, Bruce could see clouds of caddis flies bouncing around the unfolding leaves of tree branches close to the water.

"I've never seen so many flies," Amelia said. She pointed toward a stretch of water by a gnarled willow tree. Fish had just started to jump in a lane near the far bank. The rises came about a foot from the bank where the water coursed a bit faster before tailing off into the larger pool.

Both of them knew how to read streams, and this spot looked like a good place to start. A large root jutting from the base of the tree shunted the water over a shelf of submerged rocks, creating a feeding zone. One after another, the caddis flies funneled past the cover of the tree and tumbled in the current until they were snatched by a trout.

"You go first," Bruce said. "I'll net the fish."

He pulled a caddis fly from his kit and secured it to the tippet. "Tony, the fellow I told you about from the brick plant, gave me the deer hair for this fly. He knew you were coming. Catch one for him . . . He's too weak to walk a trout stream."

Amelia heard the tremor in his voice and looked at him, her lips gathered in a tender smile. "You're a good man, Bruce."

She took the rod from his hands and waded a few steps into the stream.

"You'll have to get closer," he whispered. "Three or four more steps so you can slide the line under the tree branches. Drop the fly an inch or two from the trunk and let the current take it down the chute. Just like the naturals."

Amelia sent out a few false casts away from the target so she could get a feel for the rod. Then with a smooth arc, she placed the fly on the spot Bruce suggested. The caddis bounced as it swung by the root, coaxing a large trout from under the rock shelf. With an acrobatic leap, it broke the surface and tore into the deer-hair caddis, driving the fly down into the stream. The line screamed off her reel as the trout took the fly into deeper and faster water.

"Give it plenty of room to run," Bruce said. "It's a big fish. Maybe twenty inches—best I've seen here since before the war."

Amelia knew how to manage a heavy fish, but Bruce knew the swirling currents and a fallen tree across the upper part of the stream were obstacles she hadn't encountered in the slower-moving waters of the Test. The trout was headed straight for the underwater maze of branches from the tree at the head of the pool. If it got that far, the line would break in an instant. She had a choice. Pull up on the rod and put pressure on the fish to turn, risking a snap in the line or a jerk of the fly out of the fish's mouth. Or let the big trout keep going upstream on the hope that it would run out of steam very soon.

She hesitated for a moment and then raised the tip of the bamboo as high as she could reach. The fish stopped its upstream dash and, in a sudden move, reversed course, dashing straight back at her. Amelia reeled in line with a furious rush to avoid slack that would free the trout.

Bruce stood by her side while he watched her adept handling of the fish. "Brilliant," he said. "He'll take another run toward that brush before he's done."

When the trout reached the middle of the stream only ten feet away from them, it turned again, dashing toward the far bank and the deepest part of the pool. They lost sight of it as it plunged downward. But then the trout exploded out of the water. Uncoiling its body, the fish skipped upstream, tail pirouetting on the surface, until it dived and set off in a beeline toward the head of the pool and the fallen tree. The trout was deeper in the water than its first run in this direction, and it pulled with determined force.

Amelia lifted her rod again to brake the fish's headlong race to safety. But this time the trout won. The line sagged, and the fish was gone.

She turned to Bruce with a broad grin. "Whew," she said. "Your mountain fish have a lot of fight—more than I could handle."

Bruce stepped closer and put his arm around her shoulders. "You were pitch perfect. Couldn't have handled it better. That fish wasn't going to be caught today . . . not by anybody. We'll get him another day."

"I'll count on it."

After the splashing of the trophy fish, the surface of the pool stayed calm for a few minutes. Then the rises began to pop again. A small fish straight across from them was first. Then a louder crash from the trout that had surfaced at the tail of the water when they first stalked their way to the pool. More rises came in bursts from upstream near the fallen tree.

Bruce motioned toward the tree with its branches dangling in the water. It had caved into the stream during the winter, when the high waters had eroded the bank and undercut its roots. Still alive, the branches were sprouting new leaves that dangled into the stream. "Tough casting up there," he said. "But there are lots of fish rising. It gives them cover. From the shape of the rises, I think they're good sized, but not huge. Maybe twelve to fifteen inches. Let's give it a try."

He took the first cast, shying away from the twigs until he could gauge the distance. His fly landed too far away from the seam where the fish were rising. It moved downstream, ignored by the fish. His next cast nestled between edges of two of the larger branches, giving the caddis a clear path toward the target. After hooking around the tip of a rock protruding from the water, a fish attacked as the fly coursed out of the foam and entered the prime spot of a feeding lane. In a quick maneuver, Bruce held his rod close to the water and coaxed the fish away from the tree into the middle of the pool, where he played it toward his net.

"I can see how it's done," Amelia said. "My turn."

They netted and released a dozen or more trout from that part of the stream until the sun was at its zenith, and they left the water. The boulder-strewn pocket at the tail of the pool, where a large fish still fed on the caddis, had been left untouched—a challenge saved for the afternoon.

The awkwardness, the hesitance they had felt at the beginning of their reunion, was gone. They dropped their fishing jackets, stepped out of their wading gear, and eased onto the Woolrich camp blanket with Bess's lunch basket at the corner. The harmony of their side-by-side casting had erased the last barrier. The elemental connection they knew on the Test had returned.

"How am I doing with the courtship?" Bruce asked.

"Let me show you," Amelia replied as she unbuttoned her flannel shirt and drew his face to her breast. She caressed his hair with tender strokes, bringing him closer while she pulled the wool cover around them. The picnic basket rolled to the side on the soft moss as they fell together, bathed in the midday sun.

Bruce kissed her breasts with delicate reverence, treasuring them, tasting their sweetness, while Amelia gathered him to her. They were on fire, but both knew how delicious this singular moment was—how important it was. So they slowed the pace, cherishing each other with loving traces and murmurs of knowing until the fire took them away.

# Chapter 32

## THE WAR IS OVER

With the wind picking up speed and black clouds tumbling in from the west, they had left the stream and were moving at a brisk pace toward their car. The upturned leaves on the willows and the rustling of the samaras told them that a storm was near. No birds were singing now.

Before they stepped into the clearing that funneled toward their car, they stopped, not wanting to leave this place quite yet. With Amelia's hair swirling toward him, Bruce tucked the blond strands back and kissed her again. A few drops of rain spattered their faces. Then the wind shifted, and the sun broke through the stand of trees at their backs, suffusing the forest with halos of light.

"Magical," Amelia said. "How can we leave?"

"The storm could blow over," Bruce said. "But best to be safe. Lightning can come up fast. I've seen it strike around here."

When they were halfway across the clearing, a loud crack pierced the air. It wasn't lightning. It was the bark of an M1 rifle—a concussive sound Bruce knew well from the war. And it was fired very close to them, directly in their path to the car.

"Get down," Bruce yelled to her as seven more rounds from the semiautomatic weapon fired off in a staccato burst and echoes ricocheted down the valley. His mind clicked fast as he pieced together an explanation for the shots. The familiar ping from the ejected clip at the end of the volley confirmed it was an M1 and all eight bullets had been used. The shooter would have to reload if he wanted to continue. The shots had come from about a hundred yards away, probably from the copse of trees surrounding his parking place by the road. When he strained to reconstruct the sounds from the minute gaps between the gun bursts, he found the answer. There had been low-pitched thuds of lead hitting steel. He had heard the same thuds on the slab-sides of his ambulances when the Germans shot at them.

"It's not hunting season," he whispered now to hide their presence. "Someone's attacking our car. Stay here. I'll sneak up on him."

"Don't go. Let him do what he wants."

"Could be a drunk from the tavern who thinks it's funny to shoot up a car. But if it's one of the men from the brick plant, he knows we're here. He'll wait for us. We can't just walk up to the car. And we could be dodging lightning soon if we camp out in this field. I have to go now, while he thinks we have to come the whole way from the stream."

Bruce took the fishing knife out of his creel, strapped it on his belt, and began crawling forward. The new spring growth was soft and yielding, so he could move through it without being detected. After about thirty yards he slipped into a gulley he knew carried a tributary past the pull-off for his car. Today the gulley held a few inches of water, a trickle compared to the torrent that could rush down its walls toward

Spruce Creek at the height of a downpour. He didn't mind getting wet. The gulley gave him the cover he needed to surprise the shooter. He would be out of the water before rain could swell it.

He was within ten or fifteen yards of where his ears had pinpointed the source of the shots and ready to poke his head out of the gulley when another shot rang out, followed by the sound of shattering glass—probably the windshield caught crosswise to explode all of it. Then four more shots to take out the tires. He was close enough to hear the air hissing out. The 30-06 shells must have sliced through the tires without full-throated blowouts.

Bruce could see him now, his back to the gulley, swigging on a whiskey bottle, the gun propped on a rock in front of him. The man was taking his pleasure slowly. Was he too drunk to know what he was doing? Or was he waiting for them to come from the other direction, down the main path from the creek?

Bruce couldn't wait to find out. Amelia was lying on the edge of the field, exposed to lightning if it came, and vulnerable to the rifle shots. The man showed no signs of leaving. He was occupied now with the whiskey bottle. It was time to strike.

With his knife holstered, Bruce crawled out of the gulley, crept forward, and then charged the shooter, trying to catch him off balance before he could reach for his gun. In the split second before he reached him, the man startled, hearing Bruce's approach. Swinging around and stepping sideways, he pitched the bottle like a grenade, hitting Bruce hard in the left shoulder. The exploding glass gashed his neck, but Bruce felt nothing as he bore down on the man. Bruce knew his prey now. The peg teeth and the flat, scowling face were Shorty's—the brickworker who had almost killed him once before.

Bruce's shoulder caught Shorty in the left side of his chest before he could reach the gun. A crunch of bone and a sharp wail were signs of broken ribs. But the feral attacker sprang back, clawing at Bruce's eyes and kicking toward his groin. Bruce pulled the knife, waving it to ward him off—a mistake that gave his adversary an opening. Backpedaling toward the rifle, Shorty hunched down and reached for the gun.

Bruce would have to stab a man, something he had never done, or wrestle him for the rifle. With no time to think, he charged again, dropping the knife so he could use both hands to fight.

With his force pointed to the broken ribs at the center of Shorty's coiled body, Bruce pushed past the swinging rifle to deliver a knockout blow. But a glancing strike of the gunstock put him off course. His head crashed into Shorty's jaw, driving it out of joint and splattering it with blood from the whiskey-bottle-inflicted cuts. Screaming in pain, Shorty struggled to get his right hand on the trigger while Bruce raised his fist to drive his knuckles into the broken ribs.

As he slammed his fist deep into the flailing chest, the M1 erupted with a burst of flame. Bruce felt a liquid begin to gush over his legs, but no pain. *Am I hit?* he wondered before noticing that Shorty's body had gone slack.

Switching in an instant from fighter to surgeon, Bruce scanned for injuries. The source of the bleeding was obvious—a gaping wound where the bullet had torn through his assailant's ankle, shattering the bones and almost severing the foot from a ragged stump. The rib punch had stunned him, made him pull the trigger before he was ready.

Shorty was barely conscious, and the tibial artery was pumping blood onto the ground. If he waited a few minutes, the bastard would be gone. Yet Bruce couldn't stand by. He reached into the wound with one hand, clamping his thumb and forefinger over the spurting vessel, while he reached into his jacket for a spool of heavy leader.

He hadn't heard the footsteps behind him and jerked back in defense when a hand touched his shoulder. "Thank God, you're safe," Amelia said. "Can I help?"

"Yes, grab my doctor's bag from the trunk. Be quick. He's bleeding out. I need the gauze pads and the hemostats. They look like little silver pliers."

She ran to the car while he took his hand off the bleeder to tie the cord around the leg, just above the wound. It would be hard to get enough pressure to shut off the blood flow to the lower leg—too much muscle in the way. So when Amelia delivered the instruments, he clamped the posterior tibial artery and then dissected upward in quick moves to find the fibular artery, the likely origin of the remainder of the intense bleeding.

"Do you know how to use a rifle?" he asked.

"I can figure it out. We use shotguns to hunt pheasants at the manor."

"Okay. Pick up that gun on the ground beside him. It has two rounds left. Be careful—it could have a hair trigger. I have more work to do here, and he might wake up when the bleeding stops and that punch I gave him wears off. Stand back and keep it ready. I'll take it as soon as I get this wound packed and check his chest."

"What happened? You're covered with blood."

"Most of it's from him. I have a cut on my neck. Won't be a problem. He's the guy from the brick plant that blew up my furnace. He'll be in jail for a long time, out of our way."

After Bruce put ligatures on the arteries and packed a compression bandage on the stump, he used his stethoscope to listen to Shorty's breath sounds. "Looks like four or five broken ribs from the hit I put on him. He's still moving air in both lungs. He'll hurt like hell, but he'll survive it. I'll tie him up, so you can put the gun down."

Five minutes later, Shorty was bundled in the back of Bruce's car while sheets of rain pelted at them and jagged lightning flashes illuminated the sky. He was straining at the bonds, groaning with each move.

"What the shit?" he croaked through a mangled jaw. "Where am I?"

"You're the one that needs to answer the questions," Bruce replied. "You're in my car . . . the Ford you shot up. And you put a slug in your leg. I could have let you die. So be grateful. Tell us what you were trying to do."

He grimaced and spat out a fractured tooth. "You got me fired . . . you son of a bitch. I've been waiting for my chance."

"How did you know we were here? Were you following us?"

"Nah . . . a buddy spotted your car. Called me from the tavern. I just wanted to scare you. Make you have to walk home. I should have beat it after the first round."

"Did Lucas put you up to this?"

"Hell no . . . the yellow fucker. Kept Jerry and Hap but canned me. Lucas's turn'll come. That safety shit ain't gonna work."

He tried to sit up but screamed, "Fuck. What did you do to me?"

"Enough to stop you," Bruce said. "Lie still, and it won't hurt as much. Your ribs are broken, but they'll heal. Now tell us where you parked—this car isn't going anywhere. We'll get you to the hospital after the storm passes."


With Shorty tied down and cushioned with their blanket in the bed of his rusted 1936 Chevy pickup, they were driving along the mountain road from Spruce Creek toward Altoona. The thunderstorm had ended, and shafts of light were beginning to show through the clouds.

"What were you thinking before you tackled him?" Amelia asked. "When I saw you jump out of that trench, my heart almost stopped. I was sure he'd shoot you."

"His back was to me—less risk to take him out then. He could have picked us off if he'd spotted us in that open field."

"You look like you know how to fight."

"Thank the army. We all had basic training."

"Did you have to do anything like that in the war? You spared me in your letters, but I knew it was worse than you admitted. Ever see any Germans face-to-face?"

Bruce had been steely calm until now. He'd had a purpose and stuck to it. But the face-to-face question sent a wave of emotion through him. He shuddered as an image from the most brutal night of the war jumped into his mind.

"I haven't talked about it. I've been trying to forget."

She reached to touch him. The knowing rhythms of their day on the stream, the threat they had just survived, had brought them here. "If you're brave enough to charge a madman with a gun, you can tackle the memories. Today, tomorrow, or someday soon. You can tell me everything. And I'll tell you everything . . . Nothing off limits."

"There's no better time than now," he said.

Bruce held the wheel with a tight grip but started the story with a measured cadence, recounting exactly what had happened. "It was January 23, 1945, the night my friend Blaise was killed. I'd crawled across the floor from Blaise to find my rifle, an M1 they issued when our aid station in Rohrwiller was attacked. The German shells had blasted open the roof, and I could hear the battle closing on us. The aid station was in the annex to the town hall, our command post. So we were in their crosshairs."

"You must have been terrified. How were you going to defend the hospital with a rifle?"

"Our colonel gave us a machine gun, a heavy piece that a corpsman had aimed at the door. Another corpsman was trying to pull a bazooka out of the rubble. And I had a rifle . . . if I could reach it before one of the German patients, a soldier with a stomach wound, who I thought was too sick to be tied down to his cot. He was lurching toward the cabinet where I had stored the M1. The guy had peritonitis and was pumped full of morphine and penicillin. Shouldn't have known where the gun was stored. Shouldn't have been able to get off that stretcher. Just one of the strange things that happen in war."

"Did you get there before him?"

"There were some fallen rafters I had to vault over when I saw him move toward the cabinet. But he was delirious—didn't see me coming. I smacked him in the head with a hunk of rafter as he was about to reach for the gun. First time I ever really hurt someone. Didn't know if I killed him. There was no time to check."

Bruce hesitated and said, "It got worse from there."

"Do you want to keep going? Are you okay?"

He nodded and continued. "The German tanks were in the town, pushing their way toward us. And there was no sign of our Shermans that were supposed to be coming. We had maybe a minute after the prisoner went down before a grenade hit the front door of the station. It was a fireball—like a bomb went off in the middle of your head. Blew me back over one of the gurneys against the wall. I couldn't hear anything. As I was pulling myself up, I saw the body of a corpsman jump—the one who had his fingers on the machine gun. He was gone, hit by a Nazi bullet fired through the hole where the door had been. Then another corpsman got picked off. My hearing started to come back, and I could make out screams of the German prisoners pleading to be spared.

"The shots stopped for a tick before I saw the shadow of a German edge close to the opening. I was hiding behind the upturned gurney. No protection from a bullet, but I was out of sight. After he showered the room with his Mauser, he stepped forward, right into the sights of my M1. Blaise was dead. Four or five of my other buddies were killed or wounded. I didn't hesitate, squeezed the trigger twice—the first in the chest, then one in the head to finish the job. After he dropped, two more Germans ran through the opening and started firing. I got them both."

"Did they keep coming at you? Were there more of them?"

"No. Those three were the only ones that got through to the middle of the village. None of them reached the command post before the Shermans arrived to attack the German tanks. Then an icy fog rolled over the town, and the Nazis pulled back to Herrlisheim. I'd been frozen in place behind the gurney for almost two hours with the M1 trained on the spot where the three soldiers fell. Then I heard a GI call through the mist that the Germans were gone. I started to shake and dropped the gun on the floor."

Amelia reached for him. "I had no idea you were in that much danger . . . saw that much killing."

"There's more," he said.

"Pull over to the side of the road," she said. "You stopped Shorty's bleeding. He'll have to wait for a few more minutes to get to the hospital."

After he brought the truck to a halt, he continued, "The shaking stopped when I began to work on our boys who got shot. Three were dead. But one was okay. He had a shoulder wound that wasn't deep but made him lose blood. A compression bandage and plasma were enough. The other had a head wound that took out too much of his brain to give him a chance. I loaded him with morphine and tucked him into a cot to die. Then it was time to check the Germans."

He looked away. "The prisoner was still alive. I dragged him back to his stretcher, tied his hands and feet with restraints, and moved on to the three bodies in the doorway.

"They were teenagers . . . just kids. The first one was lying with his face looking straight up at me. He was dead. But his eyes were open, like beacons stopped in their tracks. They cut through the fog, right into my gut. Then I saw the blond fuzz on his cheeks, not stubble like the GIs I knew. Something drew me down to him, and I knelt to touch that wispy hair . . . on a face that wouldn't be shaved again. The touch did it. He was a person now. He had a mother who would never see him again. I'm a doctor, took an oath never to do harm. And I had just snuffed out three lives, maybe a fourth if the prisoner didn't survive."

He paused and looked at her. "I had to shoot them, didn't I? "

"Yes, you did. You had to defend your men. And save your own life."

"Sometimes I think it would have been best to surrender. Those three would have been captured in a few hours . . . They'd be back home now. Maybe I went crazy after seeing Blaise die. Took vengeance when it wasn't needed."

"You've suffered enough. It wasn't your fault the Nazis tried to destroy us. Killed millions of Jews. You didn't give the orders for that battle in Rohrwiller. You didn't plan that grenade attack or the shots that hit your corpsman. You were just a soldier doing what you had to do. Those Germans would have killed you and who knows how many others. So put the doubts away. Be proud of what you did to save your men. I'm proud of you . . . everything you did."

She held him now as he breathed deeply. "I know I need to quit dissecting myself," he said. "But it's hard to stop."

"Isn't there a saying about doctors healing themselves? What do you need to do? I'll help you if you guide me."

"Let me talk about it . . . like we did now. Go with me to the American Legion gun range. Shoot M1s with me until they don't scare me any longer. I've avoided getting closer than a mile to that place. Don't want to hear the shots from the vets that go there. Don't want to be reminded."

"Sign me up," Amelia said. "You didn't look panicked when Shorty fired that M1. You didn't steer clear of those gunshots . . . Are you getting better?"

"I didn't think of anything except stopping him until we got into this rust heap and started talking."

He turned the key in the ignition, and the truck came to life.

# Chapter 33

## EDDIES

—◡—

Dressed in formal gear, Bruce gave a quick knock before opening Bess's door and calling up the stairs. "Amelia . . . are you ready?"

Her lilting voice sang through the hallway. "Not quite. I'm slipping into a frock you haven't seen before. I hope you'll like it."

A few minutes later, she appeared on the landing. "Do I pass inspection?" she asked as she spun to display her outfit for Glen and Mimi's wedding. With a polka dot bow at her neck, the lavender crepe dress and a white wool jacket were classy, perfect for the day. But the dress draped her lithe figure in a way that stunned him.

"Whew . . . you make me weak at the knees."

"Better have strong knees," she said as she came toward him. "A best man has to stand tall."

"The best man job doesn't worry me," he replied. "It's the next hour with you."

The significance of a wedding day hadn't escaped them. With three of the four weeks of Amelia's visit behind them, they couldn't delay discussing their plans much longer. Bruce had suggested the ground rules. Dressed for the wedding, on Bess's garden bench—a meeting in the light of day. An hour to sum up where they were, where they could go.

The path to the bench wove past a bed of tree peonies with dramatic saucer-sized flowers that would last only three or four days, then be gone until next spring. But they passed by without stopping. They were thinking about what to say.

When they arrived at the seat, Bruce didn't hesitate. He'd been rehearsing the words since he woke in the middle of the night. "It's Glen's and Mimi's time today. My mother and the judge are getting married in July. I want our wedding to be next. Here in Hollidaysburg. At the same church. Will you marry me?"

Amelia had expected the proposal, and a beaming smile signaled her pleasure. But after she pulled him close, her words revealed a corner of doubt. "I wanted you to ask me," she said. "I want to say yes. I want to tell you I can make a new home here."

"Then say it."

"I can't say it yet," Amelia replied as she loosened her embrace to face him. "I said I'd tell you everything, and I meant it. You know I love you. No questions there. I want to be with you all the time. I can't get enough of you. No questions there. If I had to live without you, I'd be miserable. The only problem is me."

"What about you? If there're any problems, I'll take them."

"My family's gone. Just aunts, uncles, and a few cousins left. So I shouldn't have so much trouble leaving England."

Amelia stood and held out her hand for Bruce to walk with her. "You can't leave your work and your people to move to England. You have a calling that's in your marrow. I respect it . . . I love you for it. And your brother would be lost if you weren't here. You aren't suited to be a squire in Hampshire, dribbling away your life. You could look after the river Test— rebuild our garden. But you couldn't be a doctor unless you went back to medical school. I couldn't ask you to do that. You'd wilt in England, and I'd wilt with you."

She stopped and turned to face him. "The only solution is for me to join you here. But I can't quite make the leap. Something is holding me back . . . and I'm trying to find the answer."

"What's wrong?" he asked. "Tell me, and I'll do anything to fix it."

"There's still all the family history, a dozen generations in the same manor. The land on the estate. The Test entrusted to me. And there's a wild idea that I haven't mentioned. Really just a fantasy. My father was a member of Parliament when he died. The party committee came to interview me, thought I might be a candidate. There are just a smattering of women in Parliament now. But the country is changing after the war. I was flattered. I have no political experience except working to help elect Daddy, but I do have a first-class diploma from Cambridge and had an important job in the war. I met a lot of influential people who think I could get elected.

"It turned out they weren't serious about considering me now. I'm too young. I don't have enough seasoning. But they want to start grooming me for the future. Told me I need to build up my résumé and wait till the time is right."

"I can see why they came after you," he said.

"The prospect stirred me. It made me think about finding a job with more heft than keeping a country estate going. My work meant something when I was in that bunker in the war. I was using my brain, solving puzzles."

She paused and reached for his other hand. "So it looks like the answer could be a tough one for us . . . A career that asks more from me than being a wife. Does that sound presumptuous? Am I being selfish? I know that loving you, having your children, should be more than enough. But I want to be fulfilled like you . . . like Sarah. Seeing her at work made me realize what I would miss. I said you'd wither if you moved to England. I worry the same would happen to me if I came here."

"You aren't being selfish. I understand what you're saying. I want you to thrive, not wither."

"There's not much use for a degree in economics here," she said. "And my connections in London wouldn't help a bit. Other than Sarah, the women who work in Hollidaysburg are secretaries or clerks at the stores on Main Street. A teaching position might be interesting, but I don't have the diploma. I've been thinking about options. Believe me."

"Let's not get stymied by trying to find you a job right now," Bruce said, trying to regain some of the momentum that had been propelling them. "Wouldn't you have the same problem in England?"

"Yes."

"We're too close to give up now. Will you keep trying? You said you liked to solve puzzles. Solve this one. It's the biggest one we have."

"Touché," Amelia said.


Glen and Bruce were the first to arrive at the church. They entered through the main door and walked down the aisle where Mimi and her father would process soon. The ends of the walnut pews were festooned with the palest shade of lilacs tied with white and yellow ribbons. At both sides of the altar, sprays of deeper lavender lilacs were mixed with cherry branches that had just come into bloom.

Glen moved forward to kneel at the altar, while Bruce took a seat in the front pew. The church was quiet as the men gathered their thoughts and prayed. Bruce doubted that prayers for intercession made much difference. How many prayers had he heard from dying GIs that weren't answered? Yet this occasion, like others full of emotion and layered with risk, drew him back to the old ways—the lessons he had learned as a child in this church.

When Glen finished at the altar, he joined Bruce in the front pew. The angle of the sun had started to change, and light was filtering through the stained glass. The reds, blues, greens, and golds showered the church in a kaleidoscope of color.

"I didn't think I'd see this day," Glen said. "Mimi's a saint to put up with me. Gave me another chance after I went nuts at Amelia's welcome party. I thought she'd give me the boot."

"You haven't been drinking. You're talking with Sarah. Waiting to see the psychiatrist from Philly when he comes in July. Doing all the right things. She knows you'll be okay."

"Thanks, cheerleader. But I was at the altar looking for guidance. I'm still asking myself if I should go through with this wedding."

Bruce put his arm around his brother's shoulders, and they sat in silence for a moment.

"It's the same story we've been over before," Glen said. "The *in sickness and health* part of the vows. Asks a lot from her."

"Mimi's made her decision," Bruce said. "And you have to trust her. Believe she's made the best choice for herself. And for you."

They heard the organist open the side door to the choir loft, and the first member of the string quartet appeared with her violin and music stand. The ushers were on their way.

"So it's time to step up. Make this marriage work. Show us how it's done."

"Yes, sir, Major Duncan," Glen replied before he rose. "I'll say my vows with conviction."

"We need to get to the minister's office before the guests arrive," Bruce said. "Let's go."

The last time Bruce had been at the Blairmont Club, the New Year's Eve celebration had turned sour when Glen got drunk. But Glen was in control at the reception—sipping a glass of ginger ale and passing up offers of champagne. He was standing with Mimi by the stone fireplace, seeming to revel in the compliments that were coming their way.

At the other end of the ballroom, Amelia and Sarah stood apart from the crowd. Were they talking about a role for Amelia in this country? Med school wouldn't be out of the question. They could move to Philadelphia for four years. It would be hard leaving Hollidaysburg, but they could drive here to visit. Another idea came to him. Law school at Penn, then a public career. There would be limits on running for office, but she could become a citizen. Opportunities would come her way. He could be flexible.

As he began to consider other possibilities, the band kicked into an upbeat rendition of "Here Comes the Bride," and Glen and Mimi walked to the center of the dance floor. "Mimi and I want our first dance as Mr. and Mrs. Glen Duncan . . . Hey, that sounds great, doesn't it? We want the dance to jump. So we've asked the band to play 'Sing, Sing, Sing.' We'll do the slow numbers later. Give us the first stanza, then everybody join in."

Amelia took the cue to move across the room to him.

"Sarah will be leaving soon," she said. "You should dance with her once . . . I won't be jealous. Even a budding spinster should dance now and then."

"What were you talking about?" Bruce asked.

"She's on our side, don't worry."

Before he could dig further, Glen and Mimi swirled by. "Come on, you two . . . get with it," Glen called to them.

By the middle of Benny Goodman's classic, the dance floor was jammed elbow to elbow with jitterbugging couples swinging to the beat. Sarah was dancing with Pete Nicholaou, who was doing double duty as a guest and a caterer. Vic and Pauline had lasted through the cascading riffs of the trumpets, but the big man didn't have the stamina to continue. He stood at the edge of the crowd as the clarinet wailed and the band raced toward the conclusion. Bruce scanned from Vic to Glen, still swaying in circles with Mimi. The groom looked exultant, not manic. *Keep him that way*, Bruce murmured to himself.

After dinner and the cake cutting, the crowd began to thin. Sarah had gone home without the dance that Amelia suggested. Alice and Bess sat with the judge, having coffee. Glen and Mimi were changing into their clothes to leave for their honeymoon. Bruce had introduced Amelia to all of his friends except the couple who stood by themselves at the bar in the next room.

"We should talk with them," Bruce said. "Lucas and Kate Glover."

"He almost killed you. Why did Mimi and Glen invite them?"

"If someone can help those men at the brick plant, it's Lucas. And he's listening to me now. My source, Tony Giordano, tells me conditions are better."

"I'm not sure I can be nice to him," she said as they walked toward the bar.

When they got closer, they could see that Lucas was staring at the painting behind the bar—a golfer on the eighteenth green.

"Wishing you were out on the course?" Bruce asked.

"Nope," Lucas replied. "Thinking I've played my last match here. I got fired this morning."

"He didn't get fired," Kate said. "He got transferred to Pittsburgh—an office job there."

"Might as well have been fired," he said as he continued to stare at the painting. "A pay cut, and we'd have to live in the city. They know I won't take it."

He turned around and saw Amelia with Bruce. "You must be Amelia. I caused you and Bruce a lot of pain . . . I'm sorry I did it. I went crazy for a while.

"You'll be safe now," he continued. "Shorty was the only one with a grudge, and he'll be in jail for a long time. The story of what happened at Spruce Creek has gotten around. I'm glad you caught him."

"I didn't want you to lose your job," Bruce said. "Was it the changes at the plant?"

"Yeah, I think so. They didn't squawk when I put in the new respirator and dust-watering policy. I did get some push-back when I ordered the exhaust fans, but it wasn't too bad. Probably could have slid by. I should have stopped there. They tilted on Thursday when I put in a requisition for an air-testing system. Said it was information we didn't need to know."

"What will happen now?"

"Hard to say. Safety placards are posted all over the plant about wearing respirators. The pipes have been installed for watering, and the fans should arrive in a couple weeks. I hope the new superintendent uses them. The men know the dangers now. They're still talking about those lungs you pulled out of the bag in Harrisburg. I think they'll stage a protest if the company tries to dump the safety program."

"How about you?"

"I'm looking for work."


As they drove home from the reception, Amelia leaned her head on Bruce's shoulder and closed her eyes. By the time he heard the crunch of gravel in his driveway, she was asleep. He turned off the engine and sat outside the garage.

It had been a day of swirling currents. He had thought Amelia would accept his proposal. All the signs had seemed to point toward success. Then the sudden crash—a feeling like all the air had been sucked out of him. Why had he been blind to something that was so important to both of them? Using their talents to the hilt. How could he expect Amelia not to use hers?

The turmoil hadn't been limited to his thwarted proposal. Glen's anguish before the wedding had grabbed at him, much more than he had allowed his brother to see. Bruce had wanted to keep Glen from bolting with fear. But he knew the score.

There was more noise in his brain from the meeting with Lucas and Kate. Walking toward them with Amelia on his arm, he'd been proud for helping the men at the brick plant. But the pride went away in a flash. He'd been naïve to think the company would let Lucas do everything that was needed. The hearing in Harrisburg might eventually do some good. But it could be a long wait.

His mind was spinning with catastrophic thoughts. Amelia would go back to England and never return. Glen would go over the edge. All of their attempts to save lives at the plant would fail. As he struggled with these fears, another image came to him. It was his friend Blaise, joking as they rode their jeeps into Rohrwiller on that blue-skied day before the battle began. *What's going on?* Bruce asked himself. *Too much happened today.*

He tried to push the memory of his army buddy away. But Blaise was smiling at him as if he wanted to say something. *Okay, it's your turn, Blaise,* Bruce said to himself. *I promised I'd live for you and the other guys who never made it home. What would you do?*

Taking Blaise's position, Bruce played the coach. *You're lucky, Bruce. Number one, you're alive. I'd take that. Number two, you have a fine woman with her head on your shoulder right now.*

*You're ninety percent there on marrying her. Don't give up—make it happen. Number three, Glen's smart. He knows what to do. Be sure he does it. Number four, the game's not over at the brick plant. Stick it out. Number five, I'm holding you to your promise. A full life, nothing short of it.*


When they walked up Bess's porch steps, she rushed to greet them with an envelope in her hand.

"Western Union just left. There's a telegram for you, Amelia."

"What could it be?" Amelia asked. "My aunts and uncles haven't been sick. There aren't any other close relatives who could have died."

"Do you want me to stay or let you open it without an audience?" Bess asked. "I'll admit, I'm curious."

"It might be better if you let me read it with Bruce. I'll let you know if I need anything."

They sat in the rocking chairs while Amelia opened the telegram and read it by the porch light. "It's from the Interservice Research Bureau in London," she said. "Should I read it aloud?"

"Yes, if you don't mind."

"It says confidential. But I have to share this with you. Will you keep it secret? Not tell anyone?"

He nodded, and she began to read.

"The pact between England and the United States of America to establish the Five Eyes surveillance program has been signed by all parties. Your wartime service makes you uniquely qualified to assume a leadership position. Please return to England to meet with me at Interservice Research Bureau headquarters. Inform me by telegram of your plans. We will arrange for a car to meet you. Signed: Colonel Patrick Marr-Johnson."

"What does that mean?"

"I know a bit about Five Eyes, but it's all hush, hush. The Five Eyes are England, the USA, Australia, Canada, and New Zealand. The intelligence service has proposed the network to collect and share information about the Soviet Union and the Eastern Bloc. I thought something would come of it after Churchill's Iron Curtain speech last month."

"So why are they after you?"

"I was at the center of the action to understand the messages that were coming at us during the war. I wasn't a spy. But I handled information they collected, radar and sonar feeds, decoded transcripts, anything we could get our hands on. Colonel Marr-Johnson taught my brother at Oxford and knows our family. Probably thinks I'd want to pick up where my brother left off—do some essential work for England."

With the revelation of each detail, he worried more that this invitation would capture her, take her away from him. "What's your reaction?" he asked, trying to remain calm. "What will you do?"

She waited to speak. "I don't know."

# Chapter 34

## FLOWING ON

### *Pennsylvania*
### *May 1946*

*H*e crawled over the broken timbers, the splintered wood sticking in his hands, elbows, and knees. Blaise didn't answer his calls. But how could he hear him? The German prisoners jumped up and down on their cots, a chorus of harpies shrieking at him. Nein, Nein, Nein, Nein . . . they cackled through their hooked beaks. He threw a loose IV bottle toward them and tried to keep going toward the stove that exploded when the shells hit. It was a magnet that pulled him through the haze of the shattered aid station.

He finally touched the boot, the same as his, crusted heavy with blood from nonstop surgery. It didn't move. The moon was gone from the open roof, no light to see. Tracing the outline of the body, he knew it was Blaise. He found the stubble on his face, his broken glasses pushed into his skin. When he put his lips down to blow air into his lungs, the stubble melted, the glass fell away. Long blond hair streamed from his scalp, breasts sprouted from his chest. It was Amelia, gray and cold, dead in his arms.

"No, no," he screamed as he thrashed at the bed sheets and woke from the nightmare.

"Bruce, it's me . . . Amelia. You had a bad dream."

He sat upright, staring ahead, his heart still pounding. "A very bad dream. First one since we caught Shorty. I hoped I was done with them."

"What was it? The war?"

"I saw Blaise lying by that stove that blew up and killed him. Then he turned into you . . . and you weren't breathing either."

"It doesn't take a psychiatrist to figure that one out," she said. "I'm leaving today. But I won't be gone forever. Come here—let me hold you. The clock says a little after four. We have till five thirty when the alarm goes off and you have to sneak back to your house."

Bruce slipped back under the covers and nestled against her. They had been sated when they fell asleep on this last night before Amelia returned to England. But he needed her again now. She stroked his cheek before she moved down to his shoulders and arms, massaging the tight cords. "I'll make you forget that dream," she said. "I'm alive . . . and I'm all yours."


Waiting on Bess's porch for Rosalie, they were talking about the farewell party Alice had hosted yesterday. The crowd hadn't included Rosalie, who was too young to attend. But a special treat was planned for her on this Saturday. The last things to do before leaving for the train station were a big breakfast Bess was preparing and a surprise for the young girl.

"My mother didn't hold back," Bruce said. "Told you she always wanted a daughter, and you were her pick. I'm sorry she put you in a spot. The Duncans can be heavy-handed."

"No need to apologize for her. She's looking out for you . . . as she should. Your mother wasn't the only one who wanted to pull answers out of me."

"What did the others do?"

"Pauline collared me in the kitchen and told me she'd skin me if I didn't come back. Vic overheard us and told Pauline to stop her pestering. But then he offered me a job—a place in the office at the railroad. Said I could work my way into a management position."

"Was he serious? The Pennsylvania Railroad is a men's club."

"I think he did find an office job I could do. Pauline or your mother must have pressured him to come up with something."

"What did you tell him?"

"Thanks. But I wasn't interested."

"Anybody else try to lure you back to Hollidaysburg?"

"The judge had a lighter touch. No job offers, just an idea to keep me busy. He wants me to do research with him on English colonists in Pennsylvania. He thinks some of my distant relatives may have been pioneers here. Sounds like a stretch to me. But all of your people are wonderful. Your mother and the judge . . . Vic and Pauline. Bess. Glen and Mimi. I'll miss them."

"Did they make any headway? Convince you to return?"

"You know I could be very happy here. But we're sticking with our plan, correct? I'm going to give Whitcombe Hall the attention it needs, do the interview for the Five Eyes program, and book you on that brand-new Pan American flight to Bournemouth for your vacation in August. Only seventeen hours from New York. I know it costs a lot, but I have the money now. Daddy's estate is settled, and I sold those stocks in New York . . . You have to let me treat you."

He grinned. "I'd be a kept man if you had your way."

"Never," she replied before Rosalie skipped up the walk to the porch.

The hours after school, before Rosalie's supper and Bruce's return from work, had been their time for the last month. Amelia had listened to Rosalie talk about her mother, who was being treated for cancer in New York, read with her, and taught her how to play chess. They had gone swimming at the Y and shot arrows at the range. Leaving after a month would be a blow to Rosalie. So Amelia had prepared something to leave her.

After they ate Bess's egg and sausage casserole, Amelia asked Rosalie and Bruce to go for a walk. Coursing down Elm Street for two blocks, they turned south toward the residential section of Union Street and stopped at the corner.

"Do you see that big yellow house with the clerestory on top?" she asked Rosalie. "It's been divided into apartments, and I have a key to the one on the second floor. Let's go in and take a look. It's going to be your new home when your mother comes next week."

"What?" Rosalie squealed. "My mother's too sick to come here . . . and we don't have the money to pay for an apartment."

"It's all settled. Our Doctor Duncan has helped her get the best treatment in New York, and she's ready to travel. She wants to be here with you and your uncle and aunt. There's a doctor in Altoona who can do everything the doctors in New York want for her. The rent's paid up for a year . . . more if we need it."

Rosalie started to cry as she hugged Amelia.

"There's a room for you, stacked with books and games. Come along so we can see it before I have to leave. I can't miss the train."

"Thank you, Miss Whitcombe. Will you come back to see my mother?"

"When I can."

They stood at the same spot where she had stepped off the train four weeks ago. It was the first Saturday in May, and the late morning sun had risen over the crest of the roof to warm the bare concrete platform. A piece of newspaper swirled toward them in the breeze and caught at Bruce's feet. It was the sports page of the *Philadelphia Inquirer*. He picked it up and showed it to Amelia.

"I forgot it's Kentucky Derby Day," he said. "Wish you could listen to it on the radio with me."

"Maybe we could go to the derby someday," she said as she read through the lineup of horses. "I've been to the Epsom Derby. It's a formal affair. Your Kentucky Derby would be more to my taste."

"Let's choose horses and make a bet between us. Best place wins . . . but we have to collect in person."

"You're distracting me from having to climb on that train," she replied. "A good idea."

"Dollars or pounds?" he asked.

She laughed. "Always the diplomat . . . How about five pounds? You can pay up when you come to England on your vacation."

"A deal . . . now pick your horse."

"I'll take Spy Song. Reminds me of my clandestine dabbling in the war."

"Assault should win," Bruce said. "He took the Wood Memorial. But I'll choose With Pleasure."

He smiled and pulled her close. "Always with pleasure."

"Always with pleasure," she replied as a whistle signaled the arrival of the Broadway Limited.

Bruce motioned to the porter to collect her bags and walked with her to the edge of the platform. "If I help you take your things inside the train, I might not get off," he said. "So we better say goodbye here."

Amelia reached into her purse as the porter loaded her bags.

"I've been saving something till now," she said. "Before you shipped out to France, you inscribed the lid from your grandfather's gold watch and gave it to me. You kept the other part. They should be together, Bruce. Hold them for us till we can find a solution . . . our bridge across the Atlantic."

There was no time to think her offer through. The train was ready to depart. Was she committing herself? Or did returning the piece of the watch mean that she might never return? He reached out to take the gold lid.

"I'll put them together," he said. "And I'll keep the watch with me until I see you again."

She kissed him and walked up the stairs to stand in the passageway. A hiss of steam hit the air as the brakes were released, and the train began to pull out of the station.

He sat on the bank with his fly rod beside him. The moss on the stream bank was greener now than when they were here a few days ago. Umbrella tops of mayapples had emerged from the forest floor, and the oaks and maples were in full leaf, filtering the rays from the midday sun. The first sulfur-winged mayflies of the season were fluttering on the surface of this section of Spruce Creek, where they had come back often after the day Shorty attacked his car. A large fish was sipping flies in the narrow feeding lane at the tail of the pool—the spot where the stream picked up speed before gushing through a boulder-edged pocket. When the caddis were hatching, Amelia mastered the tricky drift to guide her fly to where this fish was rising—a more delicate touch than he had managed. Bruce didn't try to cast to the fish. He hadn't tied a fly on his line since he came here after taking Amelia to the train.

His mind raced over the last four weeks. He thought of the day they had tipped over their lunch basket on this moss, not caring if they ate the food Bess prepared. There were better things to consume. He thought of the nights in the bedroom at Bess's house. They had become longer until last night, when they had spent the whole night together. He only slept for a couple hours. He should be exhausted. But he could still feel her with him.

He knew her so well now. Yet there was part of her that was an enigma. Amelia said she wouldn't hold back. She'd tell him everything. But did anyone ever tell everything? Was she less sure than she admitted? She had cut him off once before. Would the offer to join the Five Eyes surveillance group be too much to resist?

Bruce went deeper, questioning himself. *What's missing? She says it's finding work if she came here. But is it something about me? Was her father right? Not in her league?*

He thought about what their life might be like in this village. He could amble along as a country doctor—be consumed by treating his patients, do what he had planned when he went to med school. But it would be too quiet, not challenging enough for Amelia. Maybe not enough for him. The war had marked them. It was brutal, yet they had been more alive than they probably ever would be again. She needed to find a way to be engaged—not to a man but to life. He respected her for that quest. He had the same need. Love wasn't enough.

Then his thinking spiraled down in another round of self-doubt. *Is all of this a folly? Why did I think I could overcome the odds? Is it that streak I discovered when I flirted with Sarah? Going after the impossible? Wanting a woman who is like a holy grail?*

The sound of cracking branches startled him. It was a doe pushing through the undergrowth on the other side of the stream. She must not have seen him, because she stepped into the water to take a drink while a fawn eased in beside her.

The simple beauty of their natural movements, a mother and child together, riveted him. *No, I'm not searching for a grail*, Bruce told himself. *Just what any other creature wants.*

He watched the deer move up the hillside before he picked up the rod and walked back to his car.

When Bruce turned the key to the back door of his house, he knew something was wrong. The door was unlocked. Had he forgotten to use the key in the rush to leave for the station? *Unlikely*, Bruce thought as he cracked open the door to listen.

The radio was playing in the study, and he could hear the voice of the announcer for the Kentucky Derby. It was past six o'clock, and the race was due to start any minute. *It's Glen*, he said to himself with relief. *He has a key. And he's listening to the derby, waiting for me.*

Bruce walked into the kitchen and smelled a roast in the oven. Gazing around the room, he spotted a vase of tulips on the pine table. *Glen knew I needed this. The guy can be a good brother.*

He moved with a quiet tread through the house toward the study, where the radio was playing. The trumpeter was calling the horses to the post. "Glen," he called through the open door, "I'm home."

"Yes, we're home," Amelia responded as she jumped out of the chair by the radio, running to hold him. The words rushed out. "I turned around at the first stop. Five minutes hurtling away from you on that train was enough. Will you have me? One way or another? Here or somewhere?"

Staggered by seeing her again, he couldn't speak for a moment. Then their lips met to answer her questions.

"It all came to me when the train left the station," she told him. "I'll sell Whitcombe Hall but hold on to the stream and the cottage on the Test. We can go there in the summers when you're on vacation. It will be a slice of England for me—enough to keep me happy. And you can help me manage the Test. We can open it to let people fish when we aren't there."

"A generous plan," he said as he put his hand to his heart. "But you're sacrificing so much. What about Five Eyes? It's a chance to get back into action. There won't be anything like that here."

"They'll probably have to lift the Iron Curtain without me. But I was tinkering with an idea while I waited for you to return. Want to take a look at a telegram I might send? You can make some edits."

He opened the notepad and read the message.

*Colonel Patrick Marr-Johnson*
*Interservice Research Bureau, London*

> *I must decline your offer to interview for a position in London in the Five Eyes program. I'm marrying a Yank and will be spending most of my time in a Pennsylvania town. But I wonder if I still could be of service. Could you use a British 'Eye' in the USA? Allegheny Air flies to Washington daily, and I could be there in two hours and take assignments to complete in my new home. Please inform if an opportunity exists. Can interview in Washington now or in England in August during next visit.*

*Amelia Whitcombe*

"I wouldn't change a word. How could he resist?"

"Would you mind if I went back and forth to Washington . . . and flew to England a few times a year? I can't see them hiring me if I don't do some traveling."

"I'll be proud of you—glad you're fighting the Russians. I had a ringside seat watching them grab Berlin and East Germany. They're ruthless. We don't want another war, but we have to protect ourselves. If you can help at all, you should do it. I'll go to England with you now if they want to talk with you. Sarah would cover for me."

"I'd want you to go with me if you can."

"Would we have a wireless in the attic like the resistance fighters had in France?" Bruce asked.

She laughed. "No. But there would be a radio connection, and we would need to keep it secret. I'd need a cover story for my trips to Washington."

"I'll play my part. An adventure for both of us."

"We're getting a bit ahead of ourselves," she said. "Colonel Marr-Johnson knows what I did in the war. But he'd have to convince the American command to use me. It's a long shot.

"If he says no to my idea, we'll find something else for me to do. I'll have funds to put to work here. We can use my inheritance in a good way. I don't know what it will be—only that we'll choose it together."

He took her hand as they walked out to the front porch, where they could see the mountains to the south of the village. The flower-scented air of May enveloped them as they looked ahead, past the mountains, into their future.

"You won the bet," Bruce said. "Spy Song came in second, way ahead of With Pleasure."

"I'll take the winnings in dollars."

# AUTHOR'S NOTE

$\mathcal{T}$his story about a front-line surgeon's struggle to overcome the traumas of WWII was shaped by the suffering of relatives who experienced aftereffects of war throughout their lives and by my work as a psychiatrist in treating victims of PTSD. The choice of a surgeon as the central character was influenced by *The Other Side of Time*, a searing autobiography by Brendan Phibbs, M.D., a surgeon who fought in the battles in Alsace featured in *A Stream to Follow*. Phibbs saw vicious action at Rohrwiller and Herrlisheim in the winter of 1944–45, when the Germans fired with little or no restraint on field hospitals and ambulances. Medical personnel took heavy casualties, as did the other soldiers in this pivotal campaign.

Medical and surgical treatment during WWII is documented in other books, which helped me describe the gritty and often perilous conditions at battlefront aid stations. They include *Fighting for Life: American Military Medicine in World War II*, by Albert Cowdrey, and *Doctor Danger Forward*, by Allen Towne. Another book, *Return to Duty*, by Fran and Martin Collins, describes US Army hospitals in England, where Bruce Duncan would have been stationed before he was deployed to France and Germany.

Hollidaysburg is an actual village in central Pennsylvania. It has a rich history of being a hub for canal traffic in the nineteenth century and a major center for the Pennsylvania Railroad for several decades after WWII. Although the main street has fewer shops today than in the post-war era, the town still has considerable charm. The filigreed storefronts, attractive houses along the main streets, and the surrounding mountains and streams make it a pleasant place to live.

Blairton is a fictional town patterned after other company towns that were built near plants that mined deposits in nearby mountains to manufacture bricks and other silica-laden products for industrial applications. During and after WWII, these plants were essential businesses that were mainstays of regional economies. However, exposure to silica and asbestos took a heavy toll on the workers, and most of these factories have been shuttered. As a young man, I worked in a brick plant where I saw clouds of mineral-laden dust and the ravages of silicosis.

Spruce Creek, a mecca for trout fisherman, flows in a beautiful tree-lined valley just a short drive from Hollidaysburg. It was a favorite stream of Dwight Eisenhower and Jimmy Carter. The Test, another legendary destination for fly-fishing, is located in Hampshire, England, where Bruce and Amelia met and started their journey toward a life in Hollidaysburg.

# ACKNOWLEDGMENTS

Making a transition from writing medical and self-help books to a novel required a significant retooling of skills and much help along the way. In the beginning, Stacy Wright, a librarian and avid reader, was an enthusiastic advocate and steered me toward the interesting post-war period when America was booming and soldiers had a place of honor, yet were suffering emotional wounds in silence. Susanne and Marion Wright were steadfast champions and abided my long hours at the computer with uncommon patience and grace. A host of very sharp readers volunteered their time to dig deep into my drafts of the manuscript and give me suggestions for improving the book. Millard Dunn, a teacher of creative writing, provided much encouragement and valuable advice. David Casey, Emily Manzo, Larry Melton, Paul Ayers, Carolyn Reber, and Jean O'Brien gave insightful feedback and direction.

I want to give an especially large nod of gratitude to Will Lavender, a *New York Times* best-selling author, who showed great kindness in working with me to refine the novel and prepare it for publication. His wise recommendations were a treasure. Christine Benton, an eagle-eyed editor and astute observer of the human condition, was an essential part of the team that helped me develop *A Stream to Follow*. Shannon Green and Brooke Warner at SparkPress brought this book into print with great skill and care.

During my early years in small-town Pennsylvania, through medical school and residency training, and in my career as a professor of psychiatry, I've been privileged to hear the stories of many people who have suffered traumas and other insults to their lives and integrity. To all of these people who have helped me learn about the far reaches of emotional pain and the remarkable resilience of the mind, I give you my heartfelt thanks.

## ABOUT THE AUTHOR

*J*ess Wright is an internationally recognized psychiatrist who is a professor at the University of Louisville. He is the author of eight medical and self-help books and was the principal developer of *Good Days Ahead*, a groundbreaking online program for treatment for depression. *A Stream to Follow* is his first novel.

*Author photo © Thomas Shelby*

# SELECTED TITLES FROM SPARKPRESS

SparkPress is an independent boutique publisher delivering high-quality, entertaining, and engaging content that enhances readers' lives, with a special focus on female-driven work. www. gosparkpress.com

*This Is How It Begins* by Joan Dempsey. $16.95, 978-1-63152-308-3. When eighty-five-year-old art professor Ludka Zeilonka's gay grandson, Tommy, is fired over concerns that he's silencing Christian kids in the classroom, she is drawn into the political firestorm—and as both sides battle to preserve their respective rights to free speech, the hatred on display raises the specter of her WWII past.

*Last Seen* by J. L. Doucette. $16.95, 978-1-63152-202-4. When a traumatized reporter goes missing in the Wyoming wilderness, the therapist who knows her secrets is drawn into the investigation—and she comes face-to-face with terrifying answers regarding her own difficult past.

*Love is a Rebellious Bird* by Elayne Klasson. $16.95, 978-1-63152-604-6. From childhood all the way through to old age, Judith adores Elliot Pine—a beautiful, charismatic and wildly successful man—bound to him by both tragedy and friendship. He defines the terms of their relationship; he holds the power. Until finally, in old age, the power shifts.

*Watchdogs* by Patricia Watts. $16.95, 978-1-938314-34-6. When journalist Julia Wilkes returns to the town where her career got its start, she is forced to face some old ghosts—and some new enemies.

*When It's Over* by Barbara Ridley. $16.95, 978-1-63152-296-3. When World War II envelopes Europe, Lena Kulkova flees Czechoslovakia for the relative safety of England, leaving her Jewish family behind in Prague.

## ABOUT SPARKPRESS

*S*parkPress is an independent, hybrid imprint focused on merging the best of the traditional publishing model with new and innovative strategies. We deliver high-quality, entertaining, and engaging content that enhances readers' lives. We are proud to bring to market a list of *New York Times* best-selling, award-winning, and debut authors who represent a wide array of genres, as well as our established, industry-wide reputation for creative, results-driven success in working with authors. SparkPress, a BookSparks imprint, is a division of SparkPoint Studio LLC.

Learn more at GoSparkPress.com